LAWMEN, SOLDIERS, & OTHER HEROES

A Romance Collection

WHAT READERS ARE SAYING . . .

Lawmen, Soldiers, & Other Heroes delivers accurate depictions of the struggles our heroes in uniform face, and the book focuses on the families and friends who also sacrifice for their service.

Having served in the Army, I can identify with the reality of leaving loved ones behind. After my military service, I became a federal agent and volunteered as a police chaplain, a position I held for more than 20 years.

The struggles Derinda Babcock presents are real and impact the lives of the lawmen and their loved ones in meaningful ways.

As Babcock projects, these real-life struggles are profound, and she brings honor to those who serve by focusing on that struggle. This is a must read for those who want to understand the impact of loving someone in uniform.

—Travis W Inman, Author of Earth Fire Series and the Glenfield Series, and retired Border Patrol Agent

LAWMEN, SOLDIERS, & OTHER HEROES

A Romance Collection

DERINDA BABCOCK

Scriptures marked KJV are taken from the KING JAMES VERSION (KJV): KING JAMES VERSION, public domain

Cover and Interior Design: Derinda Babcock

Editor(s): Helene Smith

PUBLISHED BY: 4Him Press, P.O.Box 127, Marvel, CO 81329, 2024

———————————————————————————————

Library Cataloging Data

Names: Babcock, Derinda (Derinda Babcock)

Lawmen, Soldiers, and Other Heroes: A Romance Collection / Derinda Babcock

364 p. 23cm × 15cm (9 in × 6 in.)

ISBN-13: 979-8-9893327-0-0 (paperback) | 979-8-9893327-2-4 (trade paperback) | 979-8-9893327-1-7 (e-book)

Key Words: military; lawmen police sheriff marshal; K-9 dogs; mail-order bride; heroes; soldiers; American Sign Language

Library of Congress Control Number: 2023923007 Fiction

DEDICATED TO

Law enforcement officers, soldiers, first
responders, and other heroes

CONTENTS

DIAMOND IN THE ROUGH

ONE

Saige Harmony stood next to her father, Robert, and studied the run-down ranch-style house they now owned and would call home. With trained eyes, she noted the missing shingles and the fascia's chipping paint. She sighed. "This place is going to be a lot of work, Dad."

He chuckled. "When hasn't a rehab job been a lot of work? Good thing you and your brothers are between construction jobs. With their help and a few of our other crew coming on the weekends, we should have the kitchen and bathrooms finished before Christmas." He glanced at the house. "I think we have a diamond in the rough, hon."

"This diamond's going to need a lot of polishing." She looked around the yard. "Even the houses we rehabbed in Missouri and Texas didn't have as many weeds, broken glass, beer cans, and barbed wire strewn about."

"Your brothers said they'd come with more equipment and tools after the kids go back to school and after they get through Labor Day celebrations."

Saige brushed a strand of loose hair out of her face. "Okay. That gives us three weeks to get as much done as we can before they arrive. The roll-off container should be here tomorrow, so we can start demolishing the kitchen."

"Hey, hon, when we're finished with the house, let's work on the barn. I'd like to raise chickens and a few goats."

Saige's eyebrows rose. "Really?"

Red tinged Robert's cheeks, and excitement lit his brown eyes. "Yes. When we passed the fairgrounds on our way out of town, all the County Fair activity reminded me of my life on the farm when I was a boy. I can still remember the taste of fresh eggs and cold goat's milk."

She stared. Her dad hadn't been this enthusiastic about anything for a while. Two deaths within the last five years had drained a lot of his physical and mental energy, and they'd contributed to his semi-retirement from the construction industry.

She smiled. Maybe the sharp edge of his grief had dulled. Hers had. "Sure, Dad. If you want goats and pastured chickens, we'll have to fence the perimeter and cross-fence the interior. We can tell Cam to bring the pipe trailer with as many joints as he can haul when he and Brett come. I'll calculate how many we'll need to see if they can get all the pipe in one trip. While you work on the barn and coop, I can start on the fences and gates."

Robert stretched and rubbed the back of his neck. He combed through his brown hair with his fingers. "What do you want to do while we wait?"

"We need space to work." She looked up and down the county road. "I wonder if a neighbor kid wants to earn a few bucks by helping us clear the mess in the yard?"

"Yoo-hoo."

They both glanced toward the house across the road. A dark-haired, jean-clad woman in her early fifties waved one hand while she carried a plastic pitcher of water and cups in the other. She smiled as she approached. "Hello, neighbors. I'm Valerie Langdon. Welcome. I brought you cool water from one of the best wells around." Her grin widened. "Mine."

Robert returned her smile. "Thank you, Mrs. Langdon, a cool drink sounds good."

Saige wasn't used to such overt friendliness from a stranger, but she pushed down the discomfort and smiled. "Thank you. I'm Saige Harmony, and this is my dad, Robert."

"Pleased to meet you both. Please call me Val." She poured the water and studied them as they drank.

Robert returned his cup. "Thank you. Do you know of anyone in the area who might help us clean up the yard and mow the grass around all the buildings?"

Valerie stared at the trashed yard and frowned. "What a dump. I'm sure my son, Jase, would lend a hand, but he's on patrol this evening. He's a K-9 officer with the State Patrol."

A cop with a dog. Great. Just great. Saige's stomach twisted at the thought. She looked at her dad to see how he handled the news. Robert seemed paler under his tan, but he smiled and listened as the woman chatted about raising a son after being widowed.

To hear Valerie talk, Jase Langdon was the perfect son, the perfect cop, and the perfect everything else. Saige grimaced. *Perfect. A paragon lives across the road.* Her thoughts couldn't move beyond the two words: *cop* and *dog*. She massaged a spot over her heart, but the pain was too deep to rub away.

Saige returned her empty cup and refocused on the topic. "Val, do any able-bodied teens needing jobs live close by?"

"A few. The Baker boys are the closest. They live a half-mile down on the right. Their twenty acres border your twenty. Jimmy's a high-school senior and plays football. Maybe he can help after practice." She tilted her head. "If he can't come, then maybe Lincoln and Mark, the two brothers next to him in age can. Want me to ask?"

"Yes, please. Dad and I would like to get as much work done before our construction crew gets here."

She looked toward the house, her blue eyes full of interest. "I can't wait to see what you'll do with the old place." She pulled out her cell and dialed a number.

Within minutes, the sound of an ATV and a riding lawn mower signaled the brothers' approach. The one on the ATV skidded to a stop only feet from where Saige stood. Neither of the teens wore helmets, but they both wore wide grins.

Valerie introduced them, then turned to Robert. "After you and Saige finish, stop by for supper. I'll have plenty, and I'm sure you'll be tired enough you won't want to cook." She glanced toward their small motor home.

Robert looked from Saige to their neighbor. "Thank you for the invitation, Val, but we'll need to ask for a rain check. We have a lot to get done in a short amount of time."

She smiled. "Okay. I don't mean to be pushy. Forgive me. I'm just excited to have neighbors."

By sunset, Saige gazed at the heaped wire and rotted posts stacked in a neat pile near the road for pick up the next day. The boys had taken all the cans home for recycling, and the freshly mowed lawn improved the appearance of the property considerably.

After dinner and clean up, Robert stepped outside, unfolded a couple of chairs, and signaled Saige to sit. He tipped back against the motor home and linked his fingers behind his head. "Well, we're off to a good start."

"Yes." Saige slumped in her chair and gazed at the stars. The tinkling of Valerie Langdon's wind chimes and the melody of the crickets and pond frogs lulled her. She closed her eyes and let the soft breeze caress her skin.

They opened at the sound of a vehicle's tires crunching on the gravel road. Beams from the headlights sliced through the night. The driver slowed and turned into the Langdon driveway. Bright motion sensor lights came on, and Saige noted the low-profile blue and red lights on the car roof and the State Patrol emblem on the door. The cop with the dog had come home.

Jase Langdon massaged his forehead and tried to blink away the tiredness as he listened to his mother talk about her encounter with the new neighbors. He placed his fork on his empty plate and pushed them away. He wanted to get out of his uniform and into bed, but his mom always wanted to talk when he got home. She thrived on interaction with others, so he made the effort to please her, though exhaustion often seeped into his bones.

"They are nice people and hard workers. I want to have them over for dinner soon. I think you'll like Saige. She's a few years younger than you and has the prettiest brown eyes and smile I've seen. She's tall and physically strong and isn't a layabout. She got right in and did as much as her father. They didn't talk much, but they worked together like well-oiled machines. You should have seen them, Jase. Each knew what to do, and their practiced movements reminded me of a choreographed dance."

Jase straightened and crossed his arms. Images of the women his mother had tried to hook him up with the last few years passed through his thoughts. "Mom, you haven't decided to turn matchmaker again, have you? You know how I feel about that."

He made a mental note to stay far away from Saige Harmony. Brown eyes, strength, and ability had always attracted him, but they added up to more distraction than he could handle right now.

Valerie sighed. "I worry about you, Son. You're twenty-eight and so tied to your job you don't have room for anyone. If you keep going like this, I fear you'll grow into a lonely old man. God didn't intend for you to be alone."

"I have you and Dan, Mom, and no time for anyone else right now. Crime in the area is rising, and the department is understaffed."

Valerie stared into his eyes. "Dan is a dog. You warned me he's a life-saving tool, not a pet. No matter how smart he is, you can't have an in-depth conversation with him. He can't put his arms around you when you've had a hard day and tell you he loves you. He can't share your burdens or celebrate your triumphs."

"No, but he doesn't make demands either. He's happy with food, water, shelter, play, and work. When I'm ready to go, he is too. He doesn't complain about long hours or less than ideal working conditions. He doesn't care about how much money I bring home either. He lives in the moment."

Valerie shook her head and took the dirty dishes to the sink. "I hope your words don't return to bite you."

In the depths of his soul, Jase hoped they wouldn't either. He pushed the sudden yearning back into the small compartment where he kept such emotions. He couldn't afford them. He stood and brought more dishes to the sink, then he embraced his mother and kissed her forehead. "Thanks for caring, Mom. I'll be okay."

She stroked his cheek. "Though you're a tough man who wears a badge and a gun, you're still my boy, Jase. I'll always care."

He stepped away and stretched. "I'm headed to bed. Do me a favor?"

Valerie nodded. "If I can."

"Keep the doors and downstairs windows locked even during the day, especially when I'm gone. Don't open to strangers. We've had a rash of burglaries lately, and the thieves are getting bolder."

Valerie looked around the kitchen. "What are they stealing?"

"Anything they can sell quickly for drug money—jewelry, smaller electronics, guns. Some are breaking into barns and shops and stealing tools and saddles."

"Oh, Jase. Are the thieves local? I'd hate to think our neighbors are involved in this."

"I don't know. More people have moved into the area from the suburbs. Promise me you'll stay alert?" He looked out the window toward the Harmony's place. "Warn the new neighbors too, okay?"

"I will."

TWO

"Yoo-hoo."

Saige removed her safety glasses and gloves and brushed the sweat off her forehead with her sleeve as her neighbor approached. "Val, you're up early. I hope all the banging didn't disturb you."

She smiled. "I'm an early riser. I saw the truck arrive with the roll-off at first light. You've been working hard since, so I thought you might like some fresh lemonade."

Robert laid down his sledgehammer and removed his gloves. His eyes met hers. "A glass of cold lemonade sounds great. Thank you."

Valerie's eyes widened and she blushed. "You're welcome."

The pause lengthened.

Whoa. What's this? Saige frowned and looked from the neighbor to her dad. Did a look of mutual attraction pass between them? No. She had to be imagining things. Her dad wouldn't consider involving himself with the mother of a K-9 officer after what he'd been through with Chad, would he?

Saige returned her empty cup. "Thanks. If you'll excuse us now, we need to finish gutting the kitchen."

Valerie nodded. "Sure. I just wanted to warn you. Jase said thieves are breaking in and stealing things for drug money, so be careful."

Saige's lips tightened, and she met her dad's eyes. "Seems life outside the suburbs isn't as idyllic as one might think."

Robert handed Valerie his cup. "Is Jase working today?"

"No, he's off the next few days. He likes to get up early to exercise. Says he feels better when he can let off steam. He goes to an Israeli martial arts class called Krav Maga, or he takes his dog, Dan, for a run. He's at his Krav class this morning."

She smiled. "I also came over to invite you to the 4-H barbecue and livestock sale on Saturday. We can see which animals won ribbons and then go to the Exhibit Hall and look at other projects. After dinner and the sale, they have a dance on the pavilion patio."

Before Saige could decline the invitation, Robert agreed to go. Enthusiasm warmed his tones. "Thanks for the invitation, Val. I remember entering my animals in the fair when I was a boy."

He turned to Saige. "You'll have fun, hon. The carnival is set up next to the fairgrounds. I've always enjoyed the energy, the colorful lights, the smells of animals, dust, and popcorn, and the auctioneer's voice."

Valerie nodded, her words enthusiastic, "I'm glad you'll come. I got tickets for the barbecue from the Baker boys just in case. They're in 4-H and will be selling their pigs if they win blue ribbons."

Saige struggled against her wish to stay home and relax with her desire to see her dad happy again. She squelched a sigh and forced a smile. She would not quench his enthusiasm. "Thanks for thinking of us, Val."

"You're welcome. I hope you have fun. The exhibits stay open until just before the sale, so we can stroll through the animal barn first and see which 4-H animals won, then we can look at the open class exhibits in the Exhibit Hall. I enjoy the art gallery, baked goods, and quilts the most. Once the ropes are taken down to let people in, we'll take our plates and sit on hay bales or at tables—your choice."

Robert smiled. "Why don't you ride with Saige and me? I'd be happy to drive you unless you'll be going with Jase."

Valerie looked from Saige to Robert, an uncertain smile lifting the corners of her lips. "Thank you. Jase will be on duty, so I accept your invitation. We'll need to leave around five."

Saige watched Valerie walk down the drive. She turned to Robert, eyebrows raised.

He held up his hand. "Before you say anything, look across the road and tell me if you've seen any other vehicles parked in the Langdon driveway besides Jase's patrol car or that worn-out pickup truck."

She nodded. "You're right. I'd much rather ride in our comfy extended cab. Do you think that truck is modern enough to have seatbelts and airbags?"

He laughed. "Probably not, though I'm sure Jase made sure the truck has a set of belts. I can't see him letting Val drive the thing without them. Now, let's get back to work."

Jase parked his patrol car near the fairground's entrance and signaled Dan out of the car. He leashed the dog, and they walked toward the crowd.

"Okay, partner, get your game face on."

Dan looked at him, yawned, and then watched everything, his ears perked and his nostrils moving like a predator scenting prey.

A county Sheriff's Deputy walked around a group of carnival goers and approached. "Glad to see you and Dan, Jase. Thanks for helping us out tonight."

"No problem, Carl. Do you expect trouble?"

The older officer smiled. "I always expect trouble. Then, if nothing happens, I can tell my wife I had a good day."

Jase looked around. "The crowd is bigger this year."

The deputy's eyes scanned the vicinity. "Yep, so keep your eyes peeled. I have two other officers patrolling the grounds. Check the pavilion and Exhibit Hall. We'll check the carnival area and animal pens. Then we'll rotate every hour."

Jase eased through the crowd looking for known drug dealers and any unusual behavior. He searched the dark corners and out-of-the-way places. Then he entered the Exhibit Hall. As he walked the aisles in the baked goods section, he answered questions from both neighbors and strangers about Dan. Though he responded, he stayed alert to the dog's posture and to movement around him.

"Come and meet my son."

Jase turned at the sound of his mother's voice. He scanned the faces of his mother and new neighbors, but his gaze fixed on the woman. *Saige Harmony.* Jewel brown eyes. Clear, tanned skin. Strands of long brown hair that, at the slightest movement, captured the light and streaked her hair with gold. Athletic build. Self-assured posture. Ringless finger. *I'm in trouble.*

When she smiled, his gut tightened, and he sucked in a quick breath. She stood close enough he could smell her light, clean scent.

Dan looked up and cocked his head.

His mother smiled. "Jase, these are our neighbors, Robert and Saige Harmony." She turned. "Robert and Saige, please meet my son, Jase."

They exchanged greetings. As they chatted, Jase forced his gaze away from Saige to scan the area, but he couldn't look away for long. The more he saw, the more he liked. *No! Get a grip.*

A young boy approached and caught his attention. He stopped a couple of feet away and stared at Dan before his eyes traveled up Jase's uniform to his gun, badge, and hat.

"Are you a policeman, Mister?" He spoke just above a whisper.

Jase smiled. "I am. Are you okay?'

He nodded, but his lips trembled, and a tear slid from the corner of his left eye. "Mama told me to tell a policeman if I need help."

Jase knelt on one knee. "What's your name?"

The boy stared at him. "You're not a stranger, are you? Mama said not to talk to strangers."

"When I'm wearing this," Jase touched his badge, "I'm not a stranger."

"I'm Eddie. Eddie Taylor."

"How old are you, little one?"

"Five."

"How may I help you?"

"My mom is lost. I can't find her anywhere." Panic edged his words as he looked around.

Jase stood. "We'll find your mom, kiddo. How about you walk with my partner, Dan, and me? We'll go to that room over there where a person on a loudspeaker can ask your mother to come and get you." Jase held out his right hand and Eddie gripped his. "What's your mom's name?"

Eddie frowned. "Mom."

Jase smiled. "What does your dad call her?"

The boy's frown deepened, and the corners of his mouth turned down. "He calls her bad names. That's why we don't live with him anymore. He's mean."

Jase's lips tightened, but he forced them to relax. "Does your mom have a good friend?"

"Yes. Georgia."

"What does Georgia call your mom?"

He chewed on his bottom lip for several moments. "She calls her Tiffany."

Valerie gasped. "Tiffany Taylor? Jase, that's Lucy Taylor's ex-daughter-in-law. You know, Mavis and Leo Jackson's daughter? The ones who owned the property before Robert and Saige?"

Jase spoke in his softest voice, "Eddie, is your dad's name Pete?"

"Yes." He looked down and scuffed his feet.

"Okay, buddy. Let's go get your mother."

He turned. "Don't wait up for me, Mom. I'll be home late." Then he nodded at his neighbors. "Nice to meet you. Mr. Harmony. Miss Harmony."

"Call me Robert."

"I'm Saige."

He nodded. "Jase."

His gaze met hers and held. He wished he knew what the look in her eyes meant. He sensed she felt the instant tug of attraction between them, but he also recognized caution and wariness. Why would she be wary of him? Or was she afraid of Dan?

Eddie pointed at Valerie and pulled on his hand. "Mister Jase? That's your mom?"

"Yes."

"Does she ever get lost?"

"No, but come with me, and I'll tell you about a time I got lost. I've never been so scared."

THREE

No, no, no. I won't let a pair of clear blue eyes, manly jaw, broad shoulders, dark good looks, and a kind heart snare my emotions.

Saige stared as Jase Langdon led Eddie away. Her heart raced and then missed a beat. She could resist the attraction she'd felt when their eyes met, but she could never erase the image of Jase kneeling to put himself on Eddie's level, nor could she ignore the gentle tone and caring words he used to talk with the child. He'd spoken to his mother with the same grace. A man who harnessed his strength and his words to treat his mother and a lost boy with such respect breached her defenses. Kindness always trumped good looks in her book.

She sighed. *Why can't the man be a pilot, mechanic, carpenter, or butcher?*

"Hey," Valerie looked out the large open door. "A crowd is moving toward the pavilion. They must be serving dinner. Are you ready to eat?"

Robert sniffed. "Smells good. Yes, I've been ready for the last hour. Saige?"

"I'm ready." She followed a step behind her dad and Valerie but glanced over her shoulder in Jase's direction.

The PA system crackled, and a man spoke in a voice that carried through the large building and outside. "Tiffany Taylor? Please come to the lost-and-found booth in the Exhibit Hall."

Saige stepped into the pavilion courtyard as a teary-eyed woman brushed past her and rushed inside the building.

Valerie smiled. "Eddie will be reunited with his mom in no time. That's Tiffany."

Her smile faded into a frown as she looked over Saige's shoulder. "Uh-oh. Looks like Pete is here with his mother, Lucy. They're headed toward the Exhibit Hall. I don't like the angry look on his face. Hope he doesn't intend to cause trouble. Jase has been called to his house several times in the last three years for domestic violence."

Every muscle in Saige's body tightened as she turned toward the burly man and his mother. She tried to swallow the lump in her throat. Jase would be in the middle of a domestic scene, and she knew from experience how easily anger could rupture into violence. *Calm down. Jase and Dan can handle the situation.* Her lungs reached for air. Chad had been able to handle most situations too, until he couldn't. And then he ended up dead.

Saige turned and held out her ticket to Robert. "I'll be back. Grab me a plate if you get to the servers before I return."

She moved through the crowd and toward the lost and found as quickly as she could, her breath coming in short gasps. She spotted Jase talking to Eddie and Tiffany just outside the booth.

She spoke so he could hear. "Jase."

He correctly interpreted the concern in her voice and straightened. She pointed over her shoulder to the two a short distance behind her, and his eyes narrowed. He said something to Dan, and the dog stood, tense and ready.

Jase opened the door to the booth. "Tiffany, take Eddie inside. Now. Get down on the floor away from the door. Get the man in the booth down too."

Tiffany looked up and saw Pete approaching. She pulled Eddie inside with her and closed the door. The lock clicked.

Jase stepped in front of the door.

Saige moved to another aisle away from Jase's direct line of fire and watched from behind an oak display case. Her body trembled and sweat beaded the top of her lip. She wiped clammy palms down her jeans.

The few remaining fairgoers in the hall looked around, saw the situation, and ducked behind something solid and pulled out their phones.

Pete's steps faltered when he saw Jase and Dan. He stopped ten feet from them.

"Jase."

"Pete."

"Looking for my wife. I saw her go in there."

Jase said nothing.

Pete's lips thinned into a tight line, then he opened his mouth and spewed obscenities before raising his voice. "Tiffany, come out here now. I want to talk to you."

Lucy touched his arm and spoke in a soft, pleading voice. "Let's go, Son."

He shrugged off her hand. "Leave me alone, old woman. I intend to talk to my wife. Tiffany? Come out. I know you're in there."

He took a step toward the door, and Dan growled. He stopped.

"Step back, Pete." Jase's conversational tone held no threat, but Saige knew he was ready to move. She sensed the tautness of his body from where she stood.

"Please, Lord. Don't let this situation get violent." Saige kept her eyes open as she whispered the prayer.

Pete's right hand moved toward his pants pocket.

"Keep your hands away from your sides." Jase's voice sharpened, and he stepped forward. "Move your hand away now, Pete, or I'll send the dog."

Pete glared. He didn't obey immediately, but at the sight of Dan, focused and ready to be sent, he moved his hand away bit by bit. His deliberate, slow movements taunted Jase.

Saige felt the challenge and disrespect from where she stood. Her heartbeats pounded in her ears.

Pete's voice rose to a loud, wheedling whine. "I just want to talk to my wife."

Jase shook his head. "Last I heard, she has a restraining order against you. No contact."

The PA system crackled and the man in the room with Eddie and Tiffany spoke, his voice calm and clear, "Would the Sheriff or the Deputy closest to the lost-and-found booth please come immediately?" His words reached all parts of the fairgrounds.

Pete grunted.

Before Pete could say or do anything else, two deputies entered the Exhibit Hall, their hands within easy reach of their tasers. They moved to each side of the angry, belligerent man and stopped a few paces behind him.

Dan pulled on the leash.

Jase's eyes met those of the deputies. "Please detain this man while I handle the dog. After, I need to speak with the detainee. Be advised that he reached toward his right pants pocket and didn't immediately obey the order to stop."

The deputies cuffed Pete and searched him. They removed a cell phone from his baggy pants pocket.

The man sneered. "Told you. I just wanted to talk to Tiffany."

"You're under arrest, Pete, for violating the restraining order." Jase nodded, and the two deputies hauled him away.

Saige released the breath she'd been holding and slumped against the display case. Her legs continued to tremble. She watched as Jase and the two deputies walked Pete and his mother out of the Exhibit Hall.

On his way out, Jase glanced at her, and their eyes met. "Thanks." He mouthed.

She nodded and moved toward the pavilion after the shaking subsided.

Once Pete and Lucy left the fairgrounds, Jase strolled toward the pavilion. His thoughts returned to Saige's actions. After she'd warned him, she'd moved away and watched from behind the display case. He'd seen fear in her wide brown eyes—not the curiosity or excitement the other bystanders showed, but fear verging on terror. What had caused such a reaction? Her response seemed unusual given the situation. And why the wary look earlier? What secrets hid in Saige Harmony's background?

Jase returned to the pavilion just as the servers ladled the final scoop of barbecue brisket and trimmings on the plate of the last person in line. He scanned the diners still seated, and his gaze found Saige's as if drawn to hers by a magnet.

He felt her look deep in his gut.

As he approached his mother and neighbors, people moved away from Dan and gave them space.

Valerie smiled. "Everything's under control?"

Jase nodded. "At least for now."

He studied Saige's face. "Are you okay?"

Robert and Valerie turned to her with questions in their eyes.

Color flooded her cheeks. "Yes." She started to say more but closed her lips and shook her head.

"Thanks for warning me. That extra minute helped."

She nodded and lowered her lashes. "Dan is beautiful. He reminds me of a German Shepherd my eldest brother had."

"Are you afraid of dogs?"

Saige looked up and smiled. "No, I love them. If I didn't spend so many hours at work, I'd have a couple."

So, the wary, reserved look didn't come from her fear of Dan. That narrows the problem. She's wary of me. Why?

Valerie stood and brushed straw off her jeans. "The sale is about to start. If we're going to stay to see the Baker boys sell their pigs, we need to find a place in the stands. Robert, I left the blankets in your truck. We'll need them to soften the hard benches and to keep warm after the sun goes down."

Robert took out his keys. "We'll be right back, hon. Why don't you head to the sale barn and save us some seats?"

"Okay, Dad."

Jase waited for her to look at him. When their eyes met, he smiled. "I'm patrolling the sale barn and pens for the next hour if you'd like to walk with Dan and me."

Saige studied his face, a look of uncertainty in her eyes.

He tried to interpret the subtle expressions chasing each other across her face while he waited for her answer.

Finally, she nodded. "Do you want me to walk on Dan's other side or next to you?"

She's had experience with police dogs and their handlers? "Walk beside me."

She stepped to his side, and her scent quickened his pulse. Though she left him enough space to reach for a weapon without interference, she stood close enough his warmth reached out to hers.

They walked in silence until he chuckled. "I didn't expect our introduction to be so—dramatic."

A grin tugged at the corners of her mouth. "Neither did I. Maybe we should start over." Saige stopped and turned toward him, her right hand extended. "I'm Saige Harmony, your new neighbor."

He accepted her handshake. *Soft hands for a carpenter.* "Jase Langdon. Nice to meet you Saige Harmony."

They moved toward the livestock pavilion.

Jase's eyes searched the crowd as he continued the conversation. "What should I know about my new neighbors?"

Saige shrugged. "Are you asking as a cop or a neighbor?"

He chuckled. "Good question. Let's try the neighbor first."

"Nothing much to tell. My dad, brothers, and I have our own construction company. Most of our jobs are in Colorado, but several of the last ones have been in different states. We're booked out for the next two years, but we're taking time off to fix the house across from yours. Dad and I will use this as our base of operation."

"Your brothers live nearby?"

"A couple hours away. They both have families."

"Mother?"

"She died two years ago in a car accident."

"Hobbies or things you like to do?"

"Take walks. Ride my bike. Read. Cook when I have more space than that found in a motor home." Saige tilted her head. Her gaze slid to his badge and then back to his face. "What, besides the obvious signs of your career choice, should I know about you?"

He laughed. "My career choice about sums things up. I work four ten-hour day shifts for six months then switch to six months of night shifts. The schedule doesn't allow for many extracurricular activities during my days off, so, I eat, sleep, workout, take Dan for runs, go to church when I'm not on duty, and occasionally take Mom out to dinner."

"Your dad?"

"Died of a heart attack when I was thirteen."

They slowed as they approached the livestock barn.

Saige strained to see if any places to sit remained in the bleachers. "Wow, this is a popular place."

Jase pointed. "Yes, but I think I see room for you and our parents in the north bleachers."

"Hey, Mister Jase. Miss Saige."

They stopped as Lincoln Baker stepped away from his pig's pen and smiled. "Look. My pig took first place in his weight category."

"Good work, Linc. Nice looking pig."

"Mark and Jimmy get to sell too." He pointed to the ribbons hanging on his brothers' stalls.

They chatted with the excited teen until Jase spotted Robert and his mother. "You better find your places. The auctioneer just entered the booth."

Saige smiled at both Lincoln and Jase. "I'll see you around, neighbors."

Her gaze met Jase's and turned serious. She spoke just above a whisper, "Be safe, Jase Langdon."

He nodded.

FOUR

Saige frowned as she shifted the gears of Val's father's pickup and cringed at the grinding. *Why, did I agree to borrow this ancient relic when Val offered? I should have waited for Dad and my brothers to get back. Had I not been so impatient to finish the framing in the master bath . . .*

She eased out of the lumber yard gates and turned onto the highway.

The truck coughed and spluttered.

Saige glanced down at the gauges and prayed nothing would malfunction or break down between here and Val's house. The lumber yard was five miles out of town in the opposite direction, and she hadn't noticed any auto garages. She'd left her cell phone home in her haste, so, if she broke down, she'd be sitting at the side of the road, in the dark, waiting for rescue. Her mouth tightened. She was a carpenter and welder, not a mechanic, so, unless Dad and her brothers came looking for her, she'd be at the mercy of strangers.

Thunder cracked, and Saige eyed the storm clouds blotting out the last of the sun. She jumped and gasped when a jagged bolt of lightning ripped through the sky in front of her, and sudden heavy rain pelted the windshield. With trembling hands, she fumbled for the windshield wiper knob and gripped the wheel with both hands until her knuckles whitened. Her heart pounded. Chad had died on a night like this.

Though she watched the road, her thoughts raced to the time, five years ago, when she had returned to her dorm room to find the dean, her friend Ben, and her roommate waiting for her.

Ben stepped forward and took her hand. "We have bad news, Saige. Sit down, please." Her knees weakened as Ben led her to a chair.

He sat on a stool in front of her, his hand still holding hers. "Your dad called an hour ago. Your older brother died a half-hour before he called."

She crumpled and tried to blink away the darkness narrowing her vision. "How?"

The dean shook his head. "He didn't say. He wants you to remain here until one of your brothers can come and get you tomorrow."

They stayed until her screams and cries turned into silence.

The dean rose and patted Saige's shoulder. "We'll go so you can get some rest. I'll let your professors know. Don't worry about anything."

When they left, Saige packed her things with her roommate's help and started the seven-hour drive back home. *Mom and Dad need me. I'm not waiting.* She'd text her brothers when she got closer.

After she turned off the interstate two hours later, her car was one of only a few on the road for the next eighty miles. Her headlights pierced the darkness as thunder, lightning, and rain rent the sky. The rain turned to sleet and hail as she started up the first mountain pass. By the time she approached the summit of the second pass two hours later, the sleet had turned to snow. She lost traction a couple of times, so she slowed, shifted into low gear, and crept down the winding narrow road, breathing her thanks as she passed each mile marker. Fortunately, the snow hadn't deepened enough she needed to chain the tires.

Once she navigated the hairpin turn on the downhill side of the mountain and found a turnout at a lower elevation, she pulled over and tipped her head against the headrest. She closed her eyes and tried to calm herself.

Her attention snapped back to the present when a brief siren blare drew her eyes to the rearview mirror.

Red and blue flashing lights. She looked at her speedometer. *Great. Fifteen miles over the speed limit. How can a truck almost sixty years old do that?*

Saige signaled, slowed, and pulled onto the shoulder. She brushed the tears from her eyes and tried to calm her rapid breathing as she fumbled in her purse for her license. Saige opened the glove box. *I hope Val has her registration and current proof of insurance.*

Jase approached his mother's truck with caution. Mom had called earlier to say she'd lent the vehicle to Saige, so, unless someone stole the truck, he knew the driver.

He frowned. He had every intention of giving her a gentle scold for pushing the old truck so hard and maybe even a warning for speeding, but when she rolled down the window and he flashed his light across her face, he swallowed his words. Dilated pupils, shaking hands, white face, taut body, fast, shallow breathing, and tears still clinging to her dark lashes signaled she wasn't in a good space.

"Jase." Her shoulders slumped.

"Saige. What's wrong? Are you okay?"

Her fingers clenched the wheel. "No, I'm not. I don't like driving in bad weather or at night, and I didn't know if the truck would get me home without breaking down."

The pain in her voice and the catch at the end of her sentence triggered something deep inside. The woman who seemed to have herself together didn't hesitate to admit she didn't. Yet, her words were shadowed and careful, as if she restrained herself from saying more.

"I'm on my way home. I'll stay behind you to make sure nothing happens. Or do you want me to call and ask your dad and brothers to come and get you?"

She took a deep breath and sat up. "No, don't call. I'll drive the rest of the way."

He followed her home and pulled in behind her when she turned into his driveway and parked. The security lights popped on, and she got out of the truck.

He signaled Dan out of the car and walked toward her.

Saige's hand shook when she held out the key. "Will you tell Val I said thanks for the loaner?" Her voice cracked. "Thanks, Jase."

"Wait." His hand on her arm stopped her from walking past him. "You're not okay, Saige. Something is wrong. Tell me?"

Saige didn't say anything for several moments as she stared into his face. Tears glazed her eyes and her breathing turned ragged. "Nights like this remind me of one of the most painful times in my life. I—" She sobbed and pinched her lips closed. "I'm sorry. I still can't talk about what happened."

He embraced her and let her cry on his neck. Her arms encircled his torso like he was a life preserver and she a drowning woman. Jase inhaled her scent and let the feel of her warm breath and soft hair heat his blood. His heart rate increased. If he lowered his chin and turned his head, their lips would touch. He could imagine how soft and warm hers would be. Temptation grew.

Back off. Now. He resisted the warning in his brain before drawing a breath. He stood and let her cry. He would not take advantage of her vulnerable state to steal a kiss.

Saige calmed, and her grip loosened. Her hands slid to his waist where they brushed against his pistol grip and handcuffs. She stiffened and stepped away with a look on her face he guessed to be discomfort. She dropped her hands and stepped back. "I'm sorry for blubbering all over your collar, Jase. I won't do so again."

"Saige—"

"Goodnight. Cam and Brett will unload the truck tomorrow morning early." She turned and left.

Though she walked away, he sensed she fled his presence at an emotional level. *Why?*

FIVE

What were you thinking? You let a cop embrace you. You participated. Saige's conscience pricked her with each step. *Not smart.*

I know. I know. But he's solid, like a rock in a storm. I felt safe in his arms. At least, she had, until she realized she'd hugged a man wearing body armor under his uniform and weapons at his waist.

"There you are." Robert flipped on the porch light and stepped outside. "The boys and I were getting ready to come after you."

"I'm okay, Dad."

"You don't look okay, hon. I thought the storm might bother you. Have you been thinking about Chad?"

She nodded. "I'm going to bed."

"Maybe you should sleep in since tomorrow is Saturday."

"No, Dad. We have too much to do."

"Did you call the Baker boys? Are they coming over to help?"

"Yes. They'll be here by eight."

"Good. The sooner we get the fences and gates built, the sooner we can get the animals."

She reached for the door handle on the motor home.

Dad put a hand on her shoulder. "The master suite will be ready soon. In fact, I think you can move in next week."

She lifted an eyebrow. "The master suite? But that's your room."

"No. I'm taking the room across the hall. I like the front view better."

The front view. The windows faced the county road . . . and Valerie Langdon's house.

"Are you sure?"

He nodded. "I'm sure. Now, go get some sleep."

Saige introduced her brothers to the Baker boys, then gave them instructions. "You'll each be a welder's helper. Your main job is to make sure the grass doesn't catch fire while we have our hoods on. You have backpack sprayers filled with water. If anything starts to burn, you spray the flames. Okay?"

They nodded.

"My brothers and I will use a lot of welding rods, so watch to see when the rod burns down and hand us another one. We'll drop the used stubs into coffee cans you'll hold out to us."

Jimmy gave a thumbs up. "Understood."

"Then you'll use this little pointed metal hammer to knock off the slag from the weld."

She handed them each a set of safety glasses and earplugs. "Use these while we're running the generators and welding. Don't look at the arc directly. Questions?"

Lincoln looked from Brett to Cam. "Who's my welder?"

Saige grinned. "Take your pick. Both my brothers get cranky if their helpers don't pay attention, so be warned."

Jimmy stepped forward. "I choose you, Miss Saige. You're much prettier than your brothers." He wiggled his eyebrows, and Cam and Brett laughed.

"No doubt about that." Cam adjusted his hood. "Just don't get any ideas."

Brett laughed and reached for his heavy leather gloves.

Jimmy eyed her brothers' muscular builds, then smirked and saluted.

Saige grinned. She was a woman in a traditionally male-dominant career, so she was used to all the testosterone surrounding her. Jimmy seemed to have his fair share of the hormone. She'd bet he was the star football player all the cheerleaders wanted to date.

They'd dug the post holes and set the posts earlier in the week then cut the dips in the top of the posts yesterday. Dad had lifted the top rail in place with the forklift and waited until they screwed the threaded ends together.

All they had to do today was weld the top rail to the posts. *All? You're funny. Twenty acres of perimeter fencing, or 3,743 linear feet, not including interior cross-fencing, wire stretching to contain the animals, gate construction, and the building of a new pipe entry? All?* She didn't think they'd be finished for a couple of weeks. Cam and Brett would return to their homes tomorrow afternoon, so she and Dad would be the ones to continue until her brothers came back.

She cranked the engine, connected the ground, put on her gloves, and tilted the hood over her face. She smiled. Competing with her brothers to see who had the best welds and got the most done by the end of the day inspired her to be quicker and better than them. She didn't always win, but she tried her best.

Saige touched the rod to the steel and didn't stop welding until Jimmy tapped her shoulder.

She raised her hood.

He pointed to a small delivery van. "Your dad says to come."

Ah, lunch.

Jase slowed as he passed the Harmony crew and the Baker boys in his silver SUV. None lifted their heads from their work.

After he parked in the back, Mom signaled him to join her at the table under the large cottonwood tree in the front yard.

"I've got lemonade or water, Jase. Help yourself." She chuckled and waved toward the Harmony's place. "Watching the neighbors work is as entertaining as a good movie."

He poured a glass of water and sat. "I'm glad to see the Baker brothers working so hard. They tend to get into mischief if they aren't occupied. When football season ends, I hope Jimmy finds something better to do than hang out with his trouble-making friends. I don't want to haul him to jail again."

He watched the activity across the street. His gaze followed Saige, and his admiration grew. Each of her movements counted. From what he could tell at a distance, she was fast and accurate and didn't expend extra energy to do her job. She moved in rhythm with her brothers, and they accomplished a lot.

He kept an eye on her as he mowed the lawn and emptied the clippings into the compost pile.

When the Soups, Salads, and Sandwiches delivery van drove up, Mom turned from setting the water and shaded her eyes. "Let's join them, Jase. I made a fresh zucchini cake to contribute."

He remembered Saige's expression from last night. "You don't think we'd be imposing?"

"No. Robert invited us. He ordered for us too. Come on."

"I'm not sure, Mom. I don't think Saige likes cops."

Valerie turned, her eyebrows raised. "What? How do you know?"

Jase shrugged.

His mother's eyes met his. She grinned. "Well, you're not in uniform, so maybe she won't notice."

Won't notice? Ha. She's as drawn to me as I am to her regardless of how she feels about my job. She'll notice.

"Maybe." Jase leashed Dan and waited for his mother to grab the cake, a knife, and some paper plates.

Robert saw them approach and waved them closer. "Jase. Val. Come on over. Food's ready."

Saige looked up from her plate and scanned him from head to foot before meeting his eyes.

He stopped next to her and smiled. "No uniform today."

Her eyes met his. "Even if I didn't know you, Jase, I could identify you as law enforcement or military from ten yards away whether you wear a uniform or not."

Jase quirked an eyebrow. "Really? How?" *Experience? Is that why she's leery of me? Did she date a cop and the relationship went south? Has she been in trouble with the law?*

At first, he didn't think she'd answer. "The short haircut, the way you carry yourself, the self-assurance, the watchful stillness, the controlled calmness. And Dan, of course."

She smiled and tilted her head toward the van. "Better get your food."

Jase gave Dan the signal to sit-stay and dropped the leash.

When he returned with a full plate, he smiled at Saige. "Any more room at this table?"

She hesitated but moved over a space.

He sat down, and she slid a little farther away from him.

Why does she resist me? Has a cop hurt her? The more she eludes, the more I want to chase. This is bad. I promised myself I wouldn't get involved, yet, here I am letting her intrude into my thoughts more and more each day. You're pitiful, Langdon. Get a grip.

SIX

Saige followed her dad into the sanctuary and glanced around.

Val waved. "Over here, Robert. Saige. We saved you seats."

Jase stood when they approached and shook Dad's hand. He smiled at her. "Hi."

Her heart missed a beat when she saw the warmth in his eyes. "Hi."

He sat, and Saige slid in next to him. Dad took the aisle seat.

Valerie leaned forward to look around Jase. "I'm so glad you could come and so pleased you agreed to have lunch with us after service."

The music started and encouraged worshipers to settle, but Saige had a hard time doing this. Jase sat close enough she could feel his heat and smell his aftershave. Every nerve fired at his nearness. When they stood to sing, his smooth, rich bass weakened her knees. *Stop. Focus.*

Saige straightened and stared at the words on the screen then joined her alto to the rest of the congregation's voices. "In Christ alone, my hope is found, He is my light, my strength, my song."

She closed her eyes. Truly, Christ had been her firm foundation through the darkness, pain, and storms filling the last five years. He had been her Comforter and her All in All. Tears slid out the corner of her eyelids as she sang.

Her eyes remained closed. The voices of those around her blended into a beautiful tapestry of praise that lifted her spirit and her hands.

When the song ended, she opened her eyes and brushed away tears before glancing at Jase. Their eyes met and held until the musicians played the next song.

They sat for the sermon, and Jase's arm rested against hers. He didn't break the contact and neither did she. With a slight movement, he slid his little finger over the top of hers.

Startled, she looked into his face.

His eyes asked a question.

She gazed at their little fingers. If she wanted to keep him at a distance, she should move her hand away. *But I don't want to. I remember how safe I felt in his arms.*

She turned her hand over and let him rest his fingertips in her palm. Slowly, she curled her fingers around his.

His smile made her breath catch.

Jase struggled to focus. What had he done? His heart thrummed against his ribs. After all his determination to stay away from Saige Harmony, his emotions wouldn't let him. They had broken out of their compartment and flooded his soul with yearning from the beginning of their acquaintance.

The more he chastised himself for allowing her so much of his mental real estate, the more he thought of her. The more he told himself to stay away, the more he wanted to be near her. She was a larger distraction than he'd anticipated, and he knew a relationship with her would complicate his life. Yet, he'd initiated the first touch. He half-expected her to reject the contact, but she hadn't. *Now what?*

At the end of the closing prayer, Jase brushed his fingertips across her palm and stood. He wanted to offer her a hand up but thought another touch might be too soon. Already, caution filled her eyes.

He smiled. "See you at the house."

Saige nodded and followed Robert out of the sanctuary.

His mother touched his arm. "I'm ready if you are."

"Mom," Jase eased out of the parking lot and onto the highway, "has Robert or Saige said anything about a traumatic experience they had in the past? Maybe something related to storms or cops?"

"Robert lost a son several years ago, but he didn't tell me how. He said his wife died two years ago when a drunk driver swerved into her lane and hit her head-on. Why?"

"I pulled Saige over for speeding the other night. When she rolled down the window, she'd been crying. Later, she told me the stormy night reminded her of one the most painful times in her life."

"Oh, Jase. Surely, you didn't give her a ticket."

"No. Not even a warning."

"You like her, don't you?"

Jase sighed. "Yes, Mom, too much for my own comfort. I'm not sure what she thinks of me though. I get the feeling Saige has been involved with a cop in her past. She's cautious."

Mom patted his arm and smiled. "Let's see if a delicious lunch and good company will relax their tongues."

Over lunch, Jase listened to the conversation but didn't participate much until Robert mentioned someone had trespassed while they'd all been gone on errands.

Jase leaned forward. "Details?"

Robert looked from Jase to Saige, who had stiffened. "I planned to tell you, hon, but this slipped my mind. I reported the trespass, and a Sheriff's deputy came out and took pictures and filed a report. I also warned the neighbors."

He turned back to Jase. "I intended to tell you too. They didn't take anything, though they tried to get into the barn. I saw their tracks the next morning. Looked like two people with men-sized boots. I'd already replaced the broken boards, put bars on the windows, and added a heavy-duty clasp and lock on the door after you told us people were stealing tools."

Saige's jaw tightened. "We're finishing the entry and the gate this week then. The cross-fencing can wait. So can the stalls."

Robert nodded. "I ordered security lights and a couple of cameras. Cam and Brett will install the cameras when they return on Friday."

Valerie frowned. "Jase, do you think those tracks could belong to the same two homeless guys the sheriff arrested for burning down Cooper's old barn? The ones who said they were looking for a place to hole up for the winter and didn't mean to let their campfire get out of control?"

Jase rubbed his jaw. "Unlikely. I haven't seen them around since a Good Samaritan gave them blankets and food and bought them bus tickets to a warmer climate."

He glanced toward Saige. "Do you want to take a walk after the table is cleared?"

Valerie shook her head. "Don't worry about the dishes. Robert and I can handle them. You two go ahead."

They walked in silence for several moments.

Jase glanced at her. "May I ask you a personal question?"

Saige tilted her head. "You may ask, but I may not answer if your question is too personal."

Jase laughed. "Fair enough."

"What's your question?"

"Do you think—will you—do you feel—?" Jase groaned. He couldn't ask what he really wanted to know. *Do you feel the same attraction for me I feel for you? Did a cop hurt you? Is my occupation a bar to a relationship?* "I'm sorry, Saige. What I want to ask isn't coming out the right way."

She raised her eyebrows. "You have my attention. Just ask."

"Will you come to dinner with me next Saturday?"

She didn't answer for several breaths. Finally, she nodded.

SEVEN

Saige pushed up her welding hood and stepped back to look at the finished entry. Satisfaction spread through her and put a smile on her face.

Dad stepped up beside her. "Looks, great, kiddo. Functional and beautiful."

Cam and Brett pulled into the drive and stopped. They got out and studied the sturdy pipe structure.

"Nice work, Sis." Brett stared at the center piece, twelve feet above his head. "How'd you place this? The verticals, horizontals, and diagonals are made of four-inch pipe. Heavy stuff."

Saige removed her hood and wiped her forehead. "We rented a large forklift. A couple of our other guys came out to help. Dad operated the lift."

An older sedan pulled in behind Cam and Brett. Cam hopped in the truck and moved to the side of the road. The car entered and stopped.

The driver rolled down her window. "Hello. I don't know if you remember me—"

Saige nodded. "You're Eddie's grandmother, Lucy Taylor, right?"

"Yes. This was my folks' place. I happened to be in the neighborhood and saw all the activity. This may sound silly, but I got homesick and wondered if I might . . ."

Something about the dark circles under the woman's eyes and the bruise on her cheek filled Saige with pity. She'd never seen such sad, hopeless eyes. Val had said she'd had a hard life, and Saige could see the evidence stamped in her face.

Dad smiled. "Would you like to come inside for coffee, Mrs. Taylor?"

Her face brightened. "Please."

Lucy got out of the car and looked around. She said nothing for several moments. "I wish I could've made the place look like this. I just didn't have the money, energy, or knowledge."

"Come inside." Dad opened the door and stood aside so Lucy could enter.

Saige followed them to the kitchen as the woman *oohed* and *ahhed*. "Looks like a kitchen right out of one of those fancy magazines—all the stainless steel appliances, granite countertops, and tile backsplash."

"Have a seat, Mrs. Taylor, and I'll get you something to drink." Saige opened the refrigerator doors. "We have ice water, lemonade, or tea if you don't want coffee."

"Coffee, please."

Robert walked to the cabinet and pulled out two mugs. "I'll get the coffee, hon. I want some too."

Saige nodded and reached for her water bottle.

Lucy's gaze touched everything in the room. "You know, when I was younger, all I could think of was getting out of the house and away from my dad. He wasn't a nice man to be around even though he mellowed out near the end of his life. Had the place looked like this back then, I might have stayed longer. This feels like a haven."

Saige's heart hurt for Lucy Taylor. Based on how Pete turned out, she guessed her dead husband hadn't been a kind man either.

They toured the bedrooms and shiny new bathrooms. Tears tracked down Lucy's face. "My, my, my. I wish Momma could see this. She longed for pretty things."

On the way out, Lucy pointed to a closed door near the entry. "That used to be the storage room where Daddy kept all his fishing gear. He had a table and light set up so he could tie flies."

Robert opened the front door for them. "Saige and I use that room as our office."

Lucy stared at the closed door then stepped outside. "Did you do much to the barn? The hayloft is where I spent many hours staring out the loft door and wishing."

Robert took out his keys, opened the heavy lock, and flipped on the light switch. "Come in."

Saige watched Lucy's face as her eyes moved from the bars on the windows to the pens and stalls Dad had built for the chickens and goats. She stared at the small doors cut into the barn wall to give the animals access to the outside, then peered into the darker corners.

Lucy pointed. "I recognize those old milk cans and some of the other junk piled in the corner. Nothing of value there, but I see a few knick-knacks Momma used to have in the house. Daddy made a fuss about them collecting dust and told her to get rid of them. I guess she brought them here. I should come and get them out of your way."

"You can have any of the stuff that's yours." Dad pointed to the loft. "Do you want to take a look?"

Lucy glanced at the ladder and shook her head. "I'm not as young as I used to be. I don't climb ladders or trees anymore."

Dad chuckled. "Okay. Anything else?"

"No, thank you. You've been kind. I should go." She hesitated. "When is the best time for me to bring the truck and haul off this stuff?"

"We're busy until the end of next week. How about then?"

Lucy nodded. "See you."

Saige watched her drive away, then turned and hugged her dad.

"What's the hug for, hon?" He stroked her hair.

"I love you. I'm glad you're not like Lucy's father or son."

"I love you too."

She kissed his cheek and smiled. "Shall we get back to work?"

"You're such a slave driver. Yes, let's get back to work."

Jase checked his image in the mirror one more time to make sure the holstered gun on his belt didn't show under his shirt then reached for his jacket. He didn't know why he felt so antsy. He'd had dates before. *Yes, but none of the others pulled at your insides like Saige Harmony.* He felt as if he stood on the edge of a precipice and gazed into his future.

Mom glanced up from her book when he entered the living room. "My, you look handsome tonight. I always liked that silky blue shirt on you. The color makes your eyes look bluer and your hair blacker."

Jase grinned and picked up his keys. "Thanks, Mom. Make sure you lock up as soon as I leave."

"I will. Have fun."

He drove across the street and through the Harmony's new entry. Security lights came on as soon as he passed through the open gates. More came on when he stopped in the driveway.

Robert opened the door to his knock. "Come in, Jase. Saige said she's almost ready."

Jase shook his hand. "The entry's impressive, Robert, and I'm glad to see you got the security lights mounted."

"Yes. The boys got the camera system installed too. At least they mounted the cameras. I'm not sure if they're hooked up or not."

Robert continued to speak, but Jase didn't hear a word after the first sentence, because Saige walked into the living room. Her appearance sucked every bit of air from his lungs.

He thought her attractive no matter what she wore, but this elegant and noticeably feminine version widened his eyes. She looked like a model. Her silver, sparkly blouse and black slacks shimmered in the light, and the diamond drops in her ears glittered. She'd put her hair up, and the skin on her neck lured him.

Robert chuckled and elbowed him. "Breathe."

"Wow."

Brett whistled. "Better set a curfew, Dad."

Robert smiled at Jase. "I'm tempted, but since you're both of age, I'll mind my own business. Just take care of my girl, Jase."

"I will. We're going into the city to try out that new five-star restaurant. What we do after will be Saige's choice, though I don't think that outfit is suitable for bowling or skating."

She laughed and patted the sequined bag at her shoulder. I've packed comfortable shoes and a change just in case."

Jase turned onto the county road and headed toward town. He glanced at Saige. "You look more than great."

She smiled. "You do too. And you smell really good."

He laughed. "I wanted to tell you the same but didn't know how you'd take my words. I should've known you can handle such frankness."

"Mom and I lived with men all our lives, so we picked up on some of their ways. Dad and my brothers never beat around the bush or tried to figure out softer ways to say things. Mom was the one with more tact. Sometimes, I should be more tactful."

"How did you gain such skill as a carpenter and welder?"

"From the time I could walk, I trailed Dad and my brothers. I asked so many questions, they gave me a hammer, nails, and wood and told me to build something.

"When I turned seven, Dad got me my own welding hood, leather gloves, and apron and showed me how to do simple welds. As I grew up, I loved being creative and making things. I attended a year of university then switched to a vocational-technical college and took classes, but I learned the most from Dad."

Saige titled her head. "What caused you to choose law enforcement?"

"I took college courses at the same time I worked to finish my high school diploma, so I graduated early, then enlisted in the Army. I deployed overseas for four years. When I came home, law enforcement seemed the best fit for my skills."

The more they spoke of normal things, the more Jase lost the antsy feeling. They chatted all the way to the restaurant.

Saige stared at the line. "I hope this is a sign the food is as delicious as the restaurant advertised."

"Good thing I made reservations." Jase slotted the SUV into one of the few remaining spaces.

After they ordered, Jase leaned back and looked at her. He liked what he saw.

Saige lifted a brow. "What? Do you want to say something."

He smiled. "This environment suits you."

She glanced at the glittering chandeliers and the sparkling table settings. "Don't be fooled, Jase. I'm not a gold, silver, and crystal kind of person. I'm a carpenter in a fancy outfit. I'm a rough diamond compared to those who truly fit in this environment." She grinned. "Though, we can pretend for a night."

They left the restaurant two hours later. Jase shrugged into his jacket as they stepped outside. "Okay, what's next?"

"Let's go to the Pumpkin Patch. We'll need to stop so I can change my clothes someplace."

He laughed. "I haven't been to the Pumpkin Patch in years. Let's get out of the city. When we get to town, we'll stop at a grocery store or gas station. Will that work?"

"Yes."

EIGHT

Saige changed as quickly as she could in the gas station's restroom while Jase filled up. She felt more herself as she tugged on jeans, cotton shirt, warm sweater, and comfortable shoes.

She snapped into her seatbelt just as Jase got in.

He buckled up but leaned forward instead of starting the vehicle. He frowned. "I don't like what I'm seeing." He unbuckled.

Saige stared at the group Jase had fixed his eyes on. "Is that Jimmy Baker?"

Jase's mouth tightened. "Yes. And the man standing to his left is a drug dealer those on the streets call Slick. His name is Stuart Choll."

"Who are the two unkempt men standing next to Slick?"

"Those are the transients who burned down Thad Cooper's barn last year."

"Oh, Jase. I hope Jimmy isn't involved with them." She pulled out her phone, turned on the video, and zoomed in.

"I want to show Dad what those guys look like in case they come around."

Slick seemed to be talking. The unkempt men listened, but Jimmy repeatedly shook his head. When Slick reached out and grasped Jimmy's arm, Jase opened the door. "Stay here, Saige."

Saige watched the drama, her heart in her throat, and her video on.

Jase approached the group, his hand held near his right side. *Of course. He's armed. How could I forget? I went to dinner with a cop. They're always armed.*

Jimmy jerked his arm away from Slick, his face sullen.

Jase tilted his head and said something, and Jimmy turned and walked toward his pickup truck parked near the dumpster. He revved the engine, peeled out, and headed in the direction of home.

Slick's mouth moved, and he gesticulated as if explaining something to Jase.

Saige prayed none of the men would make threatening motions like moving toward a gun or knife. Attacking a cop often resulted in a lethal outcome. Chad had told her that.

Slick turned away and opened the door of a black sports car.

Jase moved toward the rear of the car as the man drove away and watched until Slick turned onto the highway.

Saige let out the breath she'd been holding and shut off the camera.

Jase approached the homeless men and spoke to them for a few more moments before they all went back into the gas station. The two came out with sodas and bags of chips, while Jase returned his wallet to his pocket as he strode to the SUV.

He slid into his seat and peered at her. "Are you okay?"

"Yes. What happened?"

"Slick opened his mouth and lies slid out. None of the others denied or confirmed his words, but I think he was threatening Jimmy in some way. The boy didn't say much. I plan to have a talk with him tomorrow."

"Do you think they're involved in the rise in crime in the area?"

"Slick, for sure. I don't know about the other three."

Saige sighed. "Do you think we can visit the Pumpkin Patch another evening? Maybe we can do something less exciting for the next few hours?"

"Like what?"

"A movie?"

"Where?"

"Your house or mine. Doesn't matter to me, just as long as I can get warm. I should have brought something heavier than a sweater."

Jase looked at his watch. "I'm sure Mom is watching a Hallmark movie as we speak."

Saige laughed. "Dad and my brothers are probably watching hunting shows or sports." She sighed. "I'm not in the mood for either, so I guess we'll watch Hallmark. Are you up for that?"

Jase sighed. "If you are. Maybe we can convince Mom to up her game a little."

"Do you have hot chocolate and popcorn?"

"Yes."

"We're on then."

Val smiled when Saige asked if they could watch a movie with her. "Of course. I felt like a Meg Ryan movie tonight. Would you prefer *You've Got Mail*, *Kate & Leopold*, or something else?"

Saige looked at Jase who shrugged. "*Kate & Leopold*. Thanks, Val."

"I'll go pop us a big bowl of popcorn. I have hot chocolate if you'd like."

"May I help?"

"No. Get comfortable. I'll be right back."

Jase scooped up a fuzzy blanket draped over the back of the couch and handed this to her. "I'm going to change. Be right back."

He returned dressed in jeans and a blue plaid lumberjack shirt just as Valerie sat the popcorn on the coffee table.

Jase headed to the kitchen. "I'll bring the chocolate and mugs, Mom."

Valerie sat in a recliner next to the couch. "Did you and Jase have a good time?"

Saige nodded. "The restaurant is pricey, but the food is as good as the reviewers say."

Jase set the steaming mugs on coasters, loaded the movie, and sat next to her. She spread the blanket over her lap and relaxed into the cushions. "Where's Dan?"

"In his kennel. I try not to upset his routine."

Thirty minutes into the movie, Valerie lowered the recliner back and raised the footrest.

Jase looked at his watch and whispered near Saige's ear. "She'll be sound asleep in five."

Saige chuckled. "Is this upping her game?"

"Depends on what the game is."

They returned their attention to the movie until Val's soft snores turned their heads.

Jase looked at his watch. "Six minutes. She lasted longer than I expected."

Saige smiled and studied his face. The smile faded at his serious expression.

"What's wrong, Jase?"

"You want the truth?"

"Always."

He hesitated. "I want to kiss you, but I'm not sure I should. I get the feeling my job is a bar to a relationship with you. Am I wrong?"

Saige stilled. "No, you're not. I'm trying to work through this though."

"Did a cop hurt you?"

"No, but his death did. He was killed when a drug deal turned bad."

"He was your . . . ?"

"Brother, Chad. He, too, was a K-9 officer. He and his dog, Mitch, were both killed five years ago."

"Ahh. That explains your reactions." He stroked her hair. "I'm sorry."

She leaned her head into his palm.

He put an arm around her and drew her close.

Saige rested against him and closed her eyes. His warmth and rhythmic breathing lulled her. She relaxed and didn't protest when he pulled her onto his lap and more fully into his arms. He draped the blanket around them and cradled her. She slept.

Jase kissed the top of her head and whispered near her ear. "Wake up, Saige. The movie is over. I'll walk you home."

Saige's eyes fluttered but didn't open.

He smiled and stroked her cheek. "Wake up. Time to go home."

She opened her eyes and straightened. "Sorry, Jase. I hope I didn't drool all over your shirt."

"You didn't."

Saige slid off his lap and glanced at Valerie who still slept in the recliner. She grinned. "What a pair we are. Leaving you to watch a romance all by yourself."

Jase stood and stretched. "I think I slept through most of the movie too."

He touched Valerie's shoulder. "Mom, time for bed. I'm going to walk Saige home."

The security lights popped on when they approached the Harmony front door.

Jase looked up. "I hope your brothers didn't hook up the cameras yet."

"Why?"

"Because if they did, they'll see this." He drew her into his arms and kissed her. When she didn't resist, he tightened his embrace and deepened the kiss.

Saige slid her arms around his neck and snuggled closer.

When someone switched on a light upstairs, she removed her arms and brushed one of his cheeks with her fingertips.

She shrugged out of the borrowed jacket. "I better go. Thanks for dinner, Jase."

NINE

Saige carried the last of the boxes out of the barn and stacked them beside the drive as Lucy Taylor pulled through the open gates.

Saige waved, and Robert walked to meet her. "Sorry, we've had to postpone you the last few weeks."

Lucy glanced at the stack. "I could've helped."

Robert smiled. "I'm remodeling that section of the barn, so I needed the room."

Jase drove up behind Lucy in his patrol car just as she closed the door of her truck. He got out, leashed Dan, and walked over. "Mrs. Taylor. Robert. Saige."

Lucy mumbled a hello and looked down at her feet.

"Saige. A word?" Jase moved toward her, but Dan lifted his head and perked his ears. His body tightened, his tail lifted, and he sniffed the air. Then he put his nose to the ground and tugged on the leash.

Jase frowned and followed.

The dog sniffed every box and gave his full attention to the milk cans.

Jase looked up. "Robert and Saige, as the property owners, do you give me permission to search these containers?"

They nodded in unison.

He opened the lids and pulled out a quart-sized plastic bag of white powder from each.

Saige stepped next to him. "What's that?"

Jase studied the bags. "The crystals in the powder indicate meth, but I'll check. I have a test kit in the car."

They turned to Lucy who'd lost all color in her face. "I don't know anything about this. I just came to pick up Momma's things."

Jase shook his head. "You'll have to wait to take anything, Mrs. Taylor."

"Can I go?"

"Yes, after you give a statement."

Lucy gave her statement, then left.

Jase went to his car and returned with crime scene tape. He encircled an area around the boxes and milk cans.

"What's next?" Saige walked with him to his car.

He pulled out his phone and touched a number on speed dial. "I'll have someone at the station go to the courthouse and request a search warrant from the D.A. and magistrate judge. Once I get this, I'll need to search the property."

"Fine." Robert looked toward the barn. "I suppose this means I need to find something else to do until you and Dan search the barn?"

Jase nodded. "I'll need to search the house and sheds too."

"Then I'll work on the cross fencing until you're finished."

"Thanks, Robert."

Saige waited until he stopped typing. "Do you think Lucy is involved somehow? The way she tore out of here makes me think she does know something about what was in the milk cans."

Jase shrugged. "All conjecture at this point. When the guys from the station get here, I'll give them a report.

She tilted her head. "I assume you came here for a reason."

"Yes, to tell you the Drug Enforcement Agency requested my assistance with an investigation in the southwestern part of the state. Dan and I may be gone a week, maybe longer. Will you keep an eye on Mom? Maybe have her over for dinner a few times?"

His words injected instant fear into her bloodstream. "Yes." She chewed on her lip. "She'll be upset if you miss Thanksgiving dinner." Her words sounded cracked and brittle to her own ears.

"Saige?" He studied her face. Concern edged his words. "Your pupils just dilated and you turned as pale as wax. What's wrong?"

She didn't speak for several moments. "These last several weeks together have been amazingly good, Jase. The Pumpkin Patch was the most fun I've had in a long time.

"When we're shooting apple cannons at spinning targets, trying to figure our way out of a glowing corn maze, zipping down a giant slide, jumping on a trampoline wearing bungee cord harnesses, or talking like normal people, I can forget you wear a badge and gun and carry the burden of dealing with criminals and those who despise any kind of authority.

"Yet when I get news like this, I'm sent back to that dark, pain-filled place—a place where I never want to return. If the DEA calls, then you will be involved in something big and ugly."

"What are you saying, Saige?" He placed a hand on her arm.

She brushed at a tear. "Losing Chad and Mom within a few years of each other was hard, but, for me, knowing a bad guy killed Chad in his prime hurt worse than knowing a drunk driver hit Mom. Chad left a wife and two young children. I've felt their pain and seen their struggles since his death."

Jase nodded. "I understand, Saige. I've endured the pain of losing friends in the same way, but that is the nature of the job. If Chad and I and a host of others don't step up to protect and defend, who will?"

"I know, Jase. I've heard the arguments before. My head agrees, but my heart is fragile and rebels at the idea of such a sacrifice from someone I—" Her voice caught.

He stroked her cheek and said nothing for several moments. When he spoke, his voice was low and soft, "From someone you love?"

She nodded.

"When Mom described you, I promised myself I'd stay far away. You offered more of a distraction than I needed, but no matter how much I tried, I couldn't stop thinking about you or finding reasons to be near you. I love everything about you, Saige,—your beauty, your strength and vulnerability, and your honesty."

Saige pulled in a quivering breath and grasped his hand. "I love you too, Jase, but this is the hardest part. Loving you is risky—maybe too risky. I don't know if I can endure such pain again. I see visions of kissing you goodbye one morning, then getting word in the evening you're resting in the morgue.

"I've been around enough law enforcement officers to know how a relationship with a cop works. Things may be fine at the beginning, but then he must work overtime to get ahead of the bills. The wife may have a job, and their schedules never fit. They seldom see each other. He misses anniversaries. Then if children come, he misses birthdays and parent-teacher conferences.

"Little by little, the stressors add up until the relationship disintegrates. I've read the statistics, Jase. Cops have one of the highest divorce rates. I don't want this to happen to us. I don't want to be another statistic."

His phone rang, and Saige stood close enough to hear, "The search warrant is approved, Jase. I'll bring this by."

She lowered her hand.

Jase's voice roughened. "What you say is true. But don't give up on us, Saige. Can we talk about this when I get back?"

She nodded. "I'll go help Dad. The front door is open." She looked into his eyes. "Goodbye, Jase. I'll leave you and Dan to your search."

She turned and walked toward her father.

Jase left the Harmony property and turned toward the interstate. Saige's goodbye left him with a squirmy feeling in his gut, and the look in her eyes worried him.

He prayed throughout the eight-hour drive.

When he got to his room, he called his mom.

She picked up immediately. "Jase?"

"Just want to let you know I got here safely. I'll meet with the task force first thing tomorrow morning. You may not hear from me for several days, but don't worry. I'll call when I can. Do me a favor?"

"Sure. What?"

"Talk to Saige about your relationship with Dad. She doesn't know he was a cop unless you've mentioned this. Tell her what you and Dad did to make your marriage work."

"You're going to ask her to marry you?"

"I want to, but her brother's death haunts her. She can't get around the 'what ifs.' She thinks I'm too high risk."

"Okay. I will."

"Night, Mom."

"Goodnight, Son. I'm praying for you."

TEN

Saige couldn't settle. She'd start something and then stop, her mind on Jase. She hadn't heard a word from him for almost two weeks, and her imagination ran wild.

When Val walked up the drive toward her, Saige removed her gloves. Her lungs constricted, and she had trouble breathing. Val's cry-reddened eyes and splotchy face told Saige the news she brought would probably crush her.

"Saige—" Her voice cracked, and tears streamed.

"Jase?" Saige whispered. A tremble started from her middle and spread to her extremities.

Val dabbed at her eyes with a tissue. "No. Dan. They were caught in an ambush. Jase survived. Dan didn't."

Saige covered her face with her hands and sobbed.

Robert approached. When he heard the news, he put an arm around each of them. "Come inside."

"How badly is Jase hurt?" Saige forced out the words as they walked toward the house.

Val sniffled. "Extensive bruising where the bullet hit his vest. He'll be home tonight."

Saige dabbed her eyes. "This kind of life didn't bother you for the sixteen years you lived with your husband?"

Val grimaced. "Of course, things like this bothered me. But my choices were to worry each day he wouldn't come back or to enjoy his company in the time God gave us. I tried to make every day count."

Robert nodded. "None of us know when we'll die, hon, so why spend so much time worrying? You're not going to escape pain, either, because this is part of life. But you can choose how you're going to handle your pain."

They sat at the table and drank hot tea.

Val couldn't relax. She put her cup in the sink and turned. "I think I'll head back. I want to rest a little."

Robert walked Val home, and Saige paced the living room. She prayed and cried and prayed some more.

When Jase pulled into the drive, she raced across the road.

He stepped out of the car, and she opened her arms.

He went into them and buried his face in her neck. He grasped her as a drowning man might reach for a life preserver. She held him and let his tears soak her collar.

When his ragged breathing calmed, he lifted his head and leaned back so he could see her face. "Is this the straw that broke the camel's back, Saige?"

She shook her head.

He placed her hands on his chest and linked his arms around her waist. "You once told me you were a rough diamond, but I think our relationship is too. If we're going to have a life together, we've got to seek help and allow God to knock off our rough edges and polish us. Do you agree?"

"Yes."

"Then, will you marry me? Will you take a chance on us?"

She slid her hands down to encircle his waist. Her hands brushed his pistol grip and handcuffs. She moved her hands higher, ignoring the feel of his Kevlar vest. "Yes, Jase. I will."

EPILOGUE

"So, the task force discovered Lucy was Pete's dealer?" Val passed the platter of turkey. "I feel sorry for her."

Jase nodded and forked dark meat onto his plate. "Yes. Pete and Slick were the instigators and up to their eyeballs in the crime in the area. They'll all go to jail, but Lucy might get a lighter sentence considering Pete forced her do to his dirty work. They'll offer her a plea bargain to turn evidence against her son and Slick."

Saige put her hand on his thigh. "What about Jimmy?"

"He wasn't involved with drugs. Slick tried to rope him into the burglary ring, but Jimmy refused. He gave us enough information we found and arrested the culprits."

"What about the tracks?" Robert glanced across the street at their newly painted barn.

"Mom was right. They belonged to the two who burned down Cooper's place. They admitted Pete offered them money to bring him the milk cans. When they couldn't get in, Pete sent his mom with instructions to get the drugs and to scope out the interior of your house. The men will probably get off on a plea bargain if they give evidence against Slick."

"Enough of this." Val smiled. "Robert and I want to discuss something with you both."

Jase looked from one to the other. "What?"

Saige straightened. "What, Dad?"

"I've asked Val to marry me, and she said yes. But we want to make sure you're okay with this."

A grin tipped up one corner of Jase's mouth. "I've seen this coming for a while. I have no objection, Robert. You're a good man. You'll treat Mom well."

Val's lip trembled. "Saige?"

Saige smiled. "I like you a lot, Val. I have no concerns either."

Val looked from Saige to Jase and back. "Then, since we have many of the same friends and family, would you object to a double ceremony after the New Year to make travel easier on them?"

Jase shrugged. "Fine with me."

Saige laughed. "Sounds fun, though I don't want anything fancy—just close friends, close family members, and the congregation at our small church."

Val agreed.

Saige grinned. "We better put our heads together to see how we're going to answer the musical houses question though. We're sure to be asked."

Val stared. "What?"

Saige grinned. "Who will live in the Harmony's diamond, and who will live in the Langdon's haven?"

Robert chuckled. "Maybe we should draw straws."

Jase reached for Saige's hand. "I don't care which house we live in as long as my wife lives there with me."

"Ditto." Robert smiled and entwined his fingers with Val's.

ROCKY MOUNTAIN HOMECOMING

HOPE WARREN STARED OUT THE WINDOW and twisted her wedding band. She did not watch the softly falling snow or wonder about the people in the cars as they inched their way through the streets of her Deep Springs neighborhood to admire the Christmas lights. Instead, she pinched her lips together and brushed at a tear. She tried to shut off the constant mental replay of the breaking news report from seven days ago but couldn't.

American soldiers killed or injured in Afghanistan's northern Kunduz province today after a roadside IED exploded. Sources say . . .

Though the news videographer panned the area without focusing on specifics, Hope caught sight of the patch on the sleeve of a bloody soldier being carried away on a stretcher by grim-faced medics. Creed's unit.

Hope's heart raced and her insides twisted.

"Come away from the window, Granddaughter. Sit. Have a soothing cup of hot tea with me." Grace Leland placed a steaming teapot and cups on the coffee table coasters, sat on the comfy sofa, and patted the cushion beside her.

"Thanks, but I don't think I could swallow a drop. My stomach is upset."

"Then come sit beside me and let me hold you."

Hope eased onto the sofa next to her grandmother. When Grace's arms encircled her, she leaned into her warmth. Words rose from the depths of Hope's soul and choked her in their rush to be spoken. "I don't understand, Grace. Why would God give Creed and me only a week to be together as newlyweds before sending him to one of the most dangerous places on the planet for more than nine months? Why would he take his life just as Creed's deployment ended?"

"Darling, we don't know if Creed was one of the soldiers injured or killed."

"Then why haven't I heard anything from him if he's alive? If he's wounded or dead, wouldn't I have received a call by now? He was supposed to be here a week ago." Hope's lips trembled.

Grace kissed her cheek. "I don't know, but I believe no news is good news in this case."

Hope sat up and reached for the wedding album on the coffee table. She opened the cover and turned the pages. She studied each image and traced the shape of her husband's firm jaw, broad shoulders, and wide grin. She wished she could run her fingers through his close-cropped, dark hair and smell the scent of his warm skin. "He's only twenty-seven, Grace. He's too young to die."

"Yes, and at twenty-four, you're too young to be a widow, but—" Grace lowered her eyes.

"But?" Hope glanced up from the images.

Her grandmother's voice softened. "When you married an active duty, special forces soldier, love, didn't you consider death might be a real possibility?"

Hope closed the photo album and stood. "Of course, I did, but when Creed returned from his first tour of duty safe and sound, I hoped . . ." She returned to the window and gazed out with unseeing eyes. "I just never expected this to happen."

"Did you plan for such an eventuality?"

Hope turned away from the window and looked at her grandmother. "Yes. I'm too much of a Colorado, snow-country girl to enjoy North Carolina, so I planned to return to Deep Springs or search for a place to live in the Durango area if Creed didn't return." She choked on the last words.

"I can do my job almost anywhere as long as I have good internet service, but—" She bit her lip. "I don't want to live without him, Grace. The thought of losing Creed hollows me out from the center. Right now, I feel like I'm walking around as half a person."

Several moments passed before Grace spoke, "If the Lord took your husband, then you and I have only each other. I'm not getting any younger, and I planned to leave you this house anyway, so consider this your home. You're welcome to stay here for as long as you need. I like having you with me."

Hope looked around the comfortable living room. Her eyes teared. "I love you, Grace."

"I love you too, Granddaughter." She glanced at the clock over the mantle. "Three o'clock. Shouldn't you be getting ready?"

"My heart is heavy. I'm not in the mood to sing tonight."

"But several people are counting on you. The churches are getting together to make this Christmas special for the community. You wouldn't want to disappoint them. What would Creed want you to do?"

Hope sighed. "He'd want me to go."

"Then go."

"You're not coming?"

"No, I'm tired. I need a nap. If I wake refreshed, I may come. I want to hear you sing."

Hope bent and kissed Grace's cheek. "Okay. I'm going to shower."

An hour later, Hope picked up her car keys and opened the door. She shivered and turned up the collar of her coat as she stepped into the cold air. Her heart twinged when she didn't see Creed's car parked behind hers. She blinked away tears and took a deep breath. She'd have to make arrangements with their friend, Dave, to get her husband's car from Denver to Deep Springs within the next few weeks if . . . no, not yet. She wouldn't think about the car. The vehicle was safe, and she had other, more pressing things on her mind.

Her vibrating cell phone startled her. Creed? Her hands shook as she recognized her best friend's name. She coughed to clear the lump in her throat before she answered. "Hi, Raylene. What's up?"

"Hope, I know you're probably on your way to the event, but I locked my keys in the car. Can you stop by my apartment and pick up my extra set from Joel? He'll bring them out so you don't have to go in. I'll wait for you at the hot springs in the resort parking lot. Please?"

"How many times in the last month have you locked yourself out?"

"Three. That's why I'm having an extra set made to keep on your key ring."

Hope sighed. "All right. I'll be there soon."

When Hope pulled into the parking lot, Raylene waved and finished her animated conversation with Damon Briggs, ex-Army Ranger turned business owner.

She got out of the car and held out the keys.

Raylene grabbed them and hugged her. "Thanks. I'll rush home and change. See you in a few."

Damon stepped next to her as they watched Raylene wheel out of the parking lot, tires skidding and slinging icy bits of snow into the air.

"She sure has a lot of energy, doesn't she?" He stared until Raylene turned onto the main street.

"Yes."

He glanced down at her and lowered his voice. "Heard about Creed's unit. I'm sorry."

She looked into his eyes. "Tell me the truth, Damon. Do you think Creed might still be alive even though I haven't heard from him for more than a week, and no one from the military has contacted me?"

"If your husband were dead, you would have heard within twelve hours, and the notification team would have shown up on your doorstep. I'd say he has a good chance of being alive."

"But—"

"Unexpected delays can happen between Afghanistan and Deep Springs, especially in the winter. I think your soldier will show up."

Hope wanted to believe him, but the trembling, empty feeling inside filled her with doubt.

"Thanks, Damon. I have to go." She reached for the door handle.

"Hope?"

She stopped and turned. "Yes?"

He paused as if trying to find the right words. "War changes a person. Creed might need support when he gets back. Just want you to know I'm here for him—anytime night or day."

Hope nodded. "I saw him change after the first deployment. When he came back, he couldn't tolerate large, noisy crowds.

"The Army provided his clothes, food, shelter, and medical care, and the members of his unit gave him a sense of camaraderie and family. He told me he had a hard time getting used to the idea he was responsible for himself and a future wife and family. This scared him.

"He was also used to Army discipline and schedules. When he returned state-side, any kind of disorder in his environment or upset to his daily routine made him uptight. I did what I could to help him adjust."

She looked into Damon's eyes. "I wonder what changes I'll see if—when—he returns."

Damon's lips tightened. "He lived, Hope. Some of his buddies didn't. Survivor's guilt is a possibility. If he starts exhibiting symptoms of post-traumatic stress, you call me, night or day."

"What are some of the signs I should watch for?"

"Symptoms can vary widely depending on the person. The length of time Creed was exposed to injury or traumatic events may increase the likelihood he'll develop symptoms." Damon straightened. "If he has nightmares and flashbacks that cause him to shake or have panic attacks, you call me."

Hope was afraid to hear more. "What else?"

"He may avoid situations, people, and places that remind him of the trauma. He may have exaggerated negative beliefs about the world. People who suffer from PTSD may be easily irritated or jumpy. Sudden angry outbursts aren't uncommon."

Pain squeezed Hope's heart and tears pooled. "I will certainly call, Damon, if I see such behaviors. Thank you."

Hope slotted her car into one of the few remaining spaces in the reserved lot. Several churches in the community and the local supercenter got together and hosted the annual "Christmas in the Parking Lot Extravaganza." People came for miles to see the luminarias and Christmas lights and to hear the holiday music. Judging by the crowds milling around the specialty booths and participating in the contests, this was the largest crowd in Deep Springs's history.

Hope stood and watched the excited, red-cheeked children and their relaxed, happy parents. She inhaled the cold air and tried to calm her nerves.

A man assigned to emcee the event tapped on the microphone. "Gather round, everyone. Dinner is ready. Are you hungry?"

The roar of the crowd signaled their agreement.

"Before we start, let's give a round of applause to those who made this happen."

The sponsors stood and waved at the crowd.

The emcee smiled. "Let me explain how this is going to work. We'll have a time of silence for those who want to offer thanks. Then those of you sitting at the outside tables will get up and move to the back of the parking lot and then come to the serving line on each side of the center aisle. Have your tickets ready and make sure to grab your silverware, napkin, and plate from the table when you get to them. If you need help getting food for someone in your party, let one of the servers know, and we'll help you. More servers will be around with coffee, water, and hot chocolate when everyone is seated."

Hope eased into a seat close to the sound system and opened a thermos of hot, herbal tea. Her stomach would not tolerate anything heavier. She shivered and wrapped her muffler around her neck.

She smiled at the others who joined her at the table and listened to their chatter and the soft Christmas music the musician at the keyboard played.

Videographers and reporters from local television stations moved through the crowds getting candid shots and stopped to interview the Extravaganza's participants.

Joy permeated the air, and Hope's spirit lightened. *I can get through this. I can.*

Floodlights spaced around the large parking lot provided plenty of light when the winter sky darkened. Hope studied the community members and the out-of-town visitors as they chatted, laughed, and enjoyed the food. Volunteers from the different churches refilled coffee cups or cleaned up. Her heart warmed. This was Christmas. This was home.

When the musician playing the keyboard finished "Jingle Bells" and switched to the opening notes of Handel's *Messiah*, the crowd quieted. Hope stood and sang in a clear, strong soprano, "Hallelujah. Hallelujah. Hallelujah. Hallelujah. Hallelujah!"

A tenor from a local church stood on his chair and repeated the hallelujahs, and the diners' heads swiveled from her to him.

Raylene and her husband, Joel, stepped into the aisle and continued with, "For the Lord God Omnipotent reigneth."

Soon, more and more singers of different ages stood and joined the flash mob. "The kingdom of this world is become the kingdom of our Lord and of His Christ, and He shall reign forever and ever!"

Men, women, and teens from the community pulled out their phones to video the performance, and children stared wide eyed as each new person joined the chorus.

The singers from the different churches who participated in the performance raised their arms at the last triumphant note, and fireworks exploded in the sky above them.

Those present stood, clapped, yelled, and whistled for several moments as the fireworks dissipated.

Hope smiled through tears as joy swelled her soul. *King of Kings, and Lord of Lords!* She tried to catch her breath. Though the song demanded her best skills and most of her energy, the music lifted her out of her troubles. *For the Lord God Omnipotent reigneth. Hallelujah! Hallelujah!* The words touched her core. Regardless of her situation, the Lord was still on his throne. He knew the beginning from the ending, and she trusted him.

She took a deep breath and smiled at friends and neighbors. When the television reporter stopped her and asked questions about the flash mob, Hope answered and tried not to let the idea of being on television bother her.

The woman reporter smiled. "Watch for the video on tonight's ten o'clock news."

Hope turned toward her car but stopped when a low, deep voice spoke her name. She knew that voice.

"Creed?" At the sound of her high-pitched cry, people turned to look.

Her soldier stood under a floodlight dressed in camouflage and holding an American flag.

Hope cried out again, raced forward, and launched into Creed's outstretched arms. She wrapped her legs around his waist, clutched the back of his shirt with both fists, and buried her face in his neck and sobbed. "I thought you were dead."

He draped the flag around her shoulders and drew her closer. He lifted his hand to cradle her head. "I know, Babe. Grace told me. I'm sorry my delay caused you such pain."

People clapped and cheered as Creed held her and moved in a slow circle, but she ignored them and the television news videographer who moved around them getting shots from different angles. She lifted her face to kiss him.

He returned her kiss and gave her more.

When she unwrapped her legs and slid to the ground, Creed held her close. "I've missed you so much." He rested his forehead against hers and looked into her eyes. With his thumbs, he brushed away her tears. "I tried to get here sooner, but my flights were delayed."

"Why didn't you call?"

"I couldn't, Babe, because my cell phone bit the dust during the flight from Afghanistan to Germany. I didn't have enough time to get another once I got to the base in North Carolina, because I had to scramble to make the commercial flight to Denver. Then weather and car crashes on I-25 slowed me down. The roads were snow-packed and icy from LaVeta Pass all the way here."

She caressed the dark stubble on his cheeks. "You're here now, and that's all that counts. I love you, Creed Warren."

He kissed her. "I adore you, Hope Warren. Now, let's go home. Our future awaits."

MAIL-ORDER MARVEL

CHAPTER 1: An inciting event

Hattie Atwell pushed the library door open three inches but stopped when she heard her parents talking about her. She stepped closer to the opening.

Her pale-faced mother wrung her hands. "What are we going to do with Harriette, John? We aren't getting any younger, and I'm so frightened to think what will happen to her if we—."

"Calm yourself, Lillian. We aren't in our graves yet." Father put another log on the fire.

"We are getting a step closer each day."

Her father leaned forward and patted Mother's hand. "Now, now, dear. You know Harriette. She's like a cat with nine lives. She lands on her feet any which way you throw her."

"Don't be vulgar, John. This isn't a time to joke."

"I'm not joking."

Mother sighed. "Had I not given birth to her myself and held her in my arms the moment she left the womb, I might have believed Harriette was a changeling. She is not like any of our other children in personality."

Hattie had often thought the same. In appearance, she and her two brothers had the height of the Atwell males.

Both brothers, even Max, the fourteen-year-old, were several inches over six feet, and she was a few inches under. Her older sister, Liza, and her younger sister, Carrie, inherited their mother's petiteness and social personality. The only thing she had in common with all of her siblings were chocolate-brown eyes and brown hair.

"I think I've failed her, John. Society doesn't take to her like I'd hoped, and I don't know why. Her looks are not off-putting, and she can set fine stitches, play the pianoforte, and manage a household with the best of us, but the eligible men are either put off by her height or her conversation. She is still as blunt as ever, and I haven't been able to break her of that habit.

"Only last night at the Petersons' dinner, Mr. Harris told me he made a comment to Harriette, and she looked at him as if he were a bug that had crawled from under a rock. I soothed his ruffled feathers as best I could, but I don't think he'll come courting, no matter how well-endowed Harriette's bank balance."

Heat rushed into Hattie's face. What her mother said was true. She couldn't abide insincerity or inanity in any form, and she didn't like the games the rich and entitled played. If she had her way, she would forego all such parties and would spend her evenings in her father's well-stocked library, lost in one of his comfortable armchairs, and nibbling on whatever food she found in the kitchen. His books, newspapers, and journals had opened the world to her, while the strict rules and expectations of the Louisiana elite of 1895 suffocated her.

Her ability in the kitchen was another thing Mother didn't know. If she found out how skilled Hattie was at preparing all kinds of food, she'd probably have apoplexy.

For years, Hattie had snuck in and insisted Cook teach her how to bake and cook. In the back of her mind, she thought she ought to know how to prepare meals instead of just ordering them. Buried even further back in her mental chamber of secrets was the feeling she might need to know how to do so if she ever got brave enough to leave home like her older brother, Heath. He had graduated from medical school and sought his new life in the wilds of the West.

"We've got to do something, husband. Harriette is already twenty-two with no prospects."

"What do you propose?"

"Maybe you can give her a choice: find her own husband by the year's end or allow us to find one for her."

Father's eyebrows lifted. "You think that will work, Lillian? You know how headstrong she is."

"What can be so wrong about wanting our daughter to have a comfortable home with a tall, attentive man to care for her and give her children?" The plea in Mother's voice touched Hattie's heart.

"He doesn't have to be tall, Mother," Hattie whispered, "I wouldn't care if he were five feet three as long as he values me as a person and can converse with me as an equal. He wouldn't care about my money or how much time I spend reading, gardening, or drawing."

Did such a man exist? A man who wouldn't look at her as if she were a different species and say, "We have gardeners for this, my dear." If so, she hadn't met him yet.

Hattie trudged up the stairs to Liza's room.

Liza looked up from a newspaper and smiled. She patted the bed beside her. "You've got to read some of these entries in the *Matrimonial Marketplace*, Hattie. Some of the ads will make you laugh."

Hattie plopped into the oversized chair near the bed and kicked off her shoes. She poured a glass of water and sipped. "Why are you reading such a paper? You already have a husband."

Carrie bounced into the room and sat on the bed. She leaned over and glanced at the advertisements. "Doesn't hurt to look, right Liza?"

At seventeen, Carrie was far too interested in men for Hattie's comfort. Her actions never crossed the line of acceptability, but she came close. She flirted with every male who came into her sphere, no matter their age. Her vivacious ways, teasing eyes, and beautiful face and body drew every man in the area.

Liza pointed. "Listen to this."

I'm thirty years old, five-feet-five, and one hundred thirty pounds. I am of sound mind and body and have all my teeth. I'm not much to look at, but I know how to cook and clean, and I have three thousand dollars to bring with me. I'm willing to work hard to provide a comfortable home and good companionship for my husband. You must bring at least the same amount of money to the marriage. Christian men between thirty and fifty who practice their faith, please feel free to contact me.

Losers, loafers, gamblers, brawlers, drunks, and other no-goods need not apply. I won't spend my time or a penny on such as you.

Hattie smiled. "I like her honesty."

Carrie studied her. "You would. She sounds a lot like you, doesn't she Liza?"

Liza grinned. "Yes, I'd say brutal honesty is Hattie's trademark."

"I'm not brutal. I try to be polite and kind, but I don't see why honesty is so offensive."

Liza raised an eyebrow. "Not many wish to hear the truth, Hattie. They have their own ideas of who they are."

Hattie grumbled. "Then why do they ask questions that may give them an answer they don't like? Bah. I have no patience with this."

Carrie chuckled. "We know. We've seen several of your suitors rush off without a backward look." Carrie suddenly looked up. "I have an idea. Hattie should answer an ad."

Harriette straightened. "What? Why would I entertain such an idea?"

Liza looked from the ads to Hattie. "Because the obvious answer is the men around here are too obtuse to appreciate you. Perhaps a man who's seen life in the wilder parts of the country would."

Carrie clapped her hands, her eyes sparkling. "Oh, yes, we can all pour over the ads to see which man we like for our smart, talented sister. He has to be the best of the best." She smiled and winked. "What kind of man do you want?"

Hattie stared at her sisters, horror causing her usually placid mask to slip. "Do you honestly understand what you're saying? Do you know the risks associated with such actions? You may believe everything you read, but I don't. How do you know the men writing for a bride aren't cheats or axe murderers?"

Liza stared. "You really must start trusting people, Hattie. You're too tight—too controlled. You don't let many people outside us see your emotions. Maybe if you did, others would recognize how special you are."

Carrie stood and reached for the ink jar, pen, and paper on the nightstand. She returned to sit beside Liza, then grinned at Hattie.

"I'm ready."

"Ready?"

"Yes, for a list of the qualities you look for in your future husband."

Hattie choked, and her eyes watered. "Are you serious?"

"Of course. What's at the top of your list?" She poised the pen over the paper.

"You are mad, little sister. Absolutely mad."

Carrie waited.

Liza urged her to at least get her wishes on paper.

Hattie considered for several moments. "He doesn't have to be perfect, but he has to be a man who walks the walk of his Christian faith. If he does, then he knows what God expects of a husband. I don't want someone who offers lip service or who lives like there is no God."

Carrie wrote, then lifted the pen. "Okay, what's next? Rich? Handsome? Tall?"

"Those may make your list, Carrie, but they don't make mine. I've had many rich, handsome, and tall men come courting. I'm more interested in what is on the inside than the outside, though I suppose the man needs to be able to make enough money to support a family.

"I'd wish for a man who had a wide experience of people and who could carry on an interesting conversation about a variety of topics. He would be kind, gentle, and speak to me as an equal. He would value what I had to say and would view me as a help instead of a hindrance."

Hattie sighed. "I listen to myself and cringe. If such a man exists, he's going to need a sense of humor, intelligence, and some backbone if he thinks to take me to wife."

"What else?"

Hattie searched her brain. "I can't think of anything else now, you silly girl."

Liza stood and stretched. "I smell dinner. I'd better go check on the children before they get into mischief."

Carrie jumped up. "I'll come with you. I haven't seen my two nieces for several hours. I wonder if Max took them outside and encouraged them to climb trees again, or if they headed to the pond to fish."

Liza grimaced. "Yes, Maxwell is determined to turn the girls into tomboys every chance he gets. Let's go."

Hattie watched them leave, then moved to the bed and read the ads from each page. Her thoughts whirled. Why would anyone consider aligning themselves with strangers? She had a hard time wrapping her mind around the idea.

Hattie understood why people placed such ads after the Civil War thirty years ago. Widows and orphans had to fend for themselves after their men didn't return. Many faced life-threatening hardships, so the ads brought these struggling women into contact with the single men who headed to the gold fields of California or the timberlands of Washington and Oregon after the war.

Hattie thought about the ads all through dinner. *Stop!*

She needed to focus on something else for a while, so she eased into the library and glanced at the latest paper Father left on his desk. The headline immediately caught her attention, so she took the paper and sat in her favorite chair.

ALLAN PINKERTON, SCOTTISH COOPER, ABOLITIONIST, DETECTIVE, AND SPY?

Hattie read until her eyes blurred. The information fascinated her so much, she didn't think about the wanted ads more than half a dozen times before heading to bed.

When she pulled the sheet up to her chin, her mind churned with a multitude of ideas. She tossed and turned until the blankets wrapped around her legs.

Hattie sat up, groaned her frustration, lit the lamp, and reached for her stack of sketchbooks. As soon as she touched the covers, her whirlwind thoughts calmed.

She smiled at the childish images she had drawn in the first sketchbook Father had given her for her tenth birthday. For the next twelve years, she filled more and more sketchbooks with pencil, charcoal, and watercolor images.

As her skill grew and she mastered the art of drawing, her sketches showed astonishing complexity and detail, but only she could see this. No one else had seen her work except for the drawings she gave her sisters, brothers, and parents on special occasions—and Doctor Eber.

Though she enjoyed landscapes, her heart thrilled to portraiture. She had pushed herself over the last few years to capture the essence of each person in their unposed, daily lives as quickly as she could. For a while, her first attempts had been sloppy and didn't capture the likeness.

Her frustration grew until she saw a medical skeleton hanging in Doc Eber's office when she was eighteen. She convinced him she would like to have a smaller model she could use to study the bone structure of the human face and body. She had to show him a few of her drawings to prove her sincerity.

Only after Father approved her request did Dr. Eber order the model for her. She knew he thought her a strange creature, but she didn't care. Many people had the same opinion.

Hattie looked at the small, child-size skeleton hanging on a stand near her desk and smiled. "You've been a great help, Katy. I wouldn't have improved so much without you."

She returned the sketchbooks to the nightstand and turned out the lamp. Perhaps tomorrow would reveal the answer to what she should do to plan for her future.

CHAPTER 2: THINGS COME TO A HEAD

TEXAS PANHANDLE, EARLY SUMMER 1895

"LOOK, UNCLE BEN. I'M MAKING US BISCUITS FOR SUPPER." Sarah's blue eyes sparkled, and pride permeated her tone.

Town sheriff and Deputy United States Marshal Benjamin Cole stepped into his home and closed the door. Flour covered his ten-year-old niece from head to toe as well as the floor and counter around her. Bowls and utensils spread over the rest of the space.

He glanced around the room at the disorder poking at him everywhere he looked. Since he'd taken guardianship of the children two years ago after his brother and sister-in-law's deaths, chaos had built. His job taxed his thoughts and energy to the point cleaning and cooking took a back burner to surviving. He closed his eyes and fought the headache pounding at his temples and behind his eyes.

"Are you okay, Uncle?" The uncertainty in Sarah's voice opened his eyes and forced a smile to his lips. "Everything's fine, darlin'. I'm just tired."

She nodded, her blonde curls bouncing. "That's why I decided to make biscuits. I overheard Mrs. Norwood telling Miss Hastings how she made hers, and I thought this sounded easy enough." Her lips puckered. "The only thing is, I couldn't remember how much of each ingredient."

"Looks like you tried to start a fire in the stove too."

"I did, but I ran out of wood, so Jeremy said he'd chop some more."

The hairs on the back of Ben's neck raised. All he needed to make his life spiral out of control was a niece with first-degree burns and a nephew who chopped off his leg.

When the fourteen-year-old entered with his arms full of wood, Ben searched him for blood. Seeing none, he relaxed enough to nod. "Good job, Jem. Let me wash up, and I'll help get supper ready."

He eyed the chaos. "Darlin', will you put the flour away and take the dirty dishes to the sink? I'll fry us some steaks while you do so."

She looked around and made a face. "I sure did make a mess. I'm sorry, Uncle Ben."

"Well, I'll give you high scores for trying."

Sarah scooted to the utility closet and pulled out the broom and dustpan. She dabbled at the mess without thought to the most efficient way to get the job done. When she finished, broom strokes showed through the flour remaining on the floor.

Ben sighed.

They sat down a half hour later to steaks, biscuits, and gravy.

Sarah reached for the flat, odd-shaped bread and took a big bite. Her face turned red, and she spit her culinary efforts into her napkin. "Ugh. That's the worst biscuit I've ever tasted. Even Buster and the chickens won't eat this."

Jeremy laughed, and Sarah burst into tears. "Don't laugh, Jem. I tried so hard to make things nice for us."

Instantly, Jeremy stopped laughing and patted Sarah's hand. "You did good, Sarah. Mama would be proud."

"She would?" Sarah brightened. "I'm glad. I'll try harder next time."

"She certainly would." Ben pushed down the panic threatening to consume him. These two needed more than just a bachelor uncle who dealt with criminals, drunks, and cranky citizens all day and sometimes at night. He didn't have much energy to invest when he got home, though he tried. He knew his efforts weren't good enough.

Sarah would be a woman in a few years, and he didn't have a clue how to prepare her, and Jem needed someone to teach him the things men should know.

Ben took a deep breath and forced each muscle to relax.

"You okay, Uncle Ben?" Jeremy looked into his face.

"Yes, just tired." He stood and smiled at both of them. "How about we have an early night? Then you'll be fresh for church tomorrow."

Sarah hugged him. "Will you tuck me in?"

He kissed her forehead. "Of course. That's my most important job."

She trotted up the stairs.

Jeremy watched him, a knowing look on his face. He nodded and turned to leave, but Ben gripped his shoulder. "Thanks for your help, Jem."

His nephew's eyes traveled from his face to his badge and then to his holstered guns. "We don't make things easy for you, do we, Uncle?"

Ben tightened his grip. "You and Sarah are the best gifts God has given me, Jem. Never doubt this. We'll get through life's ups and downs together—as a family."

Jeremy said nothing for several moments. "You need a wife, Uncle Ben, and Sarah needs a mother."

Shock widened Ben's eyes. "What do you need, Jem?"

Jeremy chewed on his bottom lip. "I'd like to have a mother too. I'll be grown soon, but I'd still like to have a mother who cares what happens to me." He looked around the room and grimaced. "Besides, without a woman, this place is likely to fall in around our ears. I had a nightmare the clutter got so high and the dust so thick, I suffocated."

Ben laughed. "I had the same nightmare. Let me think about what you said. We may have to talk soon."

Jeremy nodded, and Ben followed him upstairs to Sarah's room.

"Are you ready, princess?" Ben smiled at the little girl.

Sarah tilted her head. "When you smile like that, I can see why Miss Hastings says you're the handsomest man in Texas. The other single ladies agree."

"What?" Startled, Ben stared. "The ladies are talking nicely about me instead of complaining about something? That's unusual."

Jeremy smiled. "I've heard them too. They say your black hair, blue eyes, and sun-brown skin make you look like a pirate or swashbuckler, whatever that is."

Ben laughed. "I'm sure they would hate me to be a pirate or swashbuckler."

Sarah sat up. "Why?"

"Well, a pirate is a man who sails the seas and robs other people who sail the seas. They are violent men. A swashbuckler is a swordsman, soldier, or adventurer who swaggers around fighting. You'd call him a daredevil."

Jeremy frowned. "Sounds like if you took the pirate off a ship and gave him a horse and a gun, he'd be one of those no-good outlaws who robs trains, banks, or stages."

Sarah's eyes widened, and she shook her head. "I wouldn't want you to be a swash-swash-whatever either. We have too many cowboys who come in from a long drive. All they want to do is drink themselves silly, then swagger around and fight. They do the stupidest things, and you have to put them in jail and fine them."

Ben tucked the covers around her and kissed her cheek. "Exactly. Good night, darlin'."

Ben spent another hour cleaning up the kitchen and living areas, though his efforts did little to bring order out of chaos.

When he entered his room, he had only enough energy to remove his boots and hang his gun belt close to hand before sprawling across the bedspread.

Ben pushed his empty breakfast bowl away from him and leaned back in his chair. "Okay, you two. I need a couple of deputies to watch my back. You up for the jobs?"

Sarah's eyes widened. "Me? You'll let a ten-year-old be a deputy?"

"For this job, yes."

"Will you let me wear a badge and gun?"

Ben chuckled. "No, darlin', you won't be needing either, but you will be needing good eyes and ears."

Jeremy eyed Ben. "What did you have in mind?"

"I thought about what you both said the ladies were saying. Seems a few may be setting their sights on me for a husband."

Sarah giggled. "You think so?"

Ben shrugged. "I don't know, but if they are, I need you both to make sure the wrong one doesn't lasso and hog-tie me."

Jeremy frowned. "How do we know which are the wrong ones? They all look alike to me."

"Maybe we should start a list. You know, my wife will be your mother, so we have to make sure we pick the right one—a woman who will make our lives safer and better."

Sarah blinked. "Safer? She'll have to carry a gun?"

"Not that kind of safe." He looked into the cloudy sky. "Do you remember the huge storm we had the other day when the sky turned dark and lightning struck the ground? The hail pelted our skins, and we were chilled and hungry."

They nodded.

"How did you feel when we rushed into the barn and closed out the weather?"

Jeremy smiled. "Safe. Warm. Comfortable, especially after we lit a lantern."

Ben caressed Sarah's cheek. "That's the kind of safe I'm talking about. If we're going to invite a mother-wife into our home, we have to feel safe with her. Do you agree?"

They nodded again.

"What I want you to do is watch the single women who you think like me. Are they kind? Do they gossip? Do they treat others with respect, especially you? Do they love God and their neighbors? How can you tell?

"My deputies are known for their ability to keep their mouths closed. You'll need to be able to do the same. We can only discuss our findings when we're in the privacy of this house, okay?"

Sarah clapped. "This is going to be fun, Uncle."

"Yes, but this is a serious matter too. I'm counting on you to see and hear things I may not be able to. We'll make a list. After you watch possible mother-wives for three weeks, we'll see if one woman stands out, or if we need to keep looking."

"Should Sarah and I start a conversation with them?"

"Only if this feels natural, Jem. They'll suspect something if you start asking them a bunch of questions. Just watch."

Someone rang the church bell, and Ben stood. He straightened his tie and jacket and checked the loads in his pistols. "Time to go. We don't want to be late."

Sarah grabbed his hand. "Let's go. I want to start looking today."

Three weeks later, they sat around the table and Ben picked up the list. "Let's review. Sarah, you said you wanted a mother who could teach you how to cook. You also wanted her to smile a lot and do fun things with you. After watching our possibilities, do you want to add or change anything?"

"Yes. She must like dogs, horses, and other animals, and she shouldn't mind getting her clothes or hands dirty."

Ben added to the list and looked at Jeremy. "Jem, you wanted a woman who could like the things you like and who wouldn't get angry at a few practical jokes. Anything else?"

Jeremy nodded. "She should smell good."

Ben chuckled and wrote. He looked at the list. "I want a woman who can carry on an intelligent conversation and who will love you two the way I love you. I want a partner to share the load when the heavy things in life come, and I'd like her to smell good too. Oh, and if she can give good back rubs, then all the better."

The children laughed and nodded.

"Okay, now that we know what we want, what do you think about the women on our list?"

Sarah frowned. "We should mark Miss Hastings off. She's pretty, but she doesn't like dogs or getting her clothes dirty. She screeched at me when I accidentally bumped into her on the sidewalk the other day, and she acted as if I'd committed a crime."

Jeremy agreed. "I offered to run some errands for her. She treated me like dirt and didn't say thank you. She tried not to touch my skin when she put the coins in my hand."

Ben drew a line through the woman's name. "How about Miss Jacobs?"

For the next two hours they discussed the pros and cons of each of the ten women on the list. By the end of their conversation, all the women's names had been crossed off, and they looked at each other.

Ben stared, then scratched his head. His stomach hollowed. "Uh-oh."

Jeremy straightened. "You said we may have to keep looking. Where do we do that?"

"I'll show you." He stood and walked to the stack of newspapers shoved onto the settee. He searched through several, then brought one to the table.

Sarah studied the letters. "What's *Marriage Marketplace*?"

Ben spoke without looking up. "People who run this newspaper let men and women seeking spouses advertise. They write from all over the country. The men pay so much for thirty words and extra for more than that, but the women don't pay until after the thirty words. If the man and woman marry, they send a donation to the paper." Ben's gut roiled. Had he actually sunk to writing for a mail-order bride?

Sarah and Jeremy took turns reading and laughing at many of the ads. Ben listened until the tops of his ears burned. What could he offer a woman beside an instant family, a house in chaos, work enough for three, and a husband who worked long hours in a career that could leave him maimed or dead in a heartbeat? What woman would be crazy enough to consider him if he did write?

Sarah hopped up and returned to the table with pencil and paper. "What do we want to say?"

Jeremy studied the ads. "Both the men and women have to tell their age, height, and weight, and what money they bring to the marriage. Then they can tell what kind of person they're looking for, though they don't have to say the words in that order."

Ben smiled and took the paper and pencil. "How about I start and you both check out what I say to make sure I get the words right. We need to keep things simple and tell the truth."

Jem looked out the window. "How long after we send the letter will a woman write to us, Uncle? If the letter takes a while, she may be traveling in bad weather, or we may be in school."

"A few weeks, I'd imagine. If someone is interested, she'll write to us, and then we'll exchange letters until we're sure we all want each other."

"Then we don't have much time." Sarah pointed to the pencil and paper.

Ben nodded. "First, though, I think we'd better pray and ask God if having a mother-wife is what he wants for us, and if so, ask him to speed her to us."

No sooner had they bowed their heads, made their requests, and said "amen," than someone pounded the knocker.

Deputy Wilson shouted from the other side of the door. "Sheriff, we need you. A poker game got out of hand at Muldoon's saloon, and the men are fighting and cutting each other."

Ben stood up so fast, he tipped over his chair. He righted the chair and looked at the children. "You know what to do, right? If you get too scared listening to those ornery cusses yelling and shooting, go next door to Mrs. Norwood's boarding house and wait for me."

Jeremy nodded. "We'll be all right. I'll take care of Sarah." They heard the commotion spilling into the street.

Ben shrugged on his jacket and gripped Jeremy's upper arm. "Good man. I know you will."

Sarah rushed around the table and hugged his waist. "Don't let them hurt you, Uncle. Come home soon."

"I'll try my best, little darlin'."

CHAPTER 3: THE ULTIMATUM

WESTERN LOUISIANA, EARLY SUMMER 1895

HATTIE HELPED MRS. SALLY HANG THE LAST SHEET ON THE LINE.

The elderly woman grabbed a clothes pin from her mouth and pressed this onto the sheet. "Now, bless my heart girl, you're an odd one, aren't you?"

Hattie laughed. "Several say so, ma'am, but I don't think helping a person who's been laundering for most people in the town makes me odd."

"Well, only you know why you want to help an old lady like this, but whatever the reason, I thank you. This is the last load to dry. Why, I'll be able to sit down to an early supper and prop my feet up for a while before bed."

Hattie smiled and folded the last of the shirts and blouses. "All done. If you don't need me anymore today, Mrs. Sally, I'll head home."

"Shoo, girl. Best get home to your supper." She turned to her grandson. "Jeb, walk Miss Hattie home."

The young man emptied the last of the wash tubs and dried his hands. "Sure thing, Grammy."

Hattie slipped in through the mansion's side door and rushed up the stairs. She changed her clothes faster than she ever had and brought her hair back under control. She couldn't do anything about the high color in her cheeks or the sparkle in her eyes.

She turned to leave, but Carrie stood in the doorway. "You're late."

"I know. Sorry. Time got away from me."

"Your face is flushed and your hands are chapped. Have you been meeting a man on the sly?"

Hattie glared at her younger sister and pulled on her gloves. "Of course not. I've been helping Mrs. Sally wash and hang laundry. The poor woman needed help."

Carrie's eyes rounded and her jaw dropped. "Laundry? You?" She burst into laughter.

"Shh." Hattie pushed open the dining room door and put on her best social mask.

The males in the room, including Max and her father, stood when she and Carrie entered, but Mr. Flynn added a smile and bow.

Hattie's emotional mask tightened around her. She wanted to sigh but didn't. Instead, she tilted her head and returned his smile because Mr. Flynn was another of Mother's tall, handsome, and rich candidates for Hattie's hand.

Mother waved. "Come, girls. Dinner is served. Harriette, would you take the seat to Mr. Flynn's right?"

She moved to the chair and let him seat her. "How are you Mr. Flynn? I heard you spent several weeks in the nation's capital. I hope your trip was both profitable and enjoyable."

"Yes, quite." As the meal progressed, he recounted the details of the fabulous restaurants he had visited and the exquisite dishes they had offered him. He told of the athletic matches he'd seen with such excitement and energy, Max, who sat on her right, leaned forward and conversed from around her.

Hattie didn't mind. All she had to do was pretend to listen and nod every now and then.

Carrie eyed her from across the table, and Hattie knew the young inquisitor would be in her bedroom as soon as Mr. Flynn left and as soon as she could change into her nightgown. Carrie would demand to know why she helped Mrs. Sally, and Hattie would be pressured to tell her secret.

The meal seemed interminable.

Mother rose and smiled at Mr. Flynn. "We have enjoyed your company. Thank you for coming. I'm glad your parents could spare you for the evening."

He bowed. "The dinner and company were outstanding, Madame. Thank you."

She looked at Mr. Flynn. "Perhaps, you'd like to stay a little longer and enjoy the stars with Harriette? The porch swing is comfortable, and the night is pleasantly cool."

Mother did not look at Hattie while she waited for his answer.

Mr. Flynn smiled. "This sounds like a wonderful plan." He offered his arm. "Miss Harriette?"

Hattie kept her polite mask in place, but the one time her glance met her mother's, her mother's look begged her to try.

She placed her hand in the crook of his elbow and stepped outside with him. She then dropped her hand and signaled him toward the swing. "Please, sit. I'm sure you probably don't want to talk about stars, Mr. Flynn, but I'd be happy to hear more about your trip to Washington. Did you get to tour the White House? Did you see President or Mrs. Cleveland? What about Vice President Stevenson?" She smiled and sat down as far away from him as she could.

This was the only spark he needed to start his narrative again. He droned on for another thirty minutes before Hattie stood. "What an interesting time you must have had, sir. If you will excuse me now, I must retire."

He stood and bowed. "Thank you for a lovely evening, Miss Harriette."

"You're welcome." Hattie escorted him to the door, then headed for the stairs.

"Harriette?" Her mother's voice stopped her. "Come into the library, dear. Your father and I want to talk with you."

Dread rolled around in Hattie's stomach like marbles as she followed her mother into the library and sat on the edge of her favorite chair, her hands primly folded and her eyes cast down.

Father chuckled. "Uh-oh. I've seen that look before, Lillian. Harriette's jaw is set in that stubborn way she has."

He patted her hand. "Relax, daughter. Your mother and I just want to talk to you.

Hattie lifted her eyes and forced her jaw to relax. "Yes?"

Mother twisted the edge of her handkerchief. "We're worried about you, Harriette."

"Why, Mother?"

"Because you're twenty-two and unmarried. Don't you want a home and man of your own, darling? One who will give you children and be your close companion?"

"Yes, I want that."

Father spoke in his usual blunt way, "Then why do you run off all the eligible men who come courting, my dear?"

She answered in kind, "Because they bore me to tears, or they try to tell me what I should or shouldn't be doing as a well-brought up southern woman. I don't appreciate their bossiness. Being married to any one of them would make me feel like a prisoner."

"A prisoner? Oh, dear." Mother fanned herself. "What about Mr. Flynn?"

"What about him, Mother?"

"Didn't he appeal to you at all?"

Hattie shook her head. "Him least of all."

When her parents stared at her, she looked from one to the other. "I heard you talking about me a couple of weeks ago. You intended to give me an ultimatum—choose my own husband by the year's end, or allow you to choose one for me."

Father frowned. "Listening at keyholes does not become you, Harriette."

"The door was cracked, so I did not listen at the keyhole."

Father grinned. "Well, now that you heard us, what do you say?"

"Based on past years' experiences, we don't see eye-to-eye on suitable husbands, so I will find my own by the year's end. Do not worry yourself, Mother. He will be a man of my choosing who will make me happy. He'll give me children and you grandchildren."

Mother dabbed at tears and smiled, but Father lifted a brow. "I hear an unstated 'but' in your comment."

Hattie nodded. "But I do not guarantee you will agree with my choice or that he will fit well with the Louisiana elite. Since I have to live with him and you don't, though, you have to let me take risks."

"Will you choose some nobody off the streets to wed?" The frantic look in her mother's eyes touched her.

"Of course not, Mother. Don't work yourself into a state of vapors. You and Father raised me right, and I will not turn away from the values you taught me. My husband will have the same values. He won't be a nobody because everyone is somebody in God's eyes."

When Hattie returned to her room, Carrie awaited her. "Tell. What kept you so long, and why did you help Mrs. Sally with the laundry?"

She told her about her agreement to their parents' ultimatum. Her words silenced Carrie for a few moments.

"Where do you intend to look for a man, Hattie?" Her subdued tones made Hattie want to hug her.

"I suppose the *Marriage Marketplace* is as good a place to start as any. Wasn't this your idea? To answer an ad?"

Fat tears dripped down Carrie's cheeks. "But you would have to leave if you found a man who suited you, and I'd be by myself."

"Yes, by yourself with Maxwell, our parents, the servants, all your friends, and your beaux."

She sniffed. "Why did you do laundry?"

"Because I had to learn to clean and wash clothing. Most of the men who want mail-order brides want women who can cook and clean. I know how to cook, and I do a fairly good job of cleaning, but I didn't know how to correctly launder clothing and bedding, so I went to Mrs. Sally and asked if I could help her. Why are you looking at me as if I've grown two heads?"

Carrie blinked several times. "Are you really my well-brought up southern belle sister, or are you a changeling? What have you done with Hattie?"

Hattie chuckled. "Mother swears I am not a changeling, so I guess the real Harriette Atwell is starting to take over your southern belle sister's mind."

Carrie flung herself into Hattie's arms and cried. "Be careful, Hattie. You don't know what kind of men write those ads. I better help you sift through each one. Maybe we should ask Liza to help us."

"Liza has enough on her plate running after our nieces and caring for her home and husband. Let's not put any more worry on her shoulders."

"Okay. Here." She tossed the latest *Matrimonial Marketplace* on the bed. "I haven't read any ads yet."

"Why don't I look and make notes, and you look and make notes, then we'll compare. Okay?"

Carrie yawned. "I'm going to bed. I'll look at them first thing tomorrow. I love you, Hattie."

"I love you too, Carrie. Good night."

Hattie could not sleep. She sat at her desk and read each and every ad. She drew a pencil and paper toward her and noted any man that sounded like a possibility.

She yawned and turned to the last page. Her eyes focused on the ad near the bottom, and her heart went from sleepy to racing in seconds.

Texas lawman with a steady income needs a Christian wife who can cook, clean, and care for two children ages 14 and 10. He's thirty, 6'3", and 198 lbs.

Hattie's eyes riveted to the words. She knew. This lawman would be the man she would marry if he'd have her.

She took out a fresh sheet of paper, wrote an introductory letter, and addressed this in care of the *Marriage Marketplace*. The letter would go out with the early mail and would reach the post office before Carrie awakened.

Hattie tiptoed into her sister's room and left the newspaper on her bed, then went about her work. She finished before lunch and headed to the library with a snack tray and a hot pot of tea.

"Good morning, Father. I thought you might want a little something before lunch."

"Thanks, Harriette. You're a good daughter."

She set the tray on her father's desk, filled both their cups, then nibbled on a finger sandwich as she searched through the shelves and papers for anything about Texas or Texas lawmen.

Father went to lunch, but Hattie continued to read and take notes. She finished writing the last word when Carrie burst in.

Carrie held out the paper and pointed. "Him. He's the one."

Hattie's eyes misted when her sister showed her the same ad she'd chosen to answer. "Yes, he's the one."

Liza and the nieces showed up for their monthly visit while her husband, Thomas, attended to business.

After dinner, Carrie hauled Liza up to Hattie's room where Hattie copied several of Cook's recipes.

"What's this about, Carrie?"

"Hattie is going to marry a lawman in Texas."

Liza gasped and stared. "Start at the beginning and tell me what's going on."

She sat in a chair next to the desk, but Katy's blank eye sockets and grisly smile distracted her. "Do you have to keep that skeleton in plain sight, Hattie? She's enough to make one bilious."

Hattie moved the model away from Liza. "Katy is a great help. Because of her, I can see what each man and woman's bone structure looks like under their skin."

Both sisters stared. They spoke as one. "What?"

Hattie stood and dropped two of her sketchbooks in each sister's lap.

They turned the pages but said nothing. Hattie watched them in silence. She could read fascination and amazement in their expressions.

Liza closed her sketchbooks. "These are yours? You did every one of them?"

"Yes. I've been drawing and painting for twelve years now."

"You're better than anybody I've seen, Hattie. Now tell me about this lawman."

She pointed to the ad. "I've written but haven't heard."

"You've thought this through?"

Hattie nodded. "I can't stop thinking this through. Mother and Father don't know yet, so don't say anything."

"He's a law officer, Hattie. Does this bother you?"

"No, why should his work bother me?"

"Law officers' jobs are hard and dangerous. They are on edge day and night as they deal with some of the scum of the earth. They face death on a regular basis. My guess is this man is well-versed in the use of his fists and weapons of all kinds. He may even have had to take more than one human life in order to protect his town. Are you okay with this?"

Hattie examined her heart. Was she okay with this? "I don't know. I'll have to think about your question."

Carrie stood and stretched. "I don't like to think about such things. This conversation depresses me. I think I'll see if the girls and Max want to play games."

After Carrie closed the door, Hattie cleared her throat and looked down at her hands. "Liza, I've been meaning to ask you about something—something personal."

"What?"

Hattie blushed. "I want to know what I should expect—"

Liza frowned. "Just ask, Hattie."

Hattie's face heated and her hands perspired. She took a deep breath and the words rushed out. "What should I expect on my wedding night, Liza? I have a general idea but not the specifics."

Liza blushed a deep red and nodded. "If you're going to marry this Texan, you'd better understand the basics."

The basics amazed and frightened her and sent hot and cold spears through her system. She tossed and turned for hours that night trying to slow her thoughts.

She finally calmed when she promised herself she would interview several police officers in the area to see what their jobs and lives were really like. She could then make a better-informed decision as to whether a lawman was husband material.

Deep down, she knew their information would not change her mind. The Texas lawman was the one.

CHAPTER 4: Chosen

TEXAS PANHANDLE, EARLY SUMMER 1895

BEN DABBED AT HIS BLOODY NOSE, then rinsed the rag in the bowl. He started on his bleeding knuckles.

Deputy Joseph Wilson sat in his chair at the jailhouse and propped his boots on the desk as he watched. "You're a sight, Ben, but those cowboys look worse. Maybe they'll think twice about coming into town to make trouble."

"I'm not holding my breath. They get liquored up and gain courage from the bottle."

"Hey," Deputy Ron Nelson held up a telegram. "The U.S. Marshal's Office and the Texas Rangers sent word. We may have some bad dudes coming our way." He sighed and rubbed his prematurely graying temple. "Makes me feel old. Seems like these youngsters never learn. They're voting for an early grave when they turn to a life of crime."

Ben looked up. "What are they doin'?"

Nelson shrugged. "They're forming gangs and tryin' to shape themselves after the old Sam Bass gang, Killer Jim Miller, John Wesley Hardin, Jesse James, and King Fisher."

Joe Wilson spun his feet to the floor. "You mean Deacon Jim and Hardin haven't yet met their Maker? Those are bad men. If I were Hardin, I'd be watchin' out for John Selman. He's trouble."

Nelson nodded. "These new criminals think they're untouchable. They successfully rob trains and banks and kill people without realizin' their time's comin'. Billy the Kid, Jesse and Frank James, Johnny Ringo, Clay Allison, and the other terrors are all six feet under. Most never made their thirtieth birthday."

Joe read the telegram Ron handed him, then gave the paper to Ben.

"The Bently gang, huh? Train and bank robbers from back east. Last seen in Louisiana headed west." Ben studied the date. "We'd best review our plans and see if we need to change or modify anything. I'll talk to Fred Staples on my way home. That banker's a veteran of the War and tight lipped. He won't be letting the news out to the public."

The two deputies stood. "Sure, boss. We'll mosey around the town and keep an eye on the saloon."

"Keep your eyes peeled and stay out of the light. The shine from your badges makes a tempting target."

Joe nodded. "We know. I haven't lived to be thirty without watching my step. Night, Ben."

Ben altered his route and made a detour to the banker's home. Quietly and succinctly, he shared the news in the telegram. Staples nodded. "Thank you, Sheriff. I'm sure we'll be talking soon."

Ben took a circuitous route home in case any watched. He stood in the deepest shadows cast by a rose bush and listened for sounds in the house. Sarah and Jeremy spoke to each other in normal tones, so he pulled out the side door key and slipped into the parlor.

"How are we going to read all these letters, Jem. My eyes are already tired."

"Uncle Ben will want to read them. He'll have to decide."

"I'm here. What do I need to decide?" He stepped into the light, and Sarah's gaze immediately pinpointed his cut lip and bruised hands. Before she could say anything, he strode to her and kissed her forehead. "I'm okay, princess. I had to keep some drunk cowboys in line before they tore up the town."

Jeremy tilted his head toward the mail. "Letters for us."

Ben rubbed the back of his neck. "How about we head to the restaurant for some supper, then we can come back and read them." He had no energy for cooking tonight.

Jeremy scanned Ben's face and hands and nodded.

Ben marveled at the boy's sensitivity. He studied people and said little, but nothing much escaped his watchful blue eyes.

When they returned an hour later, Ben turned up the lamp, and they sat down at the table. He stared at the mail. At least fifty letters had his name on them. Were these all from possible brides?

He took a deep breath and divided the stack into unequal thirds. "Read the letters in your pile. If the woman doesn't match what we want, put that letter in a pile to your left. If you like how she sounds, put that letter in the middle of the table, okay? If you're not sure, put the letter to your right. We'll read as many as we can tonight, and finish tomorrow after church."

Ben bathed and shaved. He put salve on his cuts and bruises and buttoned on a clean shirt. He looked forward to this day of rest. He wanted time to collect his thoughts and reflect.

After breakfast, he strolled with Jeremy and Sarah to the church on Second Street. Several people stared when they walked to the steps of the church, and matrons whispered behind their hands. Several of the single women tilted their heads in greeting but gave him frosty looks.

Sarah frowned. "Why are they looking at us like that, Uncle Ben?"

He assessed the citizens' expressions and body language. "I don't know. Did I leave shaving cream on my face?"

Sarah glanced at his chin and jaw. "No. You look fine to me."

"Knowing these people, I'm sure we'll find out sooner rather than later, darlin'. They never keep anything that bothers them a secret. I always hear when they're displeased. Ignore them. Don't let them turn your attention from being able to worship God with a calm heart."

Ben tried to follow his own advice, but his senses had been on alert for so many years, he couldn't totally ignore them. His brain continued to catalog sounds, sights, and faces. He sat where he could monitor the two doors and the windows and reviewed his exit should he need to leave quickly. Mentally, he checked the loads in his pistols and visualized the location of rifles he'd hidden around town for easy access.

Jeremy leaned closer and whispered. "Thirty people are sitting on our side of the church, and thirty-five sit across from us. Of the sixty-five present, twenty-five are women and fifteen are men. Fifteen are children my age and younger, and ten are babes in arms. Relax, Uncle. I'll help you watch."

Ben stared at his nephew.

A corner of Jeremy's mouth tipped up.

Ben whispered near his ear. "How many businesses are on Main Street?"

Without turning, Jeremy answered, "Muldoon's saloon, a hotel, a restaurant, the mercantile, feed store, Doc Weston's office, the Jacobs' tailor and seamstress services, the telegraph office, the Post Office, the Land Office, and your office."

"How many windows face south?"

Jeremy closed his eyes for a moment. "Eight of the hotel's, two each for the restaurant, feed store, Land Office, the saloon, and Doc Weston's office.

"Impressive. How many of the north-facing businesses on the south side of the street—"

"The bank has four, two on the first floor and two on the second, the Post Office has three, the Jacobs' shop has two, and the telegraph and your office both have two." He opened his eyes and smiled. "Did I get them right? "

Ben smiled. "You answered correctly. Thanks, Jem."

He nodded and focused on the minister who stepped to the pulpit, though his eyes scanned the church every few seconds.

After services, Ben followed the last of the congregants out and shook hands with the minister.

"Sheriff Cole?" Mrs. Norwood put a hand on his arm and smiled. "I'd like to invite you and the children to lunch with me at my place. Please say you'll come. The meal will be ready when we get there."

Ben glanced at Jeremy and Sarah. They both smiled and nodded.

Ben touched his hat brim. "We accept. Thank you, Mrs. Norwood."

Once they were out of hearing range of the others, Mrs. Norwood chuckled. "You have no clue why the women are acting so strangely today, do you?"

Sarah frowned. "Do you know why?"

The woman laughed. "Of course, I do. I know everything that happens in this town."

Jeremy stepped closer. "Why are they acting so upset, ma'am?"

"The women found out your uncle advertised for a mail-order- bride. They are offended he didn't choose one of them, and they're saying Ben doesn't think they're good enough."

Ben stiffened. "How did they find out? We haven't said anything."

"The postmaster couldn't keep his mouth shut after he saw the sending address and the letters addressed to you."

Sarah scoffed. "Jem and I get to help Uncle Ben choose, and we've already looked at all the women in this town. We don't want—."

Ben put a hand on Sarah's shoulder. "Thank you for clarifying, Mrs. Norwood. You've been a great help."

She laughed. "Glad to be of help, Ben. Come on inside. I made chicken and dumplings with apple pie for dessert."

Sarah swung Ben's hand. "Yum. I love apple pie."

They read the letters in silence. Several times, Sarah asked what words meant. Most of the letters she read went in the discard pile, though one or two found their way to the center of the table.

A few more of Jeremy's letters went into the center pile, but most of the others went into the discard or uncertain pile.

Ben didn't have much better success. What if none of these women worked? Was he being too picky? He felt like he'd swallowed a lead ball, and desperation filled him. These children needed a mother before they got much older. He didn't know how much longer he could hold them together emotionally.

Jeremy straightened and focused on the letter in front of him. He read and reread, then offered the letter to Ben. "Her. I found our new mother."

Sarah squealed and left her seat to stand beside Ben. "Read her letter, Uncle. Quick."

Ben studied the elegant writing and took a deep breath.

Dear Texas Lawman and his children,

I don't know your names yet, but I hope to learn them soon. My name is Harriette Atwell, but my friends and family call me Hattie. I live in western Louisiana with my parents, a seventeen-year-old sister, Carrie, and a fourteen-year-old brother, Maxwell. My older brother, Heath, is a medical doctor somewhere in Colorado, and my older sister, Liza, is married and has two children. They visit every month.

I'm twenty-two, five feet ten inches tall, and weigh one hundred sixty pounds. My hair and eyes are brown. I have an inheritance and money to bring to a marriage. I can cook several different kinds of meals including southern dishes, but my favorites are stew, chicken pot pies, and apple and cherry pies. Yum. As I write you, I can almost taste them.

Sarah smacked her lips and pointed. "Look, Uncle. She painted a picture of a cherry pie in her letter. This looks so real, I can almost smell the crust."

Ben stared. He could too, and his stomach grumbled.

If you choose me, I know how to clean and manage a home and will work hard to make us comfortable. Though our states border each other, I'm sure our lives have been different. I won't know everything I need to know at first, but I'm willing to learn. I hope you are patient, kind people.

I love to read and learn new things. I draw and paint and enjoy getting my hands dirty as I plant vegetables and flowers in the garden. Did you know many of our garden flowers can be eaten in a fresh salad or cooked in a nourishing soup?

Jeremy leaned forward. "She drew and colored flowers, vegetables, and a hand spade. I like this picture."

Ben studied the image. "I do too."

Sarah pressed against him. "What else did she write?"

I am looking to share my life with a family who loves God and loves others. I am not as interested in physical appearance as I am in what's inside of you. When I saw your advertisement, my heart said, "This one," so you all must be special. I can't explain how I know with certainty that you are the family for me, but I just know.

If you wish to contact me, here is my address.

Love, Hattie.

Ben looked up. "What do you think? Should we offer to make Miss Atwell part of our home and family?"

"Yes!" Jeremy indicated the letters in the piles. "None of the others come close. Can't you hear the love in her words?"

Ben could, but he'd dealt with too many cons to take anyone at face value. "Let's each write her a letter and tell her who we are and what we like or don't like. We need to give her the opportunity to say no if she doesn't want us. That's only fair."

He intended to send a wire to a detective friend in Shreveport in the morning. He wanted to make sure Hattie didn't have a criminal record. He wouldn't tell the children this though.

Jeremy frowned. "What if she's answered other advertisements? I think we should write her and send the letters tomorrow."

"All right. You and Sarah write your letters while I'm at the office, and when I come home for lunch, I'll mail them on my way back." He looked around. "See what you can do to make this place look a little friendlier if you can. We don't want her to panic when she steps in the door."

Sarah clung to him. "When will she come, Uncle Ben?"

"Depends on how soon she gets our letters and how long she needs to decide if we're still the ones. If she says yes, I'll send her a railway ticket right away." He stroked her hair. "This is still our secret, okay? We don't need the whole town knowing our business yet. If Hattie comes, they'll know soon enough."

"Okay." She kissed his cheek and went to the desk for pencil and paper. She gave them each a sheet. "I'm going to use my best handwriting. Maybe, I'll draw her a picture of Buster and the chickens."

"You do that, darlin'."

CHAPTER 5: An Unpleasant Welcome

Western Louisiana to Texas, Summer 1895

HATTIE WATCHED THE PASSING SCENERY for a moment before reading the Coles' letters again. She neared the end of her journey, and sudden doubts assailed her. She needed to know she had done the right thing.

She smiled at Sarah's letter and the picture of her dog and chickens.

Dear Hattie,

As soon as we read your letter, we knew you were the right woman to be Uncle Ben's wife and our mother. We really need you.

We are kind and patient most of the time, because God tells us to be. Sometimes, though, when I'm tired and hungry, I get cranky. I'm not patient when Jem plays practical jokes on me either. Will you teach me to cook?

Love, Sarah

P.S. I'm ten and have blonde hair and blue eyes.

"Of course, I'll teach you to cook, sweetheart." She chuckled. "I wonder if Jeremy loves practical jokes as much as Max?"

She read Jeremy's letter next.

Dear Hattie,

My name is Jeremy Cole. I'm fourteen. Sarah and I have lived with Uncle Ben for the last two years after our parents died in an accident.

I'm always hungry, so your stews and pies sound good. Uncle says I'm growing. I like to learn new things too. I like to work with my brain and my hands. Uncle thinks I will make a great detective if I choose a law enforcement career.

When Uncle Ben asked me what I needed in a mother, I told him I wanted someone to be interested in what I'm interested in and to care about what happens to me. I think you are the right mother for both me and Sarah. I'll be grown up in a few years, but I'd still like to have a mother to come home to.

We need you. Please come.

Jeremy

Hattie brushed away tears, and her doubts stilled. She unfolded Ben Cole's letter.

Dear Hattie,

My name is Benjamin David Cole. You can call me Ben. I'm the town's sheriff as well as a Deputy U.S. Marshal. This means I have jurisdiction over a wider area and can deal with local and federal matters.

I don't know why my advertisement attracted you, but I'm grateful. For the life of me, I can't figure out what would draw a woman of your quality to a man in a hazardous job with a ready-made family and a house needing a woman's touch.

Hattie could imagine what the house looked like with a ten-year-old at the homemaking helm.

> I will do my best to provide and care for you. The children and I look forward to your arrival. If you say yes to our marriage proposal, I'll send your railway ticket and will have the preacher waiting when you arrive.
>
> Sincerely,
>
> Benjamin Cole

She'd said yes, and her ticket arrived a week later. She'd packed her trunk and bags and went down to face her family to say goodbye.

"You've done what, Harriette?" The horror in Mother's voice sent prickles up Hattie's spine.

"I've agreed to marry Sheriff Benjamin Cole. He and his young niece and nephew live several miles south of Amarillo. He'll meet me in Amarillo five days from now."

Liza patted Mother's hand. "He sounds like a good man. Don't worry about Hattie. She doesn't make decisions lightly."

A frown creased Father's brow. "Are you sure this is what you want, Harriette? None of the other suitors you've had will do?"

"No, they won't. I said I would find a husband who suits me better by year's end, and so I did. He comes with a premade family, so you now have more grandchildren."

Max grinned. "Are you going to invite us out to meet our new relatives when you get settled?"

Hattie smiled. "Of course. I'll send letters and pictures along the way."

Hattie fulfilled her promise. She sketched the changing landscape and the different people on the train. She captured the image of anything that interested her on their stops.

She tucked the Coles' letters into her pocket and picked up the newspaper she'd bought at the last stop. The front page was filled with reports of bank and train robberies in the area, and the Bently gang figured prominently.

She'd heard about the outlaws before she left home, so she'd taken steps to secure her money before she left, just in case. She kept five silver dollars in her reticle but had sewn several more into the lining of her decorative hat as well as the back lining of her traveling jacket. More were secured to the back flaps of several of her sketchbooks.

A few hours outside of Amarillo, the train braked to a sudden stop.

"What's happening?" Several passengers rushed to the windows just as someone fired shots.

"Looks like someone blocked the tracks. Masked horsemen are now boarding us. We're being robbed!" One man yelled.

Five bandanna-masked men burst through the doors, pistols covering the passengers.

The tallest man held up a hand. "Now, you folks sit down. Stay calm, and nobody will get hurt."

The passengers complied, though most were not calm. Hattie fought to keep the quivering inside.

"My boys are going to come to each of you for a donation. You give them anything of value, you hear?" Hattie couldn't see the smirk on the man's face, but she heard this in his tone.

A heavy-set man with whiskers started to object, but one of the criminals hit him over the head with his pistol. The man crumpled.

Hattie watched everything with a sharp eye. As soon as she had access to her pencils and sketchbooks, she would draw these events. She studied each of the men to memorize details.

"You're next, lady." A masked man held open a bag.

Hattie removed the coins from her reticule and placed the silver in the bag. She opened the purse's mouth wide enough to show she had nothing else.

"Open the carpet bag."

"No, please. I don't have anything of value to you in there. Just my sketchbooks and—"

The man's eyes hardened. "I'll be the judge of that." He grabbed the carpetbag, jerked open the handles, and screamed. He dropped the carpetbag to the seat and backed away.

"What's wrong with you?" The taller man strode toward him, irritation bristling his voice.

"She's got a kid's skeleton in that bag." The man's voice sounded young to Hattie.

"What?" The outlaw's blue eyes widened. He stared at Katy's macabre grin. "Why're you carryin' around a skeleton, woman?"

Hattie tried to look innocent. She smiled and kept her tone light and conversational. "That's Katy. I take her everywhere I go. She's been helpful to me these last few years."

Both outlaws paled and stepped away from her. The smaller man took another step backward. "She's crazy. I ain't stickin' my hand in that bag for no amount of money. She may have someone's head or another body part in there."

The taller man must have agreed because he signaled to his men. "We've got enough. Let's go."

Hattie made sure Katy was unharmed, then reached for a new sketchbook and sharpened pencils. She had to breathe deeply for several moments until her hands quit shaking, but as soon as her nerves calmed, she started the drawings.

She sketched them on horseback as they rode away.

Able-bodied men from the train cleared the tracks, and they continued to Amarillo an hour later.

Would her new family still be waiting, or would they decide she wasn't coming? She pushed down her concern. She couldn't do a thing about the delay, so she might as well relax as much as she could in the muggy Texas heat.

She thought of her new family. Would they like each other when they met for the first time? What would she do if they didn't? She had no illusions she would step into a perfect dream world where problems didn't exist. Problems always came no matter what. She just wondered what kind and how soon she must face them.

Her chin firmed. They would just have to work through each issue.

Hattie dabbed at the sweat on her neck with her handkerchief and fanned herself with the newspaper. The heat in the car wilted everyone's spirits and stifled conversation.

Amarillo came into view, and Hattie straightened. The place bustled. She'd never seen so many head of cattle, though she'd read Amarillo had become the world's greatest cattle shipping market.

She grabbed her sketchbook and pencil and ignored the heat scratching at her. She laid in quick, rough strokes and tried to capture the huge expanse of sky and land, the heat, and the innumerable herds of cattle.

The train pulled into the station, and Hattie gathered her things. Her heart rate increased, and she whispered a prayer. "Okay, Lord. I need your help getting through the next several minutes."

When the train hissed to a stop and the doors opened, she waited for several upset and angry passengers to precede her and then followed.

She looked around.

"Hattie?" A petite, blonde girl rushed to her.

Hattie smiled. "You're Sarah?"

Sarah flung her arms around Hattie's waist. "Yes. We thought you'd never get here."

Hattie leaned down and returned the embrace.

A tall, black-haired man approached. When he moved, she caught glimpses of the badge and gun belt he wore under his black, hip-length suit jacket. Her heart picked up speed.

A brown-haired, blue-eyed teen followed at his side.

Her smile widened. "Ben and Jeremy?"

Ben studied her face. "Are you all right, Hattie? We just got word the passengers on the train were robbed."

"Yes, I'm fine. They took five silver dollars."

Ben's mouth tightened, but he turned to the teen. "This is Jeremy. He's been anticipating your cooking since we got your letters."

The young man held out his hand and looked into her eyes. "Call me Jem."

She smiled and took his hand but turned the greeting into a quick embrace. "I'm so glad to meet you, Jem."

He held her for a moment and closed his eyes. When he stepped back, red rushed into his cheeks. "You smell good, ma'am."

Ben took her hand and smiled. "Let's get you into the station and out of this heat. Give me your claim ticket, and I'll get your luggage."

Hattie did so but clutched the carpetbag. Now was not the time to introduce her new family to Katy.

"I'll bring the horses and wagon around, Uncle Ben." Jeremy turned to Sarah. "Take care of our new mother. I'll be right back."

His new mother. Panic raced through Hattie's veins. *Oh, Lord, please help me.*

CHAPTER 6: Joined

BEN CLICKED TO THE HORSES AFTER HATTIE'S TRUNK AND BAGS rested in the wagon bed. His eyes scanned the people and street as their wagon moved away from the curb, but his thoughts focused on the woman beside him. He still could not fathom why such a tall, elegant, and beautiful woman would choose to be his bride.

His law enforcement mind whispered that maybe she escaped from something or someone, but he smothered that thought. No, he'd looked into her eyes and seen the kind of openness and honesty not reflected in the faces of criminals.

Ben knew the moment he laid eyes on her she would be good for Jem, Sarah, and him, though he didn't know how he knew this except God had answered his and the children's' prayers and had already planted a growing sense of affection for her inside of him.

His hands twitched. He'd never been a husband before, so what would Hattie expect of him? They would need to talk soon to make sure they were pulling in the same harness. He never hid behind fancy words or said things he didn't mean, and the only way he knew to deal with issues was head on and as efficiently as possible. He hoped she could handle such honesty because he didn't know any other way to be.

He smiled at her. "I'm sure you're hungry, Hattie. I know Jem and Sarah are. I thought we'd get some supper before meeting with Reverend Griggs. We'll have to stay in Amarillo tonight and start home after breakfast tomorrow. We have quite a drive."

A delicate tint of pink stained Hattie's cheeks, and Ben wondered if the idea of staying the night with him embarrassed her. He hoped not. No such feelings hindered him. He looked forward with great anticipation to a night spent in his new bride's arms. The thought heated his belly and sent fire to his nerve endings.

Hattie nodded, then turned to the children. "Tell me about yourselves. Tell me things you didn't write in your letters."

Sarah took her at her word and chattered all the way to the hotel.

Jeremy grinned and shrugged.

Ben hopped down and helped Hattie and Sarah out of the wagon. "I'll bring your trunk and luggage as soon as we get checked in."

Sarah frowned. "I don't want to stay in a strange room by myself, Uncle. Can I stay with Jem?"

Ben raised a brow. "Jem?"

Jeremy tugged on her braid. "Yes, but only if you don't snore or kick."

"I don't snore. I don't know if I kick."

"Okay."

They cleaned up in their rooms and went to the dining room together.

Sarah grasped Hattie's hand, and Hattie smiled and gave their interlocked fingers a swing.

More warmth filled Ben. The movement had been natural and the smile sincere. He marveled again at the woman God had sent them.

As soon as they ordered, Sarah turned to Hattie. "You're going to love the ring Uncle Ben got for you. Our initials are on the inside—BJS."

Hattie's smile lit her eyes. "Now that is a ring worth having. I'll look at the initials every day and thank God he sent me to such a family."

Ben leaned back in his chair. "Tell us more about your life in Louisiana and what made you answer my advertisement."

Without hesitation, Hattie answered, "I grew up in a home much like many in Louisiana's upper class. I was taught all the accomplishments women of my station were expected to know. We have servants who live at the mansion and work in the kitchen and gardens, so my education did not include cooking and cleaning. I had to learn this on my own."

Jeremy glanced at Sarah and then back at Hattie. "How did you learn to cook on your own?"

"When I was Sarah's age, I snuck into the kitchen and begged the cook to teach me how. I went everyday for many years. No one knew I did this. I got to eat what I cooked, and since I love to eat, this was a perfect arrangement."

Ben scanned Hattie's figure while she looked at Jeremy. She was round in all the right places but didn't carry extra weight.

Jeremy laughed. "I love to eat too."

"My father and mother expected me to behave like the southern woman I was brought up to be, which meant I attended parties and helped them entertain other important people at our home. I obliged them as much as I could, but I drew the line at marrying any of the men they thought suitable."

She told them bluntly and without pretense about the ultimatum and her agreement to find her own husband. "When I read your advertisement, and my heart said to answer yours, I did. Here I am."

Ben chuckled inside. Hattie didn't beat around the bush or sugarcoat her words—she told things as they were. They would get along just fine.

The meal came, and Jeremy frowned at the extra glasses and silverware. "This place is too fancy for me. Which fork am I supposed to use?"

Hattie placed her napkin in her lap and picked up her fork. "Use this one first. You won't need two of the glasses because they are for red and white wine. The other is your water glass."

Sarah pointed. "Why is the fork and spoon at the top of the plate turned opposite of each other?"

Hattie grinned. "Those are important. They are your dessert spoon and fork."

"Yum, dessert." Sarah copied each move Hattie made. She put her napkin in her lap and picked up the correct fork."

Jeremy didn't comment, but he also copied her movements throughout the meal and dessert.

Ben pulled out his watch. "If you all are ready, Reverend Griggs is waiting. I let him know we'd be later than planned."

Hattie straightened and pushed her plate away.

Sarah tilted her head. "What's wrong, Hattie? You look scared."

Hattie looked down at her hands and then at Sarah. "I am scared. I've never been a wife or mother before, so I'm afraid of making mistakes."

Ben stood and offered Hattie his hand. "We all make mistakes, but this isn't one of those times. We belong together. We all have some learnin' and growin' to do. We just have to be patient, right?"

Hattie nodded. "Right."

The ceremony took place in Reverend Griggs's parlor. Mrs. Griggs and another woman acted as witnesses, while Jeremy stood next to him as his groomsman. Sarah's eyes shone at being Hattie's bridesmaid.

The pastor finished speaking, and Ben placed the gold band on Hattie's finger.

Reverend Griggs grinned. "You may now kiss your bride."

Ben smiled, drew his wife into his arms, and leaned in. As soon as his lips met hers, heat seared him. Hattie pressed closer and returned his kiss. He pulled her tight against his chest.

"Yay!" Sarah clapped. "We're married."

Ben leaned away but not willingly. He clasped Hattie's hand as they accepted hugs from the children and congratulations from the adults.

Reverend Griggs pointed to a table. "Please, step over here and sign the license before you leave."

They signed, and Ben handed the pastor a sealed envelope. "Thank you for performing the ceremony."

"I'm glad I could help, Sheriff. Have a safe journey home."

They loaded into the wagon and Ben clicked to the horses.

Jeremy leaned closer. "Hattie, do you remember much about the men who robbed the train? I heard someone in the hotel say the railroad people and law enforcement are looking for information."

"I remember everything. I drew them."

Ben's eyebrows raised. "Will you let me see the drawings when we get to the hotel?"

"Of course."

"I want to see too, Hattie."

"Okay, Sarah. I'll let you and Jeremy both see if Ben permits."

They crowded into the bedroom he and Hattie would share that night. Sarah hopped onto the bed, and Jeremy sat next to her. Ben took the nearby chair and watched his new wife.

Hattie reached into her carpetbag and brought out her sketchbook. She opened to the images she had drawn earlier in the day.

Ben whistled and took the book from her. "You did these?"

She nodded.

"These are exceptional, Hattie. We need to see the sheriff before we leave tomorrow. Will you part with these if he needs them?"

"Of course. Anything to help bring the outlaws to justice."

Jeremy studied the images for several minutes. "I've never seen paintings or drawings these good. Do you have more?"

Hattie laughed. "Yes. I've been drawing and painting for many years, so I have several sketchbooks." She returned to the carpetbag, patted Katy's white cheek, and brought out three more. She gave a sketchbook to each of them.

Ben studied every image and turned the pages with care. When he finished, he swapped for the other sketchbooks.

He looked up. "These are spectacular, Hattie. Not many can paint or draw the way you do."

"No one has seen them except you all, my sisters, and Dr. Eber, and he only saw a few of my earlier drawings. One of these days, I'll tell you about him and how he helped me get Katy."

Sarah looked around the room. "Who's Katy?'

Hattie smiled. "I'll introduce you when we get home. Now isn't the right time."

Ben stood. "Okay, you two, bed."

Sarah looked from him to Hattie. "Are you coming to tuck me in?"

Ben tilted his head toward the door. "Go get ready, and Hattie and I will be in to say goodnight."

He watched the children leave, then turned to Hattie and studied her face for several moments.

Hattie's tremulous smile caused a tightening behind his ribs. "I hope you weren't expecting a beauty, Ben. My sisters fit this description, but I inherited more of my father's looks."

Ben smiled. "Beauty is in the eye of the beholder. Based on how you interact with my children and they with you, I think you're the greatest beauty in the state of Texas."

Hattie chuckled. "Well, if that is your standard, then I'm glad."

"Hattie—" Ben hesitated.

"What?" She tilted her head as their eyes met.

He sighed. "I'm a straight shooter. I say what's on my mind without hiding what needs to be said with soft words. Sometimes, this may come across as tactless, so I apologize ahead of time. I deal with criminals and rough cowboys on an ongoing basis. Bluntness and maybe a fist in their guts or to their jaws are the only things they understand. Other than my mother, who died when I was five, I've never lived with a woman, so please forgive my roughness and lack of grace. I don't mean to offend."

Hattie's smile crinkled the corners of her eyes. "That doesn't bother me, Ben. I tend to prefer honesty over fancy words too. My sisters say I'm brutally honest, though I've never tried to be brutal."

He stepped closer to her. "Then will you tell me how you feel about being my wife in every sense of the word? I will respect your wishes if you don't want to consummate the marriage tonight, but I'm hoping you do."

Hattie reddened. "I know you are the man I am supposed to marry, Ben. If I am to be a mother and wife, then I don't see any reason to postpone this, do you?"

He couldn't squelch the rush of excitement and joy as he reached for her hand and intertwined his fingers with hers. "No, I don't. Now, let's go tuck in the children."

Ben sat next to Hattie as they waited in the office for Sheriff Levitt. He tried to keep an idiotic smile off his face but couldn't, not when she sat so close, he could feel her warmth and smell her clean woman's scent.

The smile came from deep inside and had stuck to his lips the moment he woke up beside her. He'd watched the early morning sunlight touch her soft, smooth skin, and his breath caught when her eyes opened and she looked at him with those dreamy brown eyes.

I bless you, Lord. Truly, you answer the prayers of your children. Thank you.

He thought about leaning over and giving her a quick kiss as she sat on the chair beside him, but the sound of footsteps on the boardwalk outside the door dampened that idea. He stood and turned.

The man who walked in was big and tough-looking and in his early forties. His eyes fixed on Ben's badge and then on his face. The tightness around his eyes relaxed a little, and he held out a calloused hand. "Sheriff, how may I help you?"

Ben shook the man's hand. "Sheriff Levitt, I'm Ben Cole from—"

"I know who you are and where you're from, Sheriff Cole. You're a Deputy U.S. Marshal also, correct?"

Ben nodded and introduced Hattie. "My wife was on the train yesterday and was robbed along with the other passengers. She is a talented artist and drew pictures of the thieves we thought you might want to see."

Sheriff Levitt indicated Ben should sit before he sat in his swivel chair on the other side of the desk.

Hattie laid her sketches in front of him, and Ben caught the lawman's startled look as he gazed at them.

Levitt placed the images side-by-side and studied each one. He said nothing for several minutes. Finally, he looked up. "Mrs. Cole, please explain everything that happened in the order they occurred. Tell me what the thieves said and anything you noticed about them down to the smallest details."

Hattie complied and pointed to the images as she told of the robbery. She repeated the words both the passengers and the thieves used. She even tried to mimic the speech patterns and tones of the outlaws.

Ben's admiration grew. As a lawman, he recognized how complete and thorough Hattie's report was. Most people remembered a few things, but Hattie seemed to remember everything. How could she do this?

"Will you leave these pictures with me, Mrs. Cole? I'd like to send copies to the U.S. Marshal's Office and the Texas Rangers."

"Of course, Sheriff. I hope they help."

"We may need to contact you again."

Ben nodded and stood. "You know where to find us. Now, if you'll excuse me, we need to stop by the hotel and get the children before we head home."

They stepped into the sunshine and Ben placed his hand in the small of Hattie's back as he guided her over the uneven planks in the boardwalk. "Do you know how exceptional you are, Harriettet Cole? I've never seen any witness do what you just did, and I've been in law enforcement for ten years."

She lifted a brow. "What did I do except give Sheriff Levitt the information he wanted?"

"You remembered all the details."

A slight frown creased Hattie's forehead. "I don't know if I captured every detail because I was frightened, but I forced myself to pay attention and to draw what I remembered."

"Excellent work, Wife."

CHAPTER 7: HOME

TEXAS PANHANDLE, SUMMER 1895

HATTIE STEPPED INSIDE HER NEW HOME AND PAUSED. She surveyed the space.

Ben stopped beside her. "As you can see, you're sorely needed."

Sarah clasped Hattie's hand. "We tried to make the rooms friendlier for you. Do you want me to show you the rest of the house?"

"Yes, but first, let me take my carpetbag upstairs and remove my bonnet. Then we'll get supper ready."

Her words put smiles on Jeremy's and Ben's faces.

Ben hung his hat on a hook. He gazed at Hattie as she descended the stairs. "What do you want us to do?"

She pursed her lips and looked around. "I need to take an inventory of what we have before I'll know what to prepare. You can show me where everything is. After supper, we'll tour the other rooms, then we'll sit down and come up with a menu for the next two weeks. We'll go to the store tomorrow or the next day. Does that suit you all?"

She laughed at their enthusiastic nods. "Good. Now let's get started."

Sarah stayed by her side as Hattie prepared the meal. She asked so many questions, Hattie barely answered one before the girl asked three more. Hattie chuckled. "You remind me of me when I was your age, Sarah. I couldn't ask my questions fast enough either."

They sat down to perfectly cooked steaks, mashed potatoes, gravy, green beans, and light, fluffy biscuits. Oatmeal cookies cooled on the drying rack.

Jeremy closed his eyes and inhaled. A smile stretched his lips, and he sighed. "I bet heaven smells like this."

Ben chuckled. "I agree. Now let's pray."

They did not rush through the meal, and Hattie enjoyed the conversation. She finally stood and reached for her empty plate and silverware. "I'll get the wash water ready. If you'll bring your dishes to me, I'll get them washed and draining. Sarah, will you clear and wash the table? Jem, will you sweep?"

Ben stood. "What can I do?"

"Bring in more wood for the stove. I'm going to need a lot for cleaning tomorrow."

"Happy to oblige, ma'am." He grabbed his hat, and Hattie smiled. Ben still placed this on his head, though the sun had set. He wore his hat, boots, spurs, and guns as if they were an integral part of him.

Jeremy returned the broom and dustpan to the closet. "I'll be right back, Hattie."

Hattie looked up just in time to see an expression she'd seen many times on Maxwell's face just before he tried to prank her. She watched him take the stairs two at a time, and wondered if he intended to put some kind of animal or bug in her bed. Surely, he wouldn't do so if Ben slept in the same bed, would he?

Hattie hoped Jeremy didn't have a snake. She'd learned not to shudder when Max used them to prank her and her sisters. Most of the snakes in Texas she knew about were venomous, so she guessed he wouldn't use a snake. What then? Max had used a baby skunk, cones from a Cypress

tree, a small rabbit, and various ugly-looking bugs. What else had he done?

When he was ten, he'd made some kind of slimy concoction she'd stuck her toes in when she slid under the sheets. She had learned to always pull the sheets down and to look under her pillow before getting into bed.

Hattie grinned. She knew how to prank the prankster. She reached for the ingredients for an apple pie.

Jeremy eased into Hattie and Uncle Ben's room and looked around. He spotted her carpetbag and smiled.

"One more test, Spike," he whispered to a large, ugly, horned lizard. "Hattie has passed all the others, but she's only been here a day. Maybe she's not as nice as she seems."

Slowly and carefully, he pulled open the carpetbag.

A skeleton grinned at him, and Jeremy fought down a scream. He dropped Spike, and the lizard ran under the bed. Why did Hattie have a skeleton in her bag? Was she like that Dr. Jekyll person who turned into Mr. Hyde? Was she a murderer? His hands shook.

Before his dad died, he'd read Robert Louis Stevenson's book aloud. Jeremy'd had nightmares for several nights after, and his mom had been angry with his father for two weeks.

He eased away from the carpetbag and slipped out the door. He needed to tell Uncle Ben. He'd know what to do. Would he handcuff Hattie and take her to jail? Jeremy thought he'd throw up. He didn't want Hattie to leave.

He descended the stairs as quietly as he could. He hoped to catch his uncle's attention without the females noticing, but as soon as he walked into the room, his little sister stared.

"What's wrong with you, Jem? Your face is white and you're shaking. You look like you've seen a ghost."

Hattie looked up and smiled, a twinkle in her eyes. "I suspect Jem opened my carpetbag to put something in there that didn't belong and met Katy before I was ready to introduce her."

Uncle Ben straightened and looked from Hattie to him.

Sarah frowned. "You carry Katy around in your carpetbag?"

Hattie wiped her hands on her apron. "I'd better introduce you. I'll be right back."

His uncle looked at him. "You planned to prank her?"

Jeremy nodded. "That was one of the things on my list, remember? I wanted to know how she'd act. I tried to put Spike in her carpetbag, but when I opened the handles, a skeleton stared at me. I about jumped out of my skin."

Ben frowned. "Katy is a skeleton?"

Jeremy nodded, and Sarah looked at him with wide eyes.

Hattie came down the stairs carrying a child-sized skeleton on a stand. She placed the grinning Katy on the table and turned to them. "I'd like you to meet Katy. She has been with me for many years and has helped me understand the underlying bone structure of the human body. Doctor Eber got her for me after I convinced him I needed help to make better drawings. Here." She handed around sketchbooks. "Look at my drawings before Katy."

Jeremy looked from the drawings to Katy and back again. His hands stopped shaking, and he tried to figure out how Katy had helped improve Hattie's drawings. They were noticeably better after she used the model. He stepped closer to the skeleton and looked from her to the drawings.

"Will you draw me?" Sarah closed the sketchbook.

"I would love to draw you all. I can send the pictures home to my parents and siblings with my letter."

Ben smiled. "I think we should wait until tomorrow when we're all fresher."

Jeremy offered Hattie a tentative smile. "Did you bring any books you can read to us? We've read all the books we have."

"I did. I brought my favorites: *Pride and Prejudice, The Adventures of Huckleberry Finn, The Adventures of Tom Sawyer*—Tom and Huck are friends—*A Christmas Carol, The Adventures of Sherlock Holmes, Moby Dick, Treasure Island, The Three Musketeers, David Copperfield, Oliver Twist, Grimm's Fairy Tales, Twenty Thousand Leagues Under the Sea,* and *A Connecticut Yankee in King Arthur's Court.*"

Jeremy searched Hattie's face to see if she was angry with him. "Which do you like best?"

"I like them all, Jem, but if I'm going to read them aloud, I think we should start with *The Adventures of Sherlock Holmes.* Sherlock is a detective. You probably won't enjoy *Pride and Prejudice* just yet. We'll save this one for last."

Jeremy smiled. "Yes, please. Will you read a chapter before bed?"

Hattie glanced at Ben, a question in her eyes. He looked toward the stairs, shrugged, and smiled instead.

She brought the book and sat in the comfortable rocker.

Jeremy's eyes misted when Sarah eased onto Hattie's lap and snuggled.

Hattie opened the book and read the title of the first story, "A Scandal in Bohemia."

He listened carefully to Hattie's explanation of the setting and some of the hard words, and then he relaxed into the sofa cushions as he listened to the cadence of her words. She changed her voice whenever different people spoke, so she made the characters come alive.

He listened intently to how Sherlock arrived at his conclusions and wondered if Uncle Ben agreed.

Hattie got up early, made breakfast, and put more water on to boil. She'd already cleaned every surface in the kitchen and rearranged and organized things to make them handy. She had taken down the curtains and put them to soak in the wash tub while she washed the window glass.

She turned at the sound of footsteps and smiled. "Good morning, you two. I have flapjacks and sausage in the warming oven. The butter dish and syrup are on the table. Your uncle has already eaten and gone to work."

Jeremy looked around. "This is so much better, Hattie. I don't know how you figured out where to start. I never could. All the clutter and dust overwhelmed me."

Hattie signaled them to sit down at their places and brought the food. "You'll learn soon enough that I need order and cleanliness. I can think and focus on details. I'm counting on you both to help me. We'll get so much more done together."

Sarah nodded. "Where do we start?"

"Let's make a plan." Hattie drew a tablet and pencil toward her. "I've already started a list. We'll begin with the rooms we all live in and with those visitors will see if they stop by. Then we'll work together in the same room to bring order out of chaos. We break large jobs into smaller ones."

Jeremy searched her face. "That makes sense."

They worked for three hours until someone knocked on the front door. Hattie wiped her hands and face with the bottom of her apron and patted her hair in place.

Sarah watched and did the same.

Hattie opened the door to a middle-aged woman with a kind face. She held a covered dish.

Sarah stopped beside Hattie. "Hello, Mrs. Norwood. This is my new mother, Hattie."

Mrs. Norwood handed Hattie the dish. "Nice to meet you Mrs. Cole. I'm Pauline Norwood from next door. I own the boarding house. I figured you would be up to your elbows in work, so I brought you my famous chicken and dumplings.”

Hattie invited the neighbor in. “Please sit and have some tea or coffee with the children and me, Mrs. Norwood. You’re thoughtful.”

“I’ll take tea. Thanks.”

They sat at the kitchen table and chatted. Sarah leaned against Hattie. “Mrs. Norwood says she knows everything that goes on in this town.”

Mrs. Norwood grinned. “I do. You want to know something, you just ask. I don’t gossip, but I grew up here, and the people are important to me. I want to know if something or someone is trying to disturb our peace. We have to watch out for each other, you know?”

“Thank you, Mrs. Norwood.”

Mrs. Norwood stood. “Please call me Pauline. Now hand me an apron. I intend to help you with whatever needs to be done.”

Hattie took the woman at her word and handed her an apron. “I’m Hattie. Thank you so much. If you ever need help with any of your projects, please call on me.”

Ben’s stomach growled. He anticipated more of Hattie’s cooking. She’d sent a lunch, but that had long since worn off. He opened the door, stopped, and brushed a hand over his eyes. Had he stepped into the wrong house?

He looked around. No, he recognized the furniture and crockery, but the place looked clean, shiny, and smelled fresh. Had Hattie done all of this since he said goodbye this morning? The woman must be a miracle worker.

He sniffed and opened the warming door of the stove. Apple pie and chicken with dumplings. Ah, Mrs. Norwood had stopped by. He hung his jacket and hat on the hooks and followed the sound of voices to Sarah's room.

At his booted step, Hattie and the children turned.

Sarah raced to him and hugged him. A huge smile stretched her lips. She waved her arm in a broad gesture. "Uncle Ben, look at my room. We're rearranging and getting rid of the dust bunnies and cobwebs. We already did Jem's room."

He bent and kissed the top of her head. "I see, darlin'. Your room looks cozy."

His eyes met Hattie's. "This is unbelievable. Thank you."

"My pleasure. Jem and Sarah worked hard. They are great help."

"Mrs. Norwood stopped by?"

"Yes, and stayed for a couple of hours to help. She is a treasure."

Ben looked around again. "I'm assuming with all this work, you didn't get to the store?"

"No."

"We'll go first thing in the morning."

Jeremy's stomach growled. He leaned the broom in a corner and looked at Hattie. "Will we eat supper soon?"

"Yes. Wash up, and we'll go down now."

After they ate the chicken and dumplings, Hattie took the pie out of the warming oven and placed the dessert on the counter. She reached for the knife and turned her back to the others so they couldn't see what she did.

With a grin, she put the largest slice on Jeremy's plate and smaller slices on each of the other plates. She schooled her features before she turned around and set the dessert plates in front of her family members.

Jeremy looked from his plate to the others, raised his eyebrows, then shrugged.

"This is delicious, Hattie." Ben shoved another bite into his mouth.

Sarah licked her lips. "Yum. Will you teach me how to make this?"

Hattie nodded and watched Jeremy take a big bite.

The young man's lips puckered and his eyes widened. He grabbed for his napkin and mumbled, "Excuse me." He stepped outside but came back in a few moments.

Hattie grinned when he returned to the table. "Is everything all right, Jem?"

He watched Sarah and Ben demolish their pie and then gave her a grudging smile. "You got me good, Hattie."

Ben looked from him to her and back. "What?"

Jeremy laughed. "Hattie pranked me, Uncle. She did a good job too. Here, taste."

Ben took a bite of Jeremy's pie and immediately reached for his coffee cup. "She put salt in your pie instead of sugar."

Sarah frowned. "Why did you do that, Hattie?"

Hattie cut a slice of the regular pie and sat the new piece in front of him.

Jeremy smiled and picked up his fork. "She did this to show me I couldn't out prank a prankster, right, Hattie?"

Hattie put a hand on his shoulder. "My brother, Max, taught me many things, Jem. Once I caught on, I was no longer his prime target for practical jokes."

Jeremy grinned. "Can we declare a truce? I won't prank you again if you won't prank me, okay?"

"Okay, Jem, I promise." Hattie returned to her chair.

Sarah scraped her plate. "Will you draw me now, Hattie?"

"Yes, as soon as the dishes are done and the kitchen is ready to use again tomorrow."

They all stood and did what needed to be done.

"Shall I bring Katy down, Hattie?"

"Yes, Sarah. I'll get my sketchbook and pencils."

CHAPTER 8: THE GAUNTLET

TEXAS PANHANDLE, SUMMER 1895

HATTIE ADJUSTED HER HAT AND STEPPED OUTSIDE where Ben and the children waited. The early morning sunshine lifted her spirits.

Ben pointed. "As you can see, we're the last house to the east on Second Street. Mrs. Norwood's boarding house is next door, and—"

He stopped and turned to Jeremy. "Face our house and close your eyes. Tell me the buildings on our street."

"On which sides of the street, Uncle?"

"Both. Second runs east and west parallel to Main. Which buildings are on the north side of the street facing south?"

Jeremy thought for a moment before speaking. "The buildings on the north back to the buildings on Main.

"The building across the street from us is where deputies Wilson and Nelson live. The undertaker lives in the house next to them, then Pastor and Mrs. Gordon, and the banker, Mr. Staples, live in the next houses. The school is the last building on the street a few hundred yards from the banker's.

"Next to us on our side of the street is Mrs. Norwood's boarding house, the empty house the Johnsons just sold, the Hastings' place, and the church."

Hattie marveled at his accuracy.

Jeremy smiled. "Uncle has played the 'details' game with us since we came to live with him."

Hattie turned to Ben. "Why?"

Ben shrugged. "Lawmen must pay attention to their surroundings if they want to stay alive. I thought Jem and Sarah would benefit from developing this skill regardless of what they choose to do later in life."

The unspoken message his eyes communicated was clear—a lawman's family might be targets of vengeful criminals. Hattie nodded. "Details are important when I'm drawing."

They took the alley between the preacher's and undertaker's houses to reach Main.

Hattie stared. "Is the town always so busy?"

Ben looked from one end of Main to the other. "Only on Saturdays when the ranchers and their wives come in to shop or have lunch."

Hattie's fingers itched for her pencils and a sketchbook.

Ben offered his elbow, and Hattie placed her hand in the crook. "Now we run the gauntlet, Hattie. Better to do this now rather than later."

"What's a gauntlet?" Sarah held Hattie's right hand.

Ben explained, and Sarah nodded. "They were angry with us for not choosing them, weren't they?"

"Yes, darlin'."

Hattie's middle tightened. She had to live with these people, so she'd better try to be agreeable. She had experienced the games women, and some men, played, and she had no patience with them.

Townsfolk nodded and spoke as they passed. The women stared and watched their progress down the street.

"Sheriff. Mrs. Cole." A young, attractive woman dressed in the latest fashion stopped in front of them. Her posture and attitude demanded attention.

"Miss Hastings." Ben tipped his hat. "I'd like to introduce my wife, Harriette Cole. Hattie, this is Miss Lorraine Hastings. She lives a couple of houses down from us to the west."

Hattie smiled. "Nice to meet you, Miss Hastings."

The woman's frosty look and slightly raised chin told Hattie she had just started her run through the gauntlet. The coolness of Miss Hastings's "The same, Mrs. Cole," indicated she was not mistaken.

Lorraine Hastings eyed Hattie from head to toe.

Hattie grinned inside. She, also, was dressed in the latest fashion for her first exposure to the town's citizens. When the woman's mouth tightened, Hattie knew she had chosen her dress wisely.

Ben smiled. "If you'll excuse us, we must buy supplies. Good day to you, Miss Hastings."

She moved out of their way, but Hattie felt the critical woman's gaze as she strolled hand-in-hand with Sarah to the mercantile.

Inside the store, Hattie gave Ben and the children each a sheet of paper. "Grab a basket and get what's on your list. We'll be finished quicker."

Jeremy looked around. "The store is suddenly crowded with women."

Ben glanced at the new arrivals and chuckled. "Sure is, Jem. They're pretending they don't see us, but I guarantee you, they're watching our every move. I wonder if they've heard the expression 'curiosity killed the cat?'"

Hattie grinned and placed jars of canned peaches in her basket. "You can't blame them. I'd be curious too."

Sarah gazed at the women and then at Hattie. "What do you think they're thinking?"

Hattie laughed and studied the spice rack. "Oh, they're sure to be wondering where I got my clothes and hat. They'll be criticizing my height and looking for reasons to find fault.

After all, I married their sheriff. Several had eyes on him as possible husband material, so they'll look for excuses to dislike me. Some will whisper to their friends that they don't know what Ben sees in me. This helps them feel better about themselves."

Jeremy frowned. "Doesn't their thinking bother you?"

She looked up and smiled. "Not a bit. I don't have the patience for such pettiness. I've seen the same patterns played out multiple times, and I think this game is boring. If they like me, fine. If they don't, fine.

"I've been criticized for my height ever since I grew taller than some of the men. I have no control over how many inches I grow, but if I had the choice to be tall or short, I'd choose tall every time." Her eyes met his, and she touched his cheek. "I'm content with who I am, Jem."

Ben's eyes shone. "I'm content with who you are too, Hattie."

"So am I," Jem and Sarah spoke at the same time.

By the time they finished their shopping and stopped for lunch at the restaurant, Hattie had met the women of the town and some of the ranchers' wives. Most of the single women responded like Miss Hastings, the ones Hattie called The Gauntlet Gals, but the married women welcomed her.

Hattie didn't know how she would remember all of their names until Jeremy told her the secret of how he remembered. He paired each woman's characteristics with her name in a bizarre, exaggerated way, or rhymed the name with something ridiculous.

Hattie marveled at how easily the names came to her as she reviewed each of the associations in her head. "You're a genius, Jem."

He grinned. "My dad played this game with us from the time Sarah and I could talk. He especially liked numbers. Remembering gets easier with practice."

"You'll have to show me how to deal with numbers."

Pleasure wreathed Jeremy's face. "Yes, I can show you after dinner, before you read more about Sherlock Holmes."

Mrs. Norwood spotted them from her yard just as they turned onto Second Street. She waved and signaled them to come and talk.

Ben touched the brim of his hat in greeting. "Mrs. Norwood."

She fanned herself with her apron. "Did you hear the news?"

Sarah leaned forward. "What news, ma'am?"

"The couple who bought the Johnson's place next door will move in tomorrow."

They all looked toward the vacant house.

Hattie hoped the wife would be a friend—one she could talk to and share recipes with. As newcomers to the town, they could face the others together.

Jeremy looked from the house to their neighbor. "Do you know anything about them, Mrs. Norwood?"

"I hope they have kids—maybe a girl my age and boy Jem's age." Sarah's wistful tone touched Hattie.

Pauline shook her head. "I don't know much, but I don't think they have children."

Sarah's face fell.

Mrs. Norwood pulled a handkerchief from her sleeve and dabbed her sweaty neck. "Glen at the Land Office said Mr. Charles, the new owner, sent a message saying he and his lady wife would stop by tomorrow to pick up the key. They'll probably show up while we're in church."

Sarah grimaced. "I hope not. I want to see them."

Ben smiled. "Thank you for telling us, ma'am. We'll be on the watch for them."

Mrs. Norwood nodded. "I think I'll make an extra apple pie to take over. They might not be in the mood to cook."

Hattie tapped her lip. "Do you know the status of the interior? Sarah and I could slip in and dust. We could open the blinds and make the place a little more welcoming for them. We could bake cookies and leave them on the counter next to your pie with welcome notes."

"According to Mrs. Johnson, they were leaving the place fully furnished. They didn't want to bother themselves with packing and moving, since the home Mr. Johnson inherited in Virginia is already furnished. I'll talk to Glen to see if he'll let us in a couple of hours from now, okay?"

"Fine, Mrs. Norwood." Hattie looked down when Sarah tugged on her hand. "If you'll excuse us, home awaits."

Hattie, Sarah, and Pauline Norwood removed furniture covers and swept and dusted. Before leaving, they set the pie and cookies on the table with notes welcoming the couple to the community.

As they walked toward their house, Sarah swung Hattie's hand. "That felt good—to do something nice for someone. I hope the new people are surprised."

Sarah studied Hattie's face for several moments. She opened her mouth as if to speak but no words came out.

Hattie stopped. "Do you want to say something to me?"

She nodded. "Hattie, do you think—can I—?

"Can you what, Sarah? Don't be afraid. Speak."

Sarah twisted a lock of hair. "I know you haven't known me long, but may I call you Mom? Since my mom is dead, and since Jeremy and I picked you . . ."

Hattie's heart threatened to pop out of her chest. She stooped and swung Sarah into her arms. "My darling, you may certainly call me Mom or Mother, whichever you like. And I'll be proud to introduce you as my daughter, okay?"

Sarah hugged her neck. "Yes, please."

"How about we fix supper so we can read longer?"

Ben sat in the rocker and watched Sarah snuggle beside Hattie on the sofa as she read more of Sherlock Holmes's adventures. Jeremy sat close on Hattie's other side and rested his arm against hers. His eyes didn't leave her face as she read "The Red-Headed League."

Deep contentment spread through Ben. *If I could draw as well as Hattie, I'd sketch this exact scene.*

Earlier, Sarah had called Hattie, Mom. The first time she did this, Ben thought the word was an accidental slip, but Sarah continued addressing Hattie as her mother throughout Jeremy's lesson on how to remember numbers. All Hattie did was smile and caress Sarah's cheek.

Ben's heart warmed and swelled. He thought he would explode with joy. This is what he had wanted for his children—comfort and emotional safety. He smiled, and a load rolled from his shoulders. He looked toward the ceiling. *Thank you.*

Hattie finished the last word and closed the book, so Ben stood and tilted his head toward the stairs. "Okay, you two, time for bed. We'll be up as soon as you brush your teeth and put on your night clothes."

Ben held his hand out and helped Hattie to her feet. He pulled her close and kissed her. "Words cannot express what I'm feeling right now, wife. To see Sarah and Jem so content— Thank you."

Hattie glanced around the church as Ben indicated she and the children should sit on the back pew to the right side of the door. Several interested congregants watched their arrival. The nearby chatter hushed as she slid into the pew, Ben and Jeremy on each side of her.

Ben whispered close to her ear. "I always sit here. I can get out quickly if I need to."

Hattie studied the location of the doors and windows and nodded. As she looked around, her gaze contacted those of others.

She smiled and nodded at anyone whose eyes she met. Several returned the nod, but the Gauntlet Gals pasted stiff smiles on their faces and turned away. Hattie chuckled under her breath.

Jeremy, who sat on Hattie's left, looked into her eyes. "Why are you laughing?"

"People are so predictable sometimes, Jem."

His gaze flew to the stiff, upright postures of the single women. They studiously avoided looking at Hattie. "I can feel their dislike from here." He frowned. "I hope you can make friends."

She touched his hand. "Don't worry about me, Jem. I'm sure I'll make friends after they get over their miff about me marrying Ben. If they don't want to be my friends, then I'll content myself with those who do."

The service started, so Hattie focused and stood to sing with the others.

During the message, Jeremy's subtle movements caught and held her attention. He had his eyes closed, and his lips moved as he spoke in a slight whisper to himself.

"Lukewarm water. Toes. Mice." He didn't move his lips for several moments, then he whispered, "Mat. Priest."

Hattie watched him from the corner of her eyes. When she realized he was coding the scripture passages about Jesus's parable of the Good Samaritan using his peg words to remember each verse, her eyes widened. She straightened and leaned closer.

Lukewarm water represented the gospel of Luke. He connected this in a bizarre way with the peg word for ten, which was toes, and then he used the image of mice to represent verse thirty. He connected the first number picture to the second, then the second to the third, and the third to the fourth. By doing this, he could remember the verses in or out of order.

She saw in her mind each of the pegs as he whispered them, because they'd practiced the numbers through fifty. Her brain was already trained to see images.

After he coded the passages through verse thirty-six, when Jesus asked who the Samaritan's true neighbor was, she whispered near his ear, "Toes. Match. Mercy. He that showed mercy on him. Go, and do likewise."

Startled, Jeremy opened his eyes. His huge smile showed his pleasure. He nodded and whispered. "You're a fast learner—Mom."

The deliberate use of the word Mom by someone as special as Jeremy, sent a powerful rush of love through her. She squeezed his hand and then returned her attention to the service, though her mind now raced through the peg words as she listened more intently. Would Jeremy challenge her to repeat the verses over lunch?

He didn't wait for lunch. He challenged her as soon as they left the church and walked down the street toward their house.

Ben and Sarah joined in and asked them which verse said such and such. They didn't stump either her or Jeremy.

"I'm proud of you both." Ben's eyes smiled his pleasure.

Sarah pointed. "Look. The new neighbors must be here. I saw someone peek at us through the curtains." She waved.

A feminine hand returned Sarah's wave, but the movement was furtive, and the hand quickly disappeared behind the drapes.

Ben stared and then shrugged. "I'm ready for delicious food. How about you all?"

"Yes!" Sarah and Jeremy's emphatic head nods made Hattie chuckle. "The food is in the warming oven waiting for us."

Sarah reached for Hattie's hand. "Will you read some more after we eat?"

Hattie interlaced her fingers with Sarah's. "Of course. Once we finish Sherlock's adventures, I think we should read *The Adventures of Tom Sawyer*. Sometimes, Tom is too clever for his own good. He reminds me a little of my brother, Maxwell. Max is quite creative when he gets bored or doesn't want to do what he's supposed to."

Sarah swung Hattie's hand. "I want to hear more about Max and Carrie and my new grandparents. Do you think they'll come and see us?"

"I hope so."

Jeremy tilted his head to one side. "Will they like us?"

"They'll love you, Jem."

CHAPTER 9: MR. & MRS. CHARLES

TEXAS PANHANDLE, SUMMER 1895

HATTIE OPENED THE DOOR TO A TALL, LEAN MAN dressed in stylish clothes.

"Mrs. Cole, I'm your new neighbor. You can call me Charles if you'd like, or Mr. Charles if you prefer something less informal." He smiled and held out the cookie plate she'd left on his counter with her note. "My lady wife and I appreciate yours and Mrs. Norwood's kindness. What a nice welcome. Thank you."

Hattie took the plate. "I hope we'll have the pleasure of meeting your wife soon."

The expression on his face saddened. "Unfortunately, she has a delicate constitution and is extremely susceptible to the smallest ill wind that blows. She must stay indoors."

"Oh, how unfortunate. Perhaps I should call so she doesn't have to get out. I can bring her more cookies."

He shook his head. "You are kind, Mrs. Cole, but my wife is sickly and keeps to her rooms."

Hattie frowned. "Poor woman. I will give you the cookies to share with her. What is her name?"

He hesitated. "Call her Mrs. Charles. That's what she's used to. I had hoped to catch Sheriff Cole at home today. Is he here by chance, or will I find him at his office?"

"Try his office."

"I will. Thank you again. Good day."

Mrs. Norwood stopped by after lunch and sipped tea while Hattie taught Sarah how to make crust for a peach pie. She watched Hattie's instruction with interest. "Our new neighbor sure has made the rounds. He stopped by every business and introduced himself. He stayed longer at the bank and Mabel's restaurant. By now, everyone in town knows Mr. Charles. They feel sorry for his poor, sickly 'lady wife.'

"He ordered lunch at the restaurant and said he'd stop by later to pick up his dinner order. Seems like Mrs. Charles is too ill to cook. Mabel is pleased she'll have a steady customer for breakfast, lunch, and dinner."

Sarah wiped her hands. "Once I learn how to make a pie, I'll take her one. Maybe this will help her feel better."

Hattie nodded.

Jeremy looked up from reading the latest Amarillo newspaper. "Did you find out anything about them, Mrs. Norwood?"

"Well, when I stopped by the bank to make a deposit, I stood in line next to Fred Staples's office. His door was open a few inches, and I heard Mr. Charles chatting about his family in New Orleans and their estates. He said they had one within the city limits and another outside. Fred asked an occasional question, but our neighbor did most of the talking."

Jeremy put the paper down. "Is he rich?"

Mrs. Norwood shrugged. "Hard to tell. You never know about those large estates. They could be encumbered with debt, though I did hear Fred thank him for his sizable deposit."

Hattie put the pie in the oven and brushed the flour off Sarah's cheek with the bottom of her apron. "Did he say where in New Orleans the estate was? My elder sister, Liza, and her family live there."

"I didn't hear." She finished her tea and stood. "I'd best get back. I got a new tenant this morning, so I'd better think about preparing something for dinner for him and the other four."

"A new tenant?" Hattie raised her eyebrows.

"Yes, a Mr. Dillon. He seems like a nice young man—polite, respectful, and a bit shy. He rode in from Amarillo."

Interest brightened Jeremy's eyes. "What's he doing in our town?"

Mrs. Norwood put the teacup in the sink. "He's got something to do with railroads, but I'm not sure what."

Jeremy straightened. "Do you think someone is interested in bringing a railroad branch from Amarillo here?"

"I don't know, Jem." She waved and left.

He turned to Hattie. "If we had a line into Amarillo, we could go to the city in the morning, then return home in the afternoon. This would be a much faster way to travel than by wagon."

Hattie nodded and thought of Sheriff Levitt. Had her sketches done any good?

Ben entered as she and Sarah took the pie out of the oven.

Hattie smiled and sat the dessert on the counter to cool.

Ben kissed her. "That smells delicious."

Sarah beamed. "This is the first pie I did almost by myself, Uncle Ben. Hattie helped with the crust, but I did the rest."

Ben smiled. "I can't wait to try your pie."

Jeremy chuckled. "And I watched to make sure neither of them put a bunch of salt into the pie instead of sugar. That was an ugly experience."

They laughed, but Hattie's thoughts still dwelt on the success, or lack thereof, of her sketches. "Have you heard anything from Sheriff Levitt, Ben?"

He nodded. "Your sketches were key to the Rangers capturing and identifying three of the members of the Bently gang. Seems like law enforcement shared your images and information with railroad lines and banks in neighboring states. Two men were caught near the Oklahoma border as they attempted to rob a teller, and the other was caught in Amarillo when he tried to cheat at cards."

She studied his face. "What about the others?"

He hesitated. "Not yet. The robbers were offered a reduced sentence if they gave up Bently and the others."

"Did they?"

Ben shook his head. "Sheriff Levitt sent me a letter. He shared the report from the officers who caught the two near Oklahoma. They denied knowing where Bently or the others were. The three men's stories agreed. All said the gang had a falling out and split up after the last train robbery."

Jeremy stepped closer. "Do you believe them?"

"About breaking up? Yes, even if this split is only temporary. About not knowing where the leader is, I'm not so sure. I think they might know the general area, but again, they might not. The men were upset with Bently for taking the majority of their ill-gotten gains and leaving in the middle of the night with his nephew." He glanced at Hattie, worry in his eyes.

She stiffened. "What? What are you not telling me?"

"Sheriff Levitt was one of the law enforcement officers who interviewed the outlaw caught cheating at cards. The man insisted he didn't know where Bently was, but after hours in the interrogation room, he unwittingly gave more insight into the leader's character. Levitt passed this information on to me."

Jeremy chuckled. "I'd wager that wasn't a pleasant interview for the crook."

Hattie waited. "Continue, Ben. What else?"

"Bently is a man who holds grudges. His ex-gang member described the outlaw's violent temper as one of the reasons he and the other two left. He spoke of Bently's particular rage when he saw one of the wanted posters—a poster created from one of your images, Hattie.

"The criminal said Bently realized the artist had to have been on the train to Amarillo to capture such detail, and he promised vengeance and a slow, painful death to whoever drew the pictures that were sure to slow or halt their activities in the area."

Sarah paled and rushed to embrace Hattie's waist. "No, Uncle! We can't let anyone know Mom is the artist. We have to keep her skills secret."

Ben's expression remained serious. "Agreed."

Hattie took a breath and put her arm around Sarah. "Ben, do you think Bently can actually find enough clues to lead him here, or do you think his talk is all bravado?"

"Criminals always have their network of spies and people who will turn away from morality and integrity when offered enough money to do so, Hattie. I don't know how large Bently's network in Amarillo might be, if he has one, but criminals tend to be drawn to other criminals and crime. They thrive in the filth and darkness of their sin."

Ben frowned. "Did either of the men who came to you on the train see your face?"

Hattie closed her eyes and relived her encounter. She opened them. "I don't know if they saw my face clearly. They were so focused on Katy and what other body parts might be in my bag, that they only looked at my face once. I didn't get the impression they paid more attention to me than they did to the others."

Ben's jaw hardened. "We can't take chances, Hattie. We need to come up with a plan to keep you safe. I want to err on the side of caution instead of hoping nothing happens."

Jeremy stepped to Ben's side. "I'll help."

Sarah glared and clung to Hattie's hand. "I will too. No outlaw is going to hurt my mother."

Ben walked to the windows, stood to the side of them, and closed the curtains. He turned. "Lesson one. Keep these closed at night, and don't silhouette yourselves in the windows. Lesson two. Keep the doors locked, even in the day. You have keys, so use them."

Hattie kept her voice calm, though her heart raced. "Thank you. I feel much safer knowing you all are watching out for me." She smiled down at Sarah. "How about we make some cookies for Mrs. Charles?"

"Yes!"

"Hattie?" Jeremy touched her arm and smiled. "Will you make extra? I'm hungry for cookies."

"Of course, Jem. I'm sure your uncle wants some too."

Ben grinned. "You got that right."

Hattie tilted her head toward the open book on the stand in the living room. "Why don't you read to us while we bake?"

Ben brought the book to the kitchen table and sat next to Jeremy. He thumbed to the last story and began.

Hattie could listen to his soft, deep drawl for hours. His voice soothed some of her worry.

Ben finished the story just as Hattie removed the cookies and set them on the counter to cool.

Sarah made a face. "Most of those Sherlock stories are strange, if you ask me, though I did like 'The Speckled Band.' I'm ready to hear about Tom Sawyer tomorrow night. I want to know how he and my Uncle Max are alike."

Hattie wondered how Max would react to being called Uncle. Liza's children called him Max most of the time, or Maxwell when he displeased them, but they never called him Uncle.

What would Max's face look like if Jem decided to call him Uncle too? She grinned.

Sarah's brows furrowed like they always did when she tried to remember the mnemonic devices for higher numbers. She tapped on her lips. "Uncle Max is fourteen like Jem, right, Mom?"

"Yes."

"So what should Jem call him? Uncle? That seems odd."

Jeremy chuckled. "I'll call him Max. If he makes me irritated, then I might call him Uncle."

Ben's eyes crinkled at the corners when he smiled. "Don't you think you're getting the cart before the horse? Max is in Louisiana. You're in Texas. I haven't heard of any plans to visit, so this shouldn't be an issue."

Sarah's face lit. "I know. We should write to him." She turned to Hattie. "Will he answer if we do?"

"Oh, yes. Max is certain to be curious about you both and would welcome an opportunity to have contact with you, even if this is by mail service."

"Have another cookie, Mrs. Norwood." Hattie pushed the plate toward her next-door neighbor. "I've got a plate ready to go to the Charles's home, and one for the children and Ben when they get home from bringing back the new laying hens. Ben built a better chicken coop and a protected run off the side of the barn. Maybe we won't lose so many birds to predators now."

"One more, then I'd better run." She picked up the oatmeal cookie and dipped the sweet treat in her tea.

Hattie leaned forward and picked up her teacup. "You were saying you heard Mr. Charles tell about his estate outside New Orleans?"

"Yes, he was chatting with Miss Hastings in the mercantile." She grimaced. "The way Lorraine watched him with wide, admiring eyes made me blush for her. What is she thinking looking at a married man that way?"

"How did Mr. Charles respond to her attention?" Hattie hoped her new neighbor wasn't prone to immoral behavior, or that Miss Hastings wouldn't succumb to his charms. *Poor Mrs. Charles.*

Pauline Norwood shook her head. "He didn't rebuff her as I expected. On the contrary, he ate up her admiring gazes and became more expansive with his descriptions. I think I must caution Lorraine when I get the chance."

"Where did he say his estate was located?"

Mrs. Norwood repeated his words, and Hattie nodded. "My sister lives in the same area. I wonder if she's met Mr. and Mrs. Charles? I'll have to write her to see."

When Mrs. Norwood left, Hattie collected the cookies, pulled the ribbon that held the key from her bodice, and locked the door. Ben insisted they all do this, even if they intended to be gone for only a few minutes. She understood his reasoning.

Hattie walked to the Charles's front door and knocked. She had seen Mr. Charles meet and leave with Mrs. Norwood's new tenant, so she knew his wife was by herself.

Mrs. Charles did not answer, so Hattie set the cookies on the bench near the door. She caught movement at the window, even though the drapes were closed. She suspected Mrs. Charles watched. Hattie waved and pointed to the cookies.

Tentatively, a woman's hand returned her wave and then disappeared behind the curtains.

Poor woman. To be forced to remain inside due to ill health would be a burden Hattie would find hard to bear. She didn't ever remember being sick.

Hattie turned and took the shortcut to Main. She wanted to pick up a few more items for dinner tonight. She grinned when she thought of her family's enthusiasm for the chicken pot pie she intended to bake.

She stepped through the door of the mercantile and reached for the only remaining basket. *Busy place.* Several shoppers nodded to her, and she returned their greetings.

Hattie glanced up when Mr. Charles entered with Lorraine Hastings. She lowered her gaze, but her ears picked up on his enthusiastic conversation as Lorraine shopped.

The man straightened his vest and continued his narration. "My brother owns a large property in the south. You should see his beautiful tobacco fields, Miss Hastings. Row upon row of them."

Startled, Hattie looked up. Farmers didn't grow tobacco in the south. They grew sugar cane. Tobacco was grown in the northeast along the Mississippi River.

Hattie forced her attention away from the two as she paid for her supplies. She must write to Liza as soon as she got home.

Did Mr. Charles intend to seduce Miss Hastings and leave his sick, lady wife?

CHAPTER 10: CLUES

TEXAS PANHANDLE, SUMMER 1895

HATTIE REREAD LIZA'S LETTER, and acidic worms twisted in her belly.

Dear Hattie,

Neither Thomas nor I have heard of people by that last name owning an estate in the area. I've asked our neighbors, and they don't know of anyone either. The courthouse will have records. I'll check when I go into the city next week.

How is life with your Texas lawman? Max said he received letters from your stepchildren. He was delighted to get them and sent a response. Sarah and Jeremy should get his correspondence soon.

Max and Carrie have changed since you left, Hattie. I think Max grew an inch and put on another ten pounds of muscle, but the most notable change is they both mope around and are dissatisfied with everything. Max wears a serious expression more often than his fun-loving one, and Carrie flits here and there and never settles. She's making mother crazy. Our parents think she needs to choose one of her beaux to marry, so she can settle down to raise children. Carrie stalks out of the room and slams doors whenever they suggest this.

She doesn't attend as many parties these days. I caught her reading in her room the last time I came, instead of socializing with visitors who had an eligible son waiting downstairs. I'm a little worried about her, Hattie. She reminds me of a keg of gunpowder ready to explode.

Hattie sympathized with her parents. They had calmer dispositions and had never been comfortable with Carrie's mercurial temperament. Over the years, her sister had mellowed as she got older, so things must be really bad if Liza described her as being ready to blow up. She hoped Carrie wouldn't do anything she'd regret.

She tucked the letter into her apron pocket, rubbed her upset stomach, and reached for her sketchbook and pencils. Hattie let the process of drawing calm her emotions.

By the time Jeremy and Sarah came in from collecting eggs and cleaning out the stall where Ben kept his horses, her stomach no longer roiled.

Sarah's eyes tracked to the sketchbook. "I want to see." She set the eggs on the counter and stopped next to Hattie.

Jeremy washed his hands and joined Sarah at Hattie's side.

Without a word, Hattie turned to the latest drawing, and Sarah studied the image on the page. "Is that Aunt Carrie? She's beautiful, but she looks upset."

"She is. My sister, Liza, is worried about her." Hattie stood and caressed Sarah's face. "Are you ready to help me with dinner? Ben will be home in a couple of hours."

Sarah nodded, washed her hands, and put on her apron. "Why is Carrie upset?"

Hattie stoked the fire and put the skillet on to heat. "I'm not sure exactly. Liza said my parents want her to marry and have children. They think this will settle her."

Jeremy set the table without being told. "Do your parents think marriage is the solution to most problems?"

Hattie laughed. "Not for Heath or Max or other males. That seems to be the solution for unmarried women in general and their daughters specifically. They think men should get out and experience the world before they settle down."

Jeremy's eyes sparkled. "I'm glad that was the ultimatum they gave you. Otherwise, we wouldn't have you or all your good cooking, right, Sarah?"

"Right." She turned questioning eyes to Hattie. "Mom, when I get older, will me getting married be the solution to a problem like Aunt Carrie's?"

"Absolutely not, sweetheart. You can choose who, when, and if you want to marry, though I hope you wait for several years to decide. I'm a little selfish. I like having you around, and I don't want to share you with a man unless the time is right and you know for sure he is the man God has for you."

Sarah laughed. "I'm only ten. I have time."

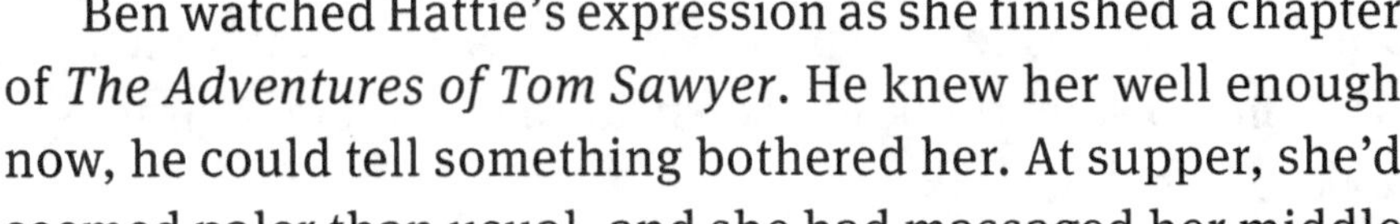

Ben watched Hattie's expression as she finished a chapter of *The Adventures of Tom Sawyer*. He knew her well enough now, he could tell something bothered her. At supper, she'd seemed paler than usual, and she had massaged her middle as if her stomach pained her. Was she sickening? He'd suggest she stop by Doc's office if she didn't get relief by tomorrow.

Once they'd said goodnight to Sarah and Jeremy, Ben followed her downstairs to the kitchen where she signaled him to sit at the table.

She poured him a cup of coffee and sat in the chair next to him.

"What's wrong, Hattie?" He stared at her face.

"Ben, I don't think Mr. Charles is who he says he is."

Of all the things he expected her to say, this was not one of them. "Explain."

Hattie related everything she'd seen and heard. "If he's not who or what he says he is, then I wonder if anything he's told us is true."

Ben's jaw tightened. He stared at his coffee cup with an unfocused gaze as he thought through the possible scenarios of this con.

Several moments later, he raised his eyes to Hattie's. "Until Charles commits a crime, I can't do anything. Many people choose the West to escape their pasts. Texas offers them second changes. Some make themselves seem larger, better, or wealthier than they are because they want others to respect them. We have to give him the benefit of the doubt, regardless of his lies. I'll keep my eyes on him, though, and I'll let Ron and Joe know to do the same."

He hesitated. "Is something else bothering you, darlin'?"

Hattie pulled a letter from her apron pocket and handed this to him. "I'm worried about Carrie. I haven't known her to be so restless and unsettled before."

He read and returned the letter. "What do you think she'll do? Obviously, she doesn't have your calm temperament. Will she do something nonsensical that will create issues for you and your folks?"

"I don't know, Ben, and that's what has me worried. Not only is Carrie beautiful, she's smart. Whatever she does will be well planned and well executed and will leave us all shocked and gasping." Hattie rubbed her belly and frowned. "What she might do has me tied in knots."

Ben stood and reached for her hand. "Maybe a good night's sleep will help."

⌁⌁⌁

Hattie felt better the next morning, though her stomach remained unsettled. After she finished her chores and sent the children off to visit their friends, she grabbed her wide-brimmed hat and walked next door to chat with Pauline Norwood.

"Have a seat, Hattie. I'll bring you some tea. You look a little pale. Are you okay?"

"Yes, just concerned about my younger sister."

Pauline sat across from her after she brought the teapot and cups. "You want to tell me about this?"

Hattie did, and her muscles relaxed as she talked, though her stomach protested occasionally.

"Why are you rubbing your stomach with that pained look on your face, Hattie?"

"Am I? I must have eaten something that disagreed with me."

Pauline asked her several pointed questions. "Oh, you'll be fine in fewer than nine months."

Hattie stiffened. "What?"

Pauline's satisfied smile widened. "You heard me."

Ice and fire flowed through Hattie's veins. *Pregnant?* Liza mentioned this possibility in the talk they'd had before Hattie left, but the thought hadn't crossed her mind since.

Pauline looked toward the dining room and stood. "Give me a few minutes. I need to check on preparations for dinner."

Hattie rose too. "I think I'll step out the side door and get some air."

Pauline chuckled and nodded.

Hattie paced up and down the narrow patch of sunbaked ground near the hedge separating the boarding house from the Charles's house. When she turned, she caught sight of Mrs. Charles watching her at the far end of their yard.

"Hello." Hattie waved. She couldn't see the woman's face clearly, but she noted the black hair and tall, thin frame.

"Hello." Mrs. Charles seemed to regret the greeting, because she turned and raced toward the back porch.

Hattie frowned. The woman's movements didn't seem to be those of an invalid's.

She eased into the narrow shade of the tall hedge just as upraised voices came from the Charles's back porch.

"What are you doing out here? I told you to stay inside." The hateful, mean words came from Mr. Charles's mouth, though she'd never heard him speak to others in such a manner.

"I wanted some fresh air, Bent. I'm tired of being cooped up like a prisoner."

Bent? The sound of a stinging slap reached Hattie, and anger replaced the ice and fire flowing through her.

"What's wrong with you, woman? Do you want the citizens to see your face and realize what you are? They'll run you out of town on a rail or allow you to take up residence in the nearest brothel." His voice threatened violence. "I won't let you mess up my plans, Sheila. For your sake and that of your invalid mother's, you better keep that ugly face of yours inside and do what I say."

Hattie froze. She'd heard the same irascible tone on the train. *Why're you carryin' around a skeleton, woman?*

Bent? Bently? Without a doubt, she knew who Charles was. Everything about him fit the man she had seen on the train. Was the younger man who'd approached her first the nephew who rode off in the night with him?

When the door slammed signaling they'd gone in, Hattie hurried inside the boarding house and bid Pauline goodbye.

She rushed to Ben's office and pushed open the door.

Ben and his deputies rose from their chairs in half a second and reached for their weapons. They moved their hands away from their guns when they saw her.

"Hattie? What's wrong?" Ben grasped her elbow. "You look like you're going to faint. Here. Sit. Joe, grab her a glass of water. Did something happen to Jeremy or Sarah? Hattie, tell me."

She gulped the water and tried to catch her breath. "They're okay. Give me a minute." Hattie took several deep breaths. "Mr. Charles is the outlaw Bently."

Ben grasped her forearms. "How do you know?"

Hattie related her experience. "I recognized his voice the moment he said those words to the woman. He spoke to me in exactly that tone. She is not a lady and not his wife, Ben. He's using her. He called her Sheila. From what he said, I think he's threatening her and her mother. What plans do you think he has that he forces her to stay inside and pretend to be his wife?"

Deputy Nelson snorted. "That's easy enough to figure out now if this is Bently, Mrs. Cole. She's a prop in his cover story."

Deputy Wilson agreed. "He wants what all criminals want, ma'am. Money. Power. Control. Respect, even if this is enforced at the end of a gun barrel and not earned."

Hattie frowned. "What does our little town offer such a criminal? Surely, if he wanted more money, power, and control, he'd go to Amarillo."

The deputies' eyes met Ben's before returning to hers.

Ben sat beside her. "Bently probably got word that a large cattle deal is going down next month. A lot of silver will exchange hands, and the seller doesn't want to lose his money to thieves.

"Law enforcement has planned alternate routes. We're one stop in that route. Bently probably got enough information to determine we might be an option."

Dread filled Hattie. How many of the town's citizens would be injured or killed? What about Ben and his deputies? Bently probably had plans to eliminate them. What should they do to stop him? How did one plan for such a situation?

No! She must have looked strange because Ben stood and helped her up. He tilted his head at the deputies. "I'm taking my wife home. We'll talk when I get back."

Ben shut their front door and pulled a chair away from the table. "Sit, love. Do you need to lie down?"

"I'm okay, but I need to tell you something. You should be the one sitting. Pull up a chair."

Ben frowned and sat. "What?"

Hattie couldn't think of any graceful way to tell him. "You're going to be a father in the spring."

His jaw dropped, and he stared at her for several moments. Then his face relaxed into a wide grin, and he leaned forward and took her hands in his. "That is the first good news I've heard today, darlin'. When do you want to tell our children?"

"Not for a few more months. After I start to show, we'll tell them. Pauline Norwood knows. If I have questions, I can ask her or Doc." She inclined her head. "Do you hope for a boy or girl?"

He stood and pulled her into his embrace. "I don't care. I hope he or she has your chocolate brown eyes, calm temperament, and loving disposition though."

Hattie laughed. "We could possibly get a child like Carrie or Maxwell, and then you'll have your hands full."

He kissed the side of her neck. "I'll take my chances." He finally pulled away. "Can you draw Bently without him knowing? I want to send his image to Levitt."

She nodded. "Now?"

"If you feel well enough to do so."

Hattie stepped outside the circle of his arms. "I'll get my sketch book and pencils. Be right back."

Hattie and her family had just finished supper when an urgent knocking shocked them all.

Ben rose and hurried to the door, his hand near his weapon. He opened to a woman dressed in traveling clothes. She clutched a carpetbag and looked at him with an expression of desperation.

"Sheriff?" Her voice came out in a strained whisper.

Hattie followed Ben to the door. "Mrs. Charles? Sheila? Come in."

The woman hesitated, then lifted her chin and stepped into the light.

Pity filled Hattie when she saw Sheila's pockmarked face and black eye. "Here, come in and sit. Are you hungry? I can get you a plate and a hot cup of tea or coffee."

Tears came and went in her eyes. "Thank you, Mrs. Cole, but I've come to warn you and the sheriff. You are in danger."

Hattie thought about sending the children upstairs but decided against this. She would not hide something as important as this news from them.

Ben went to the stove and dished food onto a plate. He poured a cup of coffee and set these and silverware on the table in front of where the woman stood. "Sit. Looks like you plan to leave. Might as well have a good supper before you do."

Sheila dropped into the chair as if her legs had turned to jelly.

Sarah studied Sheila, then hopped up and cut a slice of her apple pie and placed this on a plate. She set the dessert in front of their neighbor with a smile. "I made this all by myself—even the crust."

The woman stared, and then tears flowed down her face. She looked at Hattie. "Why are you doing this? If you know my name, then you heard Bent's hateful words. You know I'm not a lady, and I'm not his wife."

Ben offered her a napkin. "Bent is Bently, the leader of the gang who robs trains and banks?"

She nodded. "David Charles Bently."

Hattie signaled to Jeremy and Sarah. "We're going to clean up while you eat, Miss Sheila. Take your time."

Jeremy eyed the woman without commenting.

Sarah seemed to understand this was not a time for her to join the conversation. She stayed in the background and did her chores with quiet movements.

Sheila put her fork down. "Thank you. And thank you for all the cookies."

Ben sat across from her. "Now tell me how we can help you."

She grimaced. "I imagine I'm beyond help now, Sheriff. Once Bent realizes I've run off, he'll either track me down or have someone else do this. He is a mean man. He promised to kill me and my mother if I didn't cooperate with his plans to rob the bank when the silver is rerouted here."

Ben lounged in his chair. The picture of calmness. At his unsurprised response, her eyes narrowed. "You already know?"

"I recently received information that made me suspect he was not who he said he was. Where is he now?"

She startled and glanced toward the window. "He and his nephew rode out several hours ago. They were meeting up with some others in an out-of-the-way place to finalize their plans. He'll be back in a couple of days."

"His nephew? The one who has taken a room in the boarding house? Mr. Dillon?"

"Jake Dillon is his nephew. He's almost as mean as Bent, but they can both put on the smooth, pleasant act."

Hattie indicated Sarah should follow her to the kitchen. As the woman talked, she starting filling an empty flour sack with supplies. She bent and whispered in Sarah's ear.

"Make several meat and cheese sandwiches. We'll put them in the bag too. She won't go hungry for a while."

Sarah flung her arms around Hattie. "I love you, Hattie. You take care of people. You're the best mother ever."

CHAPTER 11: Plans

Texas Panhandle, Late Summer 1895

Hattie listened to the poor, abused woman's story without comment. Once Sheila started the narrative, the words flowed from her. She told everything she knew.

Ben spoke to her in a soft voice when she finished. "We will catch Bently, Miss Sheila. I need you to testify against him when he goes to trial."

She blanched. "No. I never want to see his smirking, lying face again, Sheriff. He'll kill me if he catches me. I must go. I want to get to my mother before he does. Maybe I can find a place to hide her."

"Where is your mother?" Hattie sat the flour sack next to the distraught woman.

"She lives with my aunt in Fort Worth. She isn't happy there. They've never gotten along. I want to get Mother out of that situation and into a small place where I can take care of her."

Ben lifted a brow. "What is preventing you?"

She grimaced. "Money. Work." She dropped her eyes. "I couldn't find work, which is how I started down the wrong path."

Hattie bent and whispered near Ben's ear. "I want to give Sheila money to get her to her mother. What do you think?"

Ben stilled and then nodded.

Hattie excused herself to go upstairs. She returned with a cloth-wrapped packet and a travel cloak.

She stopped next to her neighbor. "Miss Sheila, Sarah and I packed some supplies for your trip. I also have a gift for you. Do not open this until you get on the train."

Sheila stiffened. "Train?"

Hattie smiled. "How else were you planning to get to Fort Worth?"

The woman hung her head. "I don't have any money to pay for a ticket. I planned to walk and look for a job when I finally got to Amarillo."

Hattie stared. "You planned to walk at least seventeen miles?"

She nodded. "I hoped I could pick up some odd jobs with the farmers on my way."

Ben stood and moved to the counter where Hattie kept a stack of stationery and sharpened pencils. He returned to the table with several sheets. "Deputy Nelson will take you into Amarillo tonight to catch the early train first thing tomorrow. Hattie and I will get your ticket. First, I need you to do something for me. Since you won't testify face-to-face, will you write down everything you said and sign and date at the end of your document?"

She chewed on her bottom lip for several moments before nodding and drawing the paper toward her.

Ben checked his pistols, then put on his hat. "Make sure you write everything you told me. I'll be back."

Ben returned with Deputy Nelson and the banker just as Sheila finished her last paragraph. She signed, dated, and pushed the paper toward Ben. He offered the pen to Fred Staples, who signed and notarized the document.

"Miss Sheila? What is your surname?" Ben waited for her answer.

"Douglas."

"Miss Sheila Douglas, I'd like to introduce you to Deputy Ron Nelson. He will drive you to Amarillo tonight and will contact Sheriff Levitt. I want you to give Levitt your written statement and answer any questions he might have before you leave."

She nodded. "You won't tell Bent where I've gone?"

Ben smiled. "We'll continue to act as if you are still here, ma'am. Hattie and Sarah will bake cookies and take them to him as usual." He lifted a questioning brow.

Hattie nodded. "We'll give him the cookies and ask after your health."

Sheila's muscles relaxed. "Thank you."

"Here." Hattie draped the cloak around her shoulders. "You have a long drive ahead of you. You'd best get started."

Sheila's hands shook when she pulled up the cloak's hood. "I still don't understand why you would help me when you know what I am. I'm dirty. I'm a sinner."

Hattie shrugged. "God says we are all in that condition, but he offers forgiveness and cleansing through Jesus Christ if we ask. Goodbye. I hope you can find a place for you and your mother soon."

Deputy Nelson and the banker had watched the interaction without comment.

"Ma'am?" Nelson tipped his hat at Sheila. "We'd best go. We're going to be driving through the night to get to Amarillo in time for you to see the sheriff and catch your train."

She nodded and preceded him out the door.

Fred Staples watched them, then turned to Hattie. "You did a good thing, Mrs. Cole. I wish this town had more citizens like you." His eyes met Ben's. "I'll see you at the bank tomorrow so we can make plans?"

Ben nodded. "I sent a note with Ron for Sheriff Levitt. He knows the situation. I've asked him to involve the Rangers and U.S. Marshal's Office. We aren't going to let Bently and his gang get away with this robbery."

Staples nodded. "Thank you. See you in the morning."

Ben locked the door and turned toward her.

Hattie sighed her relief. "Maybe we can foil Bently's plan after all. Maybe nobody will get hurt."

"Mom, can we read?" Uncertainty tinged Sarah's voice.

Hattie nodded.

Sarah and Jeremy sat close to her as she continued Tom Sawyer's adventures. She hadn't realized how disturbed they were with the information they'd heard tonight, until their tense bodies relaxed against her. They needed the calming routine of reading as much as she did.

Bently and his nephew, Jake Dillon, returned in the afternoon of the following day. Hattie watched them stable their horses and head for their respective dwellings.

She waited for Bently to realize Sheila was gone and then picked up the plate of cookies and walked to his house.

Hattie glanced at Ben from the corner of her eyes as she walked by Pauline Norwood's hedge. He nodded at her, and she felt braver knowing he watched.

Bently cracked the door at her knock, his face a friendly mask. "Mrs. Cole. How thoughtful. My wife and I thoroughly enjoy your cookies and Mrs. Norwood's pies."

Hattie smiled. "I'm glad. I hope these treats create a bright spot in your lady wife's day, Mr. Charles. Now, if you'll excuse me, I have a little shopping to do before supper."

Bently cleared his throat as she turned to leave. "Mrs. Cole, did anything unusual happen while I was gone? Did we have any unexpected visitors, or residents traveling?"

Hattie pursed her lips and frowned as if in concentration. "No, I don't think so. Ben had to handle a couple of trouble-making drunks in the evening, but that's just part of his job." She chuckled. "Wait. Something exciting did happen yesterday. The Jacobs' pigs got loose and ran through the town. Several people chased them and tried to herd the pigs back into their pen, but they didn't want to go. I laughed until my sides hurt."

Fortunately, that had happened, so if Bently wanted to verify the truth of her story, many would tell him the same thing.

His smile looked forced. "Quite an exciting day in this sleepy little town. Nothing else?"

"No, not to my knowledge. Good afternoon, Mr. Charles. I must go."

"Good afternoon, Mrs. Cole. I'll return your plate soon."

"Thank you." Hattie strolled toward the shortcut to Main as if she didn't have a care in the world. She could feel Bently's gaze on her, and an unpleasant tingle spread across her spine to her shoulder blades. She shivered.

That evening, in the middle of Jeremy's memory lesson, he paused and looked at Ben. "How do you intend to stop the outlaws from robbing our bank, Uncle?"

"I can't give you the specifics, Jem, because the fewer who know, the better, but I can tell you I've been studying Bently's patterns and behavior from before he moved to town. From these, I'm trying to predict what he might do. Witnesses report Bently is cunning and vengeful, so, I have to determine what a smart and mean-spirited thief might do."

Jeremy frowned. "What kind of patterns?"

Ben glanced at Hattie and Sarah before answering. "He's made a great effort to disguise who and what he is. The man is smooth and practiced. He didn't learn to be this way suddenly. His manners and way of speaking indicate he had an educated upbringing. He also wants revenge. Based on Miss Sheila's report and those of the gang members we caught, Bently is preoccupied with thoughts of vengeance and the desire to get even with anyone he thinks has wronged him.

"Hattie heard him use harsh and aggressive language to threaten Miss Sheila and her mother, so the man lacks respect and empathy for people he considers weaker."

Sarah stared at him. "What is empathy, Uncle?"

"If you have empathy, Sarah, you can experience the emotions, thoughts, or attitudes of others. You can put yourself in their shoes and feel what they feel."

She nodded. "I felt afraid for Miss Sheila and her mother."

Jeremy's chin firmed. "How can I help, Uncle?"

Ben's tone turned urgent. "I need you and Sarah to stay away from Bently. Hopefully, out of sight will also be out of mind for him. Keep your eyes open and your mouths closed. Don't share your knowledge with anyone outside this room."

Hattie nodded. "If we meet him in the store or on the street, you and Jem must pretend he is who says he is. You must not look at him any differently than you have before, and you should continue to call him Mr. Charles in a respectful tone, okay?"

"Okay." Sarah and Jeremy spoke at the same time.

Hattie wondered what the thoughtful look in Jeremy's eyes meant? As intelligent as he was, he'd be trying to figure out what the thieves would do and how they might be derailed from their plans. She hoped he would share any insight with Ben.

She stood. "Enough of our lessons for tonight, Jem. Let's see how far we can get in *The Adventures of Tom Sawyer*."

The two sat close as she read. Part way through the chapter, her stomach roiled, and she flinched.

Jeremy frowned and leaned away from her to look into her face. "What's wrong, Mom?"

Hattie's eyes met Ben's. He grinned and nodded.

She smiled. "You and Sarah will have a brother or sister in the spring. Right now, the baby is making my stomach upset."

A slow smile lit Jeremy's face. Pleasure shone from his eyes.

Sarah squealed and hugged her. "Can I tell Julie, Hattie?"

Hattie shook her head. "Not yet. Once the baby grows enough I must wear larger clothing, then you can tell. Promise you won't say anything before then."

Sarah's expression fell. "All right. I promise."

Hattie snuggled Sarah to her side. "Let's finish this chapter, and then we'll have an early night."

Sarah put her palm on Hattie's belly. "Mom, do you know how to knit? I want to make my sister or brother some clothes."

"I sew but don't knit. Pauline Norwood does though. Shall we ask her if she'll teach us? She knows about the baby."

"Yes. Can we ask her after church tomorrow?"

Hattie covered Sarah's hand with hers. "Let's do."

Sarah settled. "Good. I have to learn fast because school starts next month."

Hattie glanced up from her needlework to watch Sarah. After only a week of daily instruction, she had caught on to the basics of knitting. As Ben read from *The Adventures of Huckleberry Finn*, Sarah's needles moved as fast as his words.

When Ben finished, Jeremy straightened. "Dad, can we talk about the bank robbery? I've been thinking about what the criminals might do."

Hattie smiled. As soon as Jeremy had started calling Ben, Dad, instead of Uncle, Sarah had done the same thing.

Ben closed the book. "Let's hear what you're thinking, Jem."

Jeremy spoke slowly, as if putting his thoughts in order before he let the words out of his mouth. "I asked myself who or what would stand in their way, and my only answer was you and the deputies. You would stop them, so they will want you out of the way."

Ben nodded. "Continue."

"Then I wondered how they would," Jeremy swallowed hard, "disable you. They would want to split you all up, so the outlaws would create diversions—maybe a fight at Muldoon's saloon, or an accident on the road somewhere."

Hattie's heart pounded uncomfortably. She could see the scenarios clearly. Fear tinged her blood.

Jeremy stared at Ben's face. "Bently will know the money will be sent with an armored vehicle and guards, so he will need more men than himself and Mr. Dillon. These men may hide somewhere in the area and attack the guards before they get to town."

Hattie tried to read Ben's expression as he listened to their son. He seemed more interested than upset. *Of course.* Ben had already envisioned and planned for such scenarios.

Sarah looked up from her knitting and frowned. "How many guards will ride with the vehicle?"

Ben paused as if deciding if he should speak or not. "I'd say about six total, including the driver and shotgun."

Jeremy frowned. "Six?"

Ben raised an eyebrow. "You don't think six is enough?"

"If Bently is as cunning as everyone says he is, wouldn't he have planned for this and recruited more men?"

Ben rested his crossed arms on the table. "Yes. He may have convinced up to ten more to join him and Dillon. I doubt he would ask for more, because he wouldn't want to pay them."

Jeremy's eyes widened. "So, you know you will be outnumbered even with the guards? What will you do?"

Ben studied Jeremy's face. "I'll have to even the odds, Jem, if I can."

Jeremy said nothing for several moments. He shook his head and scowled. "Something is wrong with my thinking, Dad.

"The outlaw is tricky, but the robbery scenarios so far are . . . straightforward. He will know you can figure out this much and plan for them, but I think he will do something unexpected.

"I can't figure out what yet. I don't know if he will change the time of the attack or the location. Which direction will he go if he runs? Toward the Palo Duro Canyon, toward Amarillo, or will he go east or west? Will he be a recognizable part of the gang, even if he wears a mask, or will he continue to make us believe he's a law-abiding citizen who has been robbed and keep his face unmasked? If he decides to pretend this, why would he do so? I can't believe he'd want to stay here to spend his money."

Jeremy's jaw tightened. "Seems to me like they'd split up and head to Austin, Dallas, or Fort Worth to spend their money. Maybe they would ride to Oklahoma City or Baton Rouge."

Hattie couldn't remain silent after listening to the conversation. "What about the citizens? If the silver is supposed to arrive on Saturday, many will be in town shopping. They could get hurt."

Ben nodded. "The deputies and I have been taking turns riding to the ranchers and farmers in the area to warn them not to come to town. We've not hidden the problem from them."

Hattie sighed her relief. "What about us, Ben. What do you want us to do?"

"I can't focus and do what needs to be done if I have to worry that you or the children are in harm's way. I want all three of you to stay here with the doors and windows locked. Bently is vengeful. If his plans fail, he may come looking for you."

Jeremy's gaze tracked to the shotgun over the fireplace.

Ben watched him and shook his head. "Only as a last resort, Jem. Taking a man's life weighs heavy on the soul."

Jeremy's glance moved from Sarah to Hattie, and his jaw clenched. "I will not allow anyone to hurt my mother or sister if I can do anything to stop them."

Ben nodded. "Good man."

CHAPTER 12: ARRIVALS

Hattie stared at the envelope in her hand. She read the sending address and her insides churned.

Ben stopped beside her. "What's wrong, love?"

Hattie tilted her head toward their home. "Wait until we get inside. The letter is from Carrie."

Jeremy and Sarah carried the groceries so Ben could keep his hands free just in case. They started unloading the bags without being told as Hattie opened the letter.

Sarah looked up. "Will you read what Aunt Carrie wrote aloud, Mom?"

Hattie put her hand on her stomach. "Yes."

Dear Hattie,

Max and I can't tolerate being at home another day. Mother and Father continue to pressure me to marry, and Max says life is gray and dull without you.

I hope you want to see us, because we miss you and want to visit. We'll try not to be a fuss and bother. We'll arrive in Amarillo on Thursday afternoon. I hope you will come and meet us at the train station. I'll book rooms at a nearby hotel for us.

We're traveling light. Max said I could bring only one trunk, so we have three—his, mine, and one filled with gifts for you, Ben, and the children from our parents.

Sarah said she would share her bed with me if I came, and she thought Jeremy would share with Max. If this is too cramped, I understand. We will stay next door at the boarding house. Sarah said Mrs. Norwood is kind.

Please, best of sisters, don't be angry with us. I hope to see you with a smile on your face and welcome in your eyes on Thursday.

Love, Carrie.

Sarah jumped up and down. "Yay! Aunt Carrie and Uncle Max are coming."

Hattie's gaze met Ben's. His face showed his concern.

Carrie's timing was exceptionally bad. Hattie wanted to see her siblings, but not immediately before a bank robbery attempt when they could be hurt or killed. *Oh, Lord, help!*

Jeremy studied her face. "I'm willing to share my room, but if Max is as large as you say, he can have the bed, and I'll sleep on the floor."

Sarah danced around the room. "They're bringing presents, Jem. I wonder what Grandmother and Grandfather sent to us."

Hattie read the letter again and looked up. "Can you take us, Ben?"

The lines at the corners of his eyes deepened. "I can't leave right now, Hattie. I'm sorry. I must finish final preparations before Saturday."

Jeremy straightened. "I can drive, Dad. Today is Wednesday. We'll have to leave before sunrise tomorrow morning to be in Amarillo by the afternoon." He looked at his sister. "Sorry, Sarah, but if Carrie and Max are bringing trunks, we won't have enough room in the buckboard for you, them, and their things."

Sarah's lips tightened, but she nodded. "I can go to Mrs. Norwood's for more knitting lessons."

Jeremy turned to Ben. "Dad?"

Ben searched Jeremy's face as if he weighed the advantages and disadvantages. Finally, he nodded. "Take food and drink with you."

Charles Bently watched Sheriff Cole's wife and son leave before daylight.

"What are they doin'?" Jake Dillon whispered next to Bently's ear.

They stood at the edge of town and watched the buckboard head toward Amarillo.

"I don't know, but I intend to do a little neighborly snooping when the sun comes up and the sheriff leaves his house." He looked at his nephew in the dim light cast by the moon. "Are you ready?"

"Yep. I'll check out of the boarding house this morning and head east to meet up with our men. I'll give them your instructions, then I'll ride southeast and join our second group. On Saturday, we'll come into town from the west."

Jake hesitated. "You still think the Coles had something to do with Sheila's disappearance?"

Anger and fear stirred in Bently's gut. "Who else? She disappeared off the face of the earth and left no sign."

"Do you think she told the sheriff anything?"

Bently snorted. "She probably spilled her guts and gave Cole all the details."

Jake moved uneasily. "Do you think he'll be waiting for us?"

"Of course, but he will be unprepared for the surprise we have for him."

"I hope so." Jake chuckled and returned to the boarding house.

Charles Bently looked around before knocking on the Cole's front door. He knew they were gone, but he wanted to make sure.

He held the cookie plate in his left hand as he turned the handle with his right. Locked. He grimaced. If the front door was locked, then he was certain the rest of the doors would be too. The sheriff took no chances. What about the windows?

He slid out his knife and stepped toward the window next to the door. He wedged the blade between the lower rail and the sill and applied pressure. Nothing. The windows were also locked.

Frustrated, he stepped closer to the glass and peered through the slight part in the curtains. His blood curdled when his searching eyes met the empty sockets and macabre grin of a child-sized skeleton.

His heart raced and his hands shook. He'd seen that skeleton before. On the train. The woman with the skeleton in her carpetbag had been Hattie Cole.

He took a deep breath and leaned forward to peer at the drawings on the table in front of the skeleton. They were exceptional—much like the ones law enforcement had posted in several states.

Anger churned in his gut when he realized Hattie Cole, the neighbor who brought cookies, was the artist. Of this he had no doubt. Her drawings had been instrumental in some of his gang members' capture.

His anger turned to fury and poisoned his words as he spoke them aloud. "Seems I may have to make a change in plans. Mrs. Cole will not be left alive when the bullets start to fly. I'll make sure of that. Anyone who crosses me will pay the penalty."

He left the plate on the bench under the window and turned toward his house. He muttered as he updated his plans. "Before he dies, I want that smug sheriff to know his wife will die by my hands, and his children will be left orphans. Hmm. How to do this?"

⁂

Hattie and Jeremy drove to the hotel. They had not made the trip in time to meet the train, but they were only a few hours late.

Jeremy tilted his head. "I'll take the horses and buckboard to the livery."

Hattie rubbed her aching back. "Thanks, Jem. As soon as you return, we'll eat. I'm starving. Did Ben give you enough money for the care of the horses?"

He nodded and helped her down.

Hattie walked into the hotel lobby and spotted her siblings. Carrie and Max sat on comfortable-looking sofas in the lounge area and chatted with two cowboys who sat across from them. Carrie's animated face shone with interest and excitement.

Hattie sighed. *Only three hours in Amarillo and she's already found a beau? Two beaux?* She groaned inside. She refused to be Carrie's chaperon. She just couldn't.

Carrie glanced up. She squealed and rushed to embrace her. "Tell me you're not angry with me, Hattie."

Max moved with quiet, graceful steps to them and flung his muscled arms around them both. When had her brother turned into this man who looked like their older brother, Heath?

Hattie chuckled. "Let me breathe, you two."

They took a step back and searched her face. Carrie touched her arm. "You are glad to see us, aren't you?"

Hattie nodded. "I'm glad to see you."

Carrie's smile dimmed. "I hear an unspoken *but* in your words. What's wrong?"

Hattie glanced toward the two men who watched them with interested eyes. "I'll tell you when we are alone."

"Mom?" Jeremy stepped to her side.

She put her arm around his waist. Her siblings stared.

Hattie motioned with her hand. "This is my sister, Carrie, and brother, Max. Carrie and Max, this is my son, Jeremy."

The three assessed each other in silence for several moments, then Jeremy offered his hand.

Max nodded and shook. "Nice to finally meet you, Jeremy."

"Call me, Jem, please."

Jeremy turned his gaze on Carrie. "Should I call you Aunt?"

Carrie grimaced. "Heavens, no. That makes me sound old. Carrie will do."

The two men from the sofa approached. The man in his twenties with whom Carrie had chatted earlier spoke to Hattie in a soft, drawled tone. "Ma'am?"

Hattie studied his face. "Yes?"

"Mr. Salter and I would like to invite you and your party to dinner. The table is ready."

Hattie frowned. "No, thank—"

He didn't wait for her to finish. He lowered his voice. "Sheriff Levitt is paying for the meal, Mrs. Cole, so you might as well enjoy."

Sheriff Levitt? She studied the two men. They stood silent under her critical gaze. Mr. Salter's lips turned up at the corners as more moments passed.

Hattie nodded. "Of course, lead on, Mr.—?"

"Quaid. James Quaid."

The two seated Hattie and Carrie and then sat with their backs to the wall. They had clear sight lines to the doors. Their eyes regularly scanned the people and environment.

Hattie smiled. Without a doubt, they were law enforcement officers. They had the same watchful tendencies as Ben. She picked up her menu and said in a voice only the men and her siblings could hear, "So, are you Texas Rangers or with the U.S. Marshal's Office?"

Carrie's eyes widened as she looked at the two. Her gaze remained on Mr. Quaid's easy-to-look at features.

The man in his early thirties studied his menu. "I'm Seth Salter, ma'am. I'm with the Texas Rangers."

James studied his menu and answered in a barely audible voice, "I'm with the U.S. Marshal's Office, Mrs. Cole. We're to ensure Sheriff Cole receives the packages he ordered."

Packages? Hattie could hear words within words.

They conversed over dinner as if they were good friends meeting up after a long separation.

Carrie interacted with James throughout the meal, and Hattie wondered what thoughts caused the gleam in her eyes.

Tiredness pulled at her. She brushed a hand across her forehead. "If you will excuse me, gentlemen, I'm tired and will go to my room."

The officers, Max, and Jeremy stood and waited for Hattie and Carrie to stand before they pushed in the chairs.

Salter bent close to Hattie's ear as she rose. "Bring the wagon to the back of the jail just before sunrise, Mrs. Cole." His dark eyes met Jeremy's, and her son gave a barely noticeable head tilt.

Max and Carrie entered Hattie's bedroom where she and Jeremy waited.

Hattie waved them in. "Come in and sit down. Lock the door, Max. We have a lot to talk about before we head home tomorrow."

The *packages* Hattie picked up at dawn the next day were her dinner companions from the night before.

Seth Salter and James Quaid were saddled and ready to go when Jeremy drove the buckboard into the alley behind the jail.

Sheriff Levitt waited with them. He tipped his hat. "Mrs. Cole? Please allow these officers to accompany you home. They know what they are supposed to do. I also want to thank you for the last image you drew showing Bently without a face covering. His image is being posted all over the country."

Seth Salter stared. "You drew those, Mrs. Cole? They are exceptional. I've never seen anything like them."

"Thank you, Mr. Salter." Hattie returned her attention to Levitt. "Sheriff, what about Sheila Douglas? Is she all right?"

"Yes, all because you and your husband helped her. I have her notarized statement, and I interviewed her before she left. We have enough information to hang Charles Bently once we catch him in the act of committing a federal crime."

She eyed the two men. "Thank you all for helping Ben. He knows he and the deputies will be outnumbered, and that the first steps the outlaws take will be to—" She couldn't continue.

Levitt's gruff voice held firmness. "Don't give up, ma'am. Your husband is a smart man. I've put other plans in motion to help him even the odds."

The mounted officers looked at each other, questions in their eyes, but they said nothing.

They left Amarillo at a fast walk. James rode close to where Carrie sat in the buckboard's back seat, and Seth rode ahead and acted as scout. Hattie had never seen Carrie so animated this early in the morning. She frowned. She didn't remember seeing her this animated and sincere with any of the men who had come courting. *Uh-oh.*

For the next two hours, Hattie listened to the conversation around her. At the start of the third hour, her stomach and lower back revolted.

"Stop, Jem! Stop." She covered her mouth and got out of the buckboard as soon as he did. She rushed to a bush and heaved up the remains of her breakfast. She held out her palm in a stay-back motion.

"Here, ma'am." James offered his bandanna and canteen.

Hattie reached for them, her ears burning from her public display. She sipped from the canteen, rinsed her mouth, and drank. She dabbed at her lips and the back of her neck with the bandanna.

"Hattie, are you okay?" Carrie watched her with a worried expression.

"I'm fine." Her eyes met Jeremy's sympathetic gaze. His glance slipped to her middle before James helped her back onto the wagon seat.

Five miles away from their town, Seth told Jeremy to stop the buckboard. James dismounted, removed his blanket roll and rifle, then handed Seth his horse's reins. The Ranger lifted a hand and trotted away.

Max stared. "Where is he going with your horse?"

James grinned and hopped into the back of the wagon. "Don't worry about Salter. He'll be around."

He unrolled his bedding and laid down between the trunks. "Mr. Cole, I'd be mighty appreciating if you'd avoid the potholes and ruts from here on out. When we get to town, drive the buckboard to your barn like you normally would. Mr. Atwell, I'll leave you and Mr. Cole to unload the trunks. I'll remain in the wagon until nightfall.

"Mrs. Cole, please tell Sheriff Cole I'll meet him at the jail this evening."

He chuckled and winked at Carrie. "Pardon me, if I don't seem social from here on out, but I can't be seen or heard." With that, he slid a rain tarp over himself.

Jeremy clicked to the horses, and they started home. About a mile from town, they overtook a large man riding an equally large horse and leading a big pack mule. They plodded along as if they'd come many miles.

The mule appeared to be carrying the shabby man's worldly goods. Pot handles, tin cups, and an assortment of odds and ends protruded from the mouth of the panniers.

As they passed, Hattie's gaze met his. He tipped his shabby hat, and Hattie nodded. She noted the man's frayed sleeve and holes in his jeans. Everything about him looked dirty and worn. She felt sorry for him. His long brown hair probably hadn't been washed for months.

Jeremy stared as they passed, his sharp eyes taking in everything.

Hattie glanced back once more. "I wonder where he's going."

Her son's lips tightened. "I don't know, but he could be one of Bently's men."

From the back of the wagon, James asked for a description of the rider they'd just passed. He asked pointed questions, then said, "Relax, he's one of the good guys."

CHAPTER 13: Night Whispers

Charles Bently watched the Coles return with visitors. The male who got out and unloaded the trunks looked so much like Hattie, he had to be a relative. Brother, perhaps?

Bently sucked in a breath when he saw the petite beauty who also got out of the wagon. Her hair was the exact shade as Hattie Cole's. Was this a sister? His mouth went dry. He wanted her. She was more beautiful than any woman he'd ever seen.

When they went inside, he left the shadows and stepped onto the boardwalk. He turned at the sound of hoof beats.

A huge, shaggy man plodded into town. His thick brown beard covered most of his face, and his long, dark hair hung in a tangled mass down his back. The man rode up to him and stopped.

Charles stiffened and put on his good-citizen mask. "May I help you?"

"Yep. Hopin' you can tell me if I'm headed in the right direction to get to that there Palo Duro Canyon. I been hearin' about the place for years. Finally decided to come and see for myself, so I packed up Molly and Horse and headed this way. Been ridin' for a mighty long time."

He pointed a dirty finger. "I'm also a-wonderin' if that there restaurant across the street has vittles good enough to eat. I'm hungerin' for apple pie."

"The restaurant has excellent food."

Bently startled at the sound of the sheriff's voice coming from behind him. He hadn't heard the man's soft-footed approach.

He stepped away and tilted his head at the traveler. "If you have more questions, I'm sure Sheriff Cole can answer them. Excuse me."

Bently seethed. He wished Cole already lay dead at his feet, and that he was riding out of town with the dark-haired beauty and enough silver and gold to keep him in luxury for years. Well, tomorrow would come soon enough.

Ben studied the big man as he watched Bently's retreat.

The man chuckled and turned to him. "He looks just like his wanted poster." He patted his pockets as if searching for something and turned slightly so only Ben caught sight of his badge.

Ben relaxed. "You are?"

"Just call me Little. I'm a Texas Ranger. I've brought you news from Sheriff Levitt."

"So, law enforcement can work together when they try." Humor tinted Ben's tone.

The man dropped his uneducated speech and spoke quickly and to the point. "I'm going to the restaurant for some dinner. Meet me at your office at dark. No lights."

He led his animals to the hitching rail in front of the restaurant and went inside. Ben knew the exact seat the man would take when he sat down. He would have a view of the street and the exits.

He studied the Ranger's movements as he walked, then turned his gaze on his animals. With certainty, Ben knew Little was fast and accurate with his fists and weapons, and that the appearance of fat was an illusion encouraged by his shapeless clothes. In a hundred yards, the man could probably beat him in a race over a flat surface. His animals would do the same in a contest with other horses. Though they looked dirty and tired, both the horse and mule were muscled and would most likely beat anything around.

Tightness in his chest loosened a little. Others knew his situation and cared.

Ben took a circuitous route home and stepped in the side door just as Sarah wrapped her arms around the waist of a beauty who could only be Hattie's sister.

"I'm so glad to meet you Aunt Carrie. And Uncle Max . . ." she let go of a startled Carrie and flung herself at her new uncle.

The young giant blinked and opened his arms to stop Sarah from knocking him over. He wrapped her in an embrace. She kissed his cheek, then slid out of his arms.

She caught sight of Ben and rushed to him. "Dad. They're here." She tugged at his hand, and he followed her into the living room.

Ben hung his hat on the hook, then kissed Sarah and Hattie. Slowly, he faced his sister- and brother-in-law. "Hello. I'm Ben. You must be Carrie and Maxwell."

Carrie nodded. Her eyes widened when she examined him from head to toe. Her gaze slowed when she reached his badge and the guns hugging his hips. Words seem to have deserted her.

A grin tilted his lips.

Max stepped forward and offered his hand. "Please call me, Max, uh, Sheriff, uh, Sir—"

"Ben is fine, Max."

Hattie reached for her apron. "Jem, would you see Max settled in your room? Sarah, will you show Max where to put Carrie's trunk, then come down and help with supper?"

"Okay, Mom." Sarah reached for Carrie's hand. "Come on, Auntie. I'll show you my room."

Hattie glanced at the drawings on the table. "Oh, Sarah, will you take Katy back to her place along with the sketch books?"

"Sure." She released Carrie's hand and, with careful movements, picked up the skeleton. "Time for bed, Katy-love. We have company, so you need to disappear."

Carrie continued to stare, her mouth agape, as Sarah climbed the stairs.

Based on what Ben knew about his sister-in-law's personality and upbringing, he imagined this experience had shocked the words right out of her mouth.

He swallowed a chuckle and turned to Hattie. "What do you want me to do, love?"

She brushed a strand of hair out of her eyes. "Bring in more wood and start the fire in the stove?"

With a nod, he reached for his hat and opened the back door. In less than two minutes, he carried in an armful of wood, squatted in front of the stove, and stirred the coals.

Sarah came down and pulled her apron over her head.

Ben stood and walked to the wash basin. From the corner of his eyes, he watched Carrie's face as Hattie handed Sarah a mixing bowl and spatula. His daughter knew exactly what Hattie wanted and started getting the ingredients for flapjacks. *Ah. Breakfast for supper.* His stomach growled.

When Hattie gave Carrie an apron and told her where to find the plates and silverware so she could set the table, her jaw actually dropped. Ben choked down a laugh.

Max and Jeremy returned just as Carrie moved toward the table, her hands full of plates.

Startled, Max stared at his sister, then held out his arms. "Let me help you, Sis. Tell me where these go."

Ben smiled his approval.

Within the hour, they sat down to steaming flapjacks, freshly churned butter, maple syrup, sausage, and eggs.

Ben asked God's blessing on the food, then prayed earnestly for wisdom, guidance, and help. When he looked up, he noted the solemn looks on every face.

Hattie passed around the platters of food. "Ben, we had a couple of guests accompany us from Amarillo. They were sent by Sheriff Levitt. James Quaid is from the U.S. Marshal's Office. He is hiding in our wagon until dark. He'll meet you at the office.

Ben's eyebrows rose. Another officer? Things were looking up. He nodded.

After-supper clean up started just before Ben reached for his hat. Again, he grinned to see his in-laws' shock at the process and Hattie's expectation that they would help. He glanced at her pale face and frowned. She looked tired.

He turned back, walked to her, and removed the wet dish rag from her hand. He handed this to Jeremy and led Hattie to the sofa. "Sit, darlin'. You look tired. I'll get you a glass of water."

Jeremy washed the rest of the dishes without complaint and handed Max a towel to dry the plates he put on the drainboard.

Max stared at the cloth he held, and then, with a cautious hand, reached for a plate.

Ben gave Hattie the water glass. "I shouldn't be gone more than an hour. Are you all right?"

Carrie sat down beside Hattie and reached for her hand. "I can take care of her, Ben. You do what you need to do."

For the first time, Ben looked beyond Carrie's beautiful face into the eyes of a woman who was smart and able. He nodded. "Thank you."

Carrie smiled. "My pleasure."

Carrie sensed how tired her sister was as she closed her eyes and let her body sink into the cushions. Was she ill?

"Mom?"

Hattie opened her eyes and smiled to see the book in Sarah's hands. "Yes, we'll read a chapter or two, my darling."

Hattie sat up, and Sarah snuggled close. As her sister read *The Adventures of Huckleberry Finn* aloud, the little girl eased her palm onto Hattie's belly and patted.

Carrie's eyes widened. She slid her questioning gaze to Jeremy, who watched her with a knowing expression. He dipped his head once and returned his attention to Hattie.

Sudden emotion tore through Carrie. She couldn't name the explosive combination of feelings stirred up at the sight of Sarah's loving pat given to her unborn sister or brother, but they raged through her with the strength of a hurricane. Longing choked her, and she wanted to jump and run.

Ever since she'd met James Quaid and Seth Salter, her idea of the kind of man she wanted for a husband changed. She admired their strength, toughness, and willingness to do hard, dangerous jobs to protect others and their property. Why were they so different from the men she knew?

When she met her brother-in-law, the unstated authority his badge and guns represented, and the strength oozing from him silenced her. Yet, the kindness and gentleness he displayed when interacting with Hattie and the children made her knees weak.

All three of the men wore the scent of disciplined power that attracted her like a magnet.

Her chin firmed. She would try to be worthy of such men, even if she had to learn to cook, clean, and wash laundry. She'd scrub until her hands reddened and chapped as long as she could earn the love of a man like one of these. She yearned. She longed. She wanted.

Ben cracked the back door to the jail and waited, his hand near his gun.

"Sheriff?" The whisper-soft voice barely reached his ears. "I'm James Quaid with the U.S. Marshal's Office. May I come in?"

He pushed the door wider and motioned the man inside. "I—"

Ben put a hand on his arm and leaned close. "Wait."

They reached for their weapons as stealthy movements drew closer.

"Don't shoot me." Though Little tried to whisper, his words came out as a soft, deep growl.

"Tiny, is that you?" James lowered his weapon.

"Yes. I'm coming in."

The huge man shut the door. "I don't have much time. I'm headed to Lubbock with a bundle of cash. Levitt has been leaking false information so criminals and their spy networks won't know what is actually happening. Only he and I, and now you, know the truth. I'm handing the cash off to another agent in four days. He'll take the money the rest of the way to Dallas."

Quaid's whispered words held humor. "Good thing that horse and mule of yours can outrun anything in the country. You're going to have to ride almost twenty-five miles a day to make Lubbock in four."

"Yep. That's what I planned."

Ben tensed. "What about the guards?"

"They'll be here tomorrow afternoon."

"Do they know they aren't guarding the silver shipment?"

Little hesitated. "No, and they aren't guarding anything but a box of rocks. The silver and gold part of the deal left three days ago on a train to Dallas."

A lead ball settled in the pit of Ben's stomach. "So, they may die for nothing?"

Silence.

Little turned to the door. "That about sums up the situation." He lifted a hand and stepped outside.

The only sound Ben heard was the creaking of leather as Little swung into the saddle. How many fast miles would the lawman cover tonight before stopping to rest his animals?

Ben closed the door and continued the whispered conversation. "This information changes things, Quaid."

"Sure does. How do you want to handle the situation?"

They discussed several options and finally agreed on the least likely way to get law officers and civilians killed.

"Seth is camped a few miles from town. I'll ride out and let him know the change in plans."

Before they left, James touched Ben's arm. "Sheriff? If we live through this, do I have your permission to call on your sister-in-law?"

"You've only known Carrie a day."

James chuckled. "A day is all I need. That woman is spunky and has a head on her shoulders. I can tell. If I'm not mistaken, she would make a good lawman's wife. I need to figure out a way to convince her of this."

"I think you're asking the wrong person, Quaid. You should probably address your question to Carrie or my wife."

"I'll do that."

Ben didn't return home after James left, though he wanted to. He met with his deputies, and then knocked on the banker's back door. His last stop was Barney Muldoon's place.

Ben unlocked the front door, but paused. Light streamed from the part in the curtain and reflected off Hattie's cookie plate. He frowned and glanced from the window to the dish and back again.

He grasped the plate and, with a practiced movement, stepped inside and turned the lock.

The welcome in Hattie's eyes lifted his spirit. He held out the plate. "When did Bently stop by?"

Hattie stared. "That wasn't outside when we left for Amarillo yesterday."

With a sense of growing urgency, Ben looked at the window and then at objects in the room.

Hattie put her hand on his forearm. "What's wrong?"

"I'm certain, being this close to Bently's planned robbery, he knew you were gone. He probably suspects we had something to do with Sheila's disappearance too, so why did he stop by? His would not have been a friendly visit."

Hattie paled and her knees weakened. She would have fallen had he not grabbed her. "Jem, get your mother a glass of water."

He picked her up and carried her to the couch. "Hattie? Talk to me."

Jeremy raced to the water pitcher and poured a glass.

Hattie buried her face on Ben's shoulder. "He knows, Ben. He knows I'm the artist. What shall I do?"

"Look at me, Hattie. How does he know?"

She sniffed. "We left in such a rush, I didn't put Katy or the sketches away. If he peered through the curtains, he would have seen them and remembered me from the train."

Jeremy offered her the water glass.

His children and in-laws listened to the conversation with worried faces.

Hattie drank and then took several deep breaths. She sat up. "I'm okay, Ben. Tell me what I should do to stay out of harm's way."

"You and the others will remain here. Keep the doors and windows locked."

Jeremy frowned. "Won't that be what Bently predicts you will have us do, Dad? What's to stop him from firing the house during the commotion and then shooting us as we try to escape?"

Ben stared at Jem, his mind racing. He stood and started toward the door. "I'll be back. I need to catch Quaid before he gets too far out of town." He paused. "Each of you pack a bag with two-day's worth of food and water. Take an extra set of warm undergarments. Be ready to leave when I return."

He put on his hat and turned. "Jem and Max, follow me to the barn. I want you to feed and water the chickens and horses. When they're finished eating, hitch the horses to the wagon. Do this without light or noise, understand?"

Both teens nodded.

"Hattie, you and the girls get blankets and your pillows. Get some for the boys. When you're ready to open the door and hand them to Jem and Max, douse the lights."

Ben scanned Carrie's pale but determined face as she grasped Hattie's hand. She hadn't fainted, cried, or objected. When her eyes met his, they sparkled. She rose in his esteem. *Hmm. Maybe she'll make a good lawman's wife after all.*

CHAPTER 14: Unexpected

Charles Bently rose before the sun and shaved. Today was his day. Today, he would get what he deserved.

He patted on aftershave, dressed, then opened his pocket watch. Six o'clock. Eight more hours, and he would be free of this paltry town.

With unhurried movements, he removed his freshly laundered shirts from the drawer and packed them in his saddlebags. He added his pressed slacks and undergarments, and laid the loaded pistol on top of them.

Bently made a sudden movement with his right hand. A derringer slid into his palm without hindrance. Smiling, he returned the weapon to his sleeve holster and put on his jacket. Though he'd have only two shots with the gun, this might be all he needed if he got in a bind.

Pulling on gloves, he eased out the back door with his saddlebags and into the small barn where his matching bay geldings waited. He saddled and bridled the animals and tied on the bags. He gave the horses water and an extra grain ration.

He returned to the house and put on his hat before strolling toward the restaurant, his eyes scanning every person and building.

His steps faltered when he passed the Coles' place. No smoke issued from the stovepipe, and the curtains had not been opened as they usually were at this time of day. Their irritating dog that always barked and growled at him was not in the yard, and he sensed a quiet emptiness not present yesterday.

Bently's lips pinched together. Were they holed up expecting his attack, or had they slipped away? If so, where would they have gone?

He assumed Sheila had escaped with their help, tattling on him in the process, but what if she hadn't? What if the Coles were still in the dark about who he was?

With feigned nonchalance, Bently eased down the main road and glanced toward their barn. The buckboard and horses were gone.

Cursing under his breath all the way to Main, he had to force the mask of civility back onto his face and friendliness into his voice as he walked by a few of the townspeople and returned their greetings.

Bently entered the restaurant and took his regular table.

The restaurant owner approached. "Good morning, Mr. Charles. How is your lady wife today? Will you be ordering your usual?"

Bently smiled. "She's better, Miss Mabel. Thank you for asking. Must be your good cooking."

The woman beamed. "I'll get your order in." She left, and he watched her until she entered the kitchen through the batwing doors.

He contemplated Mabel's manner toward him, as well as that of others who had greeted him on the street. He saw no sign they knew who he was. If Cole had known, wouldn't he have warned them?

Bently lingered over his breakfast another hour and watched the town wake up.

He relaxed when the deputies and sheriff walked their rounds. *Ah, back to normal. Back on schedule.*

His eyes narrowed when Lorraine Hastings stepped onto the boardwalk. She started toward the mercantile, but stopped mid-step and looked around, frowning.

What had caught her attention? He stood, laid a large bill on the table, and left the restaurant.

"Miss Hastings? How delightful to see you this morning. You're looking well."

Red stained Lorraine's cheeks. "Thank you, sir."

"What concerns you? You seem somewhat disturbed this fine day."

She frowned and looked up and down the street and at the doors of the businesses. "Today is Saturday, correct?"

"Yes."

Her frown deepened. "Where are all the ranchers and their wives who usually come here to shop? The town seems empty."

Ice slithered up and down Bently's spine. His smile disappeared. "You're right." Had the sheriff warned the outlying ranchers not to come to town today? If so, that would account for the mysterious disappearances of Cole and his deputies at different times during the last week.

Pasting the smile back on, he tilted his head. "May I accompany you to your destination?"

She hesitated, then nodded. "I'm going to the mercantile."

He walked her to the door, then bowed. "If you'll excuse me, I need to stop at the bank. My wife and I are leaving soon. I must say, making your acquaintance has made my stay here enjoyable. Thank you."

Lorraine's face fell. "I'm sorry you're leaving, Mr. Charles. Where will you and your lady wife go?"

"We'll be heading to the French Riviera. Perhaps, a change in venue will mean better health for my wife."

With a dull look in her eyes, she nodded. "I hope so."

"Too bad you can't come with us. You'd love France."

Wistfulness drooped the corners of her mouth. "I wish I could too, Mr. Charles."

He continued to reel her in. Her dissatisfaction with this small town had been obvious from the first moment he'd met her. Bently schooled his features. "Well, you have an open invitation if you choose to come. Now, if you'll excuse me?"

He chuckled inside and walked away. He wondered how long she would take to decide.

"Mr. Charles?"

That was fast. He turned back to her with a raised eyebrow and a slight smile. "Yes, Miss Hastings?"

"How is Mrs. Charles preparing for the trip?"

"She doesn't have to do much now. We'll stop in New York City and buy whatever we need before we sail. We don't like to be tied down."

Longing intensified the brightness of Lorraine's eyes. "Will she need a traveling companion to help her on the journey?"

"Yes. I will hire someone through a trustworthy agency when we start east. I will pay well."

Lorraine worried her bottom lip with her teeth for several moments. She straightened. "If Mrs. Charles doesn't mind traveling with a stranger, I'd be happy to help her."

Bently lowered his voice and looked around. "The thing is, Miss Hastings, we're leaving this afternoon. We haven't told anyone. Goodbyes are painful, don't you think?"

She started and put a hand to her heart. "This afternoon? Oh, my."

"I know. Short notice, right? But we are packed and ready. We take only the barest necessities and buy what we need later. We'll stop at our estate outside New Orleans for a rest before continuing our journey.

"If you think you'd like to join us, wait for me on the back porch of your house at about two-thirty. I don't know how quickly I can wrap up my business at the bank, so don't be worried if I'm a little late. I'll come as soon as I can. I'll bring a horse for you to ride."

Lorraine nodded and strode to her house, a smile lighting her face.

Ben watched Charles Bently's interaction with Lorraine Hastings from the shadow of a nearby building. His unease grew. He disliked and distrusted the change in Lorraine's attitude. What had the criminal said to put the color in her cheeks and the bounce in her step? What did the blackguard intend?

Around noon, Ben shielded his eyes and glanced down the road. Two riders, still at a distance, headed toward town.

Ben's muscles tightened. Bently's plan was now in motion. He walked past Muldoon's saloon and glanced at the large, red-headed Irishman who owned the place. Their eyes met. He dipped his head and continued toward the bank.

Ben walked through the bank, signaled Fred Staples, nodded to Fred's three war buddies who'd arrived during the night, then left by the back door.

The two cowboys ambled into town on dusty horses, their gazes panning each building. They pulled up to the hitchrail in front of the saloon and dismounted. They glanced around before looping the reins around the rail and entering.

Ben figured the men would drink a few shots of whiskey, watch a card game Beau Deems, Howard Grimes, and Lou Webber would most likely be playing by now, and ask to join the game. They'd eventually challenge the locals and call them cheaters. They'd start a fight, and then someone would yell for the sheriff.

Ben glanced at his pocket watch. "I'll give them forty-five minutes."

When Bently strolled from the shortcut onto Main Street thirty minutes later, Ben's eyes focused. The outlaw paused, removed his hat, and brushed his clothing before heading toward the mercantile. Was that a signal?

Ben watched and listened from the building next door to the saloon. Sure enough, chairs scraped along the floors as if pushed violently away, and the yell of *cheaters* rang clearly. Someone threw a chair through Muldoon's front window and yelled, "Fight. Get the sheriff."

Ben stayed where he was. Barney Muldoon had replaced that window once already this year, and the Irishman would be madder than mad. Ben chuckled. He'd hate to be in the man's boots who'd thrown the chair.

Ben's eyes never left Bently.

When no one moved to get the sheriff or his deputies, Bently looked up and down the street. Not a single person could be seen anywhere. All business doors were closed and windows shut. Even the restaurant's sign had been turned to "Sorry, come back tomorrow."

Good. The townsfolk had done as he'd asked. The place looked like a ghost town.

Fury twisted Bently's mouth when he realized no one could be seen on the streets for him to send. He hesitated, then walked toward the jail.

Ben chuckled again. He wouldn't find anyone there either. Joe watched from his vantage point atop the town's water tower, while Ron followed Bently's every move from the livery's rooftop.

Last night, they had greased doorknobs and poles, and removed ladders to prevent Bently's gang from gaining access to any building's roof.

Now, for part two. Ben eased out the back door and waited in the deep shadows between the mercantile and feed store. He'd worn his darkest clothing and buttoned his badge inside his pocket.

Racing hoofbeats told him he didn't have long to wait.

Two riders rode into town as if their tails were on fire, pulled their horses to a stop in front of the Sheriff's Office, and pounded on the door. "Sheriff! Come quick. There's been an accident a mile from here. Sheriff!"

They continued to pound and call out, but they quieted when they got no response.

One of them caught sight of Bently. He stood in the middle of the street, hands on his hips. "Mister, where's the sheriff?"

"He's not in his office, you idiots. He's either waiting in the bank or joining the guards to bring in the silver."

Bently's low voice carried to Ben. He smiled. He could sense the outlaw's burning rage and frustration from where he stood.

"What do you want us to do now, boss?"

Bently snarled. "Get on your horses and meet up with Jake and the others. The silver should be here soon."

Charles Bently turned and walked toward the bank. Fury consumed him. Ben Cole had outmaneuvered him. He suspected other law enforcement agencies had been involved, because he couldn't believe Cole was smart enough to do all this planning on his own. *What a time for law enforcement to start working together.* His jaw clenched and his hands fisted.

What tricks had they put in place with the silver shipment? Bently didn't intend to stick around when the bullets flew.

He would withdraw his money on the pretext his wife had taken a sudden turn for the worse and he needed to get her to a specialist back east.

He'd swing by the Hastings' place and leave town with Lorraine. He wanted the petite beauty, but she'd disappeared. Bently growled. Lorraine would likely throw a fit when she found out he had no wife, and that his intentions weren't honorable, but he didn't care. He knew how to deal with recalcitrant women.

How could the day turn sour so quickly?

Bently reached for the bank's door handles and pushed. The doors didn't budge. He blinked and turned his focus from his internal thoughts to the Closed sign hanging in front of his face.

Blood throbbed through his veins, and rage almost blinded him. He pounded on the doors. "Let me in. I have an emergency. Let me in, Mr. Staples."

No response.

Something broke inside Bently. Evil spread from his heart and consumed every inch of his mind and body. The ugly, inhuman laugh that escaped his mouth frightened him. He eased around the side of the building. He would get into the bank one way or another.

"Come have tea with me, Miss Hastings." Pauline Norwood smiled. "My boarders are gone, and I could use some company."

"I can't, Mrs. Norwood. I'm leaving town. I'm accompanying Mr. and Mrs. Charles to Europe as her attendant."

Pauline didn't let fear show on her face. "When will you leave?"

"Around two."

Pauline smiled. "That gives us an hour. Please come."

Lorraine hesitated. "All right. I'll tell my parents I'm stepping out for a bit."

Pauline's heart pounded behind her ribs. After Sheriff Cole stopped by and told her about the planned robbery,

Sheila Douglas's escape, and described Lorraine's response to that outlaw Charles Bently's conversation, he had asked her to discourage Lorraine from involving herself with him.

"Sit, my dear. Tell me all about your journey."

Pauline poured tea from the pot and stirred honey into both of their cups.

Lorraine sipped. "This is tasty." She sipped some more. Her eyes shone as she talked about her journey.

Pauline frowned. "Have you ever met Mrs. Charles? I haven't set eyes on the woman."

Lorraine lost some of her sparkle, and worry came and went in her eyes. "No, I haven't."

"Doesn't this seem odd to you?"

"Yes, but she's ill and can't expose herself."

Pauline nodded. "That's the story I've heard." She poured more tea into Lorraine's cup. "What will you do if you and the Charles' are not compatible?"

Lorraine squared her shoulders. "I will do what I have to. I must get out of this backwater town. I want to see the world." She downed the cup of tea as if daring anyone to stop her.

"What do your parents have to say about this?"

"They don't want me to go. They don't trust Mr. Charles." Her face flushed. "They're very old fashioned."

Pauline studied her guest's face. "Sheriff Cole stopped by, Lorraine. Mr. Charles is actually Charles Bently, the train and bank robber. He and his gang intend to rob a silver shipment headed our way in less than an hour, but Ben, with help from the U.S. Marshal's Office and the Texas Rangers intend to foil his plans.

"The woman he brought with him is not his wife, but a prostitute named Sheila. The Coles helped her escape several days ago."

Lorraine stood and swayed. "I don't believe this. Did Ben start such a rumor?" She put a hand to her head. "I'm going to leave—"

Pauline rushed to her and put an arm around the swaying woman. "What's wrong, Lorraine? You're pale."

"My head is spinning. I think I'm going to faint." Lorraine's eyes fluttered.

"Come upstairs and rest, my dear. I just changed the sheets in the bedroom at the top of the stairs."

"I can't. I'll be late."

"Don't worry. If Mr. and Mrs. Charles stop by, I'll wake you."

"You promise?"

"Yes."

Pauline pulled back the covers, removed Lorraine's shoes, and tucked her in. She waited until her guest's breathing indicated sleep, then returned to the teapot and dumped the contents down the sink. She washed the pot and the cups.

The laudanum had worked as expected.

CHAPTER 15: Resolved

Charles Bently smirked as he rode to the back of the Hastings' house. If Fred Staples and his minions lived, they wouldn't take him lightly again. He only wished the sheriff and his wife had been present.

The banker had planned for him to come in either the front or back doors, but no one expected him to climb the nearby tree and enter through the attic window.

On cat feet, he had slipped down the stairs and removed the revolver from an inner pocket. He'd eased himself into position.

He hadn't given the watchers warning. With four quick shots, he'd put a bullet into each of them, then moved toward the open vault in the other room. *Open vault?*

Gone. He stared. Every single bill and coin had been removed. He screamed and cursed. Where had they taken the money? His money?

Bently rushed to the place he'd seen the banker fall near the back door. Blood stained the floor, but Staples had disappeared. Where was he hiding? Had he escaped outside? Did the man wait for him, weapons drawn? How badly was he wounded?

A chill crawled up Bently's spine. He needed to get out of here. The silver shipment would arrive soon, and he didn't want to be anywhere around.

He had left the bank the way he'd come and used the long shadows between buildings to return to his waiting horses. He swung into the saddle and rode to the Hastings' back yard. He dropped the lead to the second horse and jumped the bay over the picket fence and rode to the porch.

Mrs. Hastings cracked the door.

"I've come for Lorraine, Mrs. Hastings. Will you let her know I'm here?"

The woman wrung her hands. "We don't know where she is, Mr. Charles. Lorraine's been gone more than an hour. She said she had an errand before she left with you and your wife. We haven't seen her since. We're worried."

She peered past him. "Where is your lady wife?"

He grasped for the most convenient excuse. "She left earlier with Mrs. Cole and her family."

"Oh, then they must have been the ones I heard leave in the night. I'm a light sleeper. Strange thing is, they rode east instead of north toward Amarillo. Drove right by our barn. Are they visiting someone in Childress or Wichita Falls? That would explain such an early start. They have a long journey ahead of them if either place is their destination. Do you intend to meet up with them?"

The beauty and Hattie Cole. Blood lust filled him. They would not be traveling as far as Childress or Wichita Falls. The sheriff wanted them out of harm's way when the robbery occurred, so they may be camped only a few miles from here. He probably sent a lawman to protect them.

He smiled. "Oh, yes. Those are my intentions." He tipped his hat. "Please extend my regrets to Miss Hastings. I'm sorry, but I cannot wait. I hope she finds a way to visit Europe soon."

Ben helped Fred Staples to Doc's office. The banker bled profusely from a graze to his head, but he would live.

Staples clutched his shoulder. "Please, Ben, go check on my friends."

"I will. Sit still so Doc can patch you up." He left the office and moved into the deepest shade. He looked toward the water tower. Joe gazed to the east, his face intent.

With gun drawn, Ben moved to the side of the bank's back door and listened. Groans. He eased the door open and waited. More groans.

He entered and moved away from the opening, his eyes scanning the immediate area and then up the stairs.

One of the men sat up and grimaced, his right palm pressing a wound on his left shoulder. "Check on Leo and Marc, will you, Sheriff?"

The other two men lived but needed medical attention. He rose. "I'll bring Doc."

He left the doctor's office just as hooves and whistles sounded from the north. The armored vehicle and guards raced into town and stopped in front of the bank.

Ben's eyes widened to see twelve guards surrounding the wagon instead of six.

Seth Salter looked around and frowned. "We expected to be attacked." His eyes focused on Ben's bloody hands. "Something happened here?"

Ben explained just as Fred Staples opened the front doors and stepped onto the boardwalk, his head bandaged. He signaled for the guards to bring in their shipment.

Seth frowned. "Something isn't right. I know Bently had at least ten men planning to stop us. Where are they?"

Whistles. All eyes turned to the south as many horsemen rode in. The lawmen eased their hands toward their weapons.

Rancher Carl Jenson stopped in front of Ben and waved toward the line of ranchers and outlaws who followed.

He smiled. "Brought you a present, Ben. The other ranchers and I didn't take kindly to the idea scum like these planned to kill our sheriff and rob our bank, so we took matters into our own hands. We went hunting. Caught every one of them trespassing on our places. Thought about hanging them on the spot, but figured we'd do this the right way."

Ten outlaws, including Jake Dillon, rode in front of twenty angry, armed cattlemen and their cowboys. The robbers' hands had been tied behind their backs, and rope nooses decorated their necks.

Seth Salter laughed. "Do you wish to press trespassing charges, sir?"

"We do. They killed and butchered a couple of our cows for supper, so we also want them tried for cattle rustling. We'll testify at their trials—if they live to see them."

Seth signaled the other officers. They snagged the reins of each outlaw's horse and gazed at them with cold eyes.

Carl chuckled. "No need to worry they'll fall out of their saddles to get away. We rigged the ropes so they'll hang themselves if they try a stunt like that."

The cattlemen turned and left.

His deputies stepped up beside Ben.

Joe chewed his bottom lip and looked east. "Ben, I think we have more problems. Bently escaped. He rode east like a demon chased him after he spoke with Mrs. Hastings."

Dread filled Ben. "Did Lorraine ride with him?"

"No."

Seth frowned. "Quaid took your family five miles out of town to the northeast."

Ben's heart nearly stopped. "He knows! Bently plans to go after Hattie." He whirled and raced toward his horse, his deputies on his heels. Seth told the others he'd meet them in Amarillo, then followed.

With each breath, Ben begged God for mercy. *Please, Lord, please. Save my family. Let me get there in time.*

Hattie strode the length of the wagon and back. Buster paced beside her. She patted the dog's head, then shaded her eyes toward town. Afternoon shadows grew long. What had happened? Events should be resolved one way or the other by now. Was Ben okay? Were his deputies? Were her friends?

She turned toward the law officer. "Mr. Quaid, can we return yet? I'm worried about Ben."

James looked toward the southwest. "Not yet, ma'am. Salter said he'd come for us when the smoke cleared." He lowered his voice. "Best compose yourself for the sake of your daughter."

Hattie swung around. The panic in Sarah's face prompted her to rush to the little girl and lift her into an embrace. "We have to trust God, Sarah. Give your worries to him. I will too. Come. Sit beside me while I draw."

Sarah took a deep breath and nodded. Buster crowded close when they sat.

Hattie reached for her sketchbook and pencils and added more shadow and texture to the sketch of the small grove of hackberry trees already in process.

Furtive movement near the east end of the grove focused her attention. Was that Jem? He'd wanted to collect more firewood, but hadn't he gone to the west of the grove?

Her subconscious whispered something wasn't right. She stood and reached for Sarah's hand. "Come with me."

Buster followed. Did the dog sense her distress?

She stopped in front of James Quaid, her back to the trees. She forced her voice to remain calm. "Don't look up, but I think someone watches us from the east side of the grove."

He kept his head turned toward her, but his eyes panned the area. "Get behind the wagon."

She turned, but before she could obey, the watcher fired a shot into the ground at Hattie's feet. Dirt splattered her hem.

Sarah screamed and hid behind her, and Buster snarled at the approaching rider, his hackles raised.

"Drop your weapons, lawman. Raise your right hand and unbuckle the gun with your left." The outlaw Bently followed his command with another whizzing shot near Quaid's head.

Slowly, James unbuckled, his jaw tight.

"Now kick the belt away."

He did, and spoke from the corner of his mouth as Bently rode toward them. "Get behind me, Carrie."

She obeyed, and Bently yelled, "Stand still. All of you."

Hattie froze. Where was Jem? *Lord, please keep him out of harm's way.*

The outlaw dismounted ten yards from where Hattie stood. Max inched himself partway in front of her, and Hattie's fear rose. Would he take a bullet for her? She pressed a hand over her belly.

Bently walked toward them, pistol aimed and ready. His gloating expression sickened Hattie.

"Ah, Mrs. Cole. I have a bone to pick with you." He pointed toward the sketchbook. "You are the person most responsible for the capture of my gang. I also suspect you and your meddling husband aided and abetted my—" he smirked, "*wife* to escape."

Hattie said nothing.

"What? No words to speak in your defense? I didn't think so. Well, I've found you guilty of obstructing my plans and causing me great frustration. The penalty for your actions is death. I wish your husband was here to see this."

His cackling laugh sent fear spearing through Hattie. The outlaw didn't sound sane.

Carrie moved a step away from Quaid. "Leave her alone."

James held out his arm as if to block any further movement.

Bently looked her up and down and smiled. "Or what, little beauty? Once I take care of Mrs. Cole, I have big plans for you. You won't like them, but that is the price you'll pay for being found guilty by association."

Quaid growled low in his throat.

Carrie blanched and moved an inch closer to him.

The outlaw glanced at the others, a fiendish joy in his eyes. "Too bad I can't leave any witnesses alive."

Hattie's fear turned to rage when Bently threatened her family. Her fists clenched and she stared at him through a red haze. She wished for a weapon.

Buster picked up on her emotions. His taut muscles and deep growls indicated his desire to attack.

Bently glared at the large dog and raised the gun. "Animal control. I'll start with him."

The dog snarled louder.

"No," Sarah screamed.

Hattie caught her daughter's blouse before she could put herself in front of the dog. "Stay by me, Sarah."

At the moment Hattie expected the outlaw to pull the trigger, he yelped and almost dropped the gun. Blood erupted from a wound at his left temple.

Buster sprang. The impact of his body knocked Bently to the ground. He sank his teeth into the outlaw's arm and held.

Bently yelled and cursed and tried to shake off the dog.

James and Max lunged forward only a step behind Buster. Bently turned his pistol to shoot, but James wrestled the gun out of his hand, and Max punched him hard on the chin.

Bently's eyes rolled back in his head, and he stilled.

Max glared and shook his hand. "Wish I'd hit him harder."

James frisked the outlaw and spoke without looking up. "Get the pigging string tied to my saddle horn, Max."

Max raced to the wagon and returned with the rope cowboys used to tie the legs of cattle together after they had been lassoed.

He squatted next to Quaid and watched.

"Ah, he's got something up his sleeve." James removed the hideout gun and holster, told Max to take off the outlaw's boots and socks, then rolled him onto his stomach. He looped the pigging string around Bently's wrists and ankles and hog-tied them behind his back.

Hattie's heart threatened to pound out of her chest. Her hands shook. What had just happened?

Jeremy ran toward them, his eyes wide, and a rock clenched in his fist. He panted between words. "Mom, are you okay? I didn't know if I could hit Bently with any degree of accuracy. I had to creep up close enough to make him a bigger target. I didn't want to aim at his hand in case the rock pushed his gun away as he fired and his bullet hit one of you instead of Buster."

Thank you, God.

Hattie wept and embraced him. She stroked his hair. "You're my hero, Jem."

Sarah wrapped her arms around both of them and cried.

Minutes later, they looked up at the sound of racing hooves.

"Dad!" Sarah jumped up and down and waved.

Joy replaced Hattie's fear. Ben, his deputies, and Seth Salter rushed toward them, weapons ready. Her knees weakened, and she grasped the side of the wagon.

Ben dismounted before his horse stopped and embraced her and the children. "I thought I would be too late," he whispered near her ear, then kissed her neck.

Hattie brushed away tears. "I hoped you would come, but I didn't know if you were injured or dead."

Carrie approached, the fingers of her right hand intertwined with Quaid's left. "Hattie? Ben? Can we go home now? I'm ready to sleep in a real bed and eat food cooked on a stove."

Max stepped up beside Carrie and grinned. "She and Mr. Quaid have something important to tell you. I do too."

Hattie looked from Carrie's determined face to Quaid's serious one. Carrie gripped the lawman's hand as if she'd never let him go, so Hattie already knew what her sister would say.

But what was Max's news? He had the same determined look on his face Heath had worn when he told them he was leaving. Carrie would marry her marshal, but what would Max do? Would he stay in Texas with her? She smiled at the thought. Her poor parents. She knew they'd never leave Louisiana. Good thing Liza and her family were closer.

She eased her hand to her belly. "Yes, let's go home."

Salter tilted his head toward the prisoner. "I'll haul him to Amarillo." He dismounted.

Hattie watched the Ranger replace the pigging string with handcuffs. "What will happen to him?"

Seth's smile didn't reach his eyes. "What usually happens, ma'am. Texas offers swift justice to men like him. He'll be tried and probably hung for his crimes."

Hattie snuggled against Ben. She sighed her contentment when he stroked her hair.

Maxwell cleared his throat. "Hattie, what do you and Ben think about me staying here with you? I can help with whatever you need." His pleading gaze rested on Ben. "I'd like to learn law enforcement. Maybe in time, I could be one of your deputies?"

Hattie smiled. "I thought wanting to stay might be your request. I don't mind, but the decision is Ben's."

Ben nodded. "Let's talk more tomorrow."

Jeremy gave Max a sly smile. "Thought you'd stay—Uncle Max. We're irresistible, right?"

Max nodded and Hattie chuckled.

Carrie raised her chin and grasped Quaid's hand. "We're going back to Louisiana to marry. Then, we'll return to Texas."

Hattie's gaze moved to James and then to Carrie. "You think Mother and Father will approve?"

Carrie grimaced. "Probably not, but they'll have to when I start providing them with the grandchildren they want."

Quaid's ears turned red, but he nodded and grinned. "Told you she'd make a fine lawman's wife."

Ben chuckled. "Send us an invitation."

A SOLDIER'S HEART

ONE

Madilyn Banks held the yellow plastic container in front of her and frowned. "Thirty-eight dollars for a half gallon of organic degreaser?" She squinted at the label. "This isn't even concentrated."

She sighed and moved to the self-checkout station near the exit and scanned the label on the container. The scanner beeped at her, and an error message popped on the screen. *Great. Just great. Where is the attendant?*

Maddy noted the long wait in the next three lanes over, and her irritation grew. *I'm going to be late.*

"Yeah, you'd better move to another line if you don't want to hear what I'm going to say to him."

She looked up at the belligerent tone and watched people move away from three clench-fisted, hard-jawed men as fast as they could push their carts.

"I've had enough." Maddy reached for her cell, put the phone to her ear, and stepped closer to the men. She raised her voice. "9-1-1? Yes, I'd like to report an incident at Wilson's Market. Three men look like they intend to fight. Descriptions?" She glared at them and looked into each of their surprised eyes. "They are all about six feet tall and look like weightlifters. Two are twenty-nine, the third may be in his thirties. The one who has the angry-bull attitude has light, collar-length brown hair and brown eyes. His sidekick has curly auburn hair and blue eyes. I've seen them around. I've heard them called Cory Blake and Mike Daniels. That's right. Police Chief Blake's son. The third man has dark brown hair, gray eyes, and a military haircut and posture. He may be an inch or two taller than six feet. I haven't seen him before. Okay. Thank you."

She placed the cell in her pocket, turned, and moved to the now open register.

The clerk smiled, scanned the product, and took Maddy's money. "Never a boring day when you're around, Madilyn."

"Thanks, Robin. I think." She took the bag and strode out the sliding doors.

The three men waited for her. One put his hand on her arm. "Stop, Maddy, did you really call the cops on us? Dad will be hopping mad if you did."

She glared at his hand and then at him. "Don't touch me, Cory. I'm already irritated enough after the morning I've had, and that stunt you pulled in there—What were you thinking?"

He dropped his hand and frowned before cocking his head in the stranger's direction. "I caught this guy shadowing you in the store and looking at you in a way I didn't like. He said something that made me want to punch him. Mike and I were only trying to watch out for you."

Mike nodded.

She studied the man with the gray eyes. "How was he looking at me?"

Cory didn't hesitate. "Like he was hungry."

Her brows rose, and she rested her free hand on her hip. "Mister, what did you say to make my cousin want to punch you?"

Before Cory or Mike could say anything, he answered, "Though I was speaking to myself and not to them, I said you were the most beautiful woman I'd ever seen, and I was glad you didn't wear a wedding band."

His rich bass and soft southern drawl sent tingles up her arms. He smiled, and deep dimples showed on each side of his jaw. "I'm sorry if I offended any of you. My name is Wyatt Carter, and I'm new in town."

Maddy scanned him from head to toe. "Let me guess. You're stationed at Fort Carson?"

"Yes, ma'am."

"I'm Madilyn Banks. I prefer Maddy." She gestured toward her cousin. "This is Cory Blake, and that's Mike Daniels. Now, if you'll excuse me, I'm late for work."

Mike fidgeted. "Did you really call the cops on us, Maddy?"

She grimaced. "What do you think? I didn't, though I was sorely tempted. Now, I've got to go."

Cory relaxed his stance. "Do you, Charlie, and Aunt Brenda still plan to come to the barbecue later today at our place, Maddy? Mom said you could bring a friend if you want. We'll have plenty."

"Yes."

"Good." Cory waved as he and Mike left.

Maddy hurried to her car but glanced over her shoulder to see Wyatt watching her. He sauntered toward the parking lot.

She put the degreaser in the trunk and slid into the driver's seat. She turned the key and nothing happened. She tried again. *Click. Click. Click.*

"No!" She slammed her palms against the steering wheel. "This can't be happening."

Someone tapped on her window, and she turned and looked into the soldier's face. She lowered the window. He was close enough she caught the pleasant scent of his aftershave.

"Sounds like you've got a dead battery, ma'am. May I help?"

"Yes, or I'm going to be fired for sure if I don't get to work within the next seven minutes."

"I'll take you, if you don't mind riding in a truck."

His soft, deep drawl tugged at her and urged her to trust him, but she resisted. "I don't know you."

He smiled, and the corners of his eyes crinkled. "I'm Staff Sergeant Wyatt Carter, United States Army, ma'am. As you guessed, I'm thirty years old. I'm stationed at Fort Carson until my next deployment. Regardless of the light your cousin cast me in, I'm not a stalker or an axe murder."

"All right. I accept, Sergeant. Thanks."

She grabbed her purse and followed him to his truck. He opened the passenger door for her as if this was a habit ingrained in him from birth.

He buckled in. "Where to?"

"Turn right out of the parking lot. Get in the left lane and stay there for three blocks. Then turn left on the next street. You can drop me off at the big office complex on the right-hand side."

Once they turned out of the parking lot, he glanced at her. "I meant what I said in the store, Miss Banks."

She blinked a couple of times. "What did you say? I'm sorry, but the simplest tasks went wrong for me from the time I got up this morning, and everything that happened made me cranky. If I snapped at you, I apologize."

He chuckled. "I said you were the most beautiful woman I've ever seen, and that I'm glad you don't wear a wedding band."

Maddy turned to stare at him. "Well, all I can say is that for a soldier, you must be terribly sheltered if you think I'm the most beautiful woman you've seen. Where are you from?"

"West Texas."

"Ah, that explains your limited exposure." She grinned and tilted her head. "You're used to seeing more cows than women, right? At least, I saw a lot of cattle when I visited a friend in Amarillo."

He laughed. "I've seen hundreds of cows in my life, Lady, but I haven't seen a woman with such expressive brown eyes or brown hair so thick and silky looking a man wants to touch.

"But your kindness caught and held my attention. I followed you around the store listening to you mutter to yourself. I understood you were irritated and impatient, but I watched you stop to help a man get a product too high for him to reach. He thanked you, and you smiled. A real smile. You also raised a forty-pound dog food bag high enough in a little elderly woman's cart she could pull the cans of pet food out from under the bag."

He glanced at her left hand before returning his attention to the road. "Does some man have a claim on you, but you choose not to wear his ring?"

"No. No man. No ring." She pointed. "You can pull to the curb and I'll get out."

"Did you lock your car?"

"What? Yes, I always lock my car."

"Give me your key and I'll get you a new battery. What time do you get off? I can pick you up and take you back to the parking lot."

Maddy searched his face for any signs of duplicity or insincerity before removing the car key from the ring. "Here. I get off at five. Thanks, Sergeant. I'll pay you back this afternoon."

"Call me Wyatt, please."

"I will if you'll call me Maddy instead of ma'am."

"Deal. See you at five."

Maddy hurried through the revolving door and up to the second floor. She entered the office at exactly one o'clock and rushed to her desk.

Mr. Gates waited for her with a frown and crossed arms. "I see you're enjoying every minute of your forty-minute lunch break, Miss Banks."

Maddy had learned not to speak when Gates was miffed, which he was most of the time. She nodded and placed her purse in the bottom desk drawer, then sat and logged onto her computer.

Gates tapped his toe. "Did you send all those emails I asked you to?"

"Yes, before lunch."

"I'll need the files Dance and Shawcroft sent over. Have them on my desk by two. I'm assuming you entered the needed data from the files."

"Almost. I'll finish now." Maddy turned to her screen and reached for the next file in her dwindling stack. She ignored her boss as he grumbled his way to his office.

Stephanie Loft peeked from around her computer screen and grinned at Maddy. "I wonder what he ate for lunch. Dill pickles with sauerkraut, I'll bet."

"Or nothing. He gets this way when his belly's empty."

"I don't know how you've stuck around for five years. I've been here nine months, and he's about to make me crazy."

Maddy laughed. "His bark is worse than his bite, Steph. I need this job, at least for a while. The pay is really good if you discount the boss's personality."

Stephanie tossed her long, curly black hair over her shoulder in a defiant motion. "Hard to do when he huffs and puffs and threatens to blow our houses down every day."

Throughout the rest of the afternoon, Maddy's thoughts strayed to Wyatt Carter. She didn't deny something about him drew her, but she had no intention of getting involved with an active-duty soldier. She'd been through that heartache before. The only thing remaining to her of her older brother were fading memories, a folded flag, his picture, the purple heart he'd earned for his actions in Afghanistan, a space in the cemetery, and care of his young daughter.

She walked out of the building and her eyes immediately focused on Wyatt as he leaned against his truck.

He opened the passenger side and waited for her to get inside before closing the door and getting in the driver's seat.

She smiled. "Thanks for taking time out of your schedule to do this for me."

He stared at her mouth as if he couldn't look away. Finally, he did. "No problem, ma'am—Maddy."

He made a U-turn and headed toward the grocery store. Without taking his eyes from the road, he held out his hand. "Your key."

"Thanks. How much do I owe you for the battery?"

He shrugged. "The receipt is in the glove box."

She retrieved the slip of paper, looked at the amount, and removed the cash from her wallet.

His mouth tightened, but he said nothing.

When he parked beside her car and she handed him the money, she got the feeling he wanted to refuse but didn't.

"Hey, are you hungry?"

His eyes met hers. The dimpled grin appeared. "I'm always hungry, Lady."

"Well, the least I can do is feed you. My uncle throws an annual Fourth of July party at his place. We'll have plenty of food."

His eyes searched her face. "Do you think me showing up there would be wise after my encounter with your cousin earlier today?"

"Cory said I could bring a friend. You heard him. After your help today, you are now my friend."

He chuckled. "I hope he sees the situation in the same light."

Maddy shrugged. "He might not like you to be with me, but he'll leave you alone. He won't make a scene as long as Uncle Travis is around."

"The police chief?"

"Yes. He is much like the hard-nosed, no-nonsense kind of cops you see on television, but he has a tender heart under his rough exterior. Cory is a good guy, too, once you get to know him. He's overly protective since—" Maddy closed her eyes for a moment before opening them. "I need to change clothes and get Mom and Charlie, then you can follow us to the party."

⟡

Wyatt leaned against the truck, hands in his pockets. Within ten minutes, Maddy exited the house with an elegant dark-haired woman in her early fifties and an energetic little girl of about ten. *Charlie is a girl?*

He straightened.

The curly-haired Charlie pulled at Maddy's hand. "Come on, Mom, we're going to be late."

Wyatt's gaze traveled from the girl to Maddy. Madilyn Banks couldn't possibly be old enough to be the child's mother unless she'd had a baby at a young age, which, of course, was a possibility these days.

Maddy smiled at him, and he had to remember to breathe.

"Mom, Charlie, come and meet a new friend of mine. He's a soldier, and he's coming to the party with us." Maddy stopped a few feet away. "Wyatt Carter, meet my mother, Brenda Banks, and my daughter, Charlene. She wants to be called Charlie."

Brenda held out her hand and smiled. "Nice to meet you, Wyatt."

Wyatt shook her hand. "The pleasure is mine, ma'am."

Charlie studied him with solemn eyes. "You're a soldier?"

"Yes, little lady."

She chewed on her bottom lip. "My daddy was a soldier too. He went to war and never came back."

"I guess you're sad. I'm sorry." The words sounded lame to him, but what could he say?

Charlie shrugged. "That was six years ago. I was only four, so I don't remember him too much. He was gone a lot."

Wyatt stooped and put his hands on his thighs just above his knees and looked into Charlie's face. "My daddy died when I was a little older than you. He was a rancher and a cowboy. One day, he roped a mean old bull. His horse stepped into a gopher hole, and Daddy and the horse went down. The horse fell on top of him, and he died before the doctor could come. I was sad for a long time."

Charlie patted his cheek, and Wyatt's heart melted.

"Was your mama sad too?"

"I don't know. Mama left when I was a baby. She didn't want to be a mother, and she didn't like being on a ranch. She wanted to live in a big city in Europe. Dad and I never heard from her again."

Charlie stared at him for several moments, and he wondered what thoughts passed through the child's mind.

She flung herself at him and wrapped her arms around his neck. "I'm sorry, Wyatt."

Startled, he straightened with her in his arms and returned the hug. His eyes met Maddy's. Could she tell by his expression he was out of his depth?

Maddy's eyes held his, but she spoke to her daughter. "Okay, Charlie. Let Sergeant Carter breathe. Let's go. Your cousins and friends are waiting."

Charlie kissed his cheek and squirmed to get down. "Yay. I brought my swimsuit. We can play in the pool. I hope they don't splash me. I don't like water in my face."

"I'm sorry," Maddy whispered after Charlie got into the car. "She's never done that before, especially not to a stranger."

He leaned closer. *Wow, she smelled good.* "I'm not sorry. I haven't been the recipient of hugs for a long time."

He shouldn't have said that. Before he could see a look of pity or speculation in her eyes, he lowered his head and reached into his pocket for his keys.

"Okay. Follow us. We're only a few miles away." Maddy's soft voice stirred his blood.

Wyatt looked up and watched her open the car door. She glanced at him and smiled before slipping into the driver's seat.

He sucked in a breath and got into his truck. That smile did strange and powerful things to his insides. As Wyatt eased away from the curb, he took several deep breaths.

What had just happened? Within a little more than five hours, he'd been drawn, like a magnet, to two females he'd never met before. One created a deep longing inside him, and the other showed empathy he didn't expect from someone her age. The empathy touched his soul. Wyatt shook his head as if to clear his brain. How could they turn his world upside down so quickly?

"Over there." Maddy pointed toward the food table. "I think I see enough space for our stuff."

As he carried the salsa and chips to the table, Wyatt scanned the faces of the picnickers. He spotted Cory the same moment the man spotted him.

Wyatt pitched his words so only Maddy could hear. "Your cousin doesn't look happy to see me."

Maddy turned, scanned Cory and the group he stood with, then said, "Come. I want to introduce you."

Wyatt put the food on the table and followed her, his mind and body ready in case Cory threw a punch.

Maddy stopped beside her cousin and grasped his wrist. She didn't look at him, but turned toward her uncle. "Uncle Travis, I'd like to introduce you to a friend of mine. This is Sergeant Wyatt Carter. Wyatt, this is my uncle, Travis Blake."

The police chief scanned him from head to toe and offered his hand. "Army man?"

Wyatt shook his hand. "Yes, sir."

"Welcome, Sergeant. I did some time in the Army myself. Enjoy yourself. We have games, food, drinks, and fireworks when the sky gets dark enough."

Maddy introduced him to the others in the group, and when they meandered away, she turned slightly and tilted her head toward Cory before releasing his wrist. "Wyatt, I'd like you to meet my cousin, Cory Blake. Cory, Wyatt."

She stared at her cousin, her eyebrows raised as if daring him to make a scene.

Wyatt's eyes met Cory's. "Can we start on the right foot?"

Cory glanced from Maddy to him and back again. "Are you sure, Maddy?"

"Yes, I'm sure."

Cory nodded and looked into Wyatt's eyes. "Just know, Sergeant, nobody messes with my cousin and breaks her heart. If you try, you'll have me to deal with. Understood?"

Wyatt relaxed. "Understood."

Cory eyed him. "We're getting ready for a volleyball game. Are you in?"

The hint of challenge in his tone didn't escape Wyatt. He studied Cory's face. He guessed the man acted civilized for Maddy's sake, but Wyatt could sense the distrust under his smiling façade. Cory couldn't throw a punch here, so what better way to let off steam than to face his opponent across a volleyball net? "I'm in."

Cory turned to Maddy. "Will you play?"

Maddy shook her head. "Maybe later. Charlie's still not confident in the pool. I want to keep an eye on her."

Wyatt watched her lithe movements as she walked away. "You coming?"

The sharpness in Cory's voice turned Wyatt's attention. "Yes."

They played three games with two teams of six, but when the last game ended and the players moved toward the drinks and food, Cory and Mike challenged Wyatt and an athlete named Josh to a little two-on-two.

Wyatt noted the moment Maddy and Charlie sat down to watch, but he couldn't lose focus. The tightness of Cory's jaw and the gleam in his eyes signaled the man's intent to demolish him if he could. Wyatt removed his shirt.

After four grueling, intense games, the teams tied. They had drawn quite a crowd of encouragers who whistled and clapped when the last volley ended, but their voices had blended into the background in Wyatt's mind.

He approached the net and accepted Mike's and Josh's handshakes. After a moment, he offered his hand to Cory. "Good game."

Cory studied his face, then accepted the shake. "Yes, good game, Carter." He spoke to Mike and Josh. "Let's get some food."

Wyatt turned and sought Maddy as the crowd dispersed to the food tables. She waited in the shade, a towel and his shirt held out to him.

He stepped close and accepted the towel. "Thanks." He wiped the sweat from his face and chest. His eyes slid to Charlie's as he put on his shirt. "Why such a sad look?"

Charlie shrugged and kicked at a stick.

Maddy touched her shoulder. "Do you want to tell Sergeant Carter what's bothering you?"

Charlie looked up and frowned. She brushed away a tear. "I thought I was going to drown when the kids started splashing and yelling. They got water in my eyes and up my nose. Jimmy knocked me over trying to get away from Pam, and my head went under the water. Mom had to pull me out."

Wyatt studied Charlie's anxious face. "I can teach you to swim if you want me to—I mean, I can if your mom allows."

Charlie looked into his face, hope lighting her eyes. "You know how to swim?"

"Yes, I learned in a stock tank back home."

Maddy stared. "A stock tank? Like the round or oblong-shaped metal tanks farmers and ranchers use around here to water their animals?"

He laughed. "No, a stock tank to me is a pond to you."

Charlie tugged on Maddy's hand. "Can Wyatt teach me, Mom? Please? Then I won't have to be so afraid. I want to have a swim party for my birthday next month."

Maddy looked from Charlie's pleading face into his. She remained quiet for so long, he didn't know if she'd answer. "Yes. When and where?"

Wyatt relaxed. "I train for the next six days, but I think I'll be free on Saturday. Some of my unit officers and I have been put up at a local hotel until we finish training. We can use the hotel's pool. Will that work?"

She pulled out her cell. "Yes. Text me your number in case something comes up."

They exchanged contact information, and Wyatt smiled. "I'll pick you up. Be sure to bring your swimming suit too, Maddy."

"I will. Now let's eat. I'm hungry."

TWO

MADDY FORCED HER THOUGHTS AWAY from the enjoyable time she'd had with Wyatt at the Fourth of July picnic to focus on the task at hand. Being a personal assistant to a boss like Arnold Gates demanded her full attention and the patience of Job.

"Miss Banks, did you get my—"

"You can pick up yours and Mrs. Gates's tickets at the airline counter when you arrive at the airport."

Gates nodded. "What about—"

She handed him a printed sheet of paper. "Your confirmation number is at the top, and your itinerary follows."

He looked up. "And the—"

Maddy handed him two more sheets of paper. "Your rental car and hotel information."

The lines around his eyes eased. "Are you a mind reader, Miss Banks?"

Maddy smiled. "No, sir, but you ask me the same questions in the same order every trip you take."

"Hm. Maybe I'll have to change the order next time." He glanced toward Stephanie and then back at her. "I expect the office to run as smoothly while I'm at the conference next week as when I'm here."

"Of course."

Gates smiled. An actual smile. "You and Miss Loft may leave early today."

Stephanie gasped. "Thank you, sir."

Maddy handed him a packet. "Your conference badge, meal tickets, and session information are inside. Enjoy yourself in Hawaii, Mr. Gates."

He nodded and left.

Stephanie stared at the closed door. "What happened to him?"

Maddy chuckled. "He had food in his belly and the promise of sunshine and beaches to look forward to."

Stephanie stood and reached for her jacket. "I finished the last letter, so I'm leaving. Have a good weekend, Maddy."

"You too, Steph."

As she tidied her space and rose to leave, something inside Maddy relaxed. She smiled. She would spend time with Charlie and Wyatt tomorrow.

Be careful. Wyatt is here for only five or six more weeks, and then he'll be deployed. You may never see him again. Guard your heart. Guard Charlie.

Maddy nodded at her thoughts and slid into the driver's seat just as her cell rang. *Wyatt.* Her heart rate increased, and she smiled. "Hello."

"Hi, Maddy." Wyatt's deep drawl gave her chill bumps. "We finished training early this afternoon, so I'm calling to see if you and Charlie want to get some dinner when you get off. Your mom is invited too. My treat."

Maddy tried unsuccessfully to calm the elation pumping into her bloodstream. "Thanks. Dinner sounds good. My boss gave me the rest of the afternoon off, so I'm headed home now."

"Then I'll pick you up in an hour? We can beat the Friday night dinner crowd."

"See you then."

When Maddy shared Wyatt's invitation, Charlie squealed and rushed toward the stairs, her long curls bouncing with each step. "I need to change clothes."

Brenda chuckled. "Tell Wyatt I appreciate his invitation, but I've already made plans to meet with my book club tonight. Tell him I'll take a rain check."

Maddy nodded and moved toward the stairs. "I'm going to change too. Have fun with your friends."

Brenda's eyes sparkled. "I will. You and Charlie have fun on your date."

Maddy spoke over her shoulder. "This isn't a date, Mom."

Brenda laughed. "Uh-hum."

Wyatt raised his hand to ring the bell, but before he could, Charlie flung open the door.

"I'm ready, Wyatt. Mom's coming. Where are we going? I'm starving."

"You and your mom get to decide."

"Good. Mom and I don't like the same things, so we go to the buffet. I can get what I want then."

He laughed. "That's smart. Is your grandmother coming?"

"No, she has book club tonight."

Secretly, her words relieved him. His single-cab truck wouldn't fit four comfortably.

Maddy stopped behind Charlie and their gazes met. He stilled and maintained eye contact. His chest tightened. How could one look from those brown eyes leave him speechless?

She smiled. "Looks like we're headed to the buffet."

He returned the smile. "Looks like. I'm starving too, so let's go."

Charlie chatted all the way to the restaurant about her swimming lessons. "I just hope I'm not too scared."

Wyatt walked the ladies to their front door. He didn't want to leave yet, but he didn't know what he could do or say to prolong their time together. He couldn't think of a day as enjoyable as this one.

Maddy inserted her key into the lock and pushed the door open. "Do you want to come in for something to drink, Wyatt?"

"Yes, thanks." He followed them inside and looked around. He took a deep breath. "Comfortable. Cozy. Feels and smells like home."

His gaze slid to a shelf where a framed photograph of a uniformed soldier rested next to a folded flag and an open box containing a purple heart. He moved toward the shelf and stood in front of the display.

Charlie followed and clasped his hand. "That's my dad. He was a hero."

Wyatt studied the image, then looked down at her. "You look like your dad and your mom."

"Maybe." Charlie shrugged. "I didn't know my mom. She died in a car accident when I was a baby."

"What?" Wyatt frowned. "Your mom—?"

Maddy stopped on his other side. "That's my older brother, Thad. I adopted Charlene when she was four. I had just turned twenty-one."

"I'm sorry for your loss." The standard response didn't come close to capturing the feelings inside him, but he didn't know what to say, so he remained quiet. Loss of life in a combat zone was the norm, but the loss of a loved one to those who waited back home was earth-shattering.

Maddy waved toward the sofa. "Have a seat and I'll bring you something. Would you prefer coffee, tea, kombucha, or water?"

He lifted an eyebrow. "Kombucha? What is that?"

"Fermented green and black tea."

Charlie smiled. "I like kombucha. The fizz tickles my nose and tummy. Mom won't let me drink soda, but she says kombucha is good for my insides."

Wyatt chuckled. "Then I'll try kombucha on your recommendation."

Maddy tilted her head toward the kitchen. "Charlie, why don't you get the plate of cookies Gigi left for us on the counter. Bring napkins."

Charlie hopped off the sofa and followed.

Wyatt studied the room in more detail. Once he left the Army, he wanted a home like this. The colors soothed, and the textures and materials invited him to relax.

He closed his eyes and identified the scents. Freshly baked cookies. Furniture polish. A hint of roasted meat from lunch. Chicken maybe? A clean, heady scent that could only be Maddy. He opened his eyes.

She grinned and handed him a cold bottle of kombucha. "Were you about to fall asleep?"

His eyes met hers. "No. Just enjoying a real home. I'll think of the sights and smells of this place while I'm sitting under camo netting trying to stay cool, or freezing in some mountainous environment."

Maddy's eyes clouded when he mentioned his upcoming deployment.

"My guess is the latter. My unit was sent to Fort Carson for a reason. This post offers high altitude mountain training, in terrain we might face overseas."

Charlie gazed at him with solemn eyes. "Are you scared, Wyatt?"

He searched his mind. "I'm not scared yet. I may be when I get where the Army sends me and I have to face the enemy. Scared or not, little lady, I have to do my job. Understand?"

She nodded and spoke in a small voice. "I'll miss you, Wyatt. Will you write to me when you're gone?"

"Of course. We can also text, email, or video chat if you want. I'd like to have someone to write home to." He tapped the tip of her nose. "Hey, let's not think about my leaving yet. That's weeks away. Deal?"

Her curls bounced at her nod. "Okay. I'll think about my swimming lessons tomorrow instead."

He grinned. "Good idea." Then he lifted the kombucha bottle and stared at the contents. "Are you sure I should try this? I think something's floating in mine."

Maddy laughed. "Those are scoby particles. They won't hurt you. Be brave, soldier."

He eyed the bottle one more time, then took a sip.

Maddy and Charlie waited to see what he would say. He took a bigger swallow. "I could get used to this."

Maddy nibbled on a cookie. "Do you plan to stay in the Army for several more years?"

"No. After this deployment, I'm up for reenlistment. I'll leave the military and work at a civilian job. I can make more money."

Maddy studied his face. "What kind of job?"

"I've done well in the mechanical and engineering parts of my career. I know how to operate, repair, and maintain heavy equipment like bulldozers, tractors, backhoes, cranes, excavators, and road graders. Whether I return to Texas or look for a job here, my skills are marketable in many places."

Charlie tilted her head. "Texas? Will you go back to your ranch?"

"No, not to live, but maybe for a visit. My uncle owns the ranch now. I'd probably work on oilfield equipment or on a construction site if I took a job back there."

Maddy leaned forward. "Once you get a job, then what? What do you want from life?"

Her question cut to the heart of his dreams. He didn't know if he should share, but she waited as if his words would decide something important.

Wyatt's eyes met and held hers. His voice deepened. "I want a peaceful, comfortable home like this one. I want a wife and children and maybe a couple of dogs. I want all the good things I've missed since Dad died and I've been overseas." *I want to love and be loved.*

Maddy's eyes softened. "Those are good dreams to have, Wyatt. I hope you get what you desire."

I desire you and Charlie the most. He clamped his lips shut to keep the words from leaving his mouth, but he wondered if Maddy could read the same thoughts in his eyes. They'd known each other for only a week, so he'd be crazy to say such words aloud.

Maddy smiled at Charlie. "Time for bed. Go get ready, and I'll come up to tuck you in."

Charlie started for the stairs but stopped and turned. "Can Wyatt come and tuck me in too, Mom?"

Startled, Maddy looked at him.

He recognized her uncertainty. "I don't know what tucking a young lady in involves, Charlie, but if this is something important to you, I'd be happy to do so with your mom's permission and guidance."

"Good. I'll see you in a few minutes." She raced up the stairs.

He studied Maddy's face. "You okay with this?"

She nodded.

"What does Charlie expect me to do? I've never tucked someone in before."

Maddy picked up the plate of cookies and headed to the kitchen. He followed with the empty kombucha bottles.

"Just watch and learn, Wyatt. No mechanical or engineering certificates required."

When he entered Charlie's bedroom behind Maddy, the little curly-haired beauty smiled as she lay propped on a pillow. "I'm ready."

Wyatt looked to Maddy for instruction, but Charlie spoke. "Sit on the bed beside Mom."

He complied.

"Now we say our prayers. Do you want to go first, or do you want me to?"

Wyatt's heart pounded. He hadn't spoken to God in front of people in ages. "You and your mom go first."

Charlie reached for his and Maddy's hands. "Now hold Mom's hand."

Could Maddy hear how loudly his heart pounded against his chest when she slipped her hand into his? Did she feel the electric shock when they touched? This was torture.

Charlie closed her eyes. "Dear God. Thank you for this day. Thank you for Wyatt. He's a soldier and needs you to protect him from the bad things of war. Let him come home safely. Thank you for my mom and for Grandma Gigi. They love me. Thank you for my cousins and friends. I ask you to not let me be afraid tomorrow when I get in the pool. Thank you for sending Jesus. In his name, I pray these things. Amen."

As soon as Charlie finished, Maddy began.

Wyatt listened to her tell God how wonderful he was and how she delighted in him. She gave thanks for the day, for health, and for the good things he put in her life every day. She prayed for Wyatt and asked God to keep him safe and to return him home. When she said amen, he tried to swallow the lump in his throat. His insides shook, and he sensed a waiting Presence.

"You're next, Wyatt," Charlie whispered.

Wyatt opened his mouth, but the only words he could speak were, "Oh, God—" Long-buried grief and hurt choked him. Visions of war and the loss of friends rose to haunt him. Things he'd done, said, or thought that he shouldn't have, flashed across his brain. His soul shrank.

"Forgive," he whispered to the Presence.

Maddy and Charlie waited for him to regain his control. Their silent support and warm hands eased his turmoil.

Charlie squeezed. "You and Mom pull up my covers and kiss me goodnight now."

Maddy stroked Charlie's forehead and bent to kiss her. "Night, darling. I'll see you in the morning."

"Goodnight, Mom." She looked expectantly at Wyatt.

He stooped and kissed her forehead, and Charlie wrapped her arms around his neck and kissed his cheek. "Goodnight, Wyatt. I'll see you tomorrow."

Wyatt kissed her again before standing. He refused to look Maddy in the eyes. His moment of unexpected weakness embarrassed him. "Goodnight. I'll see you both tomorrow. I can see myself out."

Wyatt got inside his truck and buckled up. He leaned his head against the rest and closed his eyes before starting the engine. He tried to calm his breathing, but his heart and lungs felt like he'd run five miles with a heavy pack. Yet, he also felt . . . lighter. Unburdened. Relieved. He opened his eyes.

The sense of God's presence filled him.

"Thank you," he whispered, and pulled away from the curb.

THREE

Maddy eased into the water and stopped beside Wyatt as he coached Charlie.

"The first thing we're going to do is have fun, so that's why I had you put on your life vest. You can't sink or drown with that on."

Charlie hesitated. "Are you sure, Wyatt?"

"Positive. Here, take my hand."

Charlie grasped his hand. He led her toward the deep end. When he drew her against his chest, she clasped him around the neck.

"Relax. Cup your hands and move them out and in by your sides like this." Wyatt bent his knees so he could get lower in the water.

"I can't touch here." Panic edge Charlie's voice.

"I know. Trust me. Let go of my neck and move your hands like I showed you. Your mom and I are right here. We won't let anything happen to you."

Charlie let one hand go at a time.

Maddy floated next to her. "Look at you, you're paddling in the deep end."

Wyatt smiled. "Good job. Now, watch my legs. I want you to move yours in the same way."

Within ten minutes, Charlie could tread water by herself. "Look, Mom. Look at me."

Some of the bare-chested men from Wyatt's unit lounged around the pool with cold drinks. They clapped and cheered.

Charlie looked up and smiled.

Wyatt gave the men a thumbs up and asked Charlie if she was brave enough to try something new.

She looked from the men to Wyatt. "Yes, what?"

"Lean back and float. Like this." Wyatt stretched out beside Maddy.

"Help me."

Wyatt pulled Charlie close. "When you're ready, put your head back and pretend you're resting on a cloud. The life vest will hold you."

Charlie made sure the men around the pool watched before releasing Wyatt and stretching out.

The men cheered. One told her she looked like a mermaid sunning herself in the ocean.

Maddy grinned. His words were sure to capture Charlie's fancy.

Wyatt floated beside her. "If you ever get tired swimming, always turn and float on your back."

"Okay."

"I brought a ball and a net. Do you and your mom want to play water volleyball?"

"Sure." Charlie lowered her legs and resumed her slow tread.

Maddy helped Wyatt attach the net to the sides of the pool, then swam to Charlie. "Charlie and I will stay on the shallow end." She grinned at her daughter. "You ready to beat Wyatt?"

"Yes!"

Once they played a gentle game of volleyball, Charlie paid no attention to her fear of water. Wyatt had engaged her competitive spirit.

"Can I take my life vest off now, Wyatt?"

"Not yet. I want you to move yourself up and down the pool several times. Down and back is one lap. See how many laps you can do while your mom and I swim, okay?"

Charlie looked toward the men.

"You got this, little mermaid," one of them said. "I'll count for you."

"Ready to burn off some energy, Maddy? Three laps?"

Wyatt's dimpled grin invited her to accept his challenge. "All right."

They stood at one end of the pool, and Maddy smiled at Charlie. "Tell us when to go."

"Ready, set, go!"

They dove into the water.

Maddy had swum on her high-school swim team years before and had enjoyed the competition, but she'd never raced against a conditioned athlete like Wyatt. She forced her arms and legs to move faster. She'd try to give him a run for his money.

The race ended as she expected, with Wyatt a lap ahead. He waited at the end, chest heaving, and arms spread and resting on the pool's edge. The grin on his face and the gleam in his eyes told her how much he'd enjoyed even a nominal competition such as this.

Her lungs and muscles burned, so she flipped on her back and floated, her hands making tiny back-and-forth motions. *Ah.* The sun felt good on her face and the water soothed. She smiled and closed her eyes.

Wyatt spoke near her ear. "I wish I had a picture of you floating so serenely. I'd take the photo out and pretend I'm floating beside you when I need to feel peace."

She didn't open her eyes. "Feel the peace now, Wyatt."

He stretched out and floated next to her, their fingertips touching.

"Mom, are you asleep?" Charlie moved next to her.

Maddy opened her eyes. "No, but I'm hungry."

Charlie nodded. "Me too."

Wyatt tilted his head toward their observers. "The guys fired the grill. Want some hamburgers or hot dogs?"

"Yes!" Charlie moved to the steps as fast as she could and shed her life vest.

Maddy turned on her stomach, pushed off the bottom, and did a couple of butterfly strokes to the stairs.

Wyatt followed close behind. "That was fun."

"Yes, though I wasn't much competition." Maddy dried and donned her wrap. "Thanks for your help, Wyatt."

He nodded. "I'll let Charlie take off her life vest next time, and I'll show her how to dog paddle, put her face in the water, and blow bubbles."

Maddy's gaze followed her daughter as she moved toward the men. "Are those soldiers trustworthy around little girls?"

Wyatt dried and draped the towel around his neck as he also tracked Charlie. "Yes. The guy cooking the burgers is my best friend, Lewis Stock. We've been through a lot together. Come on. I'll introduce you."

Sudden shyness enveloped Maddy when ten men in their prime smiled and gave her compliments and admiring glances.

One stepped forward and showed his phone to Wyatt. "Got some good shots here. I'll send them to your phone and you can share with the mermaid and her mom."

"Thanks, Joe." Wyatt received the images and smiled. "Come and look, Maddy."

She stepped close and watched as he swiped from the image of him holding Charlie close to his chest, a tender look on his face, to them both swimming close to Charlie as she floated, to a close-up of Wyatt and her diving into the pool, and then to them floating side-by-side with eyes closed. She stared at the last image for several moments.

Wyatt stared at the same image. "These are good. I want to get more pictures so I can take them with me overseas." He looked up. "You're beautiful, Miss Banks."

"And you're—" She shook her head. "I don't have the words to describe you right now."

He looked up, concerned. "Give me a hint. Good or bad?"

She smiled. "Better than good."

"That relieves my mind. Now, how about a burger and something cold to drink?"

"Please."

As Maddy chatted with Wyatt's friends over the next few hours, her shyness dissipated. She listened to their stories of wives, children, or girlfriends back home, and the plans they had after they returned from deployment.

Charlie put a hand on her knee. "I'm tired, Mom, can we go home?"

"Sure."

Maddy turned to Wyatt. "Will you take us home now?"

He stood and put on his shirt. "Yes."

They collected their things and bid goodbye to Wyatt's friends.

"Come back soon, little mermaid," Joe smiled. "We want to see how good a swimmer you become."

"Okay." Charlie clasped Wyatt's hand just as Joe snapped another picture.

Wyatt spoke over his shoulder. "Send that one too, Joe."

They got into Wyatt's truck, and he pulled away from the curb. After two blocks, Charlie slumped against Maddy, sound asleep.

She put her arm around her daughter and drew her close. "She's worn out, but she'll never forget this day."

"I won't either."

Maddy studied his face but said nothing.

"What are you two doing tomorrow? I'm training in the afternoon, but my morning should be free."

"We go to church at nine. Do you want to come?"

"Yes. I want to be with you as often as I can for as long as I can."

"Why?"

His eyes met and held hers. "Honestly, I haven't had much of a family life, Maddy. Dad did the best he could, but we worked long, hard days on the ranch. We came in, showered, ate, and went to bed. Then we started over again the next day.

"In the Army, my buddies are my family. We watch out for each other. But what you and Brenda and Charlie have is something I've only dreamed of. When I'm with you, I feel—" He shook his head. "I can't describe what I feel. The closest I can get is . . . home."

She considered his words. "Breakfast is at seven forty-five. Don't be late. We'll leave at eight-thirty. You'd better ride with us because Mom is coming. We'll take her SUV. We'll eat an early lunch so you can return to Fort Carson with a full stomach."

"Yes, ma'am."

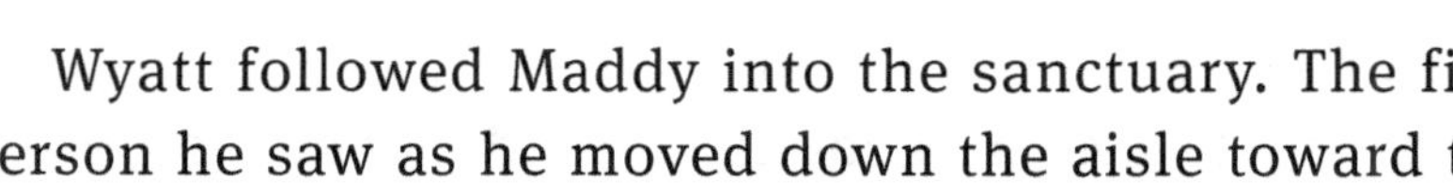

Wyatt followed Maddy into the sanctuary. The first person he saw as he moved down the aisle toward the middle section was Cory. The man saw him at the same time and frowned.

Wyatt gave him a brief head nod.

Charlie slid onto the bench next to her cousin. "Hi, Cory." She leaned forward. "Aunt Caroline. Uncle Travis."

The police chief smiled. "Hi, yourself, little munchkin."

Brenda sat next to Charlie and patted her hand. "From what I hear, Travis, she's a little mermaid now."

Charlie grinned. "I am. That's what Wyatt's friends call me."

Cory's eyebrows rose. "Wyatt's friends?"

"Yes. The other soldiers. They watched Wyatt teaching me to swim and said I looked like a mermaid."

Maddy sat, and Wyatt took the aisle seat next to her. With the police chief, his wife, Cory, and them, they sat as close as ticks on a dog. He didn't mind. He could feel Maddy's warmth next to him, and her scent heightened his awareness.

He could also sense Cory's irritation and suspicion from the other end of the pew. He hoped the younger man would leave him alone and not provoke an unpleasant situation. With a handful of weeks left and tension building in his gut, he wanted to enjoy this peace before he had to face war again.

The congregation rose to sing, and Wyatt read the words projected onto a large screen. He listened as Maddy and Brenda sang in two-part harmony. With a subtle movement, he brought out his phone and hit the record button.

When they sat for the sermon, Maddy opened her Bible and showed him the passage. Her hand brushed his, and he stilled inside.

Wyatt made himself focus on the message. The main points came from Mark 8:34 - 37.

> And when he [Jesus] had called the people *unto him* with his disciples also, he said unto them, Whosoever will come after me, let him deny himself, and take up his cross, and follow me.

> For whosoever will save his life shall lose it: but whosoever shall lose his life for my sake and the gospel's, the same shall save it.

For what shall it profit a man, if he shall gain the whole world, and lose his own soul?

Or what shall a man give in exchange for his soul?

What shall a man give in exchange for his soul? The question nagged him. He hadn't thought about his soul much. He wished he had a Bible so he could reread those verses.

At the end of the service, he leaned toward Maddy and whispered, "The man giving the announcements said they had free Bibles if a person wanted one."

She nodded. "At the table in the foyer."

"I want one. Will you mark the passage we read today?"

"Yes."

They stood just as Cory approached. He must have zipped out the aisle nearest him and around the back.

He stopped beside Wyatt and pushed his shoulder into Wyatt's personal space. "So, you're still around, Sergeant? Heard you're teaching Charlie to swim."

Wyatt held his ground and forced himself to remain calm. He kept his tone conversational. "Yes, I'm still around, and yes, I'm teaching Charlie to swim."

Maddy looked from him to Cory. She'd be blind not to recognize her cousin's aggressive stance and deaf not to hear the edge to his question.

She stroked Cory's face. "Back off. Charlie and I are in no danger from Wyatt." She kissed his cheek and gave him a gentle push. "But I love you for wanting to protect me."

Cory stepped back, his brows furrowed. "What's going to happen to you and Charlie when Carter leaves? The closer you get, the harder the separation."

Maddy nodded. "I know. We'll have to deal with this sooner rather than later. But, Cory, neither you nor I can protect Charlie from all of life's problems. She needs to develop skills to handle them."

"She's just a little girl."

"She's a young girl who will be eleven in August. She'll spend one more year in elementary school, then she'll go to middle school. I can promise you, she'll be faced with a lot of issues then."

Wyatt listened to the conversation, his emotions in turmoil. Blake had a point. Sharp spears of pain punctured his soul at the thought of leaving Maddy and Charlie. How would he feel five weeks from now if they became a regular part of his life, and then he deployed? Should he ease out of the friendship to save them heartache?

No! He couldn't. Not seeing them would be as painful as severing a limb.

He didn't say much on the return to the Banks' home, and Maddy cast him several questioning glances from the front seat.

Wyatt followed Charlie into the house and stopped. The aroma of roasting and baking surrounded him like a warm, comfortable blanket. He took a deep breath. "Ah, this is heavenly."

Brenda chuckled. "Thank you, Wyatt. Why don't you fill the water glasses while Maddy and I get the food out of the oven."

She winked at Charlie. "How about you set the table, little mermaid?"

"Sure, Gigi."

Wyatt didn't remember ever having a meal like this. The feeling of home and comfort grew. He leaned back and listened to their conversation and watched their expressions. Love. Tangible love. The longing inside him grew to giant proportions.

His gaze lingered on Maddy.

When they all started to clear the table, he stood and helped.

He stopped close to her. "Can we talk before I go?"

She nodded and searched his face. "Are you okay? You've been quiet since Cory went into protective-cousin mode."

"Yes, I'm okay."

Maddy took off her apron. "Mom, I want to talk to Wyatt before he leaves."

Brenda smiled. "Fine. Charlie and I plan to bake cookies he can take with him. We'll make enough he can share with his friends."

Moisture came and went in Wyatt's eyes, and he looked down.

Maddy touched his arm. "Come. We've got a covered swing in the backyard."

She sat and patted the cushion beside her. "What's on your mind?"

He sat next to her and turned to see her face. "Cory was right, you know. The more we're together, the harder the separation will be. I don't want to hurt you or Charlie, so shall I back out of your lives gracefully now, before things get painful?"

Maddy's eyes widened. She studied him for several moments. "No."

The tightness in his chest eased. "You're sure?"

"Yes. What else? I can tell you have something more on your mind."

He took a couple of deep breaths. "I'm seeing a Judge Advocate on the post next week after training. I'm updating my Will."

Maddy straightened and frowned. "Why? Do you have a bad feeling about this next deployment? Do you think something is going to happen to you?"

"No, but I want—" he stood and paced before stopping in front of her. "Will you come with me?"

"Sit. Your pacing makes me nervous."

He sat and looked into her face. "I'm changing my Will to make you the beneficiary."

"What?" She stared.

"I don't have parents or siblings, Maddy. Yet, in a short time, you and Charlie have become the family I never had. I know this sounds strange considering our short acquaintance, but I don't have a lot of time before I leave. Already, I can feel the predeployment tension building inside.

"If something were to happen to me, I'd want you and Charlie to benefit. I'd want to know anything I left behind could help you in some way."

Maddy brushed away sudden tears, and he reached for her hand. "Will you come?"

She stared at their clasped hands, then looked up. "Yes. When?"

"Late afternoon on Friday. I'll text you the address and get you a pass." He smiled. "I thought Charlie might want another swimming lesson on Saturday. I'm training all day Sunday and Sunday night, or I'd go to church with you."

Wyatt relaxed against the cushions, his fingers still intertwined with hers. He gave the swing a gentle push and listened to her soft breathing and the hushed sounds of a lazy July afternoon. A man could get addicted to this.

FOUR

MADDY LOGGED ONTO HER COMPUTER. "Okay, Steph. Pull up a chair. Let's make a plan. I'm sure the boss will call every afternoon after his sessions to make sure we have our noses to the grindstone, so we don't want to give him cause for more huffing and puffing."

Stephanie rolled her chair over to Maddy's desk and opened her spiral notebook. She read all the things she had on her list.

Maddy shared hers. "Let's prioritize and make sure we get the most important tasks done first."

Without Gates's constant interruptions and instructions, they accomplished much by lunch.

Stephanie stood and stretched. "I'm going to the corner café for lunch. Want to come?"

Maddy nodded. "Save me a place. I need to finish one more thing, then I'll head that way."

"Okay." She grabbed her purse and left.

Maddy finished her last task just as her cell rang. She looked at the number and smiled. *Wyatt.* "Hey, you."

"Hey, Lady. Just thought I'd call and say hello. I have a little break before we return to the field."

"Kind of hot to be outside right now."

"That's an understatement, especially wearing all my gear, but training is training, no matter the weather."

"I don't envy you. I'm headed to the corner café to have lunch with Stephanie Loft, my best friend who works in the same office. I'll enjoy the air conditioning and think of you."

"That hurts, Maddy."

She laughed and exited the building.

"Hey, Lady. Tell Brenda and Charlie the cookies were a hit. We demolished the whole bag in under thirty minutes."

"I'm sure they'll make more. I'll bring them to you on Friday."

Warmth unrelated to the sun enveloped Maddy as she walked down the street listening to Wyatt's deep voice and soft Texas drawl.

She entered the café. "I've got to go now. Talk to you later."

"Yes, ma'am."

Stephanie studied her face when she sat down. "You look like the cat who ate the cream, so that call must not have been from our boss."

Maddy blushed. "No, from a soldier stationed at Fort Carson."

Stephanie leaned forward, her eyes shining. "Tell."

Maddy opened the menu. "What do you want to know?"

"Everything. How did you meet? What's he like? The basics."

After they ordered, Maddy related her experiences with Wyatt.

"You better latch onto this one. If you don't want him, send him my way. If you do, see if he has a single friend interested in connecting with a hard-working girl like me. Hey, maybe your cousin Cory is looking. I met him once. Seems like a nice guy."

"He's a super nice guy, Steph. A little overprotective since Thad died, but I can't fault him for that."

She grinned. "Neither can I."

By the time Gates called to check on things, Maddy and Stephanie had finished all that day's work and started on the next.

"I'm impressed, Miss Banks. Glad to see the mice don't play while the cat is away. I'll check in about the same time tomorrow."

"All right. How's Hawaii?"

"Splendid, and the sessions are valuable. I'll tell you more about them when I get back." Maddy could hear the smile in his voice.

Wyatt phoned Maddy every day for the rest of the week. Sometimes he called during her lunch break or at night after he finished training and had eaten and showered.

She always sounded glad to hear from him, and he enjoyed getting to know her better.

On Thursday, he lounged in a chair beside his bed and waited for her to answer his call.

"Hi, Wyatt."

"Hey, Lady."

"How was training today?"

"Hot. Hard. Grueling. About the same as always. How was your day?"

"Cool. Easy. A little boring. About the same as always. The boss gets back on Saturday, so Steph and I are getting everything ready for his return to the office on Monday."

"Boring, huh? What would you rather be doing if you could?"

"Getting a graphics design degree. I could work for a company, freelance, or do both. As long as I had the right software and a good internet connection, I'd have a lot of options. I would set my own schedule, so I could be here when Charlie gets home from school."

"When will you start this degree?"

She laughed. "Maybe after Charlie graduates from high school. When would I have time to do this before then?"

"Maybe you should think about night school, summer school, or online classes."

Silence. Had he overstepped?

"Those are good ideas, soldier. I took some of the prerequisites before I became a mom at twenty-one."

He chuckled. "If I remember correctly, classes start in August or September. Better get your paperwork in."

She laughed again. "You're funny."

"No, I'm serious. As smart and organized as you are, I bet you could finish in under two years."

"I'll check into things."

He hesitated. "Maddy, after we meet with the lawyer tomorrow afternoon, do you want to get some dinner? I'd like to talk to you about a few other things."

"Hang on. Let me see if Mom has plans or if she can watch Charlie."

He held his breath until she returned.

"Yes, I'll have dinner with you. Is this business or a date, Wyatt? A woman has to know this kind of information so she dresses appropriately."

He grinned. "A date with a tiny bit of business thrown in."

"All right. See you tomorrow afternoon. Goodnight."

"Goodnight. Give Charlie a kiss from me. Tell her I'll see her on Saturday, and that my buddies and I really look forward to her cookies."

"Will do."

"I l—." He stopped the next words from leaving his mouth, though he thought them. *I love you.* "See you soon."

Wyatt paced the foyer of the Judge Advocate General's office while he waited for Maddy to arrive. Knowing four weeks and a few days remained before he deployed made him antsy. He had so much to do.

She pulled into a parking space and stepped out of the car.

Her appearance winded him. He took a deep breath and opened the door for her. "You're stunning, Lady. That bright pink dress looks really good on you."

She leaned forward and whispered in his ear. "You're rather stunning yourself, soldier. Dark gray silk shirts suit you."

He stopped himself from turning his head and drawing her into his arms. He wanted to kiss her right then and there. *Too fast. Don't scare her.* Instead, he clasped her hand and led her to the receptionist. "We're ready."

She nodded and tilted her head toward a closed door. "You can go in now."

An hour later, they each left the office with a packet of information.

Maddy's solemn look concerned him. He stopped her. "Are you all right?"

Her chin trembled. "I hope this all turns out to be unnecessary. I don't want you to die, Wyatt."

He stopped one of her teardrops with his thumb. "I don't want to die either, Maddy, but I have to be prepared. Anything can happen in a combat zone."

"I know. Thad's death taught me that."

He lifted her chin with an index finger. "How about we talk more over dinner?"

She gave him a watery grin. "I know. You're starving, right?"

"Always."

"Let's go. I'll follow you to the restaurant, unless . . ."

"Unless what?"

"Once we leave the post, there is a strip mall on our way home. We could take one vehicle and pick the other one up after dinner."

Wyatt smiled. "I like that idea. Shall I drive you, or will you drive me?"

She held up the keys. "You'll drive me in my car."

Wyatt didn't bring up the business side of the date until they'd finished their meal. "Maddy, I have more to ask you. Are you ready to hear?"

"Yes."

"Will you agree to be added as a signer on my checking and savings accounts, and will you help me out by paying any bills that come when I'm gone? I do most of my banking online. My government checks are automatically deposited, and the few monthly bills I have are on autopay. I'll give you my logins and passwords."

Her eyebrows raised. "In a time of rampant identity theft, you'd trust me to do this?"

His eyes met and held hers. "I would trust you with my life, Maddy. Though I haven't known you long as far as time is concerned, I know you. I've looked into your eyes and seen honesty and integrity. I've watched you interact with others.

"My buddies, who are great judges of character, say they know you're trustworthy because of the care you give Charlie and how respectfully you interact with them. They can spot insincerity and deception quickly."

"Tell me what kind of bills you're talking about."

He shrugged. "I have simple tastes some might call Spartan. What credit card expenses I incur are paid at the end of each month. I let go my half of the apartment I shared with Joe, because I knew I wouldn't re-enlist, so I don't have housing expenses yet. I pay cash for groceries. I don't have pets, so I don't need a sitter."

Maddy grinned. "What about your truck? What will you do with that while you're gone?"

"The truck isn't mine. One of the guys stationed at the post lent this to me for as long as I train at Fort Carson. In exchange, I replaced the truck's worn tires with new ones. I pay for the gas I use, and I service the vehicle."

"You're a marvel, Wyatt Carter. I don't know anyone who has fewer expenses than you. Yes, I'll agree to be a signer and pay whatever bills come."

"You don't know how much this relieves my mind, Maddy. The only thing is, I'll have to ask you to get my information to an accountant when the time comes. If you have a good one, see if he or she will accept a new client."

"I have a great accountant. Mom. She does all our taxes. Though she's semi-retired, she keeps her license. I'll see if she can work you into her schedule."

"I will pay her fee."

Maddy glanced at her watch. "I'd better get home. I want to say goodnight to Charlie."

"Shall I come too?"

"She'd love that."

Charlie's smile stretched across her face when he stepped into her bedroom. "Wyatt! You're coming to tuck me in?"

"Yes, if you want me to."

Charlie's curls bounced as she nodded.

He was better prepared for prayer time and followed their lead on how to talk to God.

He kissed Charlie's forehead. As before, her arms encircled his neck. This time, she whispered next to his ear, "You like my mom, don't you, Wyatt?"

He returned her whisper. "I love her. Is this okay with you?"

She nodded. "Do you love me?" Her whisper was so quiet, he barely heard.

"I don't have enough words to tell you how much I love you, Charlie. You're like a part of me." He put his lips closer to her ear. "Do you love me?"

She cupped her hand at the side of her mouth so Maddy wouldn't see. "Yes, I wish you were my daddy."

"Can you keep a secret?"

"Yes."

"I wish I were your daddy too."

"What are you two whispering about?" Maddy watched them from the doorway, hands on her hips and curiosity in her eyes.

Wyatt grinned. "Just a secret between the mermaid and me." He caressed Charlie's cheek. "I'll see you at the pool tomorrow."

"Night, Wyatt." She blew him a kiss.

Maddy closed the door. "Do you want something to drink? We can sit on the swing if you'd like."

"Whatever you're having."

She grinned. "Water?"

"Sure. Where's Brenda?"

"I heard her talking on the phone in her bedroom. She's probably chatting with one of her book club friends. She has a lot of them."

Maddy grabbed a couple of bottled waters and handed him one. "I'll turn on the tiny LED lights. Hopefully, they won't draw too many bugs. We'll light the citronella lamps just in case."

He helped her light the lamps, then followed her to the swing. He sat and rested his arm on the seat behind her and looked at the stars. He inhaled deeply. "Ah. This is nice."

She set the swing in motion. "Tell me what happens between now and your deployment."

"We try and put our houses and gear in order, kind of like I'm doing now."

He touched her cheek. "Tension builds inside many of those who are getting ready to leave. This may get worse within the next couple of weeks. Guys start getting on each other's nerves, and often fights break out. These are short-lived, because no one wants to pay damages or have a sergeant yelling at him. Serious injury will likely end with charges and a court martial.

"I stay away from people like your cousin during this time, because I'm super edgy, and fighting such men invites criminal charges."

"So what do you do to control this urge to snap?"

"Run. Swim. Lift weights. Avoid others if I can."

She studied his face. "What do you fear most, Wyatt?"

Images raced through his mind, and he couldn't frame a response for several moments. "Not being brave enough. Acting like a coward. Letting my friends down."

He turned toward her and lifted her hand to kiss her fingers. "My greatest fear is you and Charlie won't be here when I come back."

"This is our home. We don't plan to leave. We'll be here when you return."

Wyatt wanted more than a general acknowledgment they would be in the area. He wanted her promise she would wait for him—that she would choose him over any other man. But how could he ask her for this promise? What woman would agree to such a thing on such short acquaintance? The thought of her with any other man gave him heartburn.

Maddy closed the gap between them and rested her head on his shoulder.

Instantly, his arms encircled her and drew her closer. His heart pounded so hard, he could feel the beats in his throat, and fire raced through his bloodstream to his nerve endings. He had trouble breathing. "Maddy?"

A corner of her mouth tipped up. "Thanks for dinner, Wyatt. I enjoyed our date."

He stared at her lips, and she chuckled. "Well?"

"Well, what?" His voice roughened as he fought for control.

"You may kiss me if you like."

He didn't wait for another invitation. He kissed her as thoroughly as he could and then kissed her some more. When she returned his kisses, he groaned, set her away from him, and stood. "I need to go, Maddy. I'll see you at the hotel tomorrow."

She followed him to the front door. "Goodnight, Wyatt."

He turned and drew her back into his arms for a last slow kiss, one he hoped showed her his soldier's heart. "Goodnight."

FIVE

Maddy waved at Wyatt's friends who called out greetings to Charlie and her as they approached. The men lounged around the pool in shorts as they had done last week, but their postures indicated greater interest.

Joe signaled Charlie to him. "Thanks for the cookies, little mermaid. They were delicious."

Charlie smiled. "Mom gave some to Wyatt yesterday, and Gigi and I baked more this morning. Here." She handed him a metal container. "I used cookie cutters and made them into a lot of shapes."

"Great. We'll save them for dessert. Now let's see what Wyatt will teach you today."

Wyatt waited for them in the pool, so Maddy removed her wrap and took Charlie's hand. "Ready?"

Charlie smiled. "Ready."

Lewis called out, "I'm firing the grill. I'll have a hamburger for you when you're finished."

Then men encouraged Charlie as she put her face in the water and blew bubbles. They cheered when she dog paddled around the pool without her life vest.

Charlie ate up the attention, and Maddy marveled. She now had an inkling why Wyatt didn't want to let these men down. She didn't want to let them down either, and she wasn't even a part of their group.

"Look, Mom, I'm swimming in the deep end."

"How do you feel?"

"Great."

Joe eased himself into the water and swam to Charlie. "You made this look so fun, I thought I'd join you. Is this okay?"

"Sure, Sergeant—"

"Just Joe. Most people have a hard time with my real last name."

For the next hour, they played, or at least that's what their games probably looked like to Charlie. Maddy sat on the edge of the pool and watched Wyatt and Joe show her daughter how to move her arms and legs in the breaststroke. Charlie watched intently and copied them.

Lewis told them the burgers were ready just as Joe showed Charlie how to do a cannonball off the edge of the pool.

Charlie stood at the pool's edge and frowned. "My head will go under the water."

Joe nodded. "But only for a second. Hold your breath and close your eyes. You'll pop back up after you make a big splash."

Her gaze slid to Wyatt's and he smiled. "Joe and I will be right here waiting for you. We won't let anything happen to you, mermaid."

Charlie's lips trembled, but she nodded. She looked at Maddy.

"You can do this, darling."

"Will you show me first, Mom? Will you wait with Wyatt and Joe?"

"Sure." Maddy joined her. Her eyes met Wyatt's, and he nodded and backed up to give her room. "I need to get a little speed, so I'm going to start from here." Maddy stopped a yard behind Charlie. "Watch me."

Maddy raced forward, then leaped into the air. She grabbed her legs to her chest and hit the water with a big splash.

She surfaced with Wyatt's arms around her. She turned and smiled. "See? Wyatt and Joe won't let anything happen to you. I won't either."

"Maybe I'll just jump and not do a cannonball."

"That's fine."

The three of them moved closer to Charlie, and Wyatt opened his arms. "Jump, Charlie. Come to me."

Charlie rushed to the edge of the pool and jumped. Her head went under, but Wyatt lifted her and hugged her to him.

The observers whistled and clapped.

Charlie smiled. "I want to jump one more time."

After she dried off, she grinned and walked toward the men.

They patted her shoulder or back and told her what a great job she'd done.

She sat on the ground in the middle of them, her legs crossed, and her plate and water bottle in front of her. "I need to get good, because my birthday is at the end of next month, and I'm going to have a swim party at the Rec Center. Then we're going to Boondock's to bowl and do fun stuff."

Maddy walked beside Wyatt. "She is so looking forward to this."

He spoke near her ear, his voice soft. "We deploy before her birthday. What does she want, Maddy? I'll get her gift before I leave."

Maddy blinked away tears. "She hasn't asked for anything. I'll see if I can find out." She slipped her hand into his and squeezed. "When are you guys off next? Mom and I want to invite you to our place for food and a time to relax before—"

"Next Wednesday afternoon. Does midweek work for you?"

"Yes. About six? I can help Mom get things ready when I get home from work."

Wyatt whistled, and everyone looked up. "Maddy, her mom, Brenda, and Charlie invited us to their house on Wednesday afternoon at six for some food. You guys up for this?"

Their hoots and whistles signaled their approval, and Maddy's heart warmed toward them.

Wyatt watched Charlie interact with his buddies. He would sure miss attending her birthday party. They would too, judging by the looks on their faces. Many missed their own children and knew they would be away from home another twelve months, so they had unofficially adopted Charlie.

He turned to Maddy when an idea crossed his mind. "Hey, what if the guys and I surprise Charlie with an early birthday when we come on Wednesday? Then we won't miss seeing her open her presents."

Tears filled Maddy's eyes. "You'd do that, Wyatt?"

"Yes."

She clasped his hand and intertwined their fingers. Then she lifted their hands and kissed the back of his. "Thank you. Charlie will love this surprise."

He looked at their clasped fingers. He wanted more than a peck on the back of his hand. In one smooth motion, he lifted her chin for his kiss. He intended for the contact to be brief, but when he felt the softness and warmth of her lips, he lingered.

Lewis whooped, and Joe teased. "These shots should be worth a bundle to you, Carter."

Wyatt looked up, and Maddy blushed.

She signaled to Charlie to gather her things. "We need to get home."

Charlie grinned and looked from him to her mom. "Okay."

Wyatt walked them to their car. "See you Wednesday."

———

Wyatt rang the doorbell at exactly 6:00 p.m., or 1800 hours, on Wednesday and waited. The guys stood behind him, grins on their faces.

Maddy opened the door. She looked from him to the others. "Come in. I didn't recognize you all in camouflage."

"Funny. Training ran late and we just got off. Didn't have time to change." Wyatt looked over her shoulder. "Does Charlie suspect anything?"

She grinned. "No, Mom and I have kept things on the down low. We'll have dinner before we surprise her, or she won't eat for the rest of the evening."

They followed Maddy into the dining room, where Charlie helped Brenda put food on the table. She looked up, squealed, and ran to them. She gave hugs all around. "I'm glad you're here. Now we can eat. I'm starving."

Wyatt lifted her, and she put her arms around his neck. "Guess what, Wyatt? Mom and Gigi decided we'd have Thanksgiving today, instead of in November, though we're going to have Thanksgiving again on the real day. We get turkey, dressing, cranberries, hot rolls, green beans, mashed potatoes and gravy, and a special dessert. They won't tell me what's for dessert, but I hope they made something with chocolate. I love chocolate."

He kissed her forehead and returned her hug. "That sounds amazing, Charlie."

Just then, the doorbell rang.

Brenda waved them to the table. "I'll get that. You all sit down, and we'll have the blessing."

They washed, sat, and waited for Brenda to return. She did—with Cory Blake in tow.

Cory's glance moved from person to person. He seemed startled to see eleven men in combat uniforms sitting around his aunt's table. His eyes focused on Wyatt.

Wyatt nodded and waited.

Maddy introduced the guests, and Brenda pointed to a place at the table. "We have enough food, Cory. Grab the folding chair from the other room. You know where."

He joined them but said nothing.

Brenda asked the blessing on the food, and when they started passing platters, the noise level rose.

Charlie's eyes sparkled and her cheeks pinked, and Wyatt smiled to see her happiness.

Lewis raised his voice to be heard. "The food is great, Mrs. Banks. Maddy. We'll remember this for a long time."

Maddy smiled at each of them. "This is our way to say thank you for what you've done for Charlie and me, and to thank you for the service you provide this country. Mom, Charlie, and I will pray for your safety every day, and for the protection of your families while you're gone."

Instantly, the men quieted and spoke their thanks.

For the next half hour, they ate and chatted quietly.

Wyatt scanned Cory from the corners of his eyes, but Maddy's cousin only watched and listened as he ate. Their eyes met occasionally, but Wyatt did not sustain the contact. He didn't want to provoke the man. Besides, Maddy's eyes sparkled as much as Charlie's, and he couldn't look away from her for long. His heart ached at the thought that in three weeks, he had to leave. And he still hadn't told her how he felt.

"Let's have dessert on the patio, shall we?" Brenda rose and started clearing dishes. Wyatt and his buddies jumped up and did the same.

Wyatt's gaze met Maddy's, and she smiled and tilted her head toward the kitchen. "Wyatt and I will bring this."

Joe swooped Charlie up until she straddled his neck. She laughed as he trotted out the French doors to the patio and deposited her in an end chair.

When everyone seated themselves, Wyatt lit the birthday candles on top of the chocolate cake and carried this out.

Maddy started singing "Happy birthday, to you," and the men joined.

Charlie's eyes widened until her eyebrows disappeared under her bangs. "Today isn't my birthday."

Wyatt sat the cake in front of her and stroked her cheek. "We know, but the guys and I will be gone before your birthday in August, so we wanted to celebrate yours early."

Without a sound, Charlie blew out the candles, then stood and flung her arms around him. He lifted her, and she circled her arms around his neck. She leaned next to his ear and whispered, "I love you."

He spoke near her other ear. "I love you too, Charlie. Happy birthday." He hugged her and kissed her cheek before setting her down.

Brenda cut the cake and handed round the slices.

"Yum. Chocolate. My favorite." Charlie's eyes sparkled.

"Now, presents." Lewis handed Charlie a long, thick envelope. "We didn't have a chance to get you presents, little mermaid, so I hope this will do. We all pitched in."

Charlie opened the envelope, and her mouth dropped. "Money, Mom. Lots of money."

Joe grinned. "Each of us gave a hundred dollars. We know school starts next month and figured you could buy new clothes or supplies. If you have any left, you can use this for Christmas."

She cried, then jumped up and hugged and kissed each of them.

Wyatt's heart threatened to burst. No eye remained dry, including his and Cory's.

They laughed and chatted for another hour before Lewis stood. "We have to get back to the post, little mermaid, but we hope you have the happiest birthday party ever. We'll be thinking of you while we're gone."

Charlie hugged them all again.

Joe glanced over his shoulder. "You coming, Wyatt?"

"Be there in a few."

After the guys left, Maddy tugged on a lock of Charlie's hair. "Okay. Go brush your teeth and get ready for bed. Wyatt and I will be up in a minute."

Movement turned Wyatt's head, and he met Cory's stare. He tipped his head. "Blake."

Cory did the same. "Carter."

Brenda smiled. "Cory, let me bring you some coffee. I never did hear why you stopped by, but I'm glad you did, Nephew. Sit."

Maddy kissed Cory's cheek. "Be right back."

She signaled to Wyatt, and he followed her up the stairs.

Charlie prayed for his buddies and him for several minutes. Her words made him painfully aware their time together was short.

Charlie patted his hand. "Your turn, Wyatt."

Wyatt asked for God's protection for them all before stepping out the door behind Maddy.

When they reached the top of the stairs, she stopped and turned toward him. "Thank you, Wyatt, for—"

He drew her into his arms and kissed the rest of the words out of her mouth.

When she wrapped her arms around his neck and melted against him, he pulled her closer and buried his face in her neck. Words broke from him. "I love you, Maddy. I love you, I love you, I love you."

She leaned back to look into his face. "I love you too, Wyatt. I shouldn't after such short acquaintance, but I do. The way you treat Charlie makes me love you more."

The urgency he felt to hear Maddy's promise to wait for him intensified and fired his next kiss. Before her nearness sucked all air out of his lungs, he whispered, "Maddy, will you wait for me to get back so we can talk about our future? Will you m—?"

A noise at the bottom of the stairs turned their attention.

Maddy dropped her arms but reached for Wyatt's hand. "Cory. We're on our way down."

He waited for them to descend. "I just wanted to tell you I'm headed home."

Maddy hugged him. "I'm glad you stopped by."

Cory turned to Wyatt. Slowly, he offered his hand.

Wyatt smiled and shook. He looked into Cory's eyes and recognized resignation or acceptance. Wyatt's tension eased.

SIX

When the buses pulled to the curb to take Wyatt and the other soldiers to the airport, Maddy waited for him to store his gear.

He reached for Charlie and pulled her into his arms. "Give me a hug, little mermaid."

She squeezed him as hard as she could.

"I love you, Charlie." He kissed her cheek.

"I love you too, Wyatt. I wish you could come to my swim party."

"I do too. Listen, promise me you'll have a good time and won't be sad, okay?"

She nodded.

"Will you write to me and tell me how your first days of school are?"

"Yes."

"Good." He set Charlie on the ground and turned and reached for Maddy.

She went into his arms.

"When do you start school?"

"In a couple of weeks. Mr. Gates gave me permission to come in an hour late so I could catch the 8:00 a.m. class at the college. Of course, I have to stay an hour late in return. I'll have just enough time to get home, eat, talk to Mom and Charlie, tuck her in, and get online for my second class."

"Sounds like you're going to be busy—too busy to miss me."

"I'm already missing you, Wyatt, and you haven't left yet." She wrapped her arms around his neck and kissed him long and hard. She lifted her head and stroked his jaw. "You come back to me, you hear, Wyatt Carter?"

"I plan to. Write me?"

"Yes. You write me too."

He smiled and held up a notepad and pen. "I bought envelopes. I'll write every chance I get." He caressed her cheek. "Maddy, I love you so much. Will you m—"

"All aboard." The driver's insistent words lifted heads and created a concerted movement toward the bus.

Wyatt pulled Maddy close for one last kiss, then turned and got in line to get into the bus. Frustration mounted. Every time he'd tried to ask her to marry him, someone, or something interfered.

She said she'd wait for you. Wyatt would have to be content with that, but waiting for a whole year . . . His insides twisted. He knew of many instances where wives or girlfriends were unfaithful to their soldiers and they to their wives.

Maddy will not cheat on you. What are you thinking?

He sat the notepad on his lap and clicked the ballpoint pen.

Dear Maddy and Charlie,
I miss you already, and I just got on the bus . . .

Wyatt called, wrote, emailed, texted, and did video chats as often as he could. As days changed into weeks and then into months, and the temperature turned colder, Wyatt thought of Maddy and Charlie continually. He spent all his off-duty time writing letters and reading the study Bible Maddy had given him the week before he deployed. She had highlighted certain passages and made brief notes beside some of them.

On one particular day, he couldn't rest. He had to know how things were back home. He glanced at his watch and calculated the time difference before texting Charlie.

WYATT: Are you home from school? Can we video chat now?

CHARLIE: Yes. I'll get on my computer.

WYATT: Is your mom home?

CHARLIE: Not yet.

When Charlie accepted his video call, he almost wept at the sight of her face. "Hi, sweetheart. How are you?"

"I'm fine. Are you safe, Wyatt?"

"Yes. Hey, I don't have much time. I called to see if you'd mind if I ask your mom to marry me when I get back."

"I don't mind. Will you be my dad then?"

"If she says yes, I will be."

"Good. When are you coming home?"

"Not for several more months."

"Wyatt, can I call you Dad now?"

Tears clogged Wyatt's throat. "I'd love that, Charlie, but this must be our secret until I can officially propose to your mom. Okay?"

"Okay. I love you, Dad."

"I love you too, my sweet girl."

"Are Joe and Lewis and the other guys, okay?"

"Yes, and they talk about you often. They have all those pictures they took, and they put your photo up beside their kids' pictures. The guys talk about you a lot and miss the swimming lessons. They are really hungry for some of your chocolate chip cookies."

"Will you tell them I said hi, and that Gigi and I plan to send them some soon?"

"I will. I've got to go now. Tell your mom I'll call her when I get a chance."

"Okay. Bye, Dad."

"Bye, Charlie."

***

Finally. Wyatt sighed, and tension left his muscles. He was on a transport plane headed home. A day ago, he thought the mission might be extended another three months, so when he and the others were told to pack their gear and get on the plane, he hadn't hesitated.

He didn't call Maddy or Charlie. He wanted to surprise them. As he and the others flew back to the States, he planned his moves. He'd have to get from Fort Bliss, Texas, to Colorado Springs. He'd check flights as soon as he landed. Though he would have been flying more than fifteen hours by then, he wouldn't hesitate to fly another hour to get to Maddy.

The steady hum of the engines made him drowsy, so he slumped in his seat and envisioned his homecoming.

***

"Hello?"

"Brenda, this is Wyatt."

"Wyatt? Maddy's not here. I'm meeting her for lunch in an hour. Shall I give her a message?"

"I just landed in Colorado Springs."

"Oh, Wyatt. Does she know?"

"No. I want to surprise her. Listen, I have all my gear. May I drop this off at your house before I meet you at the restaurant?"

"Of course. I'll put the key in the flowerpot next to the door."

"I have to make a couple of stops, but I'll be there as soon as I can."

"You'll be back for Charlie's twelfth birthday tomorrow. She'll be thrilled. Maddy took the afternoon off to get ready."

"Make sure you have your camera, Brenda. I'm going to ask Maddy to marry me. You're all right with this, aren't you?"

"Ecstatic."

"See you soon." Wyatt hung up and looked around for his ride.

A gray SUV pulled to the curb beside him, and Cory Blake rolled down his window. "Get in, Carter. The trunk is open."

Wyatt slung his gear into the back and buckled into the passenger seat. "Thanks for doing this."

"Had I not seen the way Maddy and Charlie interacted with you before you left, I wouldn't have. I know both girls, and they would not have fallen for a loser." He signaled and pulled away from the curb. "Do you know Charlie calls you Dad? I overheard her talking to one of her friends on the phone."

"Yes."

"Do you intend to become her dad?"

"Yes, as soon as Maddy agrees to marry me. I tried to ask her several times before I left, but things always happened before I could get the words out. I won't let anything stop me today."

Cory raised an eyebrow. "I'm taking you to meet Maddy?"

"Please. Brenda left a key for me, so I can drop off my gear. Then, I'd like to make a couple of stops at the flower shop and jewelry store on the way to the buffet. You know which buffet?"

"Oh, yes."

⤸∾⤲

The acid in Wyatt's stomach roiled and adrenaline pumped through his system. He hadn't been this keyed up since the last time someone shot at him. He took a deep breath and opened the restaurant door.

A hostess smiled when she saw his uniform and the red roses. "Ah, yes. Follow me. I'll take you to your table."

Maddy sat with her back to him, looking at a menu, so he stopped next to her. "Hey, Lady."

She raised her head, and her eyes widened. "Wyatt!" She slid out of the booth and into his arms.

He closed his eyes and held her close. Several of the other diners clapped and cheered, but he ignored them. He focused only on the woman in his arms.

She lifted her face for his kisses, and he thought he was in heaven.

"Sit down, you two. You're blocking traffic." Brenda chuckled and took another photo.

Wyatt slid into the seat beside Maddy and handed her the roses. She sniffed, smiled, and then put them into the water pitcher the waitress left.

He took her hand. "I've missed you so much. The thought of spending another day without you and Charlie in my life is intolerable. I want us to be a family." He pulled the ring box from his pocket. "Will you marry me?"

Maddy looked into his face, tears splashing her cheeks. "Yes. When?"

He slid the engagement ring on her finger. "Well, we're too late today, and tomorrow is Charlie's birthday. The next day is Sunday, so we need to ask the pastor if he can marry us on Monday. How does Monday sound?"

Brenda laughed. "So soon?"

Wyatt shook his head. "Not soon enough. I've waited more than a year, and I don't want to wait any longer. I want Maddy and Charlie to be mine."

Maddy smiled. "All right. I'll marry you. If Pastor Morgan can perform the ceremony on Monday, we'll marry then."

The server returned with their plates and silverware.

Wyatt stood to let Maddy out. "When does Charlie get out of school? Can we pick her up early?"

Maddy grabbed her cell. "I'll call the secretary and let her know our soldier came home unexpectedly and we're stopping by to get Charlie in an hour."

Wyatt filled his plate. "Home. You don't know how amazing that sounds."

Brenda followed him in the buffet line. "Speaking of home, do you have a place to stay?"

"No. I haven't thought that far ahead."

She chuckled. "You'll stay with us, of course. We have a guest room."

"Thank you, Brenda."

She smiled. "No problem, Son."

⸺⸺⸺ ❧ ⸺⸺⸺

Wyatt stood outside Charlie's classroom door and waited for the principal to signal to the teacher.

The teacher said something about a guest, and the students' heads turned in unison.

Wyatt stepped through the door and spotted Charlie the moment she saw him.

"Dad!" She leaped from her chair and rushed toward him. Charlie flung herself into his arms and wrapped her legs around his waist. She hid her face in his neck and sobbed.

Wyatt wanted to sob too. The moisture came and went in his eyes as he held her close. "I love you, little mermaid."

Without lifting her head, she whispered, "I love you too. Did you ask Mom? Did she say yes?"

"She did. We're going to be a family soon, Charlie."

"God answered my prayers."

"He answered mine too, Daughter. Now give me another mermaid hug."

IN A STILL MOMENT

JULY 1, 1863: 6:30 A.M.

CHRISTOPHER GRANT ADJUSTED THE LEG OF THE TRIPOD one more time, then looked through the viewfinder of his camera across the tranquil fields near Gettysburg, Pennsylvania.

Birds sang in the green-leafed trees surrounding the fields, and he closed his eyes and listened to the birdsong. This tranquility wouldn't last. He had witnessed too many of the previous battles and knew the deforestation and destruction that would soon come from the cannonade.

He grimaced before clicking the shutter and repositioning the heavy camera for a shot from a different angle.

This would be the day. In the stillness of the moment, he sensed the coming battle. He knew both the Federalist Army of the Potomac and the Confederate Army of Northern Virginia, commanded by Robert E. Lee, were on the move and would meet somewhere near Gettysburg. His job was to photograph the aftermath of this meeting.

At the thought, his stomach skirmished with the contents of what remained of last night's unpalatable supper of hardtack and bacon. When he'd broken the hard biscuit open, maggots wriggled.

Christopher put the camera in its case, retracted the legs of the tripod, and carried his equipment back to the specially made wagon he shared with friend and fellow photographer, Alan Morgan. He climbed into the wagon and developed the albumen prints. When the prints were ready, he studied them with satisfaction. His employer, Mathew Brady, would be pleased.

Brady and his previous partner, Alexander Gardner, were geniuses when the time came to develop, use, and refine photographic techniques. They were so well known, European royalty and other wealthy patrons from the United States sought them out for photographs.

Christopher was humbled and grateful the men had looked at his portfolio, taken an interest in his work, and had helped him further develop his skill. They trusted him.

"Go out and make us proud, Chris." Brady had clapped him on the shoulder, pushed up his wire-rimmed glasses, and peered at him with piercing dark eyes.

Had he stood in Brady's newly opened National Photographic Art Gallery on Pennsylvania Avenue, in Washington, D.C., only two years ago? He felt he'd lived two lifetimes since then.

Battle after battle, he tried to make the men proud. His first assignment was to capture the images of the Battle of Bull Run in July of 1861. The sweltering sun and the stench and sights of blood and death overwhelmed him when he arrived. He almost turned around and went home—home to Annie. But he had remained.

Now, two years later, he gazed across the peaceful fields of Gettysburg, bone weary from trailing the Union Army through Virginia to Pennsylvania, and wishing he did not have to witness the carnage and destruction soon to come. Though the places and commanders might change, everything would remain the same—the noise of muskets, cannons, and screaming, the smell of gunpowder, blood, intestines, and gangrene, and the sight of fallen Union and Confederate soldiers sprawled in unnatural and grotesque poses, often missing faces and limbs.

Chris wondered where Alex Gardner was. He also photographed the camps and battlefields and had been assigned as chief army photographer to General McClellan. But when Lincoln dismissed McClellan from the command of the Army of the Potomac, Gardner's role lessened. He split with Brady about that time and began to follow General Burnside, then General Hooker. Meade replaced Hooker. Maybe his friend neared Gettysburg at this moment.

He'd sure like to talk to Alex. He thought of the heavily bearded, dark-haired Scotsman. "I wonder if he is as weary of all of this as I am?"

When their paths crossed a while back, Christopher had seen the stills Gardner made at Antietam. How many had died, been wounded, captured, or reported missing on that day? He tried to remember the newspaper accounts—twenty-three thousand, maybe.

Christopher built a campfire. As he moved a stump closer, he thought about the images he had taken at the First Battle of Bull Run, also called First Manassas, depending on whether the reporter was Union or Confederate—only about four thousand seven hundred dead, wounded, captured, or missing in that battle.

Then Fredericksburg. Gardner had shown him photos he'd taken after that one. About eighteen thousand fathers, brothers, husbands, and sons never returned to loved ones who waited.

Christopher poured a tin cup full of hot coffee, added a spoonful of sugar, stirred the coals, and added more wood. He nudged the water pot and cast-iron skillet toward the center of the grill, sat down on the stump to wait for the skillet to heat, and sliced bacon. Alan would return soon, and he'd appreciate a warm breakfast, even if he got only coffee, bacon, and more of the wormy hardtack.

"Hello the camp."

Christopher turned and smiled as Alan approached with his equipment. "Want some breakfast?"

Alan set the heavy field camera near his feet, accepted the cup of coffee in one hand, and picked up a piece of bacon with the other. He shook his head at the biscuit. "Know what the soldiers call hardtack?"

Christopher chuckled. "I can imagine. I know what I call them."

"They call hardtack 'worm castles' or 'tooth-breakers.' I saw a private put his on a rock, smash the bread with the butt of his musket, and then soak the pieces in his coffee. I wonder if his had worms?

"The soldiers aren't supposed to drop the biscuits in the trenches when they're laying siege, but they do anyway. The men laughed about a brigade officer who ordered the soldiers to get the hardtack out of the trenches." Alan chuckled. "A wounded soldier replied they *had* thrown the hard biscuits out two or three times, but they kept crawling back in." He grimaced. "I can't abide hardtack."

"Even when you smother the biscuits with your mother's peach preserves?"

Alan put down his cup. "That's about the only way those things are tolerable—smeared with something sweet." He stood and retrieved his equipment and moved toward the dark room. "Got to get these developed."

Christopher watched his friend hop into the wagon bed and disappear behind the black curtain of the small darkroom.

Alan, like other photographers who trailed one army or another, made a good living making photographs for soldiers who wanted to send the inexpensive prints home. He was a pacifist and believed he could best serve his fellow men by shooting their photos instead of them.

He and Alan shared the cost of materials, but most of all, they shared companionship.

Though Alan was well muscled and built like a wrestler, Christopher was tall, lean, and put together like a runner. He stared at his reflection in the sliver of mirror hanging on a nail in a nearby tree. His eyes and hair were brown, and though he had regular features, no one had ever called him handsome or remarkable. His shyness prevented him from talking to people as easily as Alan, which made him think of Annie.

He wondered what Annie saw in him. His fiancée was so beautiful and intelligent she could have the pick of the men back in Washington. Yet she had chosen him. Why?

He reached for his shaving kit and lathered his face. The razor blade slid through the cream and removed the stubble. He rinsed his face, then trimmed his mustache. His mind whispered, "Oh, Annie, I miss you so much. I miss our quiet talks on the porch swing each evening when your soft little hand nestles in mine and you lay your coppery curls against my shoulder.

"My heart about bursts when you look at me with your hazel eyes. I miss the sound of your low, soothing voice as you give wise counsel, and I miss sitting near you in the Sunday services and smelling your clean, light fragrance.

"We've been apart so long, Annie. Do you still think of me, or has someone else stolen your affections? Do you pray for me daily, my darling, as I do you?"

After Alan hopped out of the wagon, he rolled down the sleeves of his cotton shirt and shrugged out of his suspenders. They dangled at his sides. He stretched, rubbed the back of his neck and headed to the fire for more coffee.

That's when they heard the first shots.

Alan looked toward the village of Gettysburg. "Here we go again. Think we should move?"

"Not yet, but we might be wise to bring the horses in and get them harnessed."

While Alan took the horses to water then harnessed them to the wagon, Christopher secured the darkroom and made sure the volatile chemicals were safely stored. They used collodion, silver nitrate, pyrogallic acid, potassium cyanide, and sodium thiosulfate in the photographic process, and he didn't want to chance losing his supplies.

He and Alan rolled their blankets and stored them in the front part of the wagon with most of their kitchen gear. They left the two tin cups and coffee pot out until last.

Christopher faced northwest toward the sounds of firing. He knew what was happening. Men killed each other because each thought he had the cause of right and God on his side.

He remembered when so many of the young men in crisp, clean blue uniforms had flooded into the studios to have their pictures taken at the beginning of the war. They had been happy and excited, ready for a fight, and sure the conflict would be brief and end with victory for the Union.

This had not been the case.

Christopher studied the landscape. Would this war ever end? How many more would have to die?

Alan stepped up beside him and pointed toward the sounds of battle. "Do you think you'll ever be able to capture the sights and sounds of all this?"

Christopher nodded. "I know the idea is in Alex Gardner's mind. He tried to capture movement at Antietam, but with no success. With the likes of Brady, Gardner, Tim O'Sullivan, William Pywell, George Barnard, and Thomas Roche experimenting with and expanding the art, and new technologies being developed, I think we'll see moving photography one day. Maybe the images will include sound and color."

Alan shook his head. "Hard to imagine. I'm thinking this won't happen in our lifetime."

"No, probably not."

The shots ceased, and the two of them listened.

Alan nodded toward the south. "I bet they're regrouping and waiting for reinforcements. Each general is sure to try to get his troops in the best position possible." He pointed. "Do you know what the locals call that hill over there?"

Christopher nodded. "Cemetery Hill. Those hills over there are Little Round Top and Round Top." He studied the geography. "Good place for a battle."

Alan looked toward the trees. "I'm getting an odd feeling. What if the troops are moving this way? We might get caught in the crossfire."

"Let's return to Gettysburg and take cover."

Christopher swung himself into the driver's seat of the wagon and waited for Alan to slide onto the seat next to him. He clicked his tongue to urge the horses forward.

They headed northeast toward the village and Alan breathed his relief. "I'm thinking this is going to be my last battle, Chris. I'm tired of traipsing around like a vagabond. I'm going home to see Mother and Lucy."

He patted the satchel next to him. "This money will give me a new start. I'll ask Lucy to marry me. I didn't want to think of marriage a few years ago, but I'm ready to settle down now and start a family." He frowned. "I hope she'll have me after all this time."

Christopher remained silent for several moments, but when he spoke, his voice was low and strained, "I'm thinking the same thing. Brady wanted the world to have a record of what happened here, but I'm wondering how many more images of mayhem and carnage the world needs to understand the grisliness of war."

Alan smiled. "You're thinking of Annie, aren't you?"

"Yes. She's so beautiful, I can hardly hope she'll be waiting for me."

"When is the last time you heard from her?"

Christopher grimaced. "About a year ago. I've sent her letters, but haven't received any in return."

Alan grasped his shoulder. "Don't lose hope, Chris. You know how unreliable mail delivery is. Maybe she wrote you, but you haven't been in one spot long enough to receive the letters."

He reached into his pocket and removed the daguerreotype of his sweetheart he carried with him at all times. He smiled and talked to her image. "I'm coming home soon, Lucille Miller. Wait for me."

Just as their wagon reached Gettysburg, cannons and muskets belched their projectiles. The ground rumbled. They looked toward the northwest. Smoke filled the air over McPherson's Ridge.

Alan shook his head. "Here we go again."

Christopher unharnessed the horses inside the stone barn they had rented in exchange for photos of the owners.

Alan forked hay into the mangers and filled the water trough. Then he stood in the doorway and looked toward the sound of battle.

They waited. As the hours passed, the battle moved closer to them.

At noon, they heard the noise of troop movements on the roads north of Gettysburg and saw soldiers in Union blue.

Gray-clad Confederate soldiers charged them, and soon the disorganized Union divisions fled through town.

Alan studied the fleeing soldiers. "The Johnny Rebs are pushing hard. Those look like General Howard's XI Corps. I photographed some of them recently."

A musket ball slammed into the door frame, and they both dropped to the ground.

Christopher whistled. "That was close."

They listened to the sound of shots and pounding feet as the Union soldiers rushed toward the southern wheat fields and peach orchard Christopher had photographed earlier that morning. The Confederates followed hard on their heels.

Alan lifted his head, raised to all fours, and listened. "Wonder where they'll stop running and make a stand?"

Christopher shrugged. "Maybe they'll join up with the Union forces on Cemetery Hill. I think General Hanock's II Corps is there."

He stood and waited for the troops to pass. The Confederates drove the Union soldiers south of Gettysburg and continued to fire until late in the afternoon.

Chris reached for the harness. "Let's drive to the south. We have work to do."

Dead and wounded littered the wheat fields, and Christopher shook his head. He couldn't count all the casualties.

The moaning and screaming of the injured continued even after the last shots of the day had been fired. The haggard, grim-faced medical assistants from both sides of the conflict gave aid to those in need, but their help was often too little, too late. The task was devilishly impossible.

Christopher was glad he had nothing in his stomach, though he struggled to keep down the bile as he and Alan got out the field cameras and took their photographs.

"Water."

He and Alan turned at the croaking whispered words coming from a shallow gully nearby.

A Confederate soldier sprawled near the base of a boulder. Shrapnel had torn a gaping hole in the man's side.

Alan went for the canteen, and Christopher hunkered next to him. He glanced at the insignia on the man's uniform. "We'll do what we can for you, Corporal."

He lifted the wounded man's head as Alan tipped the canteen.

The soldier drank and tried to smile, though the pain turned his smile into a grimace. "Much appreciated."

Christopher eased him to the ground. "Can you tell us what happened?"

Slowly and with gasping breaths between each word, he spoke, "I'm with Heth's infantry division. Marched eastward down Chambersburg Pike this mornin'. Blue Bellies spotted us from the Lutheran Seminary. General Hill ordered Pender's division to join ours."

Alan gave him another drink before the soldier continued. "We seized McPherson's Ridge. Pushed the Blue Bellies back to Seminary Ridge. We regrouped with Doubleday's I Corps. Started pushin' the Federalists south."

He coughed, and blood splattered his shirt front.

Christopher touched the fallen man's shoulder. "Don't talk if you don't want to."

The man drank again and continued. He grimaced. "I got in their sights. Here I lie."

He looked at them with pleading eyes. "I ain't gonna live boys. Do me a favor?"

Christopher nodded. "If we can."

"Got a letter to my wife inside my jacket. Mail it, okay?"

Alan nodded. "Sure, soldier." He reached inside the man's jacket and pulled out a blood-stained letter.

"Another favor?" He coughed, and more blood flowed. "Take a photo of me while I live? Send to her? Just my face."

Alan got the camera, and Christopher covered him from the neck down with a blanket. They leaned him next to a boulder, and the man smiled, removed his right hand from under the blanket, raised his hand, and spread his fingers in farewell.

Christopher snapped the image with trembling hands.

The soldier slumped, tears in his eyes. His words faded as his life flowed from him. "Tell her. See her in heaven."

They bowed their heads and remained silent for several moments.

Alan's voice shook. "I'll dig the grave and carve his name and date on a cross. You develop the pictures."

Christopher did. He stared at the images of the dead man. He couldn't shake the depression enveloping him and threatening him with suffocation. *How many more, Lord? How many must die?*

In the twilight, Christopher stood in the doorway of the barn and listened to troop movements from both sides. "They're getting ready for tomorrow's battle. I can image General Lee and General Meade are using the last of the light to strategize and to move their men into the best defensive positions."

"You think much about dyin', Chris?"

Christopher turned. His gaze met Alan's. "Every day. You?"

Alan nodded and crouched beside the small fire he had kindled in a rock ring on the barn floor. "I don't want to think about dying, but given the circumstances . . ." He poked at a burning stick. "I'm still stickin' to the plans of dying in my bed as an old man. Maybe I'll have several tall grandsons to take me to my final resting place." He looked into Christopher's eyes. "Are you afraid to die?"

Moments passed before Christopher responded. "Yes, and no."

"What do you mean?"

"I'm not afraid of death, Alan, because my soul is secure. I believe what Jesus said when he told his followers he was going to prepare a place for them, and that he would, without a doubt, come for them and they would be together with him forever."

"You really believe that, Chris?"

"Yes."

Alan looked toward the roof. "Hard for me to trust in a God that lets this kind of horror happen. Too much dyin'."

Christopher studied his friend's face. "Do you think to escape death?"

Startled, Alan stared at him. "No, I guess not. I suppose death will come to me whether I'm in my bed or on the battlefield. Never thought of death that way."

Christopher nodded.

Alan's low voice trembled. "If your soul is safe, why are you afraid to die?

Christopher stood and paced to the door and back. "I'm not sure I'm ready to go yet. So much life still awaits. I want to do many things, and there's Annie—" He took several deep breaths and sat down again.

"When I stand before the Lord to give an account, will I be ashamed? All my motives will be exposed, and all of my life's work will be burned as if by fire to see of what quality the works were. How much will be wood, hay, and stubble? How much will be gold, silver, or precious stones?" He looked into Alan's eyes. "Will I be ashamed or unashamed when I stand before my Lord?"

Uneasiness tightened Alan's voice, "I don't think you have anything to worry about, Chris. You're a good man. You're honest, dependable, caring, and you go the extra mile for people in need. You have integrity."

"There is none righteous, Alan. Not one. Scripture is clear about this. Our own goodness is like filthy rags in God's eyes." He poked at the fire. "No, what we do with Christ is the only thing that counts. Our obedience gives him pleasure." He hung his head. "I don't always obey."

Several minutes passed before Christopher spoke again, "As hard as I try to do right, sometimes, I fail miserably."

The words of the Apostle Paul to the Romans spoke to his heart.

For the good that I would I do not: but the evil which I would not, that I do.

Now if I do that I would not, it is no more I that do it, but sin that dwelleth in me.

I find then a law, that, when I would do good, evil is present with me.

For I delight in the law of God after the inward man:

But I see another law in my members, warring against the law of my mind, and bringing me into captivity to the law of sin which is in my members.

Christopher groaned and closed his eyes. He turned his face toward the night sky, and in an anguished voice quoted the last verses in the last chapter of Romans seven.

O wretched man that I am! who shall deliver me from the body of this death?

The answer was quick in coming.

I thank God through Jesus Christ our Lord.

JULY 3, 1863: 3:30 P.M.

CHRISTOPHER SAW, HEARD, AND SMELLED. Battling, battling. Wheat field, peach orchard, Devil's Den, Little Round Top, Culp's Hill. Explosions. Orchards, trees, fields, fences, and homes destroyed. Broken animals and soldiers. The stench of rotting human and horse flesh. Clouds of smoke, cannon fire, muskets. Screaming, moaning, and cries for mothers. Disorder and chaos all around. The color of death.

Christopher willed himself not to see, hear, or smell, but the frightful images branded themselves into his memory. He gagged as he stared at the mounds of amputated arms and legs and the rows of bodies waiting just outside the field hospitals for burial.

He wanted a drink, but the water in the nearby creek ran blood red and stank. His body shook. Though the camera was focused and ready, he could not press the button that would immortalize the results of the first three days of the Battle of Gettysburg. He could not. He wondered if Alan had been more successful.

"Chris?"

Christopher turned at the accented voice and watched both Alexander Gardner and Mathew Brady approach. Both were pale and dusty.

He couldn't generate enough energy for a smile.

The two grasped Christopher's shoulder, and then they turned and contemplated the sights in front of the lens.

"Come." Brady pointed away from the scene toward his specially outfitted wagon.

Christopher packed the camera and walked with them. Though the shaking in his hands quieted, the tremors inside continued, even when Brady handed him a cup of the hot coffee he'd been heating on the small cook stove.

"Why are we doing this?" Christopher stared at the two men he wanted to please so much. His voice cracked with strain.

Brady shrugged. "I had to. A spirit in my feet said, 'Go,' and I went." He took off his glasses and rubbed his tired eyes. "I'm still going. My vision fails a little every day, so I hire others like you to go on my behalf."

Gardner stiffened.

Christopher knew this employer-employee relationship was the reason the talented photographer had dissolved his working relationship with Brady.

As an employee, Gardner's photographs had been credited to Brady. That was the nature of this business. Christopher understood, because the same thing happened with his work. He didn't bear a grudge, but he couldn't blame Alex for breaking away and starting his own business. He wondered how Brady felt to know Alex had hired many of his previous employees.

Christopher flung his arm toward the fields of Gettysburg. "I'm finished, Matt. This will be my last battle. I can't take the death and destruction anymore." He brushed a hand over his eyes. "How do those poor soldiers endure day after day? When will the bloodshed end?"

Both men remained silent.

Brady finally spoke. "I know how you feel, Chris. I was almost killed at Bull Run, and when I tried to get away, I got lost. I wandered around for three days until I eventually stumbled into Washington, almost dead from starvation. I wanted to give up then, but I couldn't."

Christopher said nothing. He listened as the conversation turned to the business of photographing war and the complications associated with this.

When Brady mentioned he had been allowed to photograph Jefferson Davis, P.T.G. Beauregard, Stonewall Jackson, and others, Christopher straightened. "How were you able to get behind Confederate lines to do this, Matt?"

Brady's eyes met Gardner's. Both pairs of eyes held secrets. Brady shrugged. "Let's just say I have connections."

"Would the connection be to Mr. Allan Pinkerton via Alex? I've seen him several times. He's the man the soldiers call General Allan." He looked at Alex. "He has a Scottish accent much like yours." When he realized what he'd said, he flushed. Had he not been under such strain, he would never have asked such a pointedly rude and personal question.

"I'm sorry. Who your connections are is none of my business." He lowered his eyes and was grateful when Brady ignored the question and changed the subject.

Brady chuckled and pointed at his wagon. "The soldiers can't figure out my strange-looking means of transportation. They don't know what this is, or why I'm following the army. They've started to call my wagon the What Is It. The only thing most of them know is that I and my wagon are heavily guarded by cavalry when we move. They don't pay much attention to me now."

He shook his head. "President Lincoln doesn't want our work to get into the wrong hands."

The late afternoon sunshine weighted Christopher's muscles and increased his lethargy. He listened to the two photographers talk about what they had seen and heard earlier in the day, but he had a hard time staying awake.

"From what information I have," Gardner began, "General Meade couldn't decide whether to fight or retire after yesterday's battle. Hancock advised him to fight. Apparently, General Lee also decided to fight, even though he'd been unsuccessful in his move against both Union flanks yesterday. He probably figured the Union morale was down. My sources said Lee overruled Longstreet's objections."

Brady nodded. "The firing we heard up until thirty minutes ago was most of the one hundred forty cannon overshooting Hancock's position on Cemetery Ridge. I think they're running low on ammunition."

Christopher blinked his eyes awake, rose, and shook hands with the men. "I'm glad I got to see you both. I hope to see you in better times when this war is over. Take care of yourselves."

Alan returned to the wagon when Christopher walked up and rested the camera on the wagon seat. The camera seemed heavier than usual, so he alternated hands and massaged each bicep before rubbing the muscles on the back of his neck.

"I thought about what you said earlier, Chris." Alan looked at Christopher from the other side of the wagon. "I thought about your words a lot. Sure would like to know my soul is safe."

Christopher nodded. "Come. Walk with me."

They walked and talked for a quarter of an hour until Alan stopped and knelt on one knee, his head bowed.

Christopher placed a hand on his friend's shoulder and looked into the sky.

A hair-raising rebel cry issued from the throats of thousands of Confederate soldiers and shattered the peaceful moment. They advanced across a nearby field toward Cemetery Ridge, and the Union artillery opened fire and mowed them down.

Alan pointed. "Those are General Pickett's men, Chris. They're—" His words ended in a gurgle of blood as a musket ball entered the right side of his neck and exited his chest just under his left arm.

Surprised, he looked into Christopher's eyes. "Lucy—?" he managed to whisper before he crumpled in a heap at Christopher's feet.

"No!" He screamed and reached for Alan. Something red hot singed the top of his left shoulder and numbed his arm all the way to his fingers. He jerked up his right hand to cover the pain, but blood flowed around his palm. "No, God, no!"

In desperation, he crawled to the wagon wheel and pulled himself up so he could reach inside the bed for the rolls of bandages and other medical supplies they carried.

With great difficulty and much pain, he stripped off his shirt, cleaned the wound, and bandaged the injury to the best of his ability.

As bullets whizzed overhead, Christopher crawled toward Alan and pulled his body along the ground. He tried to force his left arm to help the right, but the pain was so great, he passed out. During periods of consciousness, he tugged Alan with one hand then rested.

Finally, his strength at an end, he gave one last yank and sank to the ground next to the wagon wheel. Alan's head and outstretched hand lay near his lap.

The horses, already in a panic from the artillery fire, snorted and twisted to get away from the smell of blood and death.

He could not go to them. No strength remained. "You're okay, girls. Calm down. I don't want you to run away and leave me here by myself."

They plunged even more and pulled against their ropes.

Sing.

"Sing, Lord?"

Yes, sing.

"Sing when my friend was killed before my eyes? Sing as my blood joins the blood of thousands to water the fields of Gettysburg?"

Sing.

Christopher closed his eyes and opened his mouth. He didn't know if the words he sang made sense, or if the syllables actually made words, but the mournful, quiet tones soothed the horses.

Their eyes stopped rolling and their ears perked toward him, and as the sounds of battle moved away from them, their tense muscles relaxed.

Christopher remained seated and hummed the monotonous syllables until he passed into unconsciousness again.

Pain seared him, and he awoke, groaning. Every nerve, muscle, tendon, and joint throbbed, and his throat was so dry, he could barely swallow. When he touched his forehead, he burned with fever. He must drink water.

Groaning again, he pulled himself up using the wagon wheel for support and reached into the bed for his canteen. He drank until the thirst left him.

The sounds of battle could still be heard, and the sudden urge to run, to get away, overwhelmed him. Yet, as he turned, he saw Alan's sprawled body. He couldn't leave his friend for the scavengers to molest. They came from the sky, the woods, and holes in the ground at the smell of blood and death, and the vision of their feasting was too horrible to consider.

He trembled as his thoughts warred against what he wanted to do and what he should do.

Still shaking, he reached into the wagon bed for the coiled rope. He knew he could not lift Alan with his own strength, so he used the resources he had. He tied a loop at the end of the coil, wrestled the body around with his one good arm, and slipped the rope around Alan's chest. When Christopher saw his hands and bare chest were smeared with his friend's blood, he fell to his knees, gagging, shaking, and crying.

"I can't do this, God! I can't! Where are you? Why did you let this happen?"

Minutes passed. Glassy-eyed and trembling like a leaf in the wind, he stood and walked to the tree they used to shade the wagon. He studied the sturdy limb.

After several attempts, he got the loose end of the rope to flip over the branch in such a way that when he tied on to one of the horse's harness tugs, he could lift the body into the wagon bed.

None of the horses wanted anything to do with the blood smell on him, and they plunged and twisted at his approach.

He stopped and swayed back and forth, fighting the panic threatening to drown him. He closed his eyes and the mournful, toneless humming vibrated his throat.

Christopher didn't know how long he stayed in that position, but when he opened his eyes, the horses had relaxed and were looking at him. He continued to hum as he approached the calmest of the horses. Though her head came up and she flicked her ears at him, she didn't spook.

He tied the end of the rope into the harness tugs, pulled Alan's body into the air, and backed the mare slowly to lower him into the bed.

With many groans and much pain, he harnessed the horses to the wagon and turned toward Gettysburg. He clicked at them, and they started. He knew to move now was risky, but to stay was riskier.

He slumped on the wagon seat and faded in and out of consciousness. Several times he jerked awake just in time to save himself from tumbling out of the wagon.

"Whoa, there. Whoa, girls."

The horses stopped.

Christopher squinted, trying to see through the haze clouding his eyes. He knew that voice. "Alex?" His words came out as a croak, and he struggled to stay upright. "Alex, is that you? Alan's dead. I—" His grip on the reins loosened, and he slumped forward.

Gardner hopped into the wagon and examined Christopher's injuries before laying him down on the seat. "Rest now, Chris. I'll get you to help."

The grotesque images of blood and death faded as Christopher relaxed, and his mind went dark.

JULY 31, 1863: 8:30 P.M.

Annie McCarthy sighed and studied the darkening sky as she snuggled into the cushions of her porch swing. The heat of the day had cooled into pleasant twilight. She slipped off her shoes, pushed hard to put the swing in motion, curled her legs under her wide skirts, and closed her eyes.

The day had been long and hard, but the estate was finally settled and the last debt paid. She no longer feared losing the only home she'd ever known. Though the house was empty of the one she loved, the place was hers.

She listened to the squeak of the swing chains and to the serenade of the crickets. In the still of this moment, time slowed. Yet she knew that time never stopped, regardless of those who wanted this to happen. She demanded time respect the loss of her mother, but, second by second, time advanced, dulling the hard edge of her grief.

Annie tipped her head back and thought of the verse in Ecclesiastes the preacher had read on Sunday.

> To everything there is a season, and a time to every purpose under the heaven:
>
> ... A time to weep, and a time to laugh; a time to mourn and a time to dance.

She knew about weeping and mourning and wondered when her time to laugh and dance would come.

As the rocking slowed, she drifted into the space between dozing and dreaming. The swing bumped slightly and gained a little momentum, but this was not enough to make her open her eyes.

She relaxed, and the memories of better times replayed themselves in her mind. The memories helped her believe during the times she almost lost hope.

Annie wished Chris sat beside her. She could almost feel the strength of his shoulder he offered as a pillow, the security as his large hand enveloped hers, and the love he had for her when he kissed her.

"Oh, Chris, where are you my darling?"

"I'm here, Annie." The answer was whisper-soft and took moments to register in her brain.

Her eyes snapped open. Christopher cradled her against his heart, and his right hand covered hers. She looked into his eyes, and in the light of the full moon, saw the love shining from them.

She cried, reached up and put her hands around his neck, then buried her face in the soft material of his shirt. His arms tightened around her, and he rocked her until she leaned back, looked into his face, and smiled. "I can't believe you're here beside me. I've often wished for you to be, especially after Momma got hurt, then—"

"Your mother?" Christopher eased his left arm from around her, and she saw him wince.

"What's wrong, Chris? Are you hurt?" She leaned away to better examine him.

"The wound is healing. Tell me about your mother."

"Is your right arm hurt?"

"No."

"Then slide to the other side of the swing so you can hold me."

He smiled and did as she asked. When she cuddled against his side, her legs folded under her, she lifted her arm and, with a finger, traced the lines of his freshly shaved jaw. "You're thinner, my love. Are you sure you're all right?"

Christopher hesitated and bowed his head. He stroked her cheek and kissed her. "Tell me about your mother."

"She fell down the stairs and broke a hip a few months after you left. That winter, she sickened with pneumonia. She felt a little better after the doctor treated her, but the illness returned in the spring and her health deteriorated. She died a year ago this month."

"I'm so sorry, darling. I wish I had known."

"I wrote you, Chris. Didn't you get my letters?"

"No."

Annie sighed. "In a way, I'm glad. When you didn't answer, I worried you were dead. Not responding was not like you."

He tensed. "Did you get my letters, Annie?"

"The only letter I got from you this year told me you were moving toward Gettysburg." She whispered and touched his cheek. "The newspapers reported almost twenty-eight thousand men were either killed, wounded, or reported missing during the four days of that battle. They said General Lee lost more than a third of his Confederate army."

She paused. "Even though you are a photographer and not a soldier, I thought you might have been one of those who died."

He trembled, and when the shaking increased, Annie's concern rose. "Chris?"

"Hold me, Annie. Hold me. Don't let go."

She embraced him, and he returned the embrace.

Moans rose to his lips, and he clenched his teeth. His arms felt like steel bands around her. The mournful, monotonous hum that came from deep inside his chest frightened Annie, and she tried to move, but couldn't escape his arms. "Chris?"

Pain and fear emanated from him, and he couldn't answer.

She watched him before pushing the swing. As they rocked together, she laid her cheek on his chest and hummed with him. The humming released some of the pain and fear she'd felt over the last two years.

When his muscles finally relaxed, she looked into his face.

He dropped his head. "Forgive me, Annie."

"Shh. Just rest." She slid to the edge of the swing. "Lie down and put your head in my lap."

Christopher did. When he closed his eyes, she stroked his face until he slept.

As Annie rocked, she studied the lines and planes of his face. War had changed him, but how much she didn't know. Some of the soldiers had returned with all kinds of debilitating conditions that made her cringe inside. She always read the newspaper accounts of the battles, but they could never fully describe what Chris had seen through the lens of his camera.

Her heart hurt for him, and she didn't know what to do to help. She had barely been able to help herself through troubling times, now trouble seemed to have landed in her lap.

Christopher awakened at first light. Several moments passed before he could determine where he was, but when he realized his head still rested in Annie's lap, and that she had sat up all night to comfort him, shame filled him. He should have been the one to comfort her.

He sat up, and she opened her eyes. Even with her hair coming unpinned and her clothing wrinkled, she was the most beautiful woman he'd ever seen.

She smiled. "Good morning."

How could she look at him with such a sunny expression when she should be rejecting him as a damaged, unworthy fellow? He'd cried and shown weakness. He had not been able to control the trembling and humming when he was reminded of Gettysburg and Alan's death. He could not staunch the panic, and all he wanted to do was hide. The war had made him less of a man, and he didn't deserve a woman like Annie.

He didn't return her greeting, and her smile faded. "What's wrong, Chris?"

She reached out and touched his arm, but he stiffened.

"I didn't mean for you to see that last night."

"Why?"

"Because I—" He shook his head. "I can't tell you what is wrong, Annie."

She studied his face for several moments then took his hand. "Come." She led him toward the door. "I'm going to fix you some breakfast. No, don't argue. Come."

He followed her inside and sat at the kitchen table while she put on coffee and started breakfast. She moved with grace and dignity, and her beauty tugged at his heart.

Christopher yearned to wake up every day to see her face and feel her energy, but how could he?

When the meal was ready and the plates placed before them, Annie looked at him. "Will you ask for God's blessings, or shall I?"

Christopher frowned and indicated she should.

They ate in silence for most of the meal, then Annie pushed her plate away. "Look at me, Chris."

He raised his eyes.

"What's wrong? Have I offended you in some way?"

"No, Annie, you haven't. Mine is the issue. I'm ashamed."

"Why?"

His words stuck in his throat. He shrugged and shook his head.

She lifted her eyebrows. "Do you love me, or have your feelings changed?"

Christopher's eyes widened. "I love you so much I hurt, Annie, but you deserve someone better than me. I'm not whole anymore. The things I've seen . . . they've changed me. I'm not the same man I was before I left."

"Who are you to judge what I need?" Her tone sharpened. "Thousands of other men have changed also. Some of them return with missing limbs and eyes, but do you think the women who wait for them cast them out? I haven't seen one yet."

He remained silent for some time. "Out of all the men you could've had, why did you choose to love me?"

"The most important thing to me is your love for God. You live to please him, and I can't go wrong with a husband who does this. You understand how he expects you to love and care for me, because you've read the scriptures. The others didn't."

"God!" The name hissed through his teeth. "I haven't seen his mercy and grace lately. I'm wondering if he even exists. If so, why would he allow this war? Why would he permit so many to be killed?" He could barely speak around the constriction in his throat. "Why would he let Alan die only moments after he had put his faith in God? Why would he let me return to you with an unstable mind? Why, Annie, why?"

"Have you asked him? Have you searched his Word for answers? I don't know everything, Chris, but I do know he has promised to never leave us or forsake us. He's the friend who sticks closer than a brother—the One who said he'd go with us through the valleys.

"These last two years have been dark for me. I couldn't see the light. If I didn't have these promises to lean on and the sense of his presence, I don't know what I would have done." She rose and led him to the sofa. "Sit." With deliberation, she sat in his lap, spread her skirt to cover her feet, and looked into his eyes.

He embraced her and rested his cheek on her hair. She smelled so good.

"Tell me about Alan, Chris."

He hesitated. How could he tell her about Alan without describing the ugliness of his friend's death? He wanted to protect her from that. "I'm afraid if I start remembering, tremors and moans will come, and I can't control them. I don't want to frighten you."

"Are we not taught to bear each other's burdens? Perhaps I can bear some of yours and you can bear some of mine."

"You're so little, Annie. My burdens would crush you. They're crushing me."

"Try me. Tell me about Alan. If the tremors come, they come. I won't leave you."

Christopher took a deep breath and began. She chuckled at some of their adventures, grimaced at the wormy hardtack incident, and cried when she heard about the Confederate corporal. The closer he got to Alan's death, the slower his words. They were often punctuated by long pauses.

She grasped his hand. "Don't you see the Lord's grace evident in Alan's salvation, Chris?"

He stared at her.

"You asked him if he thought to escape death, and this is what made him realize he could die in any place, and at any time, right?"

Chris frowned. "So how is this grace?"

"Had you not shared, he could've died before he trusted We know of the consequences of that. Yet God extended one more opportunity for Alan to come into relationship with him.

He considered her words.

She tilted her head and looked at him. "What happened to Alan's savings?"

"After I got out of the hospital, I took the money to his sweetheart, Lucille Miller. She was grateful because hard times had come upon them."

"Why didn't you keep the money for yourself? No one would have known."

He stiffened. "What? Why would you ask me such a question? The Lord and I would have known."

Annie smiled. "Exactly. You know God exists, and he expects righteousness from his people. Don't tell me you don't think he exists."

Christopher's grin felt lopsided. "You're always the wise one, aren't you?"

"I don't know, but one thing I do know. I love you. I want to live the rest of my life with you. I don't care if you limp or have episodes. Nothing will erase the images you have seen, but maybe time will dull the pain. Perhaps the Lord will release you from the captivity of the tremors and humming, but maybe he won't. He will give you grace to overcome. We'll live with whatever comes. Don't quit on him, Chris. He hasn't quit on you."

Christopher buried his face in her neck and hugged her. "What would I do without you, Annie?"

"You would trust the Lord to get you through, but I do not intend for you to do without me, Christopher Grant." She looked around the comfortable room. "I'm tired of living here by myself."

"Then how soon will you marry me, love?"

She smiled. "Give me a week to get ready and notify our friends. We have no reason to wait longer."

Christopher stood on the sidewalk in front of Brady's National Photographic Art Gallery in New York City and stared at the sign advertising the special Civil War display.

Annie's hand rested in the crook of his elbow, and her presence strengthened him.

"You can do this, Chris." She patted his arm.

He watched people enter and exit the gallery and tensed. His breath felt trapped in his chest. "What if the tremors come? I don't want to embarrass you or myself."

"Look at me, husband."

He looked into her beautiful eyes.

"They haven't affected you for the last several months. Take a deep breath and let the air out slowly."

He complied.

"Do this again." She watched him, and the muscles of his arms relaxed. "Now remind me what we're going to do if you start to feel shaky."

"I'm going to breathe, and you're going to take my hand and walk me into one of the backrooms." He grinned. "Annie?"

She tilted her head. "Yes?"

"Will you hold my hand before I start to tremble?"

Annie chuckled, and she extended her left hand. "Certainly. Are you ready?"

He nodded, breathed in the crisp November air, took her hand, and walked inside. At a leisurely stroll, they studied the portraits of men, women, and children hanging in the first section of the long gallery. Images of many famous people from both the United States and Europe hung on the walls.

Christopher admired the prints. "Pure genius. Brady is such an artist." He explained how the images were made, and she asked intelligent, thoughtful questions. Her interest warmed him.

Sooner than he wished, the Civil War images came into view. He stopped, closed his eyes, took a deep breath, and looked at Annie. She watched him.

Though the rhythm of his heart increased, he stepped forward and looked at the image of camp life.

"Tell me what you're thinking when you look at these, Chris. I want to hear, see, smell, and feel what you felt."

"Annie, I—" He hesitated. This experience could turn ugly.

She squeezed his hand "I'll be fine. Let me share some of your burdens, sweetheart. I can't do this, if you refuse to talk."

The sincerity in her eyes and voice urged him on.

"I'll try." He related many of his experiences and the difficulties of capturing battlefield images. Annie was a good listener and asked questions to keep him talking as the moved slowly down the row of photographs.

He stopped and pointed. "Look, Annie. This is one of mine."

She studied the landscape for several moments. "Where was this taken?"

He paused. "Gettysburg. Just before the fighting started." His eyes traveled down the row of images, and his breath caught. "I don't know if I can continue."

Annie put her arm around his waist and held him close. "We don't have to go on if you don't want to."

The pressure in his chest spread to his stomach and the queasiness started. Soon after, the shaking would start.

"Breathe, love." Annie stood in front of him and tugged at his hand until he looked at her. "Would you like to go outside for some fresh air?"

Be strong and of good courage. Do not fear.

He took a deep breath and whispered, "Lord, I can't do this without you." The pressure and queasiness eased, and he stepped forward. "No, I must overcome this."

Annie read the information plaque below the image. "Dead Confederate soldiers at Antietam." She looked at him, a question in her eyes.

"You can't imagine the noise and smells, Annie."

She snuggled her hand into his. "What are you thinking?"

He spoke his first thoughts. "Explosions. Sulfur. Smoke. Screaming. Blood. Intestines. Gangrene. Death. Eternity."

They moved to the next picture. Christopher said nothing as more of the dead of different battles were shown. He stood with bowed head and tears in his eyes. When he looked at Annie, tears trickled down her cheeks. She understood.

Nearby, a man gasped. The gasp changed to loud sobbing.

Christopher turned to see a one-armed man reach toward the photograph of "Union and Confederate Dead, Gettysburg Battlefield, Pennsylvania."

The man pointed to the body in the foreground. "No, no!" He cried and leaned his forehead against the picture and wept.

Christopher stepped toward the man and put his arm around him. He waited until the grieving man's shoulders quit shaking.

"My brother." He touched the image.

Tears filled Christopher's eyes. "Gettysburg was terrible. So much death and destruction. My friend died in front of me."

The man pointed to his stub. "Lost my arm there. Got word my brother had died, but to see him like this . . ."

"I know."

The two stood together without speaking.

After a long while, the man saw Annie and hung his head. He turned to leave.

Annie stepped forward. "Sir? My husband and I were going to eat at the restaurant over there." She pointed. "We would count your joining us as an honor and privilege."

Christopher smiled. His Annie was the best. He touched the man's shoulder. "Please?"

The man studied them, then nodded. "Thank you."

In a still moment one November evening, when Christopher gave of himself, his healing began.

DANCING HANDS: A HERO

The diner's doorbell jingled. Morgan Grey glanced up from wiping the long, silver counter and bar stools. She straightened and smiled at the man who entered. He returned her smile before crossing the black and white tiled floor. He seated himself in one of the red vinyl booths.

He was not familiar, though this wasn't surprising, since she'd been working in the retro-style diner for less than a month.

Alison, the other waitress on the afternoon shift, gasped, and Morgan turned toward her. "What's wrong?"

"You get to take this customer."

Morgan's eyes widened as she looked back and forth from the man to the waitress. "Why? What's wrong with him?"

He appeared to be in his late twenties or early thirties and had missed six feet by a couple of inches. Laugh lines creased the corners of his dark-lashed brown eyes. His firm, manly jaw and neck highlighted the way his dark brown hair curled just before touching the collar of his work jacket. So why was Alison unwilling to serve him?

"He's deaf. His name is Toby Randall. He's Reggie and Nancy's son. Heard he moved back in with his folks a week ago. Got a mechanic job at Harrison's garage."

"Why don't you want to wait on him?" Morgan filled a water glass, then reached for a menu and napkin-wrapped silverware.

Alison shrugged as she turned away. "He makes me uncomfortable."

Morgan couldn't read the thoughts in Toby's eyes as he watched her approach his table. His hooded expression made her hands tremble and her stomach quiver as she placed his silverware and water glass in front of him. How was she supposed to take his order?

She took a slow, in-and-out breath. "Hello. Welcome to Dad's Diner."

He scrutinized her mouth. Maybe he read lips.

She pointed to her name badge. "I'm Morgan."

His eyes followed her pointing finger, and he smiled. He gestured to the ticket pad and pencil in her black apron and made a give-them-to-me motion, so Morgan did.

"Toby," he wrote, and pointed to himself.

"Nice to meet you, Toby." She spoke and wrote on the pad at the same time. "Do you want something other than water to drink?"

The thumb, index, and tall finger of his right hand snapped closed, and then he wrote, "No, thanks. Don't need menu. Want hot turkey sandwich with extra pickles and tomatoes. No onions. Sweet potato fries."

"Cheese?"

He again made the snapping motion with his fingers and pointed to the word no.

She nodded and removed the menu. As she walked toward the order window, Morgan glanced back. Toby watched her. She smiled, and he smiled back.

Some of the other diners huddled over their French fries and burgers, gossiping, their words loud enough to be heard over the jukebox oldies song. Between bites, they stared at Toby. As she removed dirty dishes from the silver tables and sanitized the red vinyl chairs, they discussed the man's family history and background.

Toby had attended the state's Deaf Institute, played football and baseball on their championship teams, gone to college, graduated with an Associate of Applied Science degree, and received a mechanic's certificate. Until recently, he'd worked in the city. Speculation ran high as to why he left a good job to return home to a town with limited opportunities for a deaf man.

Morgan's jaw tightened. She was a newcomer to this small town too. Did the friendly people she served on a regular basis gossip about her?

When Toby's food was ready, she carried his plate to him. But before she set the basket of fries on the table in front of him, she frowned at the backs of the diners standing at the cashier's station.

Morgan turned back to Toby, who looked from the diners to her. He signaled for the ticket pad and pencil and then pointed at her.

"Why angry? Your brown eyes make sparks."

She shrugged, tucked a stray tendril of light brown hair behind her ear, and tilted her head toward the diners. Morgan put up both hands and made the yak-yak-yak motions she and her friends in school had used when they were bored out of their minds with teachers' lectures. "They talk-talk-talk."

"About me?"

Her eyes widened, but she nodded and wrote, "In the last ten minutes, I learned who you, your parents, and grandparents are, where you live, what schools you attended, and what you do."

The right side of his mouth quirked up at the corner, and his pencil moved. "Small town. No deaf people."

She nodded and turned to go, but his light, warm touch on her wrist stopped her. He wrote, and slid the pad forward.

"Please, I may ask personal question?"

Morgan looked into his eyes. Loneliness lurked. She and loneliness were well-acquainted, so she nodded and smiled.

"You married?"

She shook her head.

"Boyfriend?"

She again shook her head, and Toby's smile reached into his eyes.

"I scare you? You afraid to talk with me?"

Morgan tilted her head and studied his face. He waited and watched while she wrote.

"No, I'm not afraid, exactly, but I don't know any deaf people. I don't know sign language. How would we communicate?"

"What we do now?" He chuckled as she read his words.

She laughed. "Okay. When do you want to talk?" She passed the tablet to him.

Alison watched them from behind the baked goods at the end of the counter, so Morgan turned her body to hide her face from the woman's stare and continued their written conversation.

"Tomorrow?"

"I go to church in the morning, but I'm free after."

"Church on hill or by river?"

"By the river. I've been there twice."

"I go same church with parents when I come home. In city, I go Deaf Church."

"You'll be at church tomorrow with your parents?"

His right fist nodded his assent. "Please, you sit with me and parents?"

Morgan paused. *I wonder what consequences I should expect if I agree?* "Yes, I'll sit with you."

His smile crinkled the skin beside his eyes and relaxed the tension in his jaw, and Morgan's heart skipped a beat.

"One thing more, please? Tonight, you write information about Morgan? You bring letter with you tomorrow? You know about Toby Russell, but I know only your eyes and mouth smile at me without fear."

Morgan nodded, looked into his unhooded, friendly eyes, smiled, and placed the bill on the table before she turned to clean the dirty dishes from the vacated tables. She took these to the dishwasher, and when she returned, Toby was gone.

"Nice tip." Alison glanced toward his spot, then turned to Morgan. The woman seemed to have a hard time controlling her curiosity. "What did he say?"

"Not much. He introduced himself."

Before Alison could ask more questions, Morgan moved to clean the table. She scooped the money into her apron pocket and looked out the plate glass window. Toby stood on the sidewalk and watched her. She waved and mouthed her thanks for the tip, and he smiled, turned, and crossed the street.

The letter was the hardest assignment since her college days, and Morgan deleted the words on her computer screen with regularity before she finally settled on a letter she could live with.

> My name is Morgan Grey. I'm twenty-six years old, and I now live in this town with my aunt, Prudence Grey. I moved in with her three weeks ago, after I spent the last several months helping my sister and brother settle our parents' estate. Mom and Dad died in a car accident at the first of this year, and though both my sister and brother invited me to live with them, I just couldn't. I had to get far away from the pain, though I haven't been successful. Do you know what I mean? Have you ever felt this way?

> I graduated with a Bachelor of Arts degree and majored in modern languages. I got my state endorsement in Spanish, and for the past four years, I worked as an interpreter at a health clinic. Though I enjoyed the work, I'm ready to make a career switch. I don't yet know what I want to do, which is why we met in the diner. Maybe the Lord will give me clear direction soon. In the meantime, I do what I can to heal.

> I enjoy Shasta daisies, earthy colors, fish tacos, avocados, and softball. I don't like cauliflower or oatmeal, though I'll eat them if I have to.

She added another paragraph, reread the letter, and then clicked print.

The next day, Morgan tucked the letter into her Bible and walked toward the river church. She glanced at the dark gray sky, and then buttoned her rain jacket and fiddled with the small umbrella hanging securely around her wrist.

When she entered the church foyer, she searched for Toby. He stepped from the shadowed hall near the water fountain, and his eyes lit. She smiled, and he pointed toward one of the padded pews near the back of the sanctuary. With a question in his eyes, he offered his elbow. She accepted, and he led her toward a couple who must be his parents. The two watched their approach. Did their eyes hold interest or suspicion? Her insides quivered.

The man and woman stood as Toby ushered her into the pew. He pointed to his mother and spoke her name. His speech was understandable, though the name sounded as if he'd swallowed the vowels.

"Nice to meet you, Nancy. I'm Morgan Grey."

Toby indicated his dad and spoke his name. "Reggie."

She shook their hands and smiled. "I can see the family likeness."

"Your aunt didn't come?" Nancy looked toward the door.

"No, she's not feeling well."

The musicians played the prelude as a signal to the congregation to prepare for worship. Morgan looked around. How would Toby understand the service without an interpreter?

"Please stand as God's Word is read." The worship leader waited until everyone stood. "Today, we read Psalm 150 from the King James Version of the Bible."

The words flashed on the projection screen and Toby looked up, his eyes scanning the words.

> Praise ye the LORD. Praise God in his sanctuary: praise him in the firmament of his power.

He began to sign the words as he watched Morgan's lips.

> Praise him for his mighty acts: praise him according to
> his excellent greatness. Praise him with the sound of
> trumpet: praise him with the psaltery and harp.

Toby acted like he played a lute when he signed the word for psaltery, and Morgan's eyes widened. How could anyone express so much without words? Toby's clean, well-formed hands made graceful picture words as she recited the psalm with the others. His whole body moved with the signs.

> Praise him with the timbrel and dance: praise him with
> stringed instruments and organs.

When Toby got to the word timbrel, he mimed the actions of playing a tambourine, and when he finished the phrase, her mental image of praising the Lord with dance cleared and took on form.

> Let everything that hath breath praise the LORD. Praise
> ye the LORD.

They reached the last verse and Toby's hands and body stilled. Morgan looked into his face. If only she could see his thoughts. He returned her gaze without dropping his eyes or hooding his expression as he'd done at the diner when others stared. She smiled before turning her attention to the rest of the service.

Morgan caught Toby studying her face when no verses were projected on the screen, much as she'd done to his earlier. *I wonder what he sees? Do sadness and pain leave marks?*

At the end of service, Nancy invited her to lunch. "I've made a pot roast, Morgan. Please come and enjoy the meal with us. We'd like to get to know you better." Nancy signed as she spoke, though her signs didn't seem to be as fluent as Toby's. He nodded at his mother's request.

"Thanks. Let me check on Aunt Prudence first." Morgan pulled out her cell phone and dialed home. Her aunt encouraged her to take lunch with her new friends.

The Randalls lived on the corner of a quiet, tree-lined avenue in the historic part of town. When they pulled into the short driveway and under the breezeway connecting the main house of the quaint, Victorian-style home to a smaller apartment over the garage, Morgan gasped. "This is beautiful."

Nancy smiled. "I'm a real estate agent and Reggie's an architect. When this narrow hillside property came up for sale, we bought the lot. Reggie liked the challenge of designing a comfortable home that fit into the style of the neighborhood."

Reggie nodded. "Toby rents the apartment above the garage. There's a kitchen, living room, good-sized master suite and bath, and a usable office. We'll take you on a tour after lunch."

After lunch and the tour, they sat in the living room and talked.

Morgan clasped her hands. "Will you tell me about Toby and his earlier life, Nancy?"

Nancy signed Morgan's request, and Toby nodded. He turned his chair, perhaps so he could see their faces and hand movements as they chatted. Morgan adjusted hers to improve the sight lines.

Toby had lost his hearing when he'd fallen as a toddler. Nancy and Reggie had done everything they could to ensure their son got the best education they could provide though, at the time, they didn't know exactly what this would mean to them or to Toby.

Nancy brushed tears from her eyes. "We had to send him away to be educated. We didn't want to. Those were hard, painful years. We tried to show Toby how much we loved him throughout the school year and when he came home for breaks, but we often saw sadness and longing in his eyes when he had to return to the Institute. We cried often."

Later that afternoon, Toby drove her to the park so they could talk privately. Morgan studied Toby's profile as he parked the car. He'd experienced as much pain, if not more, than she had. When he turned to look at her, a question in his eyes, she handed him the letter and watched him read her words. He read the letter twice, then pointed to her questions and nodded his fist. He pulled out a notebook and pen, thought a few moments, and began to write. From the intent expression on his face, he worked hard to translate his thoughts from American Sign Language into English.

"I live with pain all my life. No good to run. Tried. Not so much pain when I live in city. Have good job, many deaf friends, Deaf Church. Many activities. Here," he pointed toward the town, "I remember pain. Hearing people stare like I grow two heads. No friends. No person share life's hurts. I work, eat, sleep, and do all again next day."

His emotional pain was obvious. She took the ballpoint. "Why did you return?"

"Dad sick. Maybe cancer. Tests this week."

Morgan's fingers numbed. "Oh, no. I'm so sorry, Toby. What can I do to help?"

He looked at her for several moments before he touched the side of her cheek and neck with his fingertips. He outlined her eyes and lips with his index finger, and then took the pen from her. "Smile at me with your eyes and mouth. Talk with me. Talk with Mom and Dad. Share your touch. Heal pain. Hands can sing, dance, and make hurts better."

She nodded, looked at her hands, and then caressed his face in the same way he'd touched hers. He closed his eyes and sighed. When she slowly removed her hand, he reached for it, kissed her fingers, and entwined them with his.

Fat raindrops pelted the car in a relaxing rhythm. Morgan leaned into the warmth of Toby's shoulder as the temperature dropped. When the rain finally stopped, she reached for the notebook and pen.

"Teach me signs so I can talk to you without writing."

He hesitated. "Learn alphabet first."

He wrote the letter A, and then made the sign with his hand. He continued through Z, then told her to spell easy words.

What was wrong with her fingers? Though they were long and well-shaped, they moved like they were fat and sluggish when she tried to spell.

Then he pointed to items inside and outside the car and made hand pictures for them. Morgan repeated the motions until she could correctly identify all the objects he'd shown her.

She smiled. "Pictures are easier than spelling."

His fist nodded. He pointed to her, toward the direction of her home, and started the car.

"More lessons?" Toby raised his eyebrows.

"Yes. When?"

"After work? Sundays?"

Morgan nodded. "Your house or mine?"

Over the next two months, Morgan developed more ability to communicate. Their friendship grew and warmed, and loneliness faded. Toby's patience with her as she struggled to understand and respond to signs seemed to be limitless. He'd recognize her frustration as she tried to express her thoughts more fully. Instead of laughing, he'd respond to her message, show her the correct signs and order, and wait for her to repeat the movements. Much time passed before she stopped asking him to repeat the signs or finger spell the words, or before she could understand without translating from American Sign Language into English and then back again, but the time seemed long. If her frustration neared the I-want-to-quit point, he'd reach out, clasp her hand in his warm one, wait for her to relax, and then touch her cheek with the fingers of his other. Sometimes he would offer a one-handed prayer to God on her behalf, sometimes he'd kiss her.

When she wasn't at work or with Toby, she studied sign language lessons on the internet, or visited with Reggie and Nancy. Wagging tongues, strange looks, and the relentless inquisition at work about her private life made Church, the Randalls', and Aunt Prudence's homes her only sanctuaries. Pleading for the questions to stop at work didn't faze her colleagues or Dad himself. Their dig-for-information tactics became more subtle and insidious.

Morgan chatted with the Randalls late one afternoon until Toby drove up. She stood to leave. "I'd better go. Maybe Toby'll have enough energy to load my bike and take me home."

Though grease-smeared and tired, Toby took her home.

The porch light lit his furrowed brow as he lifted her bike out of the bed of his truck.

She frowned. "What's wrong?"

"Headache." He rubbed his hand across his forehead and smeared more grease with the movement.

"Stop. Come into the house." Though her hands signed in American Sign Language, her mind now added articles, prepositions, and tense endings to smooth the sentences into English structure.

She led him to the mirror just inside the door and pointed to the blackness on his face.

"Wait. I'll bring soap and paper towels."

When his face and hands were clean, she covered a chair with an old sheet and told him to sit. He obeyed, and she massaged his head, neck, and temples. The muscles in his face and shoulders relaxed, and when she stopped, he opened his eyes. He looked at her with love. He rose and drew her close.

Morgan rested in his arms until he kissed the top of her head and walked toward the door. "Tired. See you tomorrow."

She nodded and watched him drive away. Friendship had grown into love, of this she had no doubt, but did they have a future together? Toby struggled to function in a hearing world. Surviving in the Deaf culture would certainly be as hard for her. Her experiences working with patients in the Spanish-speaking community had illuminated just how difficult living in different cultures could be. Learning the language wasn't enough because cultural thought patterns permeated everyday use.

Could a long-term relationship withstand such stress?

She tossed all night, but in the early hours, she smiled and finally slept.

"Morgan, are you going to church today?" Aunt Prudence knocked and called to her. "Toby will be here in thirty minutes to pick you up."

"Yes. I'll be down soon."

She showered quickly and dressed. When Toby knocked on the door and she opened to him, she'd already put on her coat, muffler, and warm hat. The ear flaps were turned down.

Toby smiled when he saw her. "Storm comes?"

"Maybe."

At church, Morgan stood when everyone else stood, and sang when they did, but a few people nearby glanced at her with strange looks. *Do they wonder why I continue to prefer the company of a deaf man, or do they see something different or unusual about me?* She fingered the ear flaps of her hat, and then her face. Both Reggie and Nancy asked if something was wrong, but she shook her head. Toby asked why she hadn't removed her hat or coat.

"Cold." She looked toward the pastor. Often, she fidgeted with the pages in her Bible.

Toby's hand on her arm refocused her attention. The service was over and people were leaving, so she stood and wrapped the muffler around her neck.

The Randalls looked from her to Toby, their curiosity easily identifiable. She shifted her feet. Toby signed that he'd take Morgan for a short walk, and they'd return a little later for lunch. They weren't to wait. His parents nodded and left.

"Mom say your singing not on key or in rhythm today. You not able to focus. People speak to you and you don't answer. You wear outside clothes inside. Why?"

Morgan touched his face, then looked around to make sure they were alone. She removed the hat and the ski hat beneath, then showed him the thick padding covering the earbuds. They'd been taped tightly to her ears and were connected to her iPod.

He held up the cord and frowned.

"White noise." She had to define the expression.

"Why?"

"I want to experience your world."

His eyes widened, and his lips parted. He stared at her for a few moments before signaling her to replace her head coverings.

He stroked her cheek. "Come. Today we deaf together."

They meandered through the park and shared stories before turning back. Just before Morgan entered the crosswalk, Toby grabbed her arm and pulled her to him.

An ambulance, lights flashing, passed within a few feet of them, and she finally heard the blare of horns.

She tore off the hat and reached for the ski hat. *I have to get the earbuds out of my ears. What am I trying to prove, anyway? I almost stepped into the path of an ambulance, for crying out loud!*

Toby's strong fingers encircled her wrists and prevented her from removing the ski hat.

Morgan looked in his face, and he shook his head.

When she calmed, he signed, "Not easy way. Deaf people not able fix problems by opening ears."

He handed her the hat she'd thrown on the ground, and she slipped it over the ski hat.

How difficult and hazardous everyday life could be without the ability to hear. She had taken so much for granted. Morgan walked with Toby, hand-in-hand. *I've been so focused on my own pain, I haven't seen the pain and struggle of others. Lord, forgive.*

⁓⁂⁓

Thanksgiving approached. So much information entered her ears without effort. Bells, motors, speech, laughter, music, television and radio programs, barking dogs, screeching brakes, wind soughing through bare tree branches, the patter of raindrops on metal roofs, the swooshing of windshield wipers, and the buzzing or ringing of cellphones all signaled news of one kind or another. Like most hearing people, she'd unconsciously tuned out information not important to her at the time. The ability to hear enriched her life, and Toby couldn't share this richness with her.

Toby sat across from her in a booth at the diner and questioned her about the sadness on her face. She told him her thoughts, but he smiled.

"My eyes see all you see. My nose smells all you smell. I taste what you taste, and my hands talk, dance, sing, feel. My heart beats. Better for me I focus on gifts I have, not on loss."

Morgan brushed tears from her eyes and smiled. "You teach me much about myself and life, Toby."

She started to reach for his hand, but Alison approached with their bill. The woman had watched them from the moment they'd entered the diner, and she and the other waitress, Julie, had gossiped about them when they weren't waiting on other customers. Several of the customers stared as she and Toby spoke with their hands. No wonder Toby had worn a shuttered look when she first met him. If only she were brave enough to tell them to stop eavesdropping, and to mind their own business.

"Nice to have a day off." Alison laid their ticket on the table.

"Yes." Morgan reached for the bill. Toby touched her hand and shook his head. He glanced at the ticket, took out his wallet, and paid.

When they stepped outside, they buttoned their coats.

Toby gazed at the gray sky. "I smell snow. Colder now."

Morgan nodded and wrapped the muffler around her neck.

"You drive with aunt tonight? Go friend's house with her?"

"Yes, why?"

"Not like you go. Friends staying twenty miles away in next town. Snow comes. Maybe roads slippery."

"I know, but meeting with the visiting friend is important to Auntie. The friend leaves tomorrow. We'll be okay. I'm a careful driver."

Toby clearly wanted to say more, but didn't. She pulled him around the corner of the diner and kissed him. He drew her close and returned her kisses.

"Careful. You careful, Morgan."

Toby paced up and down his parents' living room. He looked at his watch and continued pacing. Ten o'clock. Where was Morgan? She'd promised to call his mother's cell phone when she got home, but she was late. He flipped on the porch light and opened the door. The snow level had increased another inch.

"Mom, where your cell?"

Nancy handed the phone to him, and he typed a text.

MORGAN, YOU OKAY? WHERE? CALL MOM OR TEXT.

He pushed send and waited.

Ten minutes later, after no response, he dressed warmly and reached for his gloves.

"Wait, Toby. I'll go with you." Reggie grabbed his coat from the closet and followed.

They loaded the pick-up truck's bed with extra tire chains, tow rope, blankets, flashlights, and a first aid kit, then added extra weight to increase traction. Toby steered north out of town.

A thin layer of ice had formed under the snow, so he'd shifted into four-wheel-drive. The farther they drove, the tighter Toby gripped the steering wheel, and the tenser his jaw became. The plow had recently cleared the opposite lane, but his side of the road remained unplowed and slick.

Toby rounded a curve and confronted the red and blue flashing lights of a patrol car and ambulance. His heart pounded in his throat and his stomach knotted. His headlights reflected off the underside of an upturned vehicle. The car had slid off the road, ripped through a barbed-wire fence, and come to rest in a farmer's field.

"Morgan!" The cry tore from Toby's throat.

Reggie pointed toward another vehicle parked on the shoulder, just behind the ambulance, and signed, "Prudence's car."

A police officer with a flashlight and reflective vest waved him to a stop. Toby turned on his hazard lights and rolled down the window. The officer aimed his light in their faces, and said something. Toby frowned. He couldn't read the man's lips in the dark. He pointed to Reggie, who explained their purpose for being on the road on such a night.

Toby made signs to the officer. "I go check?"

The officer looked toward Reggie, then hesitated before nodding. Toby unfastened the seatbelt and opened the door. Reggie did the same, and the two walked as fast as they could toward Prudence's car.

"Morgan?" Toby called.

A figure turned and separated from a few others standing at the side of the road. Toby turned his flashlight toward the advancing person.

"Morgan!" He opened his arms and pulled her to him. "You hurt? You okay?"

With one hand he held the flashlight, and with the other he searched her face, hair, and neck for injuries.

"Fine." She leaned her cheek against his chest, and he wrapped both arms around her and squeezed.

Could she hear the way his heart pounded? Could she hear the pulsing of fear in his veins? Could she hear how every muscle, bone, and tendon cried out his love for her?

Reggie touched his shoulder, and Toby turned his head.

"The officer wants you to move your truck. The ambulance will take the patient to hospital. All people leave now."

Morgan signed and spoke. "Aunt Prudence is in the car keeping warm. Reggie, will you drive Auntie's car? I'll ride with Toby."

Reggie nodded.

When she'd strapped herself in, Toby turned, his flashlight focused on his hand as he signed. "Why you not call? I worry." Then he turned the light to the lower part of her face and the space where her hands would move.

"I saw the accident and stopped to help the people. My phone was in Auntie's car. Sorry." She turned her palm toward him and showed him the combined I, L, Y fingers—I love you. He reached toward her with the same sign and touched his bent fingers and the heel of his palm to hers. Then he kissed her, buckled up, and headed home.

Regulars and visitors to the Christmas service waited for Toby to sign several verses of "Silent Night." He'd volunteered to participate and, within hours, the news had spread all over town. Morgan smiled. Given their curiosity, Alison's presence, and that of the crew from Dad's Diner didn't surprise her, but seeing the congregation and pastor from the church on the hill did. She closed her eyes for a moment and breathed in the fragrance of pine boughs and apple-cinnamon candles decorating the sanctuary. Faint scents from the kitchen hinted at warm, spicy baked goods waiting for everyone after the service, and her stomach growled.

When the pastor signaled, Toby rose from the pew beside her and made his way to the small stage. He'd never looked better. He nodded to the pianist who played the first chords to the song, then the church blackened and a spotlight drew every eye to Toby.

No words could express the beauty she beheld or the complex emotions his movements evoked. Toby's hands danced to the silent music flowing from his soul. No eye remained dry.

Much later, Toby drew her outside away from the celebratory crowd. They stood in a patch of light from the arched window. The snow reflected the soft colors of the window's Christmas lights.

"You dance with me, Morgan?" He held out his arms. "Hands dance, but my feet dance also."

"I'll never be able to dance like you. You're . . . beautiful."

He waited.

She smiled. "No music."

He touched the place over his heart. "Music play here."

She put her left hand in his right, and her right hand on his shoulder. His left arm encircled her waist and drew her to him. She rested her cheek on his chest, and for several minutes they swayed together to the rhythm of the heart.

"Morgan?" Her name rumbled deep in his chest and she leaned back to look into his face. He made the you-me sign. "We dance together always? Through joy? Through sadness? Through pain? We become life partners? You marry me?"

She kissed him.

"Yes, Toby. Let's dance together through the rest of our lives."

ABOUT THE AUTHOR

DERINDA BABCOCK is an author and graphic designer. She lives in southwestern Colorado near the base of the western slope of the Rocky Mountains.

In her previous career as an English as a Second Language teacher, she worked with students of all ages and many different linguistic and cultural backgrounds. The richness of this experience lends flavor and voice to the stories she writes. You can contact her at www.derindababcock.com/contact

THE
JINDENTORS
A TALE OF THREE KINGDOMS
BOOK 1
DERINDA BABCOCK

THE
VINDORANS
A TALE OF THREE KINGDOMS
BOOK 2
DERINDA BABCOCK

THE
BINROMESE
A TALE OF THREE KINGDOMS
BOOK 3
DERINDA BABCOCK

DODGING DESTINY
DESTINY SERIES BOOK 1
THIRD EDITION
DERINDA BABCOCK

IN SEARCH OF
DESTINY
DESTINY SERIES BOOK 2
THIRD EDITION
DERINDA BABCOCK

DESTINY TRILOGY BOOK 3
FOLLOWING
DESTINY
DERINDA BABCOCK

HUNTING FOR
DESTINY
A DESTINY TRILOGY
NOVELLA
DERINDA BABCOCK

VOICES FROM THE
PAST
A DESTINY TRILOGY
CHRISTMAS SHORT STORY
DERINDA BABCOCK

TREASURES OF THE HEART BOOK 1
COLORADO
TREASURE
THIRD EDITION
DERINDA BABCOCK

TREASURES OF THE HEART BOOK 2
TROUBLE
IN TEXAS
COMING
DERINDA BABCOCK

TREASURES OF THE HEART BOOK 3
THE PRODIGAL
RETURNS
COMING
DERINDA BABCOCK

THINGS
NOT SEEN
DERINDA BABCOCK

DERINDA'S OTHER BOOKS

A Tale of Three Kingdoms Series
*The *Jindentors, Book 1*
*The *Vindorans, Book 2*
The Binromese, Book 3

The Destiny Series
**Dodging Destiny, Book 1*
In Search of Destiny, Book 2
Following Destiny, Book 3
Hunting for Destiny (novella), Book 4
Voices from the Past (short story), Book 5

Treasures of the Heart trilogy:
**Colorado Treasure, Book 1*
Trouble in Texas (coming), Book 2
The Prodigal Returns (coming), Book 3

**Things Not Seen, Book 1*
**Things Hoped For, Book 2*

* audiobook available